Jason,

Thank you so r

for your support [...]

back, relax & enjoy my [...]

of romance. You're such a great

sailor. Donna Brown

11/18/05

Secret Lies

by
Portuguese

authorHOUSE™

1663 LIBERTY DRIVE, SUITE 200
BLOOMINGTON, INDIANA 47403
(800) 839-8640
WWW.AUTHORHOUSE.COM

First published by AuthorHouse 10/25/05

ISBN: 1-4208-7729-1 (sc)

Printed in the United States of America
Bloomington, Indiana

This book is printed on acid-free paper.

This book was edited by Tee Royal of RawSistaz Affair in Atlanta, GA and Donna Brown, Author

Cover page illustrated by: Sgt. Eric Cromwell, United States Army

Dedication

To
Annie L. Wright

I often tell people that when you lose your mother, you lose your life. I never thought this would happen to me so soon. Many children lose their mothers at a young age, but when you have grown to know someone so beautiful and so loving, you often find yourself looking back over your life and saying, "if only I could…." I have said those words a thousand times since that day in January 2002. As long as I can remember, my mother has been a part of my life. I pray hard every day that it would be just a dream and I would wake up from it. Unfortunately, it's reality and Annie's not coming back.

Momma use to always say things like, "Girl, you're gonna miss me when I'm gone so you'd better be good to me." Then, she'd smile and say, "I'm just kidding. I'm not going anywhere anytime soon." Oh how I wish she could still say those words. Annie ran a tight but close family, loving us no matter what. Through the good and the bad, she was always there to help not only us but those around her who needed an extra hand.

Her tireless days of working on Saturday mornings at Smyrna Primitive Baptist Church in Warrington, FL meant that someone was going to be fed and they would be fed well. She'd get there early in the morning along with the other members of the Willing Workers (Mrs. Edith Mae Stallworth, Mrs. Earnestine White, Mrs. Lucille Riggins and others) to cook dinners for the church in order to raise money for fundraisers or trips. Believe it or not, that group of women taught me how to cook. I'd be right there watching everything they did, but not opening my mouth. They say you can learn a lot if you keep your mouth shut and just watch. To this day, I truly believe the saying because my mother could burn.

Annie inspired us in so many ways. From my brother and I joining the service, to my youngest brother being the great artist he is; to my two sisters working hard to raise their families, Annie was always there for advice when we needed her. To know her was to love her. Every person who came in contact with her was touched by her spirit and her friendliness. Every man around wanted her because of her beauty and sophistication. But, she only had the heart for one man, Mr. Potter. This man stood by her side regardless. From the time I was a baby until her passing, this man has been a part of her life. Even when someone else tried to come in and take his place, Mr. Potter still came around. We often said he should have been the one she married after our father. But, that's another story.

Prologue

The verdict came back not guilty. Infuriated as I was, I stormed the bench where Judge Ramona was seated, my eyes filled with anger. My life flashed before me and my chest rippled with fear as I recounted the day Mr. Brunson had his way. I thought about the lies he told in order to get out of it. My eyes flooded with tears as I recapped the birthday surprise my best friend Michelle had in store for me. How she made me—at the tender age of nine—take my clothes off and get on top of her.

Ironic as it may be, I worshipped Michelle. But to have her perform sexual acts on me disgusted me to the point of not wanting to ever be touched again. Then as I looked deeper into Judge Ramona's eyes, Keisha appeared savage as a hunter thirsting for flesh. I shook briefly as visions of her making me take my clothes off only to hide my head in shame when her mother caught us in the act. "This can't be," I screamed out loud waiting for him to change his verdict. "This ain't gonna happen," I said drifting into another world.

To make matters worse, I envisioned the wildness in Kenyon's eye as he not only snapped my back but raped me while I was already in pain. It seemed the reflexes trying to hold my lips together caused me to yell out again. "That idiot did this to me!" I wept longer. He left me helpless lying on that squeaky bed that he got from a rummage sale while he ventured off to his J.O.B.

I thought about all who wronged me and now of all things, they were letting a rapist go because he told me he wasn't interested in sex with me. He took advantage of me and left me dejected on my bed daring me to say a word. What kind of world were we living in where a rapist could have his way with you, laugh in your face about it, and the judge say you were the one at fault? This world was filled with deceitful and mistrustful people needing a quick blow across the head to get them in order. All I ever wanted was happiness. Happiness I never found in men and might I say—the world.

Judge Ramona sat in his tall pleather chair in a long black robe, swinging his gavel. How dare he set this mean-spirited rapist free? I watched as Maurice stood there slightly smiling, winking his eye at me with shackles on his hands and feet as the judge passed down his sentence of 'Not Guilty' of rape but was charged with aggravated assault causing bodily harm and inflicting excruciating pain. Maurice hunched back his shoulders as though he was a king reigning over his throne, pointed his finger at me, winked again as to say, "I knew I would beat this senseless charge" and was told to sit down before Judge Ramona changed his mind.

My mind was working overtime trying to figure out what had just happened in this circus ring they called a court room. Was I wrong to think that 'No meant no' or was society filled with too many ego struck men needing a boost of reality check?

As I looked around this court room filled with men flaunting their high tech law degrees, fancy suits and silk ties, I wanted slap some sense into them. My chest shuddered quickly as I watched the smirk on Maurice's face linger to a smile. I felt the blood pulsing through my veins, my lungs expanding as I focused on the gavel slamming over and over again on Judge Ramona's desk.

The picture in my mind was clear. My inner thighs filled with bluish purple bruises that deluded my self-esteem after one night that was supposed to prove that I still had one ounce of womanhood left in my soul. I rolled my red hot eyes towards the hunger thirsting chauvinist pig sitting at the bench. Bet he thought he was God's gift to men when it came to setting other men free after raping women. Then it occurred to me. Why ponder the thought of hatred in my soul when I knew, deep inside of me I had a game plan and somehow, I was going to live it out? This time it's going to be different. I will have my way or will I?

CHAPTER 1

The Verdict

Rising quickly from my seat as the judge gave his verdict, I screamed out at him.

"Your honor, how could you?" Rage filled my voice.

"Ms. Jenkins, that's my verdict and it's final. Take my advice and seek counseling."

He thought he was bad sitting there with that jive ass gavel in his hands and his large black robe. How dare he tell me to seek counseling? "Damn chauvinist pig," I thought to myself as I lowered my head. Terrice, my girlfriend from years past and Maurice's sister walked towards me and placed her arms around me. Maurice, excited by the judge's decision, was lead back to his cell awaiting his sentencing.

No—he wasn't given his freedom—but at the same time, he wasn't charged for rape. This man bruised my legs, kept me silenced when his sister came to the door, and then threatened my life. How could a judge be so insensitive to a victim of rape?

I hung around and spoke with Terrice for a moment. We waited two additional hours until we heard the fate of Maurice's sentencing and talked about our future connection. After all that had gone down, I didn't see fit to have her around me anymore. We decided to remain friends, but would not have the pleasure of being with each other as girlfriends anymore. Surprisingly, Maurice was given two years of confinement and six months probation.

I headed home, got in my bed, and clung to my pillow for dear life. I didn't want to see anyone or be seen in public for a while.

Days had passed since the verdict had been given, and I knew somehow I had to succumb to the shame of being raped by my girlfriend's brother. A night of passion gone badly by joyful play left a sour taste in my mouth. I pleaded with Judge Ramona that day to take back his verdict. He ordered me out of his court room and my spirits remained torn.

I shrugged as the doorbell rang and headed downstairs in my pink Victoria Secret's bathrobe. Seeing that it was Jamal, my ex-husband, boldly standing with flowers brought a pleasant smile to my face. As I opened the door, memories of the past taunted me. Some were good, but others could have stayed where they were.

"Good morning, Chantal," he said standing there all fine and slim, unlike the days I knew him. "May I come in?"

Wanting badly to say no, I allowed him past the stained glass doors where we once shared some passionate moments.

"How are you, Chantal?" He asked seeing the look upon my face. "It seems as though life's been a bit rough on you. Can I help in any way?"

"I'm managing," I said smartly like someone had thrown a glass of water in my face. "Thanks for your concern. What brings you this way so late in the afternoon?"

"You—Chantal! I've been thinking about you lately and…" I stopped him short of saying he wanted to have me in his life again.

"Jamal— just go away. It's been four years since I've heard from you— don't try and express your concerns for me now. Not now Jamal," I said as I turned away from him. "Please, just leave me alone!"

"Chantal," he said standing there all poised and desirable. "It's been far too long. You see baby, I've grown up over the years and I've come to realize that you never get over your first true love. I need you baby like a hammer needs a nail. Just one more taste of your love is all I need."

I turned around to face this asshole and to call him out for the loser he was. But, when I saw how much weight he had lost, I couldn't act like a jerk. He actually seemed as though he really cared about me. He did light my fire a time or two, but it didn't mean he could come back into my life after all this time. "Jamal when will you face the facts that I don't want to be bothered with you anymore?"

"Listen Chantal, I missed you. I've changed a lot over the years. Jennifer and I—well, it didn't last. She heard about your problems and cut out on me. She felt sorry for you and believes she caused our breakup.

"And just how is that Jamal? Jennifer knew where I was all along. We've stayed in contact with each other and you—standing there as though you didn't know who she was. That was all a lie, Jamal. You knew about my cousin and you went after her anyway."

2

"She came to Maryland and we hooked up. She didn't know you were here. I didn't know she was your cousin. I would've never—"

"That's enough Jamal. I don't worry about that anymore. I was raped, okay. He hurt me bad enough to bring down my pride. How can I hold my head up around here? Terrice hasn't visited since the trial. I just don't know—"

"Come here, baby."

"No! I'm not your damn baby," I said pulling away from him. "I'll be alright. I just need a little time."

"Let's do dinner tonight," he said hoping for a little gratitude. "It's on me."

"I don't know, Jamal. I haven't been seen in public with a man since— God, I don't even know the last time I've been seen in public with a man."

"All the better my love! But, I don't think people would even take notice that you're with a man because that's the way it's supposed to be anyway," he said giving me a slight smile. "Now go upstairs, take a warm bath, and I'll pick you up at 6:00."

"That's three hours away! I can't pull myself together in that short of time. A woman like me need hours to perfect beauty."

"You'll be amazed. I'll be back," he said softly as he headed out the door and down the driveway.

Our son Dante had gone off to college after he graduated from Woodlawn High School and I was left with an enormous house to manage. Although Terrice and I lived separately, I wasn't certain if she would ever come back into my life again. Now after years of desertion, it seemed as though Jamal was trying to make his way back to me. My mind was working overtime trying to figure out his next move. I was a catastrophe waiting to happen.

After Jamal left, I tried to pull myself together. I went into my exotic room filled will paintings from artists exploiting naked men and women. The pictures kept you wet the moment you walked in the door. I looked into my oversized walk-in closet filled with nothing but business attire and said, "What the hell am I getting myself into?" I knew Jamal was my children's daddy, but I wasn't ready to bow down and crawl back into bed with him. *"God,"* I thought, *"This better not be another screw up for me."*

Just as I got ready to step into my warm tub filled with vanilla bubbles, my oldest sister Denise called to inform me about momma's condition. She wasn't getting any better. Slowly, her health was starting to deteriorate and her legs and eyes were failing her. She was placed on a strict diet and had to receive daily care from the motored nurses. I wanted so badly to be with Mildred to monitor her health and guide her in the right direction with her eating habits. But with the way things were going in my life, I would only bring Mildred down. Mildred's life was depressing enough with all her health issues. I didn't need to add to it.

After I lost RJ's baby, the man that I thought would leave his wife for me, my world tumbled into a thousand pieces. I wanted that baby more than anything. In my mind, I thought he would leave his wife Genie and come back to me. Somehow I wished things didn't have to end so dismally. With Jamal staring me in the face demanding that I go out with him, it seemed as though I only had one option—pick my mouth off the floor and get my ass in the tub so when Jamal returned, I'd be ready to go out on the town. I grabbed my charcoal gray slacks, my black pumps, and a black blouse I had hanging in the closet and got myself ready for my big date with Jamal. My hair was pulled up in a bun just the way he used to like it. I added a little color to my face and sprayed my body with some Elige perfume by Mary Kay cosmetics.

The door bell rang. I shrugged again knowing it had to be Jamal. He stood once again with one single red rose. I could only smile, never recalling any other day of him bringing me flowers.

"Hello again sweet thang!" He said in his always so playful not wanting to grow up voice. "Are you ready for your night of pampering?"

Frankly, I didn't know what to think. This man looked good as hell standing there in his semi-baggy black khakis, Red Polo shirt, and patent leather shoes. I gave him a quick smirk and invited him in. Then he said, "You look good baby. You look just as good as the first day I saw you in Army school."

I chose my words carefully and replied with, "I can actually fix my getting-over-the-blues face to say that you look well yourself. I'm glad you invited me out Jamal. I'm really flattered, but don't read too deep into this. I don't see myself crawling back in bed with you again."

He chuckled and said, "I'm not looking to have you in my bed, Chantal. I just want your company for a while. No arguments, no sorrow or pain, I just want a piece of your mind for my own personal gain."

I looked at him and giggled. "That had a great little rhyme to it Jamal. Have you been studying poetry?"

"No baby. I just made that up right then and there. We have to go now so our reservations won't be cancelled."

"You made reservations? That's a first," I said throwing my shawl over my shoulders.

"Yeah, it's a nice little surprise. I know you will enjoy it," he replied opening the door for me.

As we walked out the door, I set the alarm, locked the outside bolt lock, and stepped into Jamal's black Mercedes. I was shocked when I first saw it. The last time I'd seen Jamal, he was sporting a gray Nissan Altima. He definitely had moved up in the world.

We arrived at the Bay n Surf off Route 1 in Laurel. I hadn't been at this restaurant since I first arrived in Maryland. I guess it finally occurred to Jamal that if he was to make me happy, he had to shower me with seafood. This place had plenty of sumptuous seafood just waiting for me to sink my watering mouth into. When the waitress came to our table, she asked if we wanted to order any drinks or appetizers. Normally, I would turn down the appetizers and wait for the main course. But, this time I ordered the Bay Country Crab Soup. Jamal decided against an appetizer and ordered a tall glass of Pepsi instead. This would be the night he had dreamed about for years.

On her next trip to the table, the waitress brought my soup and Jamal's drink. I was ready to order and immediately asked how many shrimp would be included in the Jumbo Steamed Spiced Gulf Shrimp order. When the waitress told me a pound normally consisted of fifteen to twenty, I immediately placed my order. Jamal smiled softly as he placed his order for the Orange Roughy fresh from New Zealand.

Jamal talked slowly as he asked about my ordeal with Maurice. He knew that the rape had traumatized my life and I would need a lot of therapeutic advice after being raped twice. He couldn't fathom the thought of me going through it all alone. Although he hated to admit it, Jamal was definitely out to get his first love back.

I looked at him and said, "This is not the time, nor the place to talk about my ordeal with Maurice, Jamal. I've come to the realization that men ain't worth the shit that comes from their bodies."

"That's not fair baby. I never did anything like that to you. Why are you so cold to me? I'm just trying to get a feel of what you're going through. If you don't want to talk about it, just say so and I'll leave it out of the conversation tonight."

"I'm sorry Jamal. I'll only break down if I tell you about it here. Do you remember when we first met and I told you about Kenyon?"

"Briefly," he replied. "What does he have to do with this?"

"Everything. Every time I tried to tell you about the rape, I'd break down. Kenyon was my first real love, the first man to get inside of me. He was my husband, but ripped my heart wide open after he raped me. I guess that's why it hurt so badly."

"Let's continue this later, Chantal. I can see that you're torn about this."

"It's a good thing because the waitress is coming with my shrimp." My flesh crawled as the scrumptious smell of seafood headed towards me. One

5

thing for sure the myth about seafood making a person horny, was taking a mere affect on my inner thighs.

My shrimp were covered in spicy hot Old Bay seasoning and the peelings were still attached. Every bite I took was romanticized with flavor. I thanked Jamal for such a beautiful choice of restaurants.

After dinner, Jamal took me back home and I invited him in for a quick cup of coffee. I began to explain about the rape and how it affected my life. Jamal dropped his head in empathy knowing that if he would have tried harder maybe this wouldn't have happened.

"So how are you really dealing with this Chantal? I know Dante isn't here for you anymore and it just seems right for me to be a part of your life again."

"I'm too old for this cat and mouse game of love. Maybe later on in life I'll find that special someone, but I was always told that if you make someone your ex, it's for a reason. We had our share of fun Jamal. It's time for me to look deep into who I am and what I will be doing with the rest of my life."

He took my hand, looked deep into my eyes, and in the softest voice said, "I won't pressure you Chantal. You can have all the time you need. Just let me know that there is a chance for us again."

"I can't make you any promises, but if there is, you'll be the first to know." I was already in my forties and Jamal was close to fifty. One could only assume that he didn't want to die lonely. He needed a last piece of ass so that when he met his maker, he'd be happy.

"It's getting late Chantal and unlike you, I do have a job to go to in the morning. They are doing a little research at the company and want me to be a part of it."

"You still haven't changed Jamal. I guess you are still working those crazy hours for the other man."

"I didn't strike it big like you Chantal. I can't afford to sit at home and do nothing with my life. Somebody's gotta pay my bills and child support."

I arched my eyebrows and said, "You think I'm wasting my life at home? You don't know the half of it Jamal. By the end of the day, I'm just as exhausted as you. I volunteer downtown at one of the battered women's shelters. You should see some of them that come in on a daily basis. Men can be some cruel creatures at times."

"Not all men are bad Chantal."

"You're right. Not all of them are, but the rest of them out there are either gay, married, or just don't know how to treat a woman."

"I think I'd better go before you end up throwing something at me," he said giving me one of his 'I know I can get you back baby' looks.

"You don't have to leave Jamal. I won't hurt you. It's kind of nice talking to you after all these years. You made my day."

"I'm glad to know that I was able to cheer you up Chantal. I really miss seeing you, Dante, and my boy Montel."

"He talks about you all the time you know. Now that he's older, he wants to be a part of your life. I don't want to see him hurt. Can you understand that Jamal?"

"I sure can, but I don't plan on hurting him, you, or Dante ever again."

"It doesn't matter with Dante. He's out of the house. But Montel, he's trying to understand how things were and how come his daddy lives in another house."

"Let him come and stay with me for a little while. I'll explain it all to him."

"He's old enough to make up his own mind. But, I don't think he is ready for another change like that Jamal. Let's just keep things the way they are and see how they play out."

"That might be the best idea yet, Chantal. You know, no matter what you say or think about me, I'll always love you."

After hearing Jamal say those words again, I felt compelled to tell him that I loved him too. But, it was much too soon for that. "I'm glad to know that you still have those same feelings for me Jamal."

"I guess you cannot express your feelings just yet Chantal, but I know you'll come around one day."

Now I know after a delightful dinner Jamal wanted to divide my thighs and dive right in. But no siree—a sistah was not havin' that shit. Just because we had a past didn't mean I was spreading my legs for the nigga all over again. For now on, my thighs belong to me—that is, until I find the right man deserving enough to give them to. Granted, Jamal was being kind by taking me out for my favorite food, but he still had a ways to go before he was getting anywhere near my legs, tits or lips. Maybe a quick smack on the cheek, but until that day comes, that's all he was getting from me. So I replied with, "Maybe so Jamal, but until then, let's just keep it simple."

CHAPTER 2

Jamal's Persistence

Jamal showed up the next day unannounced and looking like he had lost his best friend. I invited him in and we talked for a moment. Then he turned to me and asked if he could have another chance.

Stunned by his question, I wanted to say, Jamal go to hell, find the devil, and ask him for another chance. Instead, I stuttered and said, "Jamal I just go over a horrific ordeal with Maurice and I just can't handle another situation at this time." This saved me the time and shame of letting him down easily.

"What's the problem Chantal?" He responded. "Haven't I made an effort by coming this far to reclaim you?"

"No he didn't just beg me for another chance," I thought. I didn't want to get loud and say something that would hurt his feelings. So I came across just as smooth as I could. "I said, NO with a capital N. What part of that don't you understand Jamal?" By now I was getting a little annoyed by all of it. Then I thought about it. If I could say no to Jamal and Maurice said no to me, what case did I have to argue? It never occurred to me that a part of me forced the rape on myself. I grabbed a hold of my hair and started to scream. "Just leave me alone."

Jamal didn't know what the hell came over me. "Baby let me help you. Let me get you some help."

"Get away from me. You, Kenyon and Maurice. Stay the hell away from me." Jamal reached for me and I snatched away.

"Kenyon and Maurice aren't here. It's just me Chantal. Please baby—let me hold you for a moment."

I looked at Jamal scared as ever. Why was this happening to me? I didn't want to relive what I had already gone through. I wanted to get on with my life. I reached for Jamal, but saw Maurice's face. "He wanted me to leave him alone," I said to Jamal. "I wouldn't let well enough alone. That's why he hurt me."

"Stop blaming yourself Chantal. Maurice knew what he was doing."

"But if I only let him be like he asked…"

"It's too late to think about what would have been. Maurice is locked up for a couple years. I want to focus on us."

I slowly back away from Jamal and said, "There is no us Jamal. I can't handle us right now. Please understand. I appreciate you trying to help and all, but the only thing I need right now is peace."

"Have you thought about counseling like the judge ordered?"

"I don't need no damn counseling Jamal. I need for you to leave me the hell alone."

"Okay Chantal." He backed off slowly holding his hand up. "I hear you loud and clear. Let me make you some tea then."

"You just don't give up do you Jamal?" Then I smiled. Jamal walked me into the kitchen, sat me down in a chair, and put the tea kettle on. I didn't understand what had come over Jamal him being nice and all. Maybe he had changed.

He sat in the chair next to me and said, "Tomorrow I will come by after work and maybe we can go to dinner and catch the late show."

I was tired of trying to convince Jamal all I wanted was peace so I said, "Why don't you do that? In the meantime, will you let me drink my tea alone so I could think about some things?"

It was almost like his heart stopped beating. He sucked his lips and said, "If you promise not to think about things that will upset you. Worry can put you in an early grave."

I snickered a bit and said, "I realize now that no matter what I say to you at this point, you will have nothing but concern for me. Thank you Jamal."

Then he let himself out the door without even giving me a smack on the cheeks. I didn't care though. I was too old for that shit anyway. At least that's what I kept telling myself.

The clock struck midnight and I jumped in sweat. I could hear the chiming of the grandfathered clock in the hallway. Dong, dong, dong. The clock chimed over and over again. I thought I saw a shadow by the closet as I noticed the moon shining brightly outside my window. My heart was racing fast and the bed was soaked. "It must have been another one of those weird ass dreams," I thought. "They just won't leave me alone."

It was late, but I needed to talk to someone. My choice was slim at that time of the night. If I called my girl Shanice I might interrupt her love making with Frank again. If I called my mother I might disturb her sleep. I knew momma wasn't feeling well, but she was the obvious choice.

When I picked up the phone to call momma, it rang twice. "Hello momma," I said. "Before you start wondering what happened, I just wanted to say that everything is okay. I didn't know who to call so I chose you."

"What's wrong Chantal? Are the kids okay?"

"They're fine momma. I had another one of those dreams about you again."

"Chantal baby, I told you I'm going to be okay. Maybe if you didn't worry about it so much you wouldn't have the dreams."

"I try so hard momma, but I keep having a dream about you walking. Are you feeling any better?"

"As a matter of fact, I feel great. I got up this morning and I was able to get around better than I have in months."

"I'm so glad to hear that momma. How are Denise and the kids?"

"Denise will be Denise and the kids, well they will be kids."

"So what you are saying is Denise still is having a hard time with the kids?"

"Something like that, but don't you worry Chantal. Denise is a grown woman and she can handle her kids."

"I hope so. By the way, Jamal stopped by earlier. He wants to work things out again."

"Oh Chantal, I'm so happy for you."

"No momma, don't get the wrong impression. I don't plan on giving him another chance. I'm still dealing with what happened with Maurice."

"Baby don't let a good thing pass you by. Jamal's a good man. He may have his faults like most men do, but Jamal loves you and especially his kids. Chantal give him another chance please for my sake."

"I can't momma. I just can't. He's coming over tomorrow to take me out, but I am going to let him down as gently as I can."

"Chantal…"

"Momma look, my mind is made up. I will talk to you tomorrow after we come back from dinner."

"Don't make the same mistake twice Chantal."

"I hear you momma. I love you."

"I love you Chantal. Good night."

I wasn't trying to hear any part of that mess so I cut the conversation short. Any other time I would talk to momma for hours. "Momma must have been up too late to be talking shit like that," I said out loud yawning the entire time. "I'll just close my eyes," I thought yawning again and before I knew it, I was sound asleep.

CHAPTER 3

Dating Jamal

My phone rang once and I grabbed it fast. "Hello," I said looking at the face of the clock. It's a good thing I didn't work because I would have been late as hell.

"What's up baby?" Jamal said. "Thought I would give you a wake up call. Did I wake you?"

"It's okay. I needed to get up anyway."

"I was thinking about our date tonight. I can't wait to see you. Can I come over now?"

Once a nuisance always a nuisance. "I don't think that would be a good idea. I haven't got out of bed yet.

"All the better for me to come over."

"I don't think so. I agreed to go out with you tonight. Please don't make me change my mind."

"I'm sorry sweetheart. I don't want to rush you. I'm anxious about us."

"Okay whatever. I need to get up and get some things taken care of. I'll call you later on this evening."

"Cutting me short, huh? That's cool. I'll be over around 6:30 tonight if it's okay."

"I'll be ready."

I got off the phone with Jamal and screamed loudly. It's a good thing the boys wasn't home because I would have scared the crap out of them.

I waited until 11:00 a.m. to call Shanice. I knew she was normally at work and her office got rather busy in the morning. She picked up the phone in her ever so cheering voice. "Shanice Williams, how may I help you?"

"Hey girlfriend. Whassup?"

"Chantal, girl I've been thinking about you. I've been so busy today. What's going on?"

"Jamal. He wants back into my life like yesterday."

"You kiddin' right?"

"I wish I was. He is starting to annoy me to death. Can you save me?"

"How?"

"Get me out of having dinner with him tonight."

"Now Chantal. Think about it. It's a free dinner and you won't be alone. Give it a chance. You never know what might come of it."

"Girl my momma said the same thing. Ya'll been talkin' or somethin'?"

"Ooh, you are country as hell. No, I haven't been talking to your momma, but I think you should listen to her."

"There you go."

"Hold up a minute. My boss just stepped in." There was a pause and then Shanice said, "I'll call you back. Something major just happened."

We hung up the phone and I turned on the TV. All over the news, I heard about a plane crashing into the World Trade Center. I was glued to the TV for roughly an hour as I watched the horrific news of three planes crashing, one into the Pentagon and the other one into an open field. I was shocked.

I picked up the phone to call Denise since her birthday was on that day. She was just as shocked as I was. "Are you okay?" I asked.

"Huh, I'm scared to death. Why this shit had to happen on my birthday? If I wanted to celebrate today, there is no way in the world I could. My birthday is ruined."

"Not ruined Denise, but saved by the grace of God."

"But why Chantal? Why did it have to happen?"

"I don't know, but God has a reason for everything He does. We're not supposed to question Him."

"I'm so scared Chantal."

"I know you are. Just pray for those that didn't make it. I'm sure their families would appreciate it."

"I'll do that."

"I'm gonna go now. Have some phone calls to make. Take care of yourself and the kids for me."

"I will. Tell Dante and Montel their aunt said hello."

"I sure will. Love you."

"Me too."

I took a closer look at myself in the mirror and thought about what Jamal had asked. As much as I traveled on planes, any one of those flights could have been mine. If I had already made up my mind to kick Jamal to the curb, my heart had changed.

When Jamal showed up around 6:15 that evening, I was already dressed in one of my charcoal gray pant suits and gray pumps. I had gone to get my hair done up at Wanda's Hair Salon and Braids.

"What a sight for sore eyes!"

"Your eyes aren't sore. Thanks for the compliment though."

"You're looking good yourself."

"Let me grab my purse and I'll be ready to go." I set the alarm on the way out and turned down the lights.

"We arrived at Joe's Steak House around 6:45 p.m., placed our order, and talked until the waitress delivered our plates.

We came back to my house and I invited Jamal in. I actually enjoyed myself with Jamal and wanted to show my gratitude by offering him a cup of coffee. Jamal accepted my offer and came in. He took a seat on the sofa while I was making him some coffee and me some lemon tea. For a while, we laughed and talked about the kids and how things should have been. Jamal asked if he could tuck me in and I looked at him and said, "I know your tricks Jamal. I'm not falling for that one."

"No tricks intended. I just had such a wonderful time tonight and wanted to make sure you got to bed comfortably."

Now I knew Jamal wasn't thinking about putting me to bed. The only thing on his mind was getting in between my thighs. "No funny business okay. I'm extremely tired and need to rest a bit."

We walked upstairs and entered my room. Somehow through it all, I forgot to make my bed.

"I know what you are about to say and don't worry about it. I didn't make my bed either."

"Jamal, you never make your bed." Then I smiled at him, took my shoes off, and lay across the bed.

Jamal gave me a massage and kissed me on the neck. A part of me wanted him to stop, but the woman in me wanted him to continue. I could feel him against me as he straddled his left leg over my buttocks.

"I think you should leave," I said before he decided to take things further.

"Let me in baby. I know you want it just as much as I do."

Then, he kissed me again. I felt a slight tingle and it was on. "Only for a minute and then you have to leave," I said knowing I was telling a lie. I wanted Jamal just as much if not more than he wanted me.

Jamal undressed me and I did likewise to him. For the first time in years, I allowed him to caress my body like before. I needed closure with Jamal and if having to make love with him one last time would do it for me then so be it.

We didn't have mean sex—you know the kind where men would flip your ass over and turn you inside out. Nope, not even the predictable "V" where the legs flew up in the air and then over your head. Nah, it was the kind the women dreamed about. The kind where the missionary played very little part and the doggie style came to play. Then without notice, he kissed me in places I haven't been kissed in a very long time. My body melted like wax.

"Auh shit," I screamed. "Why'd you have to do this to me Jamal?" Then I released.

"Feels good baby."

"Yes, it does."

"Did you come for me?"

"I sure did."

"Was it good?"

"Stop the talking Jamal and fuck me okay!"

"Like this?"

"Yeahhhhhhhhhhhhh," and then I released again.

I hadn't felt this good in a long time. My body poured in sweat and Jamal trembled as he released himself inside of me. We just lay there for a moment gasping for air. The bed was soaked. I reached in the drawer next to me and pulled out two hand towels. We cleaned ourselves up and took a shower and fell asleep.

The next morning when I woke up, Jamal had already gone. He left a note behind saying that he had an early morning meeting and thanked me for allowing him to stay over. Had I known he was going to be a no show the next morning, I would have kicked his ass out the night before.

Fallin' Soldier

Muscles tensed
Amidst the thighs
Bladder bliss
Temperature rise.
Warm sensation
Hot creation
Drip drip juice
My fascination.
Shaft fall down
Dig deep
Tickling walls
Oops, defeat.
Roar the thunder
Make me hot
Fallin' soldier
Fail me not.
Rise with triumph
Defeat the fight
Stand tall wounded soldier
Feel me tonight.

Donna Marie Brown

Copyright ©2005 Donna Marie Brown

CHAPTER 4

"Deteriorating"

I was lying in bed that November 2001 debating on whether or not I should get up or just sleep in for the rest of the day. It was one of those mornings where I just didn't want to do anything, but be lazy. The phone started ringing and the decision was made for me. I didn't even want to answer the damn phone thinking it was a telemarketer or some bill collector looking for Jamal. We had started getting our lives back in order and Jamal was hanging around quite often. Montel liked that more than anyone.

I picked up the phone and said, "Hi mother," noticing the caller ID had her number on it.

"How did you know it was me?" Mildred asked.

"Technology momma. Is everything okay?"

"I have some bad news. My kidneys are failing and the doctor said I might need a donor."

"That's not a problem momma. I'm volunteering my services right now."

"No Chantal," she said. "I don't expect any of my children to risk their lives for mine. They have me on the register and one should come through soon."

"Momma that could easily be fixed today. I know someone that did the same thing for his sister and he's fine. In fact, the guy is over fifty. Please let me do this for you."

"I won't have it Chantal."

"That settles it then. I'm coming home."

"When?"

"I'll be there tomorrow. Get some rest and I'll talk to you later."

I didn't like the way Mildred sound on the phone. Her voice had changed and I was getting worried about her health. I asked Jamal if he would take care of Montel while I was gone which didn't seem to be a problem. I contacted Shanice and let her know what was going on with Mildred and asked if she would check in on Montel for me.

I arrived at the Pensacola Regional Airport about 1:30 p.m. on November 9, 2001. I could only be away for a short while with Montel being in school and all. I picked up my car from Budget Rental Cars and headed down Navy Boulevard to be with her. When I got there, Mildred looked at me and said, "There's my baby." It brought back so many memories of how I used to walk in the house, put my arms around her, and give her a great big kiss on the neck.

"Yes Momma, your baby is home." My sister Denise looked at me and started to cry. "Why the tears Denise?" I asked blatantly.

"It's so good to see you here. Every time momma calls for you, you always make your way here fast."

I smiled at Denise and said, "You don't realize something." Then I turned to Mildred and said, "you only get one momma. You have to treat her with the utmost love because her love is too fragile to waste."

Mildred shook her head and said, "Chantal—what in the world am I going to do with you?"

I kissed her again and said, "Just love me momma."

Denise walked away and Mildred and I sat and talked for hours. I didn't want to scare her, but wanted her to know that I was having some strange dreams about her being in a coffin. I still remember her saying, "Don't wish bad luck on me Chantal." I tried explaining to her that I would never wish bad luck upon her life or anyone else's for that matter. But, I believe God was just sending a message through me to prepare her for the future. Sometimes I wished God didn't use me like that.

As Momma sat in her living room that cold November day, I watched as she dozed off to sleep. I went to her closet, retrieved her favorite blanket, and tucked her in. She opened her eyes slightly, gave me a smile, and told me how much she loved me. I knew she wasn't going to live much longer, but denied myself the thought. Her skin color had changed from light brown to dark bronze. She fell asleep often and had problems walking.

Trying not to disturb her, I decided to make her favorite sour cream pound cake while she slept. But the sound of pots and pans along with the mixer disturbed her. It wasn't until she smelled the aroma of the sour cream pound cake baking that she sat straight up.

"Chantal Jenkins—what are you cookin' in there that smells so damn good?"

"Take a guess Momma." I waited for her to tell me, but she took too long. "I guess I have to spoil your surprise. It's your favorite cake Momma," I said frowning knowing that my surprise was ruined.

"Bring me a slice now!" She demanded.

Then I laughed at the fact that she couldn't have any and said, "Sorry mother, but you have to wait another twenty minutes or so. It's not finished yet."

Mildred wasn't trying to hear that she had to wait for a slice of her favorite cake. Her passion for my pound cakes was better than having sex on a good day. Not that sex on any day wasn't good. Mildred started to pout knowing she had awakened to her favorite smell in the world other than collard greens, cornbread, pig's feet, and fried chicken.

As soon as the cake emerged from the oven, Mildred had her mouth fixed to get a slice. "Nope, gotta wait til it cools off so the cake can form and it won't crumble." I tried offering her a cup of coffee while she waited, but she insisted on waiting for the cake.

"You wanna play Spades or Pity Pat momma?" I asked trying to lure her mind in a different direction.

"I'll play Pity Pat if you deal first."

I laughed and said, "I'll get the cards." Denise and her daughter Danielle joined in. Although Danielle wasn't old enough to gamble, she took us for every nickel, dime, and quarter we had.

"You're a pro at this game Danielle," I said wishing for my quarters back. "Who taught you how to play like that?"

Momma started to gag on the thought that Danielle would name her as the culprit.

"Oh, I learned this from watching granny and her friends," Danielle replied. I turned to Momma and she started whistling.

"Before you say anything, Danielle is almost seventeen and she is old enough to watch me play cards."

"I'm not going to say a word. But, you have to be careful playing cards around the kids. They might repeat it to someone and you'll get in big trouble."

"Chantal, mind your business. Where is my cake anyway?" Momma added.

I shook my head and said, "I hope you are going to share this time."

"If anybody gets a piece, I will cut it."

"There you go being selfish again momma."

"Denise, watch your mouth. You always pickin' on me. Momma took everything so serious. She was about as spoiled as a rotten egg.

"I'm sorry Momma. Tell her I was just joking Chantal. Take a chill pill won't cha!"

"Oh, I thought you were trying to be funny," I remarked. I looked at momma and said, "You know I can't stay long right?" Then I gave her a humongous hug.

"Don't I know Chantal! I really hate to see you leave so soon."

"I'll be back before you know it Momma. You are going to get so tired of me being around that you'll pack my bags and send me back to Maryland yourself." I changed the subject and said, "But before I leave, why don't I take you to Biloxi for old time sake?"

Mildred's eyes lit up like candles on a birthday cake. Mildred couldn't move fast, but the mere mention of Biloxi, Mississippi sent her storming to her room to change clothes. Denise tagged along for the ride. She wasn't interested in playing the slots. She just wanted to be there with us to get away from Warrington—a suburb of Pensacola.

We headed down I-10 towards Mobile, Alabama. The entire time momma slept. After an hour had passed, I popped in a tape and told Mildred to listen. She was half asleep, but Denise somehow got her attention to focus on what I was trying to do. I looked in my mirror, smiled at her lying in the back seat, reached behind me with my right arm grabbing her hands, and began singing to her.

One of my all time favorite songs, *Momma* by Boyz to Men was playing on the CD player. I wouldn't let go of her hand until I played the song through twice. Mildred thanked me for what I was trying to do and then she went back to sleep. Denise said, "Girl, you really know how to make Momma light up."

"It's nothing special Denise. I just love her so much," I replied trying to keep my eyes on the road while crossing the bridge going into Mobile, Alabama.

"Man, this is a long ass bridge," Denise said.

"Watch your mouth Denise," Mildred said sitting up as we went through the tunnel. "I'm still your momma and you still have to respect me," she said smiling jokingly.

"I'm sorry Momma. Didn't know you were awake. No disrespect intended."

"I'm just kidding baby. I know you're well over forty."

"Whew! Thought I was getting ready to get another one of Mildred's famous slap-in-the-face ass whippings."

"Denise. Cut it out girl!" I responded.

"Alright already," she replied.

We went back to singing more songs on the tape and Mildred placed her request for us to sing "Momma" again. We were more than happy to oblige. She especially liked the part about 'loving you is like food to my soul.' I don't know how many times we had to repeat that for her, but it was well worth it.

When we reached the Grand Casino, Mildred insisted she needed a wheelchair. Denise ran to get one while I parked the car. The place was packed with gamblers from all across the nation. Mildred told me to make myself scarce and Denise was to push her over to the Jokers Wild slot area. Her first ten dollars went so fast that she went over to the dollar slots. Mildred lost five dollars immediately and then if by fate, she put in three dollar coins instead of two and in an instant, hit five hundred dollars. You talking about a stroke of luck. Mildred was the queen of luck.

After Mildred cleared $752.50, she started to get tired and said the smoke was bothering her. She had Denise come and get me so we headed back home. We finally arrived around 9:15 p.m. We were beat. I started to pack my clothes and the doorbell rang. Karen and Shavonda, old friends from high school asked me to go to a club with them. Man, I was tired as hell and wasn't keen on going at the time but thought since I hadn't seen them in a while maybe a couple hours wouldn't hurt. I knew I had to hurry back soon to spend some quality time with momma before I headed back to Maryland.

We end up at this place called Post 93. It was located downtown just off Cervantes street. We walked in and the place was packed with niggas bumping and grinding themselves crazy.

I sat and watched as this tall, snaggle-toothed man with a tan cowboy hat and brown tie started to head towards me. There was no way in hell I was going to let this man anywhere near me. His face was round with deep cast in his jawbones and a slight cut upon his chin. *"He cannot be coming my way,"* I thought as the man introduced himself and then asked if he could sit at the table with me. I was not trying to see this man in my face. I was just chillin' with some friends and just watching them dance their hearts away in a small section of the brown wooden floor.

Most of the people were African Americans and they started to gather on the same tiny floor shaking their asses and grinding each other as though they were making love.

I was hoping my friends would hurry back so this hybrid creature could get away from me. When he smiled at me, I thought to myself, "This man hasn't seen a tooth brush in decades. I burst into laughter and he thought that I was just happy someone came over to my table to talk to me.

"Hello Ms., may I have this dance?" He asked hoping for an immediate yes.

"Sure," I replied. "Why not?"

I hadn't danced in years and I sure didn't keep up with the latest dances. My mind drifted as he stared graciously at me. "You shouldn't look so serious," he said pulling himself towards me. I kept my arms and fists close to my chest. There was no way in hell I was going to let this thing touch my body. Man, he was fishin'.

"So how often do you come to the post?" He asked.

"This is actually my first time," I replied. "I don't do clubs. I'm just here on a business trip.

"You don't seem to be having a good time." He said bluntly.

"Actually, I'm not," I responded. "The smoke is killing me and I have a flight to catch tomorrow."

"You're leaving so soon?" He asked.

"Yep, the sooner the better." Then I paused noticing how rude I was being towards this man. "I'm sorry. Where's my manners? I was actually born and raised here, but I left about fifteen years ago to join the service."

"Oh really now! I'm ex-Air Force. Served my country for twenty two years, then I had to retire. Too much overseas time!"

"That's remarkable," I said gasping for a relief of fresh air. "How do you stand being around all this smoke? You gotta be desperate to be in a place like this."

"I just put up with it myself," he said. "I never got your name." He said smiling again showing me his missing teeth.

"I never gave it to you," I replied in a smart manner.

"So, I can't have your name?"

"The name's Chantal—Chantal Jenkins."

"Chantal. That's a beautiful name for a beautiful woman. I think you should continue that lovely smile of yours so that all the men can look at you."

"I'm not interested in other men, just my husband," I replied. "I need to sit down now. I'm getting the worst headache."

"Baby, you sure you don't wanna stay on the dance floor? I'm not ready to leave yet."

"That's just too damn bad Mister whatever your name is. I need to sit down right now. My feet are killing me," I said making any excuse to get away from this man. "Besides I don't know you."

"Charlie," he said hoping I would I'll somehow ease up on him at bit. "Charlie Steele. You know like the author Danielle Steele," he said trying to add a little humor to the conversation, but I didn't crack a smile. "Alrighty then! I guess I'll just join you at your seat if it's okay with you."

Finding another excuse, I replied, "Maybe that's not such a good idea. My friends will be back soon and they might get mad if their seats are taken."

I was determined to get this loser away from me. This man—although neatly dressed—had such a horrific look that I didn't want my friends or anyone else for that matter to get the impression that I was with him.

"Damn baby, are you always this bitter? Can you at least cut a brotha a break?"

"Look, maybe I'll dance with you another time. I really need some fresh air."

Charlie went back over to his seat and watched me until my friends came back.

"What an arrogant asshole!" I said as they took their own sweet time getting back to me.

"Girl, I saw you turning the men down left and right. You need to loosen up a little bit," Karen said.

"Not if the men look like him I don't. Besides, the smoke in here is really detrimental to my health. How much longer are you going to stay in this hole in the wall?"

"Not much longer Chantal! Shavonda and I need to shake our butts a little longer. Don't playa hate because you don't have anyone worth while to dance with you."

"It's some nice looking brothers up in here. Unfortunately, they tend to be taken at the moment. I'm likely to go up to one of them and ask them to dance. Do you think that's a bit bold, Shavonda?"

"Girl women have to be more aggressive these days. Stand your ground and do whatever your heart feel is right," Karen replied while stopping the waiter asking for a tall glass of Long Island Iced tea.

"You're gonna drink all that poison? Do you know what's in it?" I asked.

"Sure do. I have them all the time," Karen replied.

"I hope you don't end up like your daddy," I said. Karen's daddy stayed just as drunk as mine. In fact, they were the best drinking partners out there.

"Girl, don't bring that man's name up around me!"

Shavonda cut into the conversation. "I saw you dancing with old snaggled tooth. Did his breath stink?"

"No, but his smile said go get a tooth brush, dental floss, and some liquid drain cleaner and scrub that shit off your teeth fast."

"You're too funny Chantal. What about the other guy that came and sat with you at first? How come you didn't dance with him?" Shavonda asked.

As the waiter walked back to the table, she handed Karen her Long Island Iced Tea and was tipped a dollar.

"Well—that guy wanted to slow dance with me. Now you know I wasn't having that. How I look with some greasy nigga grinding up against me and I never met him before?"

"I don't know. But, he wouldn't be grinding against me neither."

Karen said, "You know not to have another nigga rubbing against your ass other than Jamal. That man would kill you."

I shrugged. "Jamal don't have any power over me. He's no closer in my life than any other man I've been with."

"Yeah, that's what your mouth say," Karen responded.

"That's what I know," I replied.

Then like the Messiah had walked through the door, the DJ threw on a song, "Your Wife Is Cheating on Us," and every person in the room started to scream. I thought, "What the hell? Did I miss something here?" It was the first time I'd heard that song. People started jumping up out of their seats like some pop star was on stage. I sat back and watched as Karen and Shavonda left me again to dance with men I've never seen before. The men watched as though to give each other the eye and then another came to the table. This time it was one of the fine ones. I smiled and he sat down introducing himself as Robert Young, a businessman in the area.

We talked for a bit and then the DJ—as though he was going through a love triangle of his own, announced that he would be slowing the music down for all the lovers out there who were going through some hard times. He talked about the situation he was in with his girl and thought the song he chose would be most fitting for the occasion. The women screamed as he put, 'Before I Let You Go Away' on the turntable. Couples jumped as though a savior had come to take them away.

Despite the small area they had to dance on, Karen and Shavonda joined the crowd. I turned around to face them as they grabbed men from their seats and held them close. Most of the people seemed to be romancing more than slow dancing. A tall guy wearing a white outfit with a medium dark complexion and sporting a flabby ass got up out of his seat and worked his body worse than a prostitute walking the streets on Central Avenue. I laughed my ass off watching him shake his ass in hopes of scoring with the woman he was dancing with. It was late when we left the club, but I knew one thing for sure, it was one night I surely could not forget.

The next morning, Mildred had the house slamming with the smell of fried pork, scrambled eggs, and homemade biscuits. I ain't never tasted biscuits so fresh! Mildred had a slight limp that caused her body to twist. "Momma, you sure you're going to be alright when I leave?"

"Baby, I'll be just fine. Don't go worrying your pretty little self about me! How in the world do you continue to look so thin and beautiful?" As though she hadn't seen me in years," she said, "I know you're getting up in age."

"Now that's my secret Momma. But, if you really have to know, Shanice gave me some of that Mary Kay stuff she sells."

"Well, it sho' nuff keeps your face looking young," Mildred said finding it hard to keep her balance.

"Momma, why didn't you let me fix breakfast this morning? I still know how to burn a little."

She smiled at me and said, "When my baby comes home, I have to treat her special."

"You act like I'm some kind of actor or something," I jested.

"To me baby, you're better than an actor or actress. You're my unsung hero."

I raised my eyebrows and stuck my lips out, "I'm nothing special momma. Just have a special kind of love for you, that's all."

"I'm proud to say you're my daughter Chantal. Not many women get a chance to say that about their children."

I smirked a little, "I'm going to miss you Momma. I can't wait to come back." Then I grabbed my bags and started to pack the rest of my items from the previous night.

"Chantal Jenkins," momma called out putting the emphasis on the word Chantal. "Come here for a minute." I went back into the living room and she was holding a beautiful gold roped necklace. "This is for you baby."

I couldn't believe she had gotten me a gift and I didn't have one for her. "Oh momma," I blurted. "Why did you go and buy something for me? I don't have a gift for you."

Mildred grabbed my hands, smiled, and said, "I wasn't looking for anything in return. You have given me so many things especially this big beautiful house. I just hope the good Lord lets me live long enough to enjoy it."

I smirked, "You will be here longer than you'll ever know."

CHAPTER 5

A Frightening Dream

After I returned from my trip, I tried desperately to make things work with Jamal. We went out a few more times, but we just couldn't get it right. He had lost the one thing I use to love most about him, sense of humor. I guess after being with RJ and being turned inside out, no other man was going to ever come close to making love to me like him.

I decided to lay down for a while trying to think what was best for me and that's when it happened, the strangest damn dream I've ever had in my entire life. I could see if it had to do with me giving somebody a blow job or someone banging the crap out of me. But, this one was way in left field. I woke up around 2:00 a.m. that cold Monday morning in December 2001. I rushed around trying to find some paper and a pen noticing one sitting on the dresser across from me. Trying not to disturb anyone, I went into the bathroom and started writing. I didn't know what I was writing because I was still partially asleep.

When I woke up the next morning, I saw that I had three pages of notes from the night before. I couldn't believe my eyes. It was almost like I was seeing an event getting ready to take place, but didn't know exactly what it was. I gave my girlfriend Shanice a call. I was mesmerized by the events that had taken place that morning and needed to let somebody know. Shanice was in the process of getting her children Justin and Miranda ready for school.

Shanice had just finished ironing Justin's jeans when the phone rang. "Hello."

"Shanice. Hi, it's Chantal. I know it's early but girl, I need to talk to you. Did I wake you?"

"No girl, I've been up since 6:30. What's the problem?"

"I don't think it's a problem, but girl—I had a dream out of this world. I have to tell somebody about it. I've already called my sister Denise earlier this morning, but I wanted to wait until people in Baltimore woke up. You know how grouchy some people can be."

"Girl, don't I know that. What kind of dream was it? I mean—did you finally find the man of your dreams in your dream?" Smiling, as she turned Frankie over to rub down his bottom with Johnson's baby lotion.

"No, don't I wish. You know how I always have strange encounters and dreams about something happening to turn my life around, right?"

"Yeah."

"Well listen to this. It will knock you off your feet. Especially, the way it starts off."

"I'm all ears," Shanice said. "Go for it."

"This is how it went."

Knowing the fate of his life would soon be snatched away like a thief in the night, I held him close ensuring his gentle, but frail little body would be comforted until God called him home. Silence was in the air as I drifted into a world where my son Montel and I walked outside into a wooded area filled with open air and partially dark skies. As I looked around, I could see what seemed to be three monkeys facing the opposite direction squatting on the ground. As I pointed them out to Montel, more of them appeared. We started to back away in fear that these monkeys would come our way. People started to gather and we felt safer.

Without a moments notice, the creatures popped out of the air, out of the trees, and they came off the ground like an assault missile plunging into an army of soldiers waiting for war. Their faces were pure white and when they stood up, they were the size of humans. There was also a leader with them that stood almost seven feet. They were ripping the lives of each human as they plunged. I grabbed Montel and ran desperately seeking a place to hide from these hideous creatures. Heads were being chopped off and bodies half hung as we made our way through willowed tree lines.

As I awakened, I could see that it was just a dream and Montel was still fast asleep in my arms. As I closed my eyes once again, the dream continued with me and Montel running further into a path where bits and pieces of human flesh lay scattered upon the earth destined for more destruction. The further we ran I could see doors of trailers aligned side by side opened on a dirty path filled with tree limbs and small fractions of rocks. I closed the doors as we passed yelling to them that the monkeys were coming and to find safety.

"Hold up one moment, girlfriend. You mean to tell me you saw all of this in a dream?"

"Yeah, now let me finish okay."

Taking a slight breath, Shanice said, "all right, go ahead."

"Thank you."

As we ran further, Colin Powell was telling us to move forward and to keep the enemy behind us. He was fully dressed in his Army greens and was commanding a unit of other military personnel looking for cover.

Then out of the blue, I was back at the sight of the little baby. The fragile little baby who rested curled up in my arms had met his maker. Tears rolled down my face as I walked towards his mother giving her the unbearable news. Screams of disbelief frequented the parlor as I sat awaiting the comfort of a gentle soul. Not one of them came my way. I saw the face of the baby's uncle as his corpse lay stiffly in a mahogany coffin prepared for the sheathing of his body. The baby, only two months old, could have been anyone's baby. But it looked like my cousin's baby. She looked around waiting for the reaction of her disappearing husband who bore no resemblance to the baby I had lying in my arms. If ever there was a time I had seen the sweetness of a chocolate-coated baby, it was now.

"Whoa girlfriend! Are you at a funeral or something?"

"Yes, in the dream it's a though I'm attending my cousin's funeral, but a war is going on at the same time."

"Girl, this is too weird even for you. I know your dreams are wild, but this one takes the cake."

"Just listen to me Shanice. I know it doesn't make any sense right now, but it's like I'm seeing the future or something. Let me finish okay."

"Go ahead, but I don't have all day. I have to finish up with the kids."

"Okay, I'll make it quick."

As I passed him over to his weeping mother, I headed towards the first open room I could find, yet I drifted silently into my dream. By this time, the white-faced monkeys with their leader leading the pack had devoured the entire area. The leader's face was flushed like the whiteness of a marshmallow and the density of his skin was covered in black fur. I watched as this thing resembling a Sasquatch continuously devoured every person in site while heading towards me. With every victim, he left a dapple of secretion noting the area of his return. I could see the fury in his face as it alerted me to get the hell out of sight.

Running as fast as we could, we ducked into a trailer not suited to fill more than ten people. This thing with its enormous strength constantly pounded until the door of the rigid trailer gave way. His reach was long enough to grab two at a time and I pushed my way forward until the Montel and I were free.

Jumping from pools of sweat, I looked around to see if anyone was there. Nothing—no one, but me left alone to fend for myself in the opened sanctuary room of Union Memorial Hospital. As I rose from my seat, seeing the half plastered walls, my feet stood still as this was the worst nightmare I had ever encountered. Yet, as I moved closer to the door, I could see the last person standing there with open arms calling out to me. It was then that I realized I was not in a dream, but God had once again taken home one of his children. "The strangest part about it was I was dreaming about me being a dream."

"Girl, you done lost your mind. You are by far the weirdest person I know."

"Yeah, but I have some hellavu dreams though."

After waking and realizing I was still in dreamland, I leaped out of bed as fast as I could to write down this dream. I wrote it down piece-by-piece allowing no room for error. Eventually, going upstairs, I made a phone call to Denise, ensuring that everything was well at home. I guess she thought I was a little crazed by calling at 5:35 a.m. As I described my dream to her, she told me about the birth of her second grandson the previous day. "He looks just like Tony," Denise said as she yelled out at Danielle to hurry up and get dressed. I smiled knowing that the baby in my dreams also resembled Tony, Denise's son. My heart was eased knowing that there was no trouble lingering with my family in the Sunshine State.

As I awakened my family telling them about this elaborate dream, silence captured the room as we heard the announcer on "The Today Show" make reference to another sighting of a Sasquatch in Pennsylvania. Looking at each other, Dante said to me, "Momma, you just mentioned something like that in your dream." Shaking my head in disbelief, I said, "I know baby and this is weird as hell."

"Stop right there," Shanice said as I told her about the events that had taken place that morning. "You mean to tell me that all of this happened this morning?"

"It sure did. It was an unbelievable morning."

"That's enough, Chantal! Girl, you have some weird and I mean weird messed up dreams," Shanice said as she handed Justin a blue shirt to put on for school.

"Crazy, isn't it? But with all the shit that's going on in the world, I wonder what it really means," I said hastily.

"Yeah, like 911. Then it was the Anthrax scare, and oh who can forget all those Priest molesting little altar boys," Shanice remarked.

"That's why God is so pissed off with the world. He's not mad at us, but He's mad at them crazy ass priest. In the Bible, God said that every man should have a wife and they shall be as one. He didn't say you are exempt because you're a priest. That's why they mess with little boys because they're afraid of women," I said.

"Girl, you are sick! How 'bout them crazy ass niggas running around here talkin' about killing people in Virginia and DC?" Shanice asked.

"One thing for sure, they sure don't have any respect of people. Just like God. When He comes back, He doesn't spare the Christians with a graceful death. When it's their time to go, they can die in an airplane just like non-believers. One thing for sure though, they're gonna hang them niggas once they find them," I replied tiredly. "What possessed black men to go around shooting so many people in the first place and especially their own kind?"

"I say it's lack of sex. All they needed was a good woman standing behind them and we would have been safe. I think the brothas would've been all right," Shanice said.

"Oh, I think we were fine. It's the other people running around here scared to go outside." You have to admit. It's a shame how people of different nationalities were killed, but they tried them on the white woman from Virginia murder first. That shit bothers me and it should bother others as well."

"I guess they figure by trying them with a white woman's murder, they were sure to get the death penalty right away. It's just like the old days, hang them niggas and hang them well. Through it all, you have to admit you were just as scared as the next person Chantal."

"Not really Shanice. I figure, if it's meant for me to die, God would have taken me also. Check this out! All those people who died during 911, it wasn't a coincidence. It was a message from God. Those people could've been scattered all over the world and died one by one and no one would've given it a thought. But God allowed this to happen because He's tired of the way the world is. Check out Noah's Ark! God was tired of the whores, liars, cheaters, murderers, and corruption. You see what He allowed to happen to them? That's why I try to be prayed up. You know, just in case God calls me home."

"That's well said Chantal! But, I don't think it's over yet. I think your dream is the start of something major. We might not live through this one."

"Don't talk like that Shanice! That kind of shit scares the pants off me. I mean—how many times do our higher officials have to put our families in harm's way? I don't see them throwing their spoiled ass stuck up daughters in harm's way. We actually had some sistas killed in the last war. But it was the white girl that got all the recognition and the book deal. That bitch just laid there and waited to be rescued. But the sista, she got messed up bad."

"I know Chantal. That bothers me too. Listen, I gotta go before the kids are late for school."

"Yeah—me too. I have a lot of things to do around here. Give me a call later okay."

"Will do. I love you Chantal."

"Me too."

Dreams

They come by night
Wakin' you, shakin' you
Takin' you through fantasies, horror, pain and delight
Some come by day full of passion—emotion
Stirring up all kinds of commotion
They creep at you even sleep with you
Make you pour in sweat
Some even have the nerve to make you wet
They're classy, sassy, hot and deep
Make even an old man lose his sleep
They over power you
Keep you guessing what the outcome will be
Damn it, this one came at three
It was hairy scary made me lose my mind
About a woman, Lord knows she ain't my kind
Said I was a classy lady
Huh, to me, she seemed kind of shady
Told me she wanted to be mine
Shit—she wasn't even fine
I hate knowing she felt that attraction
Blew my mind with her distraction
I woke up with such a weird feeling
Knowing it was her I should be killing
Interrupting my precious sleep
Trying to dig deep—into my heart
She was there
Without a moment to care
Tearing my life in pieces
What's the point?
No, I won't do it
I won't
I won't
Damnit,
I did.

Copyright ©2003 Donna Marie Brown

CHAPTER 6

Hanging from the cell
(Shanice)

"Stupid tramp bitch!" Rick thought as he tied another knot in his shirt. "She never knew how good she had it. Had to go and mess with my friend. I'll show her," he said tying another knot through his shirt. He took out a piece of paper and reached for his pen and started to write:

My dearest Shanice...I remember the good times we shared and the love you gave. I brought so much distress to your life and you gave me your heart. What else am I to do? Now that you're with my best friend, I have nothing left. My kids wouldn't want to see a father in jail all the time and me....well, that's another story. There's a death threat on my life so I might as well give them the pleasure of killing myself. So many men have gotten the disease and hopes of recovering were slim. Baby, you were my everything. Why did you have to go and sleep with my friend? I saw you, Shanice. I saw you let another man make love to you. Out of all the people in the world, you had to sleep with Frank. I'm sorry Monique and I hurt you. But baby, we made our mistakes. We couldn't help what we felt. She died longing for Frank but he only had eyes for you. I knew it years ago. I just couldn't admit it to myself. They say the hardest part is letting go. Well, baby—I'm letting you go. It's time, don't you think? Huh, I think it's rather funny watching the two of you raise my damn kids! Yeah, they are getting up there in age and probably don't even remember me. I'm the one who changed their diapers one, two, three o'clock in the morning. Where was Frank then? You know, Shanice—you deserve each other. I hope you rot in

32

hell for what you're doing. I should've listened to my mother. She told me that women like you would only hurt me and turn up as whores. Huh, that's what I think of you—you back stabbing slut.

A long pause and it was over.

Rick hadn't called in weeks. I thought he had finally given up on me and decided to let me and Frank work on our relationship. I was so excited about Frank asking me to marry him.

Chantal was sitting in her black chaise lounge writing a letter to her sister when she received my call. She had been sipping on a Strawberry Daiquiri filled with whipped cream. She was still having a hard time dealing with that fact that her mother might not be around much longer. Mildred was everything to Chantal and now that the doctors had given up on her, Chantal's life was in shambles. Mildred watched over Chantal through her hard times with Kenyon, Jamal, and RJ. When I told her about my engagement to Frank and a baby being on the way, Chantal choked on the idea of me having a baby by another man while still married to Rick.

"Girl, how you gonna have another man's baby while your husband's in jail with HIV?"

"I don't see anything wrong with that, Chantal. I mean—Rick and I will never be intimate like that again. Besides, I told you that Frank proposed to me, right?"

"Yeah—you did. But, that doesn't make it right for you to disrespect Rick like that."

"Girl, what's wrong with you today? You don't seem right. Is everything ok with you and Jamal?"

"It has nothing to do with Jamal. It's not like we're having great sex these days. We just like being around each other so we can take care of our child. I don't think I'll ever feel close to him like I use to."

"That's not what he's telling everybody. If it was left up to Jamal, you have been getting it on with him since you left RJ."

"That's just not true! I don't care what he tells other people. I know I can't let myself be with him like that again." Chantal changed the subject suddenly. "I really don't want to talk about some sorry ass Jamal, girlfriend. I want to talk about this baby of yours? When is it due?"

"Two months from now," I replied with a pleasant smile.

"Two months? And you're just telling me. I thought we were friends." Chantal said grudgingly.

"We are. I haven't seen or heard from you since the breakup. I'm sure the word got around somehow that I was pregnant."

"Well—yeah, Terrice told me about it. But, I wanted to hear it from you. You my girl, Shanice! No matter what Terrice told me. You should've been the one telling me."

"Speaking of Terrice, did you and her ever…well—you know what I'm trying to say?"

"If we did, I won't spill."

"Isn't it funny how we almost got together like that?" I said.

"Oooh, that would've been the biggest mistake ever. Girlfriends just don't rub like that," Chantal replied.

"Interesting choice of words, Chantal. What'cha mean by rubbing like that?" I responded defensively.

"I didn't mean it like that. Your mind stays in the gutter."

"Girl, Frank keeps my mind like that. That man got some kind of power over me."

"I don't wanna hear that shit, Shanice. You're nasty girl, aren't you?" Chantal said laughing.

"Yeah, that's the only way to be. Men like it when you start talking bullshit while you're making love," I responded.

"I wouldn't know about that. But—one of these days, I'm going to find mister right and when I do, you'll know everything about him," Chantal said.

A loud knock came to my door. "Hold on a minute, Chantal. Someone's at the door."

Two men dressed in police uniforms stood at the door. They looked serious. My first thought was that something had happened to Frank. "One moment," I said to them. "Let me get my girlfriend off the phone."

"Chantal, I'll call you back. It's the police."

"May I help you?" I asked placing the phone on the floor.

"Good afternoon, ma'am." They took their hats off and I knew then something bad had happened. "I'm Officer Curtis and that's my partner, John. May we come in for a minute? It won't take long."

I opened the door after they presented their badges with ID. I didn't know what to expect, but I was hoping the news wasn't too bad.

"Are you Shanice Everette? Officer Curtis asked.

"Yes. What's this about?" I asked worriedly.

Reaching into his pocket, Officer Curtis pulled out a letter address to me. "We need to talk to you about your husband Richard Williams."

"He's my ex-husband," I said placing my hands on my hips.

"We didn't know at first how to contact you. It's been a few days since it happened. You see ma'am, there isn't any easy way to tell you this. Mr.

Williams hung himself a couple days ago. He left this letter behind for you. We're so sorry to bring you this news."

I placed my hands over my mouth and stood motionless. Then, I let out a loud scream and wondered what could have gone wrong. "Rick wasn't such a bad guy," I told them. *"He only denied me affection because he was HIV positive and was concerned for my well-being."* I thought to myself. Smooth talking Rick was finally gone. *"How am I going to explain this to his kids?* I thought to myself again. Then I turned to one of them not wanting to hear that Rick had hung himself and asked, "Was he murdered? Oh my God! What am I saying? Why Officer Curtis? Why did they allow such a tragedy to happen?" I couldn't contain myself at this point.

"Ma'am, we're sorry for your loss. We can't control every prisoner in our custody. According to his cell mate, he felt as though you turned your back on him when you stop coming to see him. When you're locked up, you're just as good as gone," Officer Curtis said to me.

"Well then, there should be a law protecting the innocent," I said looking at him harshly and folded my arms.

"When you come to prison, you're fair game," Officer Dawson said taking his shades off.

I stared into the air for a moment and started to reminisce about my relationship with Rick. "He wasn't so bad," I screamed at the officer.

Frank walked up the steps and saw my expression. He introduced himself and told the officers he could handle the situation from here. He pulled off his black leather jacket, hung it in the closet, and walked the officers toward the door. I ran towards him.

"He didn't deserve to die," I said pounding Frank in his chest. "He wasn't a bad man, Frank. He was misunderstood."

"I know baby. He was a good friend too," He said dropping his head. "But we know what Rick did and those people had a death warrant out on him."

"How could they do such a thing, Frank?" I shouted angrily while running towards the couch.

"Baby, don't beat yourself up over this! Rick infected several people while he was locked up. You knew he was a dead man from the start."

"But—they didn't have to kill him, did they?

"No baby, they didn't. I'll tell you what. Let's go on a little outing tonight! I'll grab a babysitter for the kids."

"Oh my God! I forgot about the kids Frank. How will I tell them they don't have a father anymore?"

He held me in his arms and said, "Very carefully honey. I know it won't be easy, but you can do this."

"Since I'm the only link to his family, I'll have to take care of it."

"Maybe you should think about cremation. Rick had too many sores on his body for him to be exposed. We don't want everyone talking badly about him in front of his kids," Frank said kissing me on the forehead.

It was 6:45 p.m. on a Thursday evening. The kids were in the basement playing and Frank had just returned home from work. Hearing news about Rick's death didn't quite make for a special evening. Today was our third year together. He had already made reservations at Rusty Scupper on the Inner Harbor. He had them set aside a bottle of their best Champagne and a booth that sat cozily in a quiet corner.

"The babysitter will be over in an hour. We need to get dressed. I wanna take you somewhere special."

"Does it have to be…" He suddenly cut me off.

"Yes baby, it has to be tonight. I have special reservations already set up," he gave me a huge smile.

I smirked wanting to smile back at him but I couldn't bring myself to do so.

"Get dolled up for me baby!" Frank said as he pinched my butt. "Tonight, it will be just me and you.

I went upstairs prowling through my crunched up clothes hanging in my u-shaped closet. "Red, now that's hot!" I said looking at my miniskirt. *"Rick use to love this skirt. Guess he'll never see me in it again."* I said tearfully. *"Get a grip girlfriend."* I said to myself. *"Things will work out fine. Frank said so himself."*

I had gained a few pounds since I last wore that red leather mini. "Dayum girlfriend! You can't even zip it up without tucking in the tummy," I said praying it would fit. My focus went towards the letter. I took it out of the envelope and read it slowly. My heart was torn as I read how Rick expressed his sadness over Frank and I being together. As I read further, I realized that Rick wasn't murdered but hung himself like the officer stated, but I was too distracted by what he was telling me. I yelled out for Frank and he ran quickly towards me.

"What is it baby?"

"Look at this!" I screamed. "They didn't kill him. Oh my God!" I said screaming louder. "He killed himself." I burst into tears while falling onto the bed. "We killed him Frank. He couldn't take us being together."

"Baby—please! Don't beat yourself up like this. Rick would have done it regardless."

"But Frank…"

"Shhhh," he said and gave me a great big kiss. Then he looked me in my big brown eyes and said, "We have a dinner engagement sweetheart. We should leave shortly." We went to the car and Frank had twelve stemmed roses inside a crystal teddy bear vase waiting for me.

I didn't feel right going out to dinner knowing that Rick had hung himself. We tried not to mention Rick's name for the rest of the night. We just sat, ate and talked about the baby that would be coming soon.

CHAPTER 7

Mildred

Her passions were chocolates, sweets, and cigarettes. It didn't matter the flavor and it didn't matter the taste just as long as she had it. Three times that Wednesday she had her son-in-law run downstairs to sneak a few candy bars and a couple of cigarettes up to her room. Momma waited until they left and then wheeled herself downstairs to the courtyard. She had one cigarette after another and headed back upstairs as though nothing happened. The doctor's said the increase in nicotine and sugar had caused her blood pressure to skyrocket.

January 11, 2002, I gave Momma a call while she was in Baptist Hospital to check on her. Another congestive heart failure landed her back in the hospital that previous Monday.

Momma was known by the neighborhood kids as the "Candy Lady." Not because she sold so many sweets, but because of her kind passionate heart and the laughter she portrayed when the kids came around her. As we spoke on the phone, I could sense Momma's health was deteriorating. I never imagined it would be the last time I would hear Momma's precious voice. Momma was concerned that I ran my phone bill up immensely checking on her daily. After explaining that her life was more important, Momma finally understood.

It bothered me to hear momma cough. It was the same nagging cough a smoker had after years of constant smoking.

"Momma, are you okay?" I repeatedly asked. "You're starting to worry me. Have you been smoking again?"

"No, Chantal." Knowing that she had had a couple cigarettes earlier, she told me as she started to yawn. "Chantal, I'm so tired of the aches and pains my body's been going through. You know baby, I have been in and out of hospitals so much. I'm just tired."

"Momma, pray about it. You know if you had the faith of a mustard seed, God would reveal His healing power to you."

"I know baby. But—you don't understand," she said. "I've been in pain for so long—Chantal, you just don't understand."

"Momma, don't talk as though you're giving up. All you have to do is touch your aching pains and cry out to the Lord, Momma. He'll heal you just like He's healed me so many times."

Mildred was suddenly silent and I heard a slight snore.

"Momma, I'm sorry that I kept you up. I'll give you a call tomorrow."

"Baby please, stop wasting your money on me! I'll be fine." Mildred said while drifting off again.

"Momma, I love you." I told her as I usually did before we hung up the phone.

"I love you too baby. Don't worry about me. I'll be fine. They might even release me tomorrow. They're just monitoring my blood pressure. They said I had a little blood in my eyes. Not to worry though. They are taking care of it."

"Momma, please pray. I'm so worried about you," I said nervously as I hung up the phone.

On Thursday morning, January 12, 2002, I got up, fed and dressed Montel, and hurried out the door. At the time, Jamal and I were living separate lives and Montel lived with me most of the time. As we walked out the door, a large black raven flew over Montel's head nearly hitting him. In the next instant, a huge white seagull flew after him. I thought about the Raven portraying death, but the sea gull was an Angel of God chasing away the darkness. It bothered me as to what it really meant. While dropping Montel off at daycare, I mentioned it to his Carmen, his provider.

She turned to me and said, "You know your momma has been in and out of the hospital. She's been really lucky. I'll pray for her, but one of these days, I don't think that she will be that lucky," Carmen said.

"I know Carmen, but Momma is strong. She'll pull through," I said as I got ready to walk out the door. "I have to hurry up and get to work. I will call Momma and make sure she's okay."

By the time I'd reached my job, it was 8:38 a.m. The office was at full capacity and my coworkers chatted amongst themselves. My jacket couldn't come off fast enough. I had to contact Momma to see if she was all right. The phone rang and rang, but no answer. I called Denise, but still no answer.

An hour later, I tried again. The only person that could be reached was my uncle Joseph. He hadn't heard anything so the coast was clear.

At 2:05 p.m., I finally got in touch with Denise who had been out shopping and had just returned.

"Is everything okay with Momma?" I asked firmly desperately seeking an answer.

"As far as I know," she said. "Momma usually calls me around seven or so, but they must have taken her to dialysis already."

"Oh that's right! I forgot she has dialysis on Thursdays," I replied with a touch of ease in my voice.

"You know Chantal, I heard Momma had a heart attack last night."

"That's not true. They probably meant to say that she had congestive heart failure."

"I don't know Chantal, my friend was pretty certain about it."

"Well—she's wrong," I said disgustingly. "I guess I'll call her later when she comes back to her room."

"Okay, I love you," Denise said dragging out her words.

"Me too, Denise."

CHAPTER 8

She's Gone

I had five projects that needed to be completed by day's end. It didn't seem probable for me to meet my deadline. The phone rang at 2:23 p.m. All I could hear was out pours of cries.

"Hello," I said. "Hello. Is anybody there?"

"Chantal, it's Denise. You tell her Michelle," Denise said screaming louder.

Michelle, one of Denise's friends got on the phone. "Chantal," screaming to the top of her lungs, "your momma…..I can't do it Denise!"

I started to worry. Denise took the phone. "Momma had a bad stroke last night. They said she won't make it through the night."

"Stop lying to me! What are you saying?" I said while remembering the birds that flew over Montel's head.

"Come home, Chantal! Please, come home."

"It's gonna be alright. Momma always pulls through," I remarked while gathering my projects. "I'll see you tonight."

I immediately made arrangements on the Internet. I contacted Jamal and Montel's daycare provider.

"Your momma always pulled through," Carmen said nervously. "I'll keep you in my prayers."

My boss was in a meeting when I interrupted him. I explained that my mother had just had a stroke and probably would not make it through the night. I proceeded to give him each project, told him what needed to be done, and headed home. I didn't even ask if I could leave.

Jamal met me at my house along with Dante and Montel. Dante was grieving hard and momma hadn't passed yet. The previous April, we had lost our cousin Catherine to breast cancer and now Mildred was leaving. I was torn. I rushed around trying to find all the necessary items for my trip. Jamal grabbed hold of me and gave me a kiss.

"I can't lose my mother, Jamal. I just can't lose her. That's my momma, Jamal!"

"I know baby. I know," he said holding me even tighter.

"I gotta go before I miss my flight. Please take care of the boys."

"I will," he said as we packed up the car and drove over to BWI.

"Why do all the people I love have to die?" A very sorrowful Dante asked.

"I don't know baby. Let's just pray that God won't take her like He did with Cathy."

"I'm so scared momma," he said. Montel didn't know what was really going on. All he knew was I was headed to Florida to see my mother.

The airport wasn't crowded, but security was tight since the bombings of the WTC and the Pentagon on 911. I flew out of Gate D on AIRTRAN and thought about Mildred the entire time. A gentleman sitting next to me saw me as I fiddled around trying to find something to write with. He gave me a pen.

"Do you need a sheet of paper also?" He offered while tearing a piece from his tablet.

"No thanks. I just need a pen! I had a thought and I wanted to write it down before I forgot."

"Okay then. I'm sorry to disturb you."

"Oh no sir," I said somberly. "You didn't disturb me at all. You see my momma"—pausing suddenly—"had a stroke and they said she wouldn't make it through the night."

"Sorry to hear that," he replied. "I'll keep you in my prayers."

"Thank you, sir." I continued to write as Rose of Mine kept seeping in and out of my head. I didn't know what it meant but had written the words down. Ironically, no other words followed.

I arrived at the Pensacola Regional Airport around 8:57 p.m. Denise and her friend Michelle stood there awaiting my arrival. When we arrived at Baptist, my Uncles Joseph and Robert were waiting. I gave them a huge hug and then Uncle Joseph walked me to the room.

The ICU was quiet and people were in great pain. Momma's room was well lit and there she lay almost as if she were sleeping. Her tongue was hung slightly to the left side of her face and a unit was connected to her dripping the massive amount of tar that had covered her lungs over the years. Uncle Joseph gave me a minute and I held Momma's hands.

"Momma," I said with tears in my eyes. "You have to wake up. They said you're already gone and the machines are keeping you alive. Momma, please wake up."

Momma didn't respond. Uncle Joseph stepped back into the room and told me he was going down the hall. Denise and Michelle soon joined me. Their outpours of screams frightened the other patients and they were starting to get agitated. I just didn't get the time I needed to be with her so that I could pray for her.

"Please keep the noise down," someone yelled out.

I offered my shoulder for support and told them they had to quiet it down some. Nothing could keep them calm. I watched Momma as she slightly smiled at me, but her eyes never opened. I knew it had to be her spirit smiling at me.

"Momma," I said again. "Don't do this to us! You have a lot to live for. Think about your grandchildren, Momma. What will they do without you?" Momma's hand tightened against mine. "She's squeezing my hand," I said with a smile.

"Mommmmma!" Denise cried out. "Please come back to us." Momma's leg reflected briefly. "She's gonna be ok," Denise said. "Chantal, the doctor's said her entire left side was paralyzed."

"That can't be, Denise! You saw it, didn't you? Momma moved her hand and leg. They're on the left side.

My uncle Joseph entered the room. "I'm gonna be here all night. Who's staying with me?"

I jumped to my feet. "I'm not leaving her side."

"I have to go home, but I'll be back tomorrow." Denise murmured tearfully.

I contacted my brother Byron before I left Maryland. He was overcome with grief. "Momma can't be dying Chantal. I just talked with her last night."

"I know Byron. So did I. Denise said that she was with her all day and her friend Lucille was the last person to hear her voice."

I explained about the blood in Mildred's eyes and how she just faded out while talking with Ms. Lucille that Wednesday night. Lucille recalled her dropping the phone while they spoke, but Mildred called her back immediately. That was after 9 P.M.

"They believe it was the last conversation she had," I said dreadfully.

An outburst came from Byron as he told me to contact the Red Cross so that he could come home on emergency leave. Byron had left home some nineteen years prior searching for a good life for himself and his family. This was the year he would end everything with a twenty year retirement in Uncle Sam's Army.

"But she can't die, Chantal! I've worked my entire life just so momma would be proud of me."

"I know Byron. Momma was always proud of you and she always will be. Please get here soon," I murmured.

Byron didn't arrive until late Friday night. In spirit, Momma could sense his presence. Her body moved immediately when he called out her name. A nurse standing there said that it was only reflexes from the life support machine.

"It's typically set at 12 to provide additional support to the person connected to it. As you can see, the unit responding from your mother is also reading 12. Unfortunately, it's keeping her alive. If she makes it through the night, her brain tissues will never function again. She would be a vegetable for the rest of her life," Nurse Bell said remorsefully.

The life support machine hadn't changed in two days and our family worried even more. I spent that Friday night alone in Momma's room curled up in a folding chair. They hadn't placed any additional chairs in her room because the room could only accompany her bed and the machine she was attached to. I struggled all night trying to find comfort. I held on to her hand until six o'clock the next morning.

When I opened my eyes seeing Momma lying there with no life in sight, I left the room and commenced with the loudest cry since I had arrived. The phone rang in the waiting lounge. Byron could tell that I had been crying and tried to soothe my hurt.

"I told you not to go back in her room." An older more powerful brother spoke out. "I'll be right over."

"I couldn't leave her by herself. She needed someone to be with her."

"I know Chantal. Don't go back in her room until I get there."

Within an hour's time, ten people had showed up. Mildred was loved by many and it showed by the overwhelming support that filled the waiting area. Three women from one of the local Pentecostal Churches entered. We didn't know them, but they were friends of Denise. They stood with us and asked if they could pray for her.

Powerful prayers of endurance and messages in tongues were spoken. After they prayed, Momma's pastor entered the room and asked if he could see her. His look was saddened as he watched one of his faithful church members lay helpless on the metal frame bed. Momma's doctor asked if everyone other than her children and her husband would leave the room.

Byron wasn't too keen on him being there, but since Momma hadn't divorced him, by law, it was his right to be there.

It had been years since the family had said words to Anthony since he distanced himself from his kids. Byron was believed to be the last person that spoke to him in over three years.

When Doctor Matlap spoke to us, he was trying to be as encouraging as possible. However, he spoke of removing Mildred from the life support system. Her condition was worse and there was no chance of recovery. He left the family to discuss the matter but Denise was determined not to let it happen. I told them how Mildred insisted on not ever letting anyone seeing her lying lifeless with her tongue hanging out. She had seen too many of her own friends die that way.

"It's not fair," Denise screamed out.

A comforting Byron put his arms around her and told her that Momma shouldn't have to suffer like this. The decision was made and Doctor Matlap came back into the room. They would put Momma into a much larger room with no support going into her system. It didn't please the family knowing that if Momma came back around, the hospital wouldn't try to revive her. She hated being at Baptist Hospital. Some thirty years prior, she had rushed her nine month old baby there suffering with pneumonia. They made her wait and then told her that there was nothing they could do for him. She'd never forgiven them for that. Yet, when her health failed, she always ended up at Baptist.

Momma was moved to the other room and as many as fifteen people surrounded her. The three prayer warriors entered also. They prayed continuously for nearly an hour. Then they had to go and see another patient at Sacred Heart Hospital. In our hearts, we felt she would make it. But God wanted her in his presence.

Later that evening, a lady by the name of Mrs. Jackson showed up with some famous Church's Chicken and all the fixings. She had been a long time friend of the family. She and Momma hung pretty close in the younger days. I hadn't eaten since Friday afternoon and here it was going on five o'clock Saturday evening.

Mr. Potter, another good friend of Mommas, came to her room. It took a lot to get him to the hospital and once he was there, he stayed by her side. He was determined not to let anything or anyone stop him from seeing Momma on her death bed. Their relationship was such a unique one. One minute they were on and the next, she was kicking him to the curb. But regardless, Momma love for Mr. Potter remained strong. Tears left his eyes as he begged her to wake up. He called her name so many times and she moved slightly. Her spirit was there, but her body was gone.

"Get up Mildred!" He said dropping his head.

Her response never changed.

Byron noticed a tube connected to Momma that had a black liquid running into a pan.

"Chantal," he said giving her a nudge. "What's that?"

"It's tar Byron. All the years Momma had been smoking is now making its way throughout her system. Her body is rejecting all the nicotine that's been backed up inside her. I tried to warn her, but she wouldn't listen." I said as I watched the line of tar streaming from the tube.

"I didn't know it would be so bad," Byron said. "I only wanted her to be happy."

Rose of Mine came back to me as I sat there wiping the mucus from Momma's mouth. I got up and grabbed a piece of paper and a pen.

"What'cha you doing, Chantal?" My father asked.

"I'm writing a poem for my mother," I replied. "It came to me while on the plane, but I couldn't find the words for it."

I wrote half the poem and my mind drew a blank.

Springtime blossom roses that shine,

Petals that fade, sweet rose of mine.

Sunshine in the morning, noon and night,

Mildred always made things alright....

Then my mind went blank. I put the pen and paper down noticing Anthony catching a glimpse of my poem. Byron had replaced me while I was writing. He wiped the access mucus from Momma's mouth. We wanted to make sure the mucus wouldn't choke her while she slept.

Momma's sister Clara entered the room. She had been sitting in the lounge waiting for the room to clear. Both of her brothers, Robert and Joseph never left her sight.

"Ooh, it's hard seeing Mildred lying like that," a saddened Clara mentioned. "Can they do anything with her tongue?"

"I'm afraid not," I said walking over to give her a hug. "Look at the fluid in her eyes." I said as I lifted Momma's right eye. "It won't be long now." I mentioned after remembering what had happened a few months prior to Uncle Robert's daughter-in-law.

"Don't say that, Chantal!" An angry Byron said.

"I've seen this before Byron. She didn't make it much longer after they took the life support from her."

"Mildred sure looks bad," Clara said as she walked over to her. "This is my only sister. How could you Lord?"

A cheerful Robert spoke up. "Yeah, that's how it is when you're on your last leg. God watches over us and He doesn't want us to suffer any more than we have to."

"Why are you so understanding, Robert? A curious Clara asked.

"I love my sister," he said. "She has suffered for so long and I've prayed over and over again. But sometimes, that's all we can do. God has a plan for all of us, Clara." She turned her head towards him. "But do we all have to suffer behind it?"

"Sometimes Aunt Clara, it's all we can do," I responded.

RJ found out from Shanice that Momma was dying. He flew from Maryland to be by my side. It had been a while since I'd last seen him. I introduced him to the family and RJ asked if I wanted to go to the lounge. There was a big reclining chair that was calling my name. As we talked about Momma, RJ somehow reflected on what we once had.

"Not now, RJ," I said. "Maybe we can pick it up when I get back to Maryland."

Jamal and I were still separated and I wasn't trying to let anyone back into my life anytime soon. I knew Momma wanted us back together so I tried to stay focused on that.

Ten minutes had passed and a frantic Robert came running into the lounge.

"She's gone," he said running breathless down the hall.

I dashed like lightning to the room hesitating as I walked in. By then, Momma's tongue was back in her mouth and she lay peacefully. It was obvious that her spirit kept me preoccupied with RJ because I hadn't left her side since I arrived in Pensacola on Thursday.

"Ten minutes. I was only gone ten minutes. What happened?" I said crying out loud.

"She died peacefully," Uncle Joseph replied. "I was the only one that saw her when her eyes popped opened. Byron was distracted by the TV. You and Denise were in the lounge.

"Mommmmmaaaa." A long disturbing cry was held out by my aroused anger. Please momma, please don't leave me. We need you."

Momma's body shook briefly. Byron noticing it tried talking to her but her response faded. "Momma, I did this for you," he said. "Please momma, don't go!"

I joined in. Mildred's body moved again.

"Ms.," one of the nurses said. "She's gone."

"But—she moved her body." I replied.

"She's gone ma'am," the nurse said again. Apparently, the nurse wasn't trying to revive her. It was the most messed up ordeal we had ever encountered. I could almost hear Mildred's spirit speaking to me as she said, "Let me go, Chantal."

"Okay," I said out loud.

"What was that?" Byron asked.

"She told me to let her go," I responded immediately breaking down grasping at my chest. Sharp pains were developing around my heart. The nurse had me sit down and took my pressure. "I'm okay," I said. "I get sharp pains in my chest when I'm upset."

"I still wanna check your blood pressure to make sure your vitals are fine."

No more than five minutes later, we had to exit the room. The nurse wanted to get Momma prepared for the morgue.

"This is all the time we get with her?" I remarked. "I guess no one gives a damn about you when you die. I see why my momma didn't like this place."

"It's procedures ma'am," the nurse replied.

"Procedures my ass!" Byron looked up at her. "This place is hosed. I will have a full investigation conducted. I know you guys must have given her the wrong medication or something for her to go this fast."

We walked away solemnly and headed to Momma's house. It was the first time I had been there since I arrived. The house was in shambles. Danielle had stayed there while momma was in the hospital. She'd been living with Momma since she was five and when Momma's health got worse, she stayed until she was seventeen.

A slow paced Byron finally walked in the door. He headed straight for Momma's room and closed the door. You could hear his outpour as he lay on her bed.

"Open the door," I said. "We need to talk about this." I said standing there with Denise at my side.

No one other than Momma's children had come there for the first hour or so. Denise left to go back home and Byron was heading out to one of his friend's house.

"Where are you going Byron? I'm gonna be here by myself."

"What about your friend from the hospital, Chantal?"

"I can't allow him over here. I don't want people talking like something's going on."

"Forget about what other people say. You're a grown woman. I think you have a mind of your own," Byron responded. "Will you be okay here by yourself?"

"I guess I don't have a choice. I mean—I don't have any transportation. I didn't rent a car this time. Kinda creepy staying here all by myself though."

"I know you're not afraid of momma's spirit."

"Nah," I replied as a knock came to the door. Keisha was standing there with her mother, Monica. Their grief poured out over Momma's death.

"See baby girl," Byron said. "Your prayers were answered."

"Keisha—Ms. Monica, how are you?" I said trying my best to smile.

"Baby, the question is—how are you and the rest of the family holding out?" Monica responded giving me a big hug. "You haven't changed a bit."

"She sure hasn't, Momma. She's still just as beautiful as ever," Keisha said.

"Come in. Denise and the kids went to the store but they'll be back shortly. Would you like something to drink?"

"Just a cup of water," Monica said.

"I'll have a Coke if you have some Chantal," Keisha replied.

"Your momma sure was a good woman. I was telling Keisha about the times we use to hang out at the Du Drop Inn. Those were the good old days. But now that I've gotten my life together, I'll never go back."

"That's a good thing Ms. Monica. Momma used to love that place. Man I would give anything to see her beautiful smiling face again." I said as my eyes drew salty water.

"I know baby. How long are you planning to be in town?" Monica asked.

"Just a day past the funeral! We have to get the place together and decide what to do with all her things. It's sad that we have to get rid of them so fast. I mean—that's just like saying that she never existed."

"I don't think that's the impression everyone will get. We all know that you and Byron live out of town. Denise would be left trying to settle things by herself. A death is very hard Chantal," Keisha said.

"Don't I know! Momma took me by surprise though. I thought she would live forever. Although, I knew she was very sick. It's just not the same without her," I said.

"Maybe you can stop by the house before you go back to Maryland." Monica said.

"I'll try my best." I replied.

"We have to make a few more stops but we'll be back soon Chantal." Monica said.

"I really appreciate you stopping by the house. I look forward to seeing you again." I said looking over at Keisha.

Keisha gave me a wink and a huge hug. "You still look good Chantal."

"Thanks Keisha. I try."

Rose of Mine

Springtime blossom roses that shine,
Petals that fade sweet rose of mine;
Sunshine in the morning, noon and night,
Mildred always made things all right.
Happy as the rose with spiritual blues,
Left no sorrow mourning without a clue.
Rise with happiness sweet rose of mine,
With a delightful smile that forever shined.
When night time comes and the sky is clear,
We knew you'd always be somewhere near.
Though your petals are closed awaiting great light,
Anytime they're opened made it all right.
You taught us to respect each petal so dear,
Oh how we wish you were somewhere near.
Although we cannot see your bright bold smile,
We knew you'd always go the extra mile.
Your battle was fought with persistence and strive,
Hoping for a miracle to keep you alive.
Guide us with hope of dignity divine,
Ever so loving sweet "Rose of Mine."

Donna Marie Brown

Copyright ©2002 Donna Brown

CHAPTER 9

Funeral Day

Anthony hadn't been seen since the day after Momma's death. Byron had his suspicions about him showing up after all these years. I was reluctant to go against him. He came over a couple days and helped around the house. He swept, mopped, and even scrubbed the stains out of the carpet. Byron stood there hoping that Anthony's ulterior motives were for the best.

"If this nigga has shown up after all these years trying to play on our sympathy, I'll kill him," Byron said looking over me.

"Do you really think Daddy has something up his sleeves Byron?"

"Momma never trusted him and why should we?" Byron replied.

"You're right about that. Momma still remained friends with him though. Maybe that was part of their agreement since they never divorced," I said.

"Now that bothers me, Chantal. You don't think he plans to waltz in here and take everything from us, do you?"

"Nah, Byron. You worry too much."

Anthony spoke up. "The funeral parlor called and said we need to come in and talk to them about the arrangements. Are you guys available tomorrow morning around nine?"

"Yeah, I guess we have to be," Byron responded.

"Is it ok if you stop by my house and pick me up Bryon? My truck isn't working so well these days."

"I guess I will have to if you're gonna be on time."

"I'll see you guys at nine o'clock then," Anthony said as he walked out the door.

"We gotta watch him Chantal. I really don't trust him."

"He's okay. You'll see."

The next morning came too soon. Byron, our Uncles, and I arrived at the funeral home around the same time. Anthony was nowhere in sight. Byron had stopped by the house, but Anthony didn't open the door. That wasn't unusual for Anthony. I remember as a little girl, he would stay locked up in his room and if our grandmother knocked on the door and told him we were there, he would say, "Get the hell away from my door and leave me alone." Byron figured that Anthony had found another way to the funeral home. We discussed the proper dressing of Momma, her casket, and how the funeral would be paid. That's when the problems started. Byron gave the funeral director all of Mildred's information and he called the insurance company. We could tell by the look on his face, it wasn't good news.

"Are you sure this policy was supposed to be in your name Byron?" He said looking him directly in the face.

"Positive. Momma had it changed some years ago after the policy lapsed."

"It doesn't appear that way. Seems like the insurance company renewed the policy with Anthony's name as the beneficiary."

"You gotta be shitting me!" Uncle Robert replied. "Mildred told me herself she had moved that policy to Byron's name."

"That's not the case here! Until Mr. Anthony comes in and agrees to all the arrangements and says he'll pay for them, then I cannot do anything with the policy."

"Man, he better not blow this," Byron said looking over at me. "I'll kill that nigga."

"He seems like a decent enough man," Uncle Joseph said. "You don't think he'll wrong his own children, do you?"

"You know the evil this man holds within him. The root of all evil is held within his soul," Byron responded.

"Come on, Byron! Daddy can't be that bad, can he?" I asked.

"Let's take this conversation outside. I'll meet up with him and discuss it. I'll swing by his house again and then we can all meet at momma's house," Byron said.

"I'll see you guys later this evening. Gotta take the wife to the doctor's office today," Uncle Joseph said.

That evening when everyone showed up at the house, guests had already started to arrive and brought food for our family to eat. Mrs. Jackson brought a pot of gumbo, cornbread, potato salad, and fried chicken. It was just enough to bring a huge smile to the faces of Denise's kids, Byron, and me of course.

Daddy showed up around 5:15 p.m. He was a little hesitant about being there with a crowd of people. He asked if we could go somewhere private. I was the only one of the three that actually cared for Anthony. Denise couldn't stand to be in his presence and Byron just didn't like him.

"How you guys holding up?"

"We're doing okay daddy," I responded. "Did you get the funeral arrangements taken care of?"

"Of course I did. I told you I wouldn't let you children down."

"Man, we're not children anymore. We just don't want anything to go wrong," Byron said.

"Everything will work out find. Don't worry about it. Now let's go take care of these guests. Mildred sure had a lot of friends," Anthony said.

"She sure did," Denise muttered. "Not like some of us."

I gave her the eye and told them we needed to go back inside. Denise had no respect for him whatsoever. I guess since he was never around, they phased him out.

Another knock came to the door and when I opened it, I saw a face that I hadn't seen in years. Kenyon, of all people, decided to drop by with his family and pay his respect. His hair had gotten even nappier than I remembered. He looked as though he had aged quite a bit since our divorce over fifteen years ago. I took one good look at him and wondered what in the world possessed me to marry someone so damn ugly?

"Do come in, Kenyon and Yvonne," I said.

"Just wanted to let you know how it saddens us to see Mildred gone," Kenyon said.

"We appreciate that. Would you like something to eat or drink?" Denise asked. "We have plenty."

"Just a glass of water," Yvonne responded.

Kenyon looked at me and asked if he could give me a hug. I was a little reluctant, but quite remorseful hearing those words from him.

"Of course you can. I don't hold grudges," I said rolling my eyes to the back of my head.

He smiled at me and held me in his arms. "I don't remember you being this uptight when I used to hold you. What gives Chantal?"

"I'm just thinking of Momma, that's all." I wanted to say, *Get your freakin' hands off me and get out of my mother's house.* But the kinder side of me just embraced him and his ugly ass wife.

A couple hours went by and people were starting to clear out. I was left putting the excess food away. Momma had a lot of old food left in the refrigerator. Danielle was useless. She left everything hosed. All she wanted to do was be with her boyfriends. Byron made her go to her room and clean up the mess she'd left behind. She had shit thrown everywhere. We were so embarrassed bringing people to the house and her room looked like a tornado had hit it.

The next morning, Byron received a call from the funeral home. They wanted to change the date of the funeral because Mildred's body was starting to deteriorate. It didn't go over well with the other family members since they lived in Georgia and Alabama. Unfortunately, many of them couldn't make it. But the ones who were in town, took her death fairly hard.

On the day of the funeral, we were led from Uncle Robert's house to Smyrna Primitive Baptist Church. Denise, Byron, Anthony, and I sat in the first black limo as they pulled in front of the church. We were told not to get out of the car until all the family had arrived. One by one we were led inside the church where Momma's body lay resting in the golden casket. Each of us was given a chance to tell her goodbye and then we were seated.

Reverend Davison stood and read the Old Testament while Reverend Standsbury read the New Testament. The choir rose and sang Momma's favorite song, "Rough Side of the Mountain." The church was rocking for a while and then one of Momma's friends sung Precious Lord. Screams poured throughout the church as Minister Coleman sang. We knew it would be the hardest day of our lives, but nothing could have prepared us for my sudden breakdown. I started screaming, "I tried Momma," letting her know that I tried to be strong for the family. But—yet somehow, losing the best friend I ever had, I would never be the same.

I was sitting next to Anthony when it all happened and he put his arms around me. I guess Byron and Denise had no intentions of being next to him. Reverend Hopkins dismissed us with the recessional and we were led to the Rest Haven Cemetery. Byron, Denise, Anthony, and I sat in the leading car. Jamal had come up from Maryland and brought Dante and Montel with him. They sat in the car behind us. Not one person was left at the church. They all followed the family to the gravesite to pay their last respects.

My friends, Keisha and Michele came over to talk to me. Being that I wasn't in the mood to talk to either of them, I hurried the conversation. They assured me that they would stop by before I left for Maryland. Michele wanted badly to talk to me, but I insisted that there wasn't much that she could say to me to make me feel any better.

Momma touched the hearts of many. But Mr. Potter grabbed a hold of her casket and planted his body next to it. "Woman, you are really breaking my heart right now," he said. "I wished a many days we had stayed together, but I guess you got tired of me or you just didn't want me to go through so much pain after you were gone. Don't you know that I would have given anything to be a part of your life? You should have given me the chance,

Mildred. I loved you just that much. You didn't need Anthony or any other man. We could have been perfect together. I'm gonna miss you baby. May you rest in peace."

Mr. Potter walked away and got back in his car. Momma's death devastated him and he left the gravesite in tears. As the preacher gave the benediction, screams poured all over the grounds. Some were so loud that they could have literally awakened the dead. All the women sitting on the first and second rows were given a carnation from the spread of flowers on Momma's casket. Anthony gave me a look of defeat and told me that he would come back over later that day. That day never came. He went home and was never seen again.

CHAPTER 10

Maryland

On the day I left heading back to Maryland, Jamal and Dante saw us off at the airport. I decided to take Montel back with me because he was still pretty young. Since they had driven down, it would take them at least a day's drive to make it back. I reached the house first. Man did I leave that house in a wreck. Things were thrown around while packing so fast. A stale cup of tea was still sitting on the table. I placed my bags down gently in the center of my living room and turned around searching for someone to talk to me. I forgot just that fast that Jamal and Dante wouldn't return until daybreak. I called Montel's sitter to see if she would watch him for a while so I could have a little time to myself.

As I headed up the stairs, I noticed my bed wasn't made. I lay across the bottom edge and began to pour in tears. "How could someone with such a beautiful heart and so young be gone so quickly?" I screamed. I kicked off my shoes and curled my body into the fetal position. I had a picture of Momma in my hands and relieved myself of screams.

I made my way to the walk-in closet and sat on the floor talking to Mildred's picture for over an hour. My legs ached like hell after being in that closet curled up for so long. When I tried to stand up, I realized that I couldn't walk. The very pain that I had received medical disability for while serving in the Navy had settled in my legs once again. I didn't know what to do since I was all alone in this big ass house of mine. I cried out loud, but no one was there to help me. I made my way over to the phone and called Byron. He was crying when he answered the phone.

"Hello," he said tearfully. Since caller ID was now a part of technology, Byron knew it was me immediately. "Chantal, I can't do this. I can't make it without my momma."

"I know Byron," he could tell that I had been crying as well. "We have each other now. Momma would want it that way. We have to stay strong for Denise and her kids."

"You don't understand Chantal. Momma was supposed to be here for me."

"She can't be here forever Byron. Momma was so sick. I didn't want to see her suffer any longer. I'm just glad she was here long enough to see us become successful adults."

"But that's the problem Chantal. I only had a few more months before I retired. Why couldn't her health linger a little while longer? I wanted her to be proud of me."

"Oh but Byron, she was. You were her heart. All she talked about was your retirement and how successful you turned out to be. She talked about Denise and her success running her business and me winning the lottery and becoming an instant millionaire. She was so proud of all of us."

"I know she was Chantal. But did she have to die?"

"It was just her time Byron. We're going to make it through this. I promise."

Then Byron asked me a question that I hadn't given any thought to. "When are you going to move back home Chantal? We really want you closer to us."

"I'm not sure, but it will be soon. I promise."

"Maybe you should really reconsider. You and Jamal are no longer together and Dante is almost in college."

"They are going to move him up two grade levels in order for him to be in college. I think it's rushing him."

"Chantal, he's a smart boy. Why shouldn't he increase his knowledge and get the free education he deserves? Some of us had to work hard for our education."

"I know Byron and that's why I'm so protective of him. I can't lose him right now."

"You won't lose him Chantal, but you have to let him grow up."

"They'll be home tomorrow and I'll see if he still wants to go Morehouse."

"That's a good school. Don't let this opportunity pass by!"

"I'll think about it Byron. I need a little time."

"Okay baby! You get some rest and try not to think about Momma too much. I know it's not as hard on you like it is for the rest of us."

"That was a front Byron. It literally killed me seeing Momma lying there helpless. I wanted to scream just as loud as you and Denise. I just had to be strong. Momma would have wanted it that way." We ended our conversation and I tried to rest, but the freshness of Momma's death kept taunting me.

We hung up the phone and my leg was still killing me.

Eventually, I gave Shanice a call, but she wasn't available. I even tried to call RJ. No answer. I lay on my bed in misery.

CHAPTER 11

I Cried Out Loud

My phone started to ring again. I was hesitant about picking it up, but it could have been Dante wanting to come home.

On the other end was a sympathetic ear waiting eagerly to listen. She didn't want to talk about anything, but mostly, wanted to listen to my grief. As I began to speak, Shanice told me that I was making her cry. She didn't quite know how it felt to lose a mother, but since we had lost our good friend Monique in a car accident, she was ready to listen to anything. I retrieved the cordless phone from my bedroom and went over to the chaise lounge to talk to her.

Shanice suddenly asked, "So how are you holding up with the passing of your mom? I know she meant a lot to you."

I replied, "In the ease of the night, I can still hear her silent whispers calling out to me," I said as I lay cozy up in my lounger. I mean—Mildred was a big part of my life—my dreams and ambitions. She inspired me the most and now that she's gone, my life has no meaning."

I switched the phone to the other side of my face and reluctantly waited for Shanice's response. Knowing that Shanice was my best friend, I admitted my regrets for leaving Jamal. Running around with RJ caused me to lose my husband and pushed Dante out of my life. Dante still had much love for me, but lost total respect after my adultery. Not an ounce of hatred or despair did he have for me. When I explained the mishaps I had encountered as a child and the complications of being raped twice, Dante hesitantly understood.

As I spoke to Shanice, I talked about RJ and the baby we had lost. She tried to comfort me, but warned against living in the memories of her past.

"Take heed to the lifestyle I've lived, Chantal," she said. "It's not fun watching your good friend suffer while you're screwing her husband. For God's sake, Monique was in the hospital dying and I—because of Rick's infidelity to me—decided to seek revenge. The phone was ringing and I knew it could have been Rick letting us know that Monique was passing. But my selfishness—ha ha—Oh my selfishness kept him in between my legs just so I could feel good for a change."

Then I asked angrily, "Was it really worth it, Shanice?"

"More than you could imagine! Frank is a jewel compared to Rick."

"Don't ever compare apples to oranges! I mean, when you start comparing one man to another, they hardly ever live up to your expectations. I did that with Kenyon and Al. I thought Al was God's gift of what every man should be. Girl, Kenyon took me away from my family and while I was away, Al promised he would always wait for me. Little Miss Naïve—Yeppers—that was me! Granted I was only 21 and Al was 33. You talkin' 'bout putting somebody through some changes, girl—Al put me through more changes than the song by Kashif back in the late 80's."

"Yeah but—it can't be as bad as what Rick and Monique did."

"You wanna bet, Shanice? Al would have me waiting for hours thinking he would come over. Then, he would say he had a headache knowing some other woman was lying in his bed. The funny part about it, my momma would sit there with me and laugh her ass off. She said, "Gurl—I can't believe you sittin' her waiting on some sorry ass nigga like this! He's worse than Kenyon." Then, she'd laugh some more. "Man, if I could get back that laughter from her! It took a while, but eventually I got over him. Then, when I went overseas, he found out where I was stationed. Said he got my address through a contact that used to be stationed there. He asked for my hand in marriage, but I had already made a commitment to Jamal. I asked him when we first met if he was married and Al flat out lied to me. Then—when I responded to his letter—I asked him again. He came clean and told me that he couldn't tell me before because his wife was leaving him. He use to go out to sea a lot and I guess she couldn't take it. Can you believe that mess? I was hot! I was so naïve back then. I told him that I had just met the man of my dreams and if it were anyone else, I would have dropped them in a heartbeat."

"Girl—you had it bad for this—Al person!"

"I sure did, but if you think that's bad, try marrying someone and then finding out that he's in love with your cousin. What kind of shit is that?"

"What? Oh hell no!" Shanice yelled out. "Your man was in love with your cousin, Jennifer?"

"Hell yeah! We use to switch off on each other when we were younger, but I never thought it would follow us to the East Coast."

"Dag girl, I heard of keeping it in the family, but that's some freaky shit!"

"When you're in high school, you do weird stuff like that. One time I walked in the girl's locker room and these two white girls were freakin' up a storm. I got the hell out of there real fast. Another time, we had to stand outside in the freezing rain while our gym teacher watched some of the girls change their clothes. Now you know Shanice that mess freaked me out!"

"Did anybody report that dyke ho?" Shanice asked as she sipped a cup of Irish Tea.

"Dyke is such a harsh word. But to answer your question—No—not one of us reported her. Girl, she was a hard looking woman too. I still recall the look upon their faces when we walked in from the freezing rain. Those white girls didn't care, but it scared the crap out of the gym teacher. Her cover was blown, girlfriend."

"Chantal, there is no way I would have stayed in that class any longer. I mean, it's bad enough that you had to put up with that old white man touching you, but having to watch yourself around females as you showered, ooh girl—I couldn't do that. Look it's getting late and I need to get out of here before Frankie is late for practice. He's growing so fast. Stop by some time for dinner or a drink. I'm sure Frank would love to see you again."

"I'll do that Shanice. Give the kids a kiss for me," I said as I hung up the phone.

I really didn't want to be bothered by anyone. As I continued to unpack my clothes, one of the pictures I brought back of my mother fell out of my suitcase. I was a real basket case then. I stroked the picture once and realized once again Mildred was gone. On the inside of my closet was a sitting stool large enough for two adult size people to sit comfortably. I had most of my small items lying there waiting to be picked up. To the right of me was an open space where I kept tons of fashionable shoes and sneakers. I gently pushed them to the side and sat in the closet talking to Mildred's picture.

"Why couldn't you live long enough to enjoy the house I bought you? Momma, it's so hard living without you. I know it's only been a week since you passed, but it seems like yesterday I was talking to you on the phone and you were telling me to stop running up my phone bill. Do you know that I would give anything to hear you say those words again?" Almost in an instant, I let out the loudest scream. "Why Lord—My God why would you inflict so much pain upon me and my family right now? How could you take the only thing in my life that was worth something to me besides my children?" I continued to beat myself up.

The tears just wouldn't stop and the screams got louder. I didn't care if my neighbors heard me or someone even called the police. Besides, the walls were so damn thin you could hear everyone's conversation anyways. "God," I said. "You promised never to put more on us than we could bear. Why is it that I can't stand to bear this pain Lord? Please—take this pain away Lord. I can't bear it all by myself." I had held my sorrow for so long while my sister and brother let go of theirs at home. They thought I didn't care, but deep inside, it was killing me trying to be strong for them. I was so overwhelmed by Mildred's death. Now that Mildred is gone, who is going to be there for me?

It was cold outside that January after I returned back to Baltimore from the funeral. Traces of old man winter were left on the ground when I arrived. I had left all the sunshine and warmth in Florida and came back to this dreadful place. I walked outside briefly to get the access mail that hadn't been checked since I left. One of my neighbors was outside at the time. She could see that my movement wasn't as swift as it normally had been.

"Is everything okay, Chantal?" Miss Mimi asked as she walked over towards me.

"Yes ma'am," I replied giving her respect. She had come outside in her flannel PJs with two yellow hair rollers for her bangs and one pink roller holding her ponytail. She was a short woman in her late sixties. "I just got back from my mother's funeral."

"Oh," she said in a bit of a shock. "I figured something was wrong when I hadn't seen you around. I'm so sorry to hear about your mother."

"It's okay Miss Mimi. I'm just gonna sit back and relax for a while."

"Did you hear what happened down the road?" She said.

"No ma'am. Was it bad?"

"Oh yes Chantal. A teenager was gunned down over a dispute with his girlfriend's ex-lover." She paused for a minute and shook her head. "It's a shame that boy had to die on these streets like this. If you were to ride around the corner, you'll see the tree where his family has memorialized his death. His picture is plastered everywhere."

"That's really sad Miss Mimi. Children are getting murdered in these streets all the time and it seems no one is doing anything about it."

"Uh Huh, Uh Huh," Miss Mimi replied. "It's the parent's fault. They need to stay home and raise their children respectfully. But no…the women are all over the streets shaking their asses and the men ain't no better."

I smiled as she apologized for her language. "You're right Miss Mimi," I said losing my balance. "My leg is in a lot of pain. Can we talk later?" I said trying my best to stand straight.

"Oh sure baby. I know you must be tired. I'll call you later."

"Thanks." I walked up my driveway, got all the mail stuffed tightly in my mailbox, sorted through all the bills, and put the rest away. I had asked the phone company and the electric company to send my mother's bills to me and I would pay them. But when they came to the house, I put them aside and waited to hear from Byron.

CHAPTER 12

The Struggle (Chantal)

Mildred's birthday was fast approaching and I wanted to go back home to be with the family. I had made plans to have a special memorial for Mildred with my brother and sister. Byron made certain that he would come down from the Carolinas. Mildred's sister and brothers attended also. We met at Sanders Beach and had a small reception. I had Dante and Montel with me. Everyone was being biten by the ants and mosquitoes. Florida was known for those red fire ants and once they bit you, your feet would swell for days. My feet were covered with big red blisters.

I stood at the grill most of the time barbecuing chicken, hamburgers, hot dogs, and sausages which my brother Byron craved. The kids weren't allowed in the water because the county said that it had been contaminated. Some people were daring though. You could see many sail boats and jet skis gliding across the waterfront area. Off to the side, stood a large beach house said to belong to a wealthy fisherman.

Byron took pictures of everyone with his new Sony Mavico digital camera and downloaded them for everyone to see. He sent some of them back home to be enlarged. By the time I finished cooking, the ants had messed up my feet so bad I had to run to the store and buy treatment. One of the pharmacists suggested I soaked them in Epson Salt and advised me to go to the emergency room if the blisters got any worse. I was hardheaded though. I figured since I was over forty, no one could tell me what to do. Guess I took that stubbornness after my daddy.

That night, the pain did persist and the swelling got worse. I went over to the Naval Hospital and was given ointments and antibiotics. I couldn't believe those small creatures tore my feet up so much.

The day before I left, I decided to pay Anthony a visit. I told my sister that I was going to visit a good friend and should be back in a couple hours. Dante wanted to hang out with his cousins which was excellent. I left the house and went straight over Anthony's. It was almost seven o'clock on a Sunday afternoon and Anthony was preparing for bed. Every morning he'd get up around five and take a long walk picking up beer cans. When I knocked on the door, he peeped out the window and to his amazement, it was me. My uncle Bill wasn't home so I had the perfect opportunity to talk to him alone. He opened the door and had a slight smile on his face. I stood there almost in tears.

"So, am I still Daddy's little girl?" I said angrily standing at his brown wooden beat up door.

He'd lived with his mother his entire life until she died in 1993. She just dropped dead one day while shopping in Wal-mart. Anthony never recovered after that day. The house which he built with his father when he was a little boy was a peeled brick red. It had a look like the ones on The Little House on the Prairie. After his mother passed, his brother moved in with him after finding out that Anthony wasn't entitled to the house. His mother had left the house to Uncle Bill instead. Since Anthony was older and had lived there his entire life, my uncle Bill having a decent heart, allowed him to continue to live there. They eventually remodeled the house taking away the darkness inside and revitalized it with a soft yellow tone.

As a little girl, I was always afraid of that house. My mother told me that demons and spirits lived in there. My grandmother wouldn't allow me inside, and we always sat on the porch on a faded crooked swing.

Anthony looked as though he had aged fifteen years since I last saw him that January. His hair was a salty shade of white. His physique was narrow and it looked as though death had run him over twice. I stared at the man I once referred to as 'Daddy.' He had on light brown khaki pants with two oil spots on each knee. Something about the look on his face rubbed me the wrong way. His nose started to point more and more. Most of his teeth were either missing or brown from all the tobacco and snuff he'd chewed over the years. He stood there all 5'6 ½" weighing barely 140 lbs. He watched me for a minute and then invited me in.

"Baby, I just wanted to see you again. I know things didn't turn out right after the funeral and I wanted to make sure that you still loved me."

"Love you? Love you? How could I love you Daddy? You took everything from us. Momma worked her ass off raising us and it was us—not you that took care of her when we got grown."

"Your momma didn't care about me. She had Mr. Potter and other men in her life."

"Damn it Daddy! If you hadn't tried jumping her when she was pregnant with me, maybe she would have stayed with you. You fought a pregnant woman. You expect her to stay with you after that? Besides, from what we were told, Grandma kept her away."

"How dare you talk about my mother like that, Chantal! She's dead."

"Maybe it's a good thing that she is so she wouldn't have to watch her sorry ass son take advantage of his children."

"You get the hell out of my house, Chantal! I don't need you, your brother or sister."

"Not until you hear what's on my mind, Daddy!"

"What could you possibly have on your mind that you haven't said already?"

"You think I wanted to be like this, huh? I loved you Daddy. When I saw you walking around, I was the one that spoke to you. What did you do in return? You'd cuss me out in front of your friends and made a mockery of me. You son of a bitch! I stood there with tears in my eyes and then you gave me a twenty, a bag of chips and a soda thinking it would take away the hurt. That's how much I use to love you."

"Chantal, you still can love me. We don't need anyone else."

"Go to hell Daddy! I don't need your kind of love. When you fell from that tree, I prayed to God that he would hurt you because you hurt me Daddy. You took my graduation card and threw it down on the ground after I gave it to you. My cousin saw me about ten minutes later and gave it to me. You threw it down, Daddy. I asked God to hurt you really bad, but not to kill you. I should've had Him finish you off. But you know what Daddy, for some strange reason, I still love you. After all that you've done to us, I still love you."

"I never fell from a tree. I don't know why people keep saying that. I hurt my head on the job."

"You're lying daddy! Byron came all the way from overseas to be with you, but when he got home, he said that he was on vacation. He didn't care to see you. Denise was right here and she didn't want to be a part of your life. But it was me Daddy who saved your life. They wanted me to make the decision for your surgery. I couldn't though. Your brother was there and I asked him to do it for me. Just a little while longer and God would have taken your sorry ass away. Why didn't I let Him while I had the chance?"

"You really wished that kind of luck on me?"

"Sure did. You hurt me so many times and I got tired of it."

"Get out Chantal! Get out of my damn house now!"

He opened the door, but I slammed it closed. Anthony didn't know what to think. All he knew was that he had hurt his daughter and I wasn't going away anytime soon.

"Daddy's little girl, huh? I'll show you daddy's little girl."

I reached into my purse and pulled out a long silver switch blade. I looked at him for the last time and said, "Daddy's little girl." Then I took the blade, pulled my hand back, and dropped it on the floor. "I can't do it," I said crying furiously. "You hurt me so much and I just can't do it. I wanted you gone Daddy, but the love I have for you is unbearable. You see what your little girl has turned out to be, Daddy? I could have killed you tonight, but it was the love I have for you that stopped me."

Anthony reached out for me, but I snatched away. Whenever I would let anger get the best of me, it was like the blood vessels in my eyes popped out. I pushed him away, left the blade on the floor, and ran through the kitchen. Since no one saw me go in and no one saw me leave, I could have easily stabbed Anthony and left him to die.

When I went back to Denise's house, I was shaking like crazy. I didn't dare tell them what had happened only that I needed time to think about some things. No one heard from Anthony in days. One of the neighbors went by the house and found his body lying on the floor. Anthony had given him a key some years ago. When he didn't see Anthony after a few days and saw his truck in the yard, he feared something was wrong.

I guess after I left Anthony, the guilt he felt was overwhelming. He used my switch blade and slit his throat. My fingerprints were still on the blade along with his. The authorities gathered a struggle had taken place before his death. Anthony literally tore the room apart making it look like someone had murdered him.

I had already gone back to Maryland where the law enforcement officers tracked me down for questioning. I told them that I was in town, but hadn't seen Anthony. We were supposed to meet at Shoney's, but he never showed up. I got upset and went to my sister's house. My explanation for the silver switch blade was that I had given it to him as a gift the previous year for his birthday. When I held it to show it to my ex-husband Jamal, my fingerprints must have been left on it.

I was already warned by Byron that the authorities were looking for me so I came up with a quick tale fast. I was devastated that Anthony was gone. Losing Mildred was bad enough, but losing Anthony six months later was unbearable. No one knew my secret about going over to Anthony's before he killed himself and I wasn't about to tell. I always told Byron that if something happened to Anthony that I would have his body cremated and thrown in the dumpster with all the other trash. That's exactly what I did. I didn't allow any of his family members to see his body after he passed. Since Anthony had left everything in my name, I told the funeral director to burn him. Against his better judgment, he did.

When I went to Pensacola Savings and Loans bank to make the withdrawal, all the money that Mildred had left behind for us was gone. In a time of desperation, Mildred's money came in on time. Anthony spent every single penny and had nothing in his bank account.

"Twenty five thousands dollars," I said. "He spent the whole damn amount. Denise and Byron are going to have a shittin' fit."

Marian, one of Anthony's sisters saw me at the bank. She gave me a nasty look and told me that she hated me for disposing of her brother's body without allowing them to see it. "I hope you suffer for what you've done," she said just as calm as she could.

"The suffering happened the day my mother laid eyes on your brother. He was the devil himself," I told her.

"He loved you Chantal. He talked about you all the time. His beautiful little Chantal."

"I'm not little anymore, Aunt Marian. I'm all grown up," I said as I walked away.

It was hard for me to go back to Byron's to give him the news. This man was supposed to take care of his children not destroy them. Denise lost every ounce of respect for him years ago. She knew what type of man he was and wasn't about to accept that he had nothing.

"You gotta dig deeper into his house, Chantal. I know that nigga got money somewhere. You still have the key to his house, don't you?" Byron asked.

"He once told me about this insurance policy he had put aside for me, but I thought he was lying. It was worth about fifty thousand at that time. If it exists, I will split it with you and Denise."

Byron looked over at me. "I say we go over to his house and look for it."

We didn't have a clue what we would find once we got there. Uncle Bill had left for work so it was the perfect opportunity to search for it. When we opened the door, there was yellow tape strapped across the living room area and blood stains on the floor. Forensics still had to come over and do more with the evidence.

A knock came to the door while I was in Anthony's room. There stood a short gray haired older gentleman with crusty lips and coke bottled glasses.

"May I help you?" Denise asked.

"I saw you churin' when you arrived. Just wanna pay my 'spects, that's all!"

"I'm sorry," Denise said, "but I didn't catch your name."

"Yo' daddy usta call me Mr. Charlie. I live over there in that house."

"Are you the same guy who had that handsome grandson some years ago when I was a little girl?"

"I sure am ma'am. You talkin' 'bout Richard. Yes, Yes, Yes—well, he passed away 'bout seven years ago. Had a terrible car accident in Norfolk. He never married you know. Said he couldn't find the woman his heart craved for."

"I'm so sorry to hear that Mr. Charlie. He seemed like a nice person when we played together."

"Nothin' but the best! He was well-educated and had his head on straight. Not too many young boys operate with a full bag of chips these days."

Denise laughed. This man came to console us, but he had me dying with laughter.

"Well Mr. Charlie, we really appreciate you coming by, but daddy left something here for Chantal and she was afraid to come over by herself. She said his spirit might still be in the house and she didn't want to come alone."

"Oh, well—he told me where he kept all his policies if that would help you out some."

Denise glanced at me and smiled. All her questions were being answered without tearing up the place. "That would be great Mr. Charlie. Byron—Chantal, come here for a minute."

"This is Mr. Charlie from next door. He said he knows where daddy kept his insurance policies."

"I remember you," I said. "You had a grandson that was finer that shit back in the day."

Denise covered her face.

"Did I say something wrong, Denise?"

"He passed away about seven years ago. Mr. Charlie said he was in a car accident."

"Sorry to hear that," Byron said.

"Me too," I replied.

"If you look behind his bed, he has a rusty old drum barrel that he kept all of his important papers in. You might even find some money back there. He didn't like taking money to the bank. He said they were a rip off."

As Byron pulled the bed out, indeed there was a rusty drum barrel sitting in plain sight. He looked at me. "Sis," he said, "I believe I will give you the honors of opening up the can, since he had your name on the policy."

"Oh, that's not true!" Mr. Charlie said. "He had something for all his kids. It's been a while since he showed it to me, but he said if he ever died, his kids would be wealthy."

Byron smiled slightly. "Could Anthony have a heart after all?" He thought. As I opened the barrel the sight amazed us. It was filled to capacity with tens, twenties, and fifty dollar bills. There were three insurance policies for all three of his children. Mine was the largest. Byron's had the least amount, but he didn't complain. His alone was twenty five thousand dollars. There was enough money in the barrel to split three ways and then still having a couple thousand a piece.

"He said he would do right by us. I thought he was lying," Byron said.

"See, I told you he wasn't all that bad. I had him cremated for nothing. Just because I was angry with him, I denied his family the right to see him off decently."

"Don't worry your conscience about it, Chantal! He wronged you earlier in life. Who knew he would be so generous when he died?" Byron said amazed by the sight of daddy's money.

"I don't know Byron, I still loved him. No matter what you or Denise say, we can't pick the parents that God gives us. We can only pray for them and try not to do the same things they did to us with our kids."

CHAPTER 13

Folk Talk (Chantal)

Before Montel and I headed back to Maryland, we got word that Aunt Millie and Uncle Joe wanted us to stop by. Though Louisiana was out of the way, I couldn't miss the opportunity of seeing them again. They were much older than my other aunts and uncles in Florida, but had the kindest hearts. They've only seen Montel once and I said, "What the heck?" I was in no hurry to get back to Maryland anyway.

I often tell people if you want to learn about life talk with an older person. We are so eager to put them into old folks homes or ignore them saying they talk out of their minds. But, if only we took the time and listened to our great-grandparents or aunts and uncles, we would be surprised at the knowledge that's held inside of them.

When we arrived at their house on 24 Under the Hill Road, Uncle Joe and Aunt Millie were sitting on an old wooded porch. The sun beamed down on our tired bodies as Auntie Millie was talking to Uncle Joe about the first time she'd used a computer. Her remembrance seemed to fade as this eighty-seven year old woman told about Montel's school project on crawling insects. She'd tried everything in this world to help the little rascal, but she just couldn't figure out how to turn the damn thing on.

Montel was sitting on the couch patiently waiting on her so they could get started. When he walked over to her, she seemed exhausted from trying to find the power button. Montel touched the round button with the partial circle and the computer came on.

"I'd be damn," Aunt Millie said when the computer lit up. Technology has come a long ways since I be a little girl," she told Montel while gumming on a piece of apple. I had invited her to stay with me in Maryland one weekend when the weather was too hot for her and Uncle Joe to stay at home by themselves. They didn't have the luxury of central air and heat like us modern folk.

Aunt Millie's house—I was told—was built back in the early 50's and black folk back in those days never dreamed of having invisible air to cool them off. They just worked from sun up to sun down and sat on the porch trying to cool themselves off. So when Montel's project was due, Aunt Millie thought she knew everything about crawling creatures since she lived in the south where most of them migrated.

Uncle Joe suddenly interrupted. "Chantal," he said. "Mighty fine seein' you and the boy hur today," he said struggling to get up from his seat.

"You sit right back down now Uncle Joe. I'll bend down and give you a hug," I said.

Aunt Millie had been really sick and I thought it would bring a brighter smile to her face seeing how much Montel had grown. Aunt Millie smiled as Montel walked over to her. He was growing up so fast. Uncle Joe, being ninety-one, told Aunt Millie to get two more glasses so she could pour up some freshly squeezed lemonade. You could tell Aunt Millie was having a time struggling as she tried to get to her feet. Her step wasn't quite the same and her feet were swollen from arthritis.

"Damnit woman!" He said missing eight of his teeth. "You'd be walkin' slower than a turtle on a half shell."

Turning around facing him, Aunt Millie said, "You'd be walkin' the same way too iffin you had Mista Lawrence chasin' yo ass all the da time," Aunt Millie replied.

"Hmmm, it sho' be nice to have them glasses so we can give the young folk dat nade sometime today," Uncle Joe said snickering at her.

"Gone now, Joe! Ain't got time for yo smart ass remarks," Her eyes started to blink heavily. "Aw shit! Now lookie what just happen'. Somethin' dun fell in my eye."

It was the funniest thing seeing these two elderly people going at it. Uncle Joe got up slowly. He could walk much faster than Auntie Millie once he got started. He looked into her eyes and said, "Justa piece of eye lash, I reckon, Millie. Need me to git it out fo yah?"

"Nah, I think I can manage on my own," she said walking into the house.

"Let me help you Aunt Millie," I said walking towards her.

"No baby, uze company. Uze jus sit right down and eyz git them glasses right away."

I felt a little foolish watching my aunt struggle with her step. "Are you sure, Auntie. I can get that much faster and you can relax."

"Nah baby. Ah'd be alright. Need to move these ole stiff bones anyways."

"Alrighty then! If you say so." I knew not to talk back to my elders. My aunt and uncle had been living in Louisiana on Under the Hill Street since the late seventies. They moved from Florida some years ago. They said the family needed to get themselves together. They didn't want to distance themselves from the family completely so they moved a few hours away. I made sure I visited them every once in a while since they were getting older.

A sudden clash of noise caught our attention. "Aunt Millie. Everything okay in there?" I asked demanding a response.

I ran in the house and Aunt Millie was lying half-way between the kitchen and living room.

"Uncle Joe! Uncle Joe. Come quickly!" I said frantically.

Uncle Joe got off the swing and high-tailed into the house. His precious Millie lay breathless on the floor.

"Sweet Laud in Heben! Millie—aye Millie! You wake up now. You hear me talkin' to you woman."

Uncle Joe was scared. He and Aunt Millie had been married over fifty years. Whenever you saw one, you saw the other. Aunt Millie lay silently on the shredded carpet linking the kitchen and living room.

"Good Lawd, my Millie's dun gone to see hu maker," he said while gripping his chest and falling to his knees.

It was the saddest thing I had ever seen. Uncle Joe had a heart attack grieving for his Millie. They both lay there motionless as I ran over to the phone. By the time the paramedics arrived, they were both gone.

Montel started to scream and I went over to comfort him. I couldn't believe that in an instant, both my aunt and uncle were gone. It was almost like fate had brought me over because they probably would have been dead for days before someone found them.

After the paramedics arrived, Aunt Jesse and Uncle Jake showed up. They didn't live too far from the house. It took them thirty five minutes to get there. They had brought their little granddaughter Nikki with them. Uncle Jake made his way inside the house and started crying at the site of his parents. Uncle Jake was the only child they ever had. Aunt Millie had gotten sick after the birth of Jake and couldn't have any more children. That was probably a good thing though. Jake was spoiled as hell and whatever he wanted, they gave it to him. When he got older, he'd always send money home to his parents. What he didn't know is that everything he sent, they put at least half of it away.

The paramedics waited for the coroner to come and remove the bodies. Uncle Jake fell to the floor. He wanted to see them one more time before the bodies were removed. They looked like two toy soldiers lying peacefully after they've been shot. Each of them had a slight smile about their faces. Jake grieved a while longer until he heard a noise outside. Aunt Jesse had been chasing Lil' Nikki around the yard and slipped on the water hose. The dress she was wearing flew up and you could see that she was wearing a pair of long tights cut off at the knee and a pair of black underwear sporting a huge hole. When Uncle Jake caught wind of her, he about fell off the porch.

"Lawd have mussy! Ah'd dun seen dah light. Dis day dun gimme a headache," Uncle Jake said. "I'm gointer help you up and then, we needin' be gittin' outa hur."

These folks had that deep Southern dialect that made you laugh every time they spoke. I couldn't help, but laugh. Momma would get mad at me earlier on in life when she was living. But, now that I was older, I actually enjoyed listening to the old folk talk. I was just glad that I'd never picked up on it. Knowing the people up North, they would have laughed me clean out of Baltimore.

After the funeral was over, Uncle Jake had it arranged for both of them to be buried on top of each other. He purchased another slot right next to them.

"I'm not wasting any time Jesse. If something happened to me today, I want you to be taken care of without worry. I'm not getting any younger, you know."

"I know Jake. Come ovah hur and gimme a hug!" She said. "I hope to have you roun' a lil' while longer. I couldn't take it if you leff me, Jake."

"If'n the good Lawd keep me hur, ah'd be hur fur yah."

"Guess I'll be heading back home!" I said eagerly awaiting the comfort of my own bed. "I only wish my visit could have been more pleasant. I'm really going to miss your parents."

"Don't cha be a stranger now! I wanna see ya gin fore I leave to meet my maker," Uncle Jake said.

"You don't have to worry about that. I'll make my way down here as often as I can."

Montel stood with me as I said my last good-byes. I wanted so much to be there with them but I had to get Montel back in school. He was on his Spring Break. The weather was perfect for everyone except Aunt Jesse. She was always cold.

The drive back home was long. Not too much was said in the car. Montel slept most of the way and I didn't have anyone else to help me drive back. I pulled off the road shortly after passing through Atlanta so I could catch some fresh air. Whenever I would drive, I always kept the windows up. I was so afraid that a bug would fly in the car while I was driving. People didn't understand how I could be so afraid of bugs being from the South. If they knew half the shit I went through with bugs, they would be afraid too. There were times in my life when the biggest damn cockroaches I'd ever seen would fly at me in 3D motion. In my defense, I would swing at them like we were at war. As a child, I would tuck all the sheets and covers under my mattress before I went to bed and then one of them bastards would be under the sheets with me. You talkin' bout someone damn dear killing herself trying to get out. That was one of the reasons I left the South so I could get away from them suckers.

I looked over at Montel and he was still fast asleep. I got a cup of coffee at the nearest 7-Eleven and started my drive back home. Dante was in college, so it was just me and Montel. That was fine though. As long as I had Montel, I really didn't need anyone else.

I thought about my plans for the next day. Shanice and I were getting together for a little shopping spree. I still didn't have to worry much about working which was a good thing. With Montel being in school, I wanted to be there when he came home. I had to work hard before Montel was born until I won the fifty million dollars with my ex-boyfriend RJ. I invested most of it and lived off the rest. I wanted to make sure that my boys would be set for life if something happened to me.

We finally arrived in Baltimore about six o'clock that evening. I was too through. My hair was all over my head and my body smelled as though I hadn't bathed in a few days. I knew that wasn't true, but traveling such a long distance had me sweating up a storm. Montel went to his room and crawled in the bed. Although he slept most of the way, he still was tired. Montel couldn't wait to tell his teacher and friends about his trip. He'd never seen a person die in front of him before. Now he could tell everyone how two of his relatives dropped like flies before his very eyes. Most people thought he exaggerated a bit, but his teacher knew it was true. All his friends told him how sorry they were to hear the news and gave him a hug. Montel really didn't know his great-great aunt and uncles, but he would hear me talk about them often.

I decided to take Montel out to eat later that evening because I wasn't in the mood to cook. His favorite restaurant was Applebee's. No matter how many times we went there, he always ordered the same thing, Bourbon Street Steak and I'd order the Sizzling Fajita Combo. By the time we had finished eating, Montel was ready for round three of his sleeping. I took him home, made me a cup of tea, and watched the local news in my bedroom.

CHAPTER 14

(Maurice)

Fifteen minutes later, the doorbell rang. I sprang quickly from my bed nearly knocking a cup of tea on top of me. To my surprise, Maurice was standing at my door with his sister Terrice and his parents. Terrice asked if they could come in and I still stood with my mouth wide opened.

I took a deep breath and said, "Come in."

Maurice spoke first. "May I sit next to you for a moment?"

He was pushing his luck, but I figured, *"Humor me. Hell I forgave my ex-husband why not give you the opportunity to speak?"*

"I'm not here to hurt you Chantal. I've replayed that night a thousand times over the past year and what I thought was being a man turned out to be a jackass."

I took a moment to pause then said, "I've also had time to think and have recurring nightmares. Do you know how it feels to jump up nightly Maurice pouring in sweat and think someone is come for you?"

"I get it now Chantal. Believe it or not, I found Christ while I was locked up. They say what goes around comes around. When the guys found out what happened, they didn't take it lightly. I was jumped several times Chantal."

"So you wanna blame me for that huh?"

"No that's not what I'm saying. I realize now I was completely wrong."

Mrs. Jones, Maurice's mother broke in. "Can't you see he's trying to apologize to you young lady?"

"Now wait a minute momma," Terrice interrupted. "Chantal has been through a great ordeal here. It's not just a one-sided thing momma."

"It's okay Terrice," I said in a calmer voice. "I will hear Maurice out."

Mrs. Jones rolled her eyes at Terrice as Maurice began to speak. "I hope in due time you can find it in your heart to forgive me. I know now you were just having a little fun, but I took it to another level."

"I forgave you some time ago Maurice. I've never been one to hold a grudge. I do believe people can change their lives through rehabilitation. Then I smiled and asked if they wanted something to drink.

"Got some Vodka?" Mr. Jones asked.

I laughed and said, "I don't carry Vodka, but I have plenty of Ginger Ale."

"Ginger Ale it is," he replied and walked over to the bar.

I thought, *"The nerve of some people."* I guess the term make yourself at home was definitely in his vocabulary. Then my focus went back to Maurice. "So what exactly happened to you in the pin?" I know he said he was jumped, but I wanted him to say that the men got a hold of him and ripped his ass or something like that. That would have given me satisfaction.

Maurice seemed stunned by my question. "You're talking religion wise or something else?"

"I mean…were there ever any encounters with the prisoners?"

"If you're asking if I was raped, the answer is no. However, I was jumped over and over again. I never had any problems with the law until that night."

"He's right about that," Mrs. Jones said angrily. "That's why I don't understand your charges."

"It's okay momma," Maurice told her. "Chantal was right and I was wrong. I know that now."

"But…"

"Just leave well enough alone," Maurice said.

Mrs. Jones pouted for a bit and Maurice turned to me again. "Chantal I am really sorry I hurt you. Please forgive me once again."

"I'm passed that Maurice. I just hope you were really rehabilitated."

Mr. Jones finished his Ginger Ale and said they needed to be moving along. Terrice asked if she could stay a while longer to catch up on old times. I was curious to know why, but allowed her to stay.

CHAPTER 15

"Relentless Love (Chantal)"

Jamal came home the next night and I begged him for hours to come closer to me. This was the last straw putting up with Jamal's arrogance. I allowed him to move back in and he still had problems making love to me. I couldn't understand what his problem was. Men found me attractive, but God must have put a damper on Jamal's manhood. I understood we had been separated for a few years, but I gave him another chance. He should have been kissing my feet or jumping at my every move.

Since Dante was already in college, there was no need to play house again. It would always be slip in—slip out, an easy way of saying, "You can have it now, but you won't see it later."

Jamal had to work another night shift and I didn't want to be alone. I'd ask if someone else could take his place, but Jamal was adamant about leaving. Tempers started to flare, but were soon halted when Dante mysteriously walked in the house.

"Dante's home," Montel yelled out.

Their relationship had a special bond. Whenever Dante came home from college, he was sure to take Montel to Laser Tag.

"I'm glad to see you buddy," Dante said giving Montel a huge hug. "My buddy," he said glancing over at Jamal. "What's up pop? Good to see you're still hanging around the house. Momma's not puttin' you out yet, is she?" He said jokingly.

"Man, get over here and give your old man a hug. And to answer your question, she can't resist me."

"Says who?" I stared and then walked through the kitchen and into the dinning area.

"Momma—Oh Momma! It's been a while. You are so beautiful Momma."

"Now that's a man who knows how to compliment a lady!" I said giving him a kiss on the forehead.

"He got it from his pops," Jamal said smiling heavily.

"Hey pops! I gotta show you something."

"Not now son. I'm on my way out the door. I'm working the midnight shift."

"No man! That can't be! I just got here."

"Should've told us you were coming home! I would have cancelled my shift for you son," Jamal said.

"You won't even call in for your son—Jamal! You have so much damn devotion to that lousy ass company of yours that it's pathetic," I said angrily. "Don't you care about your son's feelings?"

"I do Chantal. I can't get into it right now, but something major is going down at work and I need to be there."

"Go ahead then daddy," Dante said. "I'll show momma. Maybe I'll think about showing you later."

"I'll be back before you know it," Jamal said giving him a hug. "So glad you're home, son!"

Jamal gave Montel a kiss and walked out the door.

"I guess I don't matter as usual with him," I remarked.

"Momma, don't take it that way, Daddy really loves you. He's just—well, since you left him before, he gets nervous when he's around you."

"Nervous, what do you mean by nervous?"

"Momma, I told you years ago that Daddy said he felt nervous when you guys were together. He saw you when you use to walk down the stairs in your sexy nightgowns trying to seduce him. He was afraid he wouldn't be able to meet your needs."

"What? He told you all of that?"

"Actually, when I was ten, he told me everything. He didn't feel you guys were close enough to spill the beans."

"He's lying Dante. He wasn't nervous around my cousin Jennifer. I bet he gave her what she needed."

"She didn't judge him momma. She took him as he was."

"Judge him Dante." I paused to gather my thoughts. "Look sweetie, you just got back in town. Let's talk about you for a while. This is boring me."

"I did have something to show Pops, but I think you should see it too."

He pulled out a picture of a young man with similar features to his.

"Who is this Dante? He almost looks like your father."

"That's because it's his son. I ran into him at Georgia Tech. Momma, Daddy's been lying to you for years. He knew this Jennifer person for years. The boy, Juan Dobbins, is Jennifer's son.

"Those trips he was taking, you know—business related trips—they were definitely business related. Long lost business with Jennifer! They both played you like a deck of cards, Momma."

"He told you that, Dante?"

"Nah, momma. It wasn't Daddy, but Juan. He described Daddy to the "T". When I saw Daddy tonight I almost punched the son of a bitch."

"Dante! Watch your mouth. Just because you're twenty, doesn't mean that you're grown."

"Momma, why you defending him like that? He dished you like a sack of potatoes and threw the peelings in your face. You alright with dat?"

"Dante, let's hear your father's side of the story before we draw any conclusions," I said wanting to kill him myself. "Montel's upstairs sleep. He might hear you."

"I'll let it go for now, but tomorrow, Momma—it's on."

"That's a good thing Dante. You want something to snack on? Georgia is quite a drive. You gotta be hungry."

"Who you tellin' Momma? My legs started to fall asleep then Janique took over."

"Whoa baby! Who's Janique?" I asked curiously.

"Ah mom—that's my girl! She'll be over tomorrow if you don't mind," Dante said smiling brightly.

Janique was a senior at Georgia Tech. She was a couple years older than Dante and she lived in Bowie, just outside of Baltimore. Her family came from a predominantly rich area. Her family was from India.

"I guess I'm not going to get anymore information about her since you can't wipe that silly little smile off your face."

"Oh sorry Momma," he said stretching his arms towards me and giving me a huge hug and kiss. "I guess I'll turn in now Momma. I'm tired as a motha…."

"Dante! You better watch your mouth boy," I said slapping his face playfully. "Give me another hug baby. I just might need it after tomorrow."

"I can't wait for you to meet my baby, momma," Dante said hugging me back.

Overnight, the rain began to pour. Lightning flashed across the sky and a huge rainbow showed in the morning dew. When the alarm clock went off, I got up early so I would be waiting for Jamal's arrival. Jamal walked through the door, tired from working the midnight shift. I had some things to talk to him about, but wanted to make sure Montel and Dante were still sleeping.

As I walked down the stairs in my lavender Victoria Secrets PJs, Jamal made his way to the kitchen putting on the tea kettle for some Folgers's instant coffee. Appeased by my appearance, we sat at the table and he told me about his shift. It was 7:59 a.m. on a Saturday morning and I was not trying to hear about some stupid ass night shift. My main concern was Juan and why I had no clue about him being a part of Jamal's life.

When I first saw Jennifer at my party, I had no idea that Juan existed. I thought it was a bit strange that Jamal and Jennifer just happened to meet while in Maryland, but to find out that they had known each other longer, devastated me. My approach to the conversation had to be pragmatic. Easing my way through the talk about servers, receivers, and one of the employees wasn't an easy thing for me to do. Jamal loved his job and most of the time, that's where he spent the vast majority of his nights. At least that's what I initially thought.

Montel walked down the stairs. *"Damn it,"* I thought to myself. *"My chances are shot."*

"Hey little man," Jamal said. "What's up my man?"

"Good morning Daddy," a squeaky little voice replied. "Mommy, I want break tess," he said mispronouncing the word.

"It's breakfast, Montel," I said sounding it out over and over again. "Where's my good morning? Can I at least have a hug?"

"Mommy, is Dante still here?" An inquiring voice asked.

"I sure am," Dante replied picking him up and swinging him around.

"Dante," a cheerful Montel squealed. "I'm so glad you're still here."

"I'm not going anywhere ever again," he said looking up at Jamal and me. "I'm home for good."

"Dante, you're kidding….right?" I asked. "You're leaving Georgia Tech! What happened baby?"

"Janique. She's moving back home to be with her family. She said she couldn't take being away from her family anymore. I decided since the semester was over, I'll transfer my credits to the University of Maryland in Baltimore."

"Hold up son," Jamal said. "You can't just quit like that. I thought you loved it in Georgia."

"I did until I met Juan Dobbins," rolling his eyes at Jamal.

"Juan Dobbins? How? When?" Stumbling over his words. "I mean— who is he?"

"Don't try and play it off daddy, Momma already knows about him. She knows how you pretended to go on trips and detoured to Georgia where

Jennifer used to live. You lying bastard! I hate you!" Dante said running out of the room.

I immediately jumped up telling Jamal I'll talk to him about it later. I followed Dante upstairs to his old room. I had left it just the same, knowing he would be back someday. He still had his pictures of Ashanti and Alliyah hanging on the wall.

"Man," Jamal said looking over at Montel. "What a way to start the day!"

"Daddy...why is Dante upset with you? Is he going to be okay?" A curious little Montel asked.

"He's just upset right now, but he'll be alright," Jamal said hoping to be correct.

"Baby, you ok?" I asked with a somber expression on my face.

"Nah Momma! I didn't wanna come across like that so early in the morning. But he deserved it. He's lucky I didn't just knock him out and explain why later."

"Dante, I'm not happy about this either, but you gotta control your temper baby. What if it's not true and Juan told you this because Jamal left his mother? We don't know if he's just saying this to spite you or cause friction. I'll talk to your father and get to the bottom of this. How old would you say this Juan person is?"

"I don't know, maybe seventeen or eighteen. He's younger than me. I do know that much."

"I'll talk to him. If it's true, we'll work it out."

"Are you gonna leave him again Momma?" Dante inquired.

"I haven't given it a thought yet. This is a shocker to me as well."

"I'm taking a shower and heading over to Janique's house. She doesn't live that far from us. I'll bring her over later when I come back."

"Give her a call first. Her parents might have other plans for her today."

"Yeah, you're right about that Momma. I will call her now," Dante said while heading towards the shower.

Jamal started making his way upstairs. He met me on my way down. I wasn't happy at all. Jamal was a bit shocked by Dante's disobedience.

"That boy needs to learn to respect his elders."

"We have to talk Jamal," I remarked angrily.

"I'll tell you all about it when I get a little rest."

"Oh hell no Jamal! You owe me an explanation and I want to hear it now. I think I deserve that much."

"Two hours baby. That's all I need," he said making his way back to our room.

"I'll give you your two hours, but you better make sure you have your lies straight when you wake up."

"Damn it," Jamal said slamming the door after walking into our bathroom. He looked over at the picture of 'Picasso' Dream' I had hanging on the wall. "That ho mind is all messed up."

After Jamal got out of the shower, he sat on the bed searching for answers. He knew two hours wouldn't be long enough for anyone to snooze. He could hear Montel heading up the stairs wanting to play Nintendo in his room.

"Man we gotta move that game downstairs. Can't get no peace around here," Jamal said under his breath.

Dante had left for Janique's. When he arrived, he found an exquisitely tasteful mansion. The driveway was made of ceramic tile flown to the states from India. Two statues of Hindu descent pilastered the doorway as he made his entrance. Dante walked into the preserved empire and was greeted with a smile and kiss by Janique. Her mother stood in the doorway with her and also greeted him with a smile.

"Dante—This is my mother Jorjanian. I wanted her to meet you before we left for your house."

"The pleasure's all mine. You are just as beautiful as your daughter," Dante said with a smile.

Jorjanian jested and said, "Please come in. Make yourself welcome." She called Janique off to another room while Dante looked around. "Your father is not going to like this. You must correct your mistake before he finds out that you are dating a black man."

"But mother, he's kind and I know father will like him. Just give him a chance. His mother and father are well-to-do people. Dante told me all about them."

"That doesn't matter with your father Janique. You should not have brought him here. Let's grab some tea and go back into the living quarters before your friend starts to worry."

Dante made himself comfortable. He sat on the couch posted with pillows taller than the back of his head. His feet rested comfortably under the table and the TV was tuned in on BET. When he saw the ladies enter the room, he stood in their presence like a real gentleman would.

"Glad to see you ladies made it back. I was starting to worry."

"Oh there's no cause to worry Dante. My mother thought fit for us to bring you some tea."

Dante wasn't big on tea, but didn't want to hurt their feelings. "Thank you very much Mrs. Siddiqui. You have a very lovely home."

"We try very hard to keep it suitable. So, how long have you been living in Maryland?"

"Nineteen years ma'am until I went off to college. I've always wanted to go to school in Georgia."

"Ah yes. So that is where you met Janique? She's a very lovely girl. We don't want to see her hurt."

"No ma'am. I have no intentions of doing that. I respect her in every manner."

"That is good young man. Janique's family believes that culture is very important. As you will see, Janique will dress the same as I when she's home. We believe that our women have to be presentable to our men. Do you understand young man?"

"Loud and clear!" I started to wonder what she was tryin' to tell a brotha. "I was hoping to take Janique over to meet my mother and father today. I wasn't sure if she already had plans."

"I see. Her father will be home shortly. I'm sure it's okay this time. However, Janique will need to be home by sunset. We eat our last meal before the sun goes down and then we take a walk afterwards to keep in shape."

"I promise to have her back in due time. It was my pleasure meeting such a lovely lady."

"My pleasure as well."

Dante and Janique got into his black Mustang and headed back to the house.

I was still waiting for Jamal to come and explain how Juan Dobbins came about. The tension was high when Dante reached the house. As he walked in, he could tell that things weren't right. Montel was still upstairs playing one of his Nintendo games and Jamal was still in bed. Dante introduced Janique to me and left us to talk. He headed towards his father's room and opened the door slowly. Jamal was lying on the bed in his torn blue boxers and a white tee-shirt. He was still tired from his shift the night before. Awakened slightly by Dante's presence, Jamal sat up long enough to hear him say that his girlfriend was downstairs and that he shouldn't bother coming down to meet her.

Dante left the room closing the door behind. He went over to Montel's room watching him play Battle Tank. Montel smiled when he saw him come in. "Dante, look at how well I'm playing this game," Montel said. It was a level Dante hadn't seen him reach before.

"Man you're getting better than me. I have to come and play it with you one day."

"You will? Oh thank you Dante."

"Hey buddy. You wanna meet one of the most beautiful women on earth."

"Momma's the prettiest so she must look as good as Momma."

"Not quite, but she's close."

When Montel walked in the room, he looked at Janique and said, "she looks like my teacher. She wears the same type of dress like you."

Janique smiled. "What a cute little boy he is!"

"This is my little brother Montel. He likes pretty women."

"Nothing wrong with his eyesight," Janique said smiling at him. "Hello Montel. I'm very happy to finally meet you. Dante has told me a lot of good things about you."

"He has," said Montel with a huge smile on his face.

"Yes Yes. He thinks the world of you."

Dante cut her off. "Don't make him blush Janique. It will go to his head."

"Oh, but it's true. Maybe you're the one that's blushing and not Montel."

"I see both of you have your little love quarrels also. So Janique do you mind telling me about your family and your culture?"

"Sure Mrs. Lewis."

"Actually, it's Ms. Lewis. I'm not married to Dante's father. We're still in the process of working things out."

"I see. Well, my family came from very far. They left India when I was eight years old. My father was put out of his country when his father passed leaving him with many riches. According to my father, he had so much wealth that the government wanted to take control of it and have him come work for them. My father wasn't going for it. He was asked to leave the country and never return. My father already had relatives living in the United States. One of his uncles lives in Bowie. He asked if my father would come and live here also. That's how we made it here."

"That's a very interesting story Janique. And your mother, what does she do for a living?"

"She's a homemaker. Since my father has a company here, she doesn't have to work. We all live under one roof. It is our custom for the man to take care of his wife and family. It would be a disgrace for the women to work."

Montel interrupted. "Mommy, do you miss your mother? She died and now she is in Heaven."

"Montel—what made you ask that question? Of course I miss her."

"Janique was talking about her mother and I thought about Granny. I still remember seeing her lying in the big basket. Momma said they were going to cover granny's face and put her in the ground."

"Montel—sweetie, let's not talk about Granny right now okay," I added.

"Is it making you sad Momma?"

"Very."

"Okay mommy. Can I go back upstairs and play with my games now?"

"Sure you can."

Dante looked over at Janique. "Kids. They say the darnest things sometimes."

"I think he's sweet."

We waited for quite a while for Jamal to come downstairs and meet Janique. I was livid. Needless to say, two hours had long passed and he never came down for our talk. My patience wore thin and I was about to go upstairs and bring his sorry ass to meet her. He never showed up and Dante had to take Janique back home. I had never been so upset and embarrassed by Jamal's foolishness. I went to bed an angry person that night. The nerve of him making me look like a fool after I allowed his sorry ass to spend a few nights with me and Montel. *"I know this won't last forever,"* I thought as I prepared myself for bed.

CHAPTER 16

"Dominique's Physique (Chantal)"

I woke up angry the next morning. Jamal pissed me off for the last time. "To hell with Jamal," I said as I walked outside to get the morning newspaper.

Looking around the neighborhood, I noticed that the garbage men had already taken the trash, but left a trail of evidence behind. I could have easily walked over and picked up the remainders, but what would be the purpose? I was too upset to do anything other than get the paper. I grabbed the paper, said screw the trash can, and walked back inside my house.

The house needed a good cleaning, but I wasn't in the mood to touch it. After a few months of being back in the work force, I was giving it up for the second time. I had stocks and a nice settlement. I had a countersuit against RJ's wife Genie that was going to pay off substantially so why work?

"That heffa thought she could hold a sista down," I said smiling to myself.

Genie's refusal to let RJ go caused much agony in my life. Never thinking I would give Jamal another chance and his selfishness with Jennifer damn near landed me in the nut house.

I became indulgent in Shanice's life. Hoping someday to have a relationship such as hers and Frank's, I began pursuing men like never before. My birthday was fast approaching. This would be a big one for me since I was getting closer and closer to the "Big Five O."

"Face it," I said telling myself as I read the sales ad in the Washington Post, "Forty-Six is approaching and you're still without a man. Shanice has it all. Looks, a big house, a man hung like a horse (so she says), and happiness. She's gotta tell me her secret to having it all." I scratched my head while pondering the thoughts in my mind.

I decided to call my girl Shanice and see what she was up to. The phone rang twice. Answering the phone in the middle of sex didn't rub Frank the right way. Frank loved sex. More than that, he loved giving Shanice every powerful inch of himself.

"This had better be good!" Shanice said with hair wildly scattered upon her head.

"Shanice," I responded eagerly needing an ear.

"Yeah. Who this?" Shanice said in an uncertain voice.

"It's me—your girl, Chantal. Not another bad time, is it?" I questioned while quenching my face tightly.

"Girl—Frank was messing up my mind with love thumps."

"Whatever! Wanna go to Arundel Mills with me? I heard they have a big sale going on."

"Nah. You go this time. I have some unfinished business to take care of here with Frank."

"Girl, it is 12 o'clock in the afternoon! Git yo stank ass off that man's horse and come go with me the mall! PLEASE," I begged overemphasizing the word, please.

Shanice looked down at Frank and said as gentle and kind as possible, "Not in this lifetime! I'm riding the pony and once you're on, whoa baby! You can't get off. And I mean that literally." *Click.* Shanice hung up the phone.

I stood with my mouth wide open, "That nasty ho hung up on me! I'll go by my damn self!"

I got in my Benz, adjusted my mirrors, and headed down 97 south. When I arrived at the mall, it looked like people were still shopping for Christmas in March.

"Damn this place is always crowded!" I said seeking a parking space.

I was wearing my red leather pants and a black sports coat as I entered by the movie theatre. My mid-length Coach purse hung close by my side as I pulled my gold-framed glasses from my face.

"Slightly blurry in here," I said. "Better put the eyes back on the face," I said sensing my sex appeal would go unnoticed.

"This is a big ass mall for a sista to be walking by herself. Good thing Dante kept Montel for me," I thought.

After strolling around for a few minutes, I'd wished Shanice had come with me. Off Broadway Shoes Warehouse was straight ahead. It looked like the perfect resting place for me to stop. My feet were very uncomfortable and the oversized corns on each pinky toe wasn't helping with the pain. My eyes followed a pair of Jordan's that was heading in my direction. He was as tall a man as I'd ever seen. Pretending to be looking for some comfortable shoes, I gazed straight into his luring eyes.

"Hi beautiful," he said looking directly at me. "Dominique's the name."

"Chantal. Jenkins—Lewis, whichever one you wish to call me," I said blushing.

Confused by the comment, Dominique extended his hand and said, "I don't see any rings so I take it that you're single?" He asked cautiously.

"Both. I mean—I've been married—divorced, married again, and divorced again.

"Damn baby! You're not trying to break a record or something?" He asked jokingly.

"Just a lot of bad luck, that's all. And you—let me guess." I checked him over noticing an impression of where a ring used to be. "You're divorced. Am I correct?"

"Not even close," he said. "I'm a widower. Lost my wife six and a half years ago."

"I'm so sorry Dominique. She had to be quite young. How did she die?" I asked trying to show a bit of concern.

"Leukemia," he responded clearly his throat. "She was thirty-eight. We didn't even know she had it until one day she started to feel faint. You know what Chantal I prefer not to talk about her at the moment if it's okay with you. Brings back too many memories of what we use to have. You had lunch yet?"

"Nope and to tell the truth, I'm starving."

"Let's walk over to the courtyard and grab a bite. My treat," Dominique said raising one eyelid hoping for a 'yes'.

"I don't have anything else to do at the moment," I said.

"After you beautiful," a smooth talking Dominique expressed.

I looked back at him as he watched me walk flaunting my long slim body. As we passed by the Wet Seal, I couldn't help, but make a comment.

"Now there's an interesting name for a store. Who would name something so sexual if they weren't thinking that way?"

"I'm not sure. But, I think it's a cool name, if I have to say so myself."

I looked over at the Rocky Mountain Chocolate Factory and invited Dominique to take a look inside with me. Tons of chocolate were stretched on a tabletop across the room. From white to deep dark provocative chocolate, the aroma took over our nostrils.

"I think I'd better sit this one out, Dominique. I'm getting fat just looking at all of this chocolate."

"I believe you're right, my dear. Shall we continue towards the food court?" He said hopefully.

There were many places to choose from, but I chose 'Chili's Too'. Wanting a Sizzling Fajita topped with grilled peppers and onions, I chose the grilled chicken Caesar salad instead.

"Eating light, my love?" Dominique asked.

"Trying to watch my figure, that's all," I murmured.

"Baby, there's nothing wrong with the way you look," Dominique said. "I would say more, but I just met you."

"I'm flattered by your style, Dominique. It's good to finally meet a man with taste.

"Is it possible for me to have your number?" He asked reluctantly looking me over from top to bottom. "I'd like to see you again very soon. Maybe I can invite you into my domain at Los Casa de Dominique," he said smiling politely at me.

I was rusty as hell with Spanish, but it sounded good. "What's that suppose to mean?" I asked with a puzzled look.

"It means—The House of Dominique, in Spanish."

"Oh," I responded dropping my head in shame. "I guess I need to take some Spanish lessons to keep up with you, huh?"

"Nah baby! You're fine just the way you are. Look, I have to be moving along or I'll be here with you all day and into the night."

"Nothing wrong with having a little fun, is it?" I remarked.

"Not when the fun is as exciting as you," he said. "I'm glad it was me in that shoe store and not some other man. Fate comes along just when you need it the most. Let's say we get together two weeks from now at mi casa."

"I think that's a wonderful idea. I gotta ask you this so don't take it the wrong way. Are you involved with anyone? I mean—I've been through some shit with men and at the age of forty plus," smiling shyly, "I don't need any complications or drama."

Pausing for a split second, he said, "Actually, I've been in a relationship way too long and frankly speaking, it's at the point of dissolution."

Wishing I'd never asked, I came clean myself. "I was trying to build something special with my ex-husband. We have two kids together. One's twenty and let's say that I got caught with the last one. He's eleven."

"Damn baby! You had him kinda late, don't you think?"

"Actually, he's my pride and joy. Rarely do you see him without seeing me. We're attached at the hip as some would say."

Raising an eyebrow, "And this ex-husband of yours, just where does he fit in?"

"See, that's the problem. He doesn't. After Montel was born, the fire never rekindled. He still comes around to see him, but he has to call first."

"Whew! Thought a brotha had some competition for a minute!"

"Huh, Jamal! He'll never fit in my life like he used to. I think he wanted me pregnant again so he'd have an excuse to stop by when he pleased. It's a crying shame his wife left him so suddenly.

"Man, there's a lot of drama with you. I hope that's his only intention. Listen baby. I really must be leaving now. Can I see you in two weeks? I'll call you tonight, if it's all right with you."

"Sure thang, Dominique."

CHAPTER 17

"Taking Longer Than Usual"

Two weeks had come and Dominique had asked me to meet him at Jillian's outside Arundel Mills Mall. I arrived around 1:35 p.m. and Dominique called to say he would be a little late. After thirty minutes had gone by, I started to get a little restless. I saw a spot opening up, but I was afraid to move from where I had been sitting because the parking was ridiculous and I would lose my spot. I waited a while longer when this blue 4WD trimmed in gray took the next available spot. I watched the woman struggle to back her truck in. She maneuvered to the left and then to the right. After several attempts, she backed straight into the back end of a red mustang behind me. The entire car moved an inch forward and I sat in disbelief. Was this person going to be a good citizen and do the right thing or would she sit it out without a care?

Not sure of what she should do, she sat in her truck a few minutes longer. A short dark skinned woman got out on the passenger side. She was wearing an out of shape weave and baggy pants with black boots. She took a quick look, and got back in the truck. Again, they sat and waited. I'm sure they knew I had seen the entire thing. After another ten minutes had gone by, the driver got out and took a peek and got back in. I could see her watching me through her mirror.

Since I had been waiting almost an hour now, I was really starting to get restless. I picked up a piece of paper and pen and started to leave a note. It was the principle of the thing. These bitches were getting ready to leave a scene and walk into the mall without saying a word. I started my note like this:

Dear Sir/Madam,

As I sat in my truck waiting for a friend, I noticed a blue truck trimmed in grey back into your red mustang. After they left, I walked over to their vehicle and made note of the license plate number. The time was approximately 2:05 p.m. in front of Jillian's. Why am I concerned about the matter? Because I have seen incidents like this one happen to a lot of people and no one bothered to leave a note. One of the women, the driver, had a short manly dusty red haircut. She was wearing a tan jacket and a pair of black slacks. Her girlfriend wore baggy pants and a pair of black boots.

If I were you, I would definitely check into this and call the police.

Signed: A concerned citizen

I sat contemplating whether or not to put this note on the car. The women finally got out of their truck looked over at me and went into Jillian's. Just as I got ready to get out of my truck, a group of teenagers dressed like gangsters walked outside. I knew they would see me and wonder what I was doing to someone else's car. After I got up the nerve, opened my door, Dominique pulled up. *"Saved by default,"* I thought to myself as I waved for Dominique to keep driving as I got back into my truck. Although my intentions were good, I didn't get a chance to leave the note behind.

I followed him to the rendezvous point and we met with some of his friends. This place was live. The people were dressed fashionably as though they were attending an award's show. Dominique wore a black knitted shirt that buttoned down the center and I wore a long black skirt with a split down the back. We didn't seem to be dressed appropriately for this event.

Dominique had some papers he wanted to give to his good friend who used to be a professional ball player. I just sat back and watched the show taking place around me. There were women wearing bras two sizes too small making for a helluva show of boobs.

I didn't recognize this part of Dominique, but was beginning to get a feel for what he stood for. I walked over to the bar and asked for Bourbon chilled slowly. The bartender looked at me and smiled.

"You're not a regular here are you?" He said smiling at the expression on my face.

"Is it that noticeable?" I whispered looking around the room to see if anyone had heard him say those words.

"I've been around for quite some time and I've never had a woman order Bourbon chilled slowly."

I laughed softly, and said, "Actually, I'm not a big drinker. I thought I would make up my own choice of liquor. I didn't know you would take notice so easily."

"Sweetie, let me tell you something, when people come in here—they order the soft drinks trying to cover up who they really are. But deep down inside, I know who they are and what they really want. You were just bold enough to order yours."

"Is that good or bad?" I asked.

"Actually, I like a woman like you."

Dominique started to head our way. "Looks like your gentleman friend is coming for you. He's a very lucky man. I tell you if you didn't have that big ring on your finger, I'd be coming after you."

"I'm flattered," I said. "We're not married or anything. I'm not trying to go that route again."

"Been there before huh?"

"You can say that. I don't think I can do it again."

"You'll be surprised at the things you can do if you're given the chance to do it."

Dominique interrupted. "Hey baby. You ready to go?"

"Sure honey. Let me just get my jacket and I'll be heading out the door with you."

"You take good care of her mister. She's a keeper."

"Oh—I will. I wasn't born yesterday to know when I see a good thing right in front of me." We walked to Dominique's car and he said, "Was that man trying to come on to you?"

I looked at him and smiled. "Nah baby, he was just teaching me the ropes about drinks."

"Drinks? What about them?"

"Well, I'll just say, I tried to order some Bourbon chilled slowly and he almost laughed me out of that place. I didn't realize you were coming back so soon."

"You didn't make that mistake, did you honey?"

"Oh, it's funny to you. I'm glad you got the last laugh. Ha Ha."

"Now you're being funny," Dominique said. "I'm just trying to help you out for when you and Shanice go out and you don't make yourself look bad."

"Oh, I doubt if I will be placing an order like that when are out. Shanice doesn't drink and neither do I. I was just trying to impress the bartender."

"So you're the one that was flirting?"

"You busted me baby," I said giving him the puppy dog look. "Forgive me, please."

Dominique looked at me and said, "Baby, no matter what you do, I'll always find it in my heart to forgive you."

"Watch yourself!" I said. "You never know what you might have to forgive me for. Not that I would do anything to disrespect you. But, you never know what might happen to make me beg for forgiveness."

"Don't start to worry me baby! I have a lot of trust in you and I know you wouldn't defy me in any way. Besides, our day is getting closer."

"What day is that?" I asked suspiciously.

"Oh—you'll see. One of these days, you'll be mine forever."

I didn't like the sound of that since I vowed never to get hitched again. Dominique was a stockbroker and indeed a wonderful man, but I only knew him for a short period of time and a sista wasn't trying to be married anytime soon. "Can I interest you in a home cooked meal tonight?"

"You mean, you're going to cook dinner for me or will we be ordering out?" Dominique jested.

"I will be cooking up some steamed shrimp, a nice Caesar Salad, and baked potatoes. I also have a nice selection of wines to go with it," I added.

"Now how can I turn that down after you put it that way?" Dominique said.

"Great. I'd better get back in my car and get ready for tonight. Is seven okay?"

"Make it six and we'll be on track."

I was puzzled by that one. I wasn't sure what Dominique had up his sleeves, but six o'clock was fine by me. "Six it is. I'll see you then."

CHAPTER 18

"One Night of Passion"

Being the 6'5" tall, dark, and extremely handsome man he was, Dominique took his time with me despite my dying need for passion. He was smooth with the way he gently raised my legs into the perfect "V". I kept my eyes closed the entire time trying to fathom this newest member of the male species entering my body.

Passionately kissing me on the lips, he made sure not to keep his tongue in my mouth any longer than necessary. I enjoyed every move of this man's touch. I joined in the fun by licking his neck and behind his ears in hopes of finding the most sensitive part of his body.

Keeping my legs formed in the perfect "V", Dominique held his member of passion at my open entrance. Instead of the force I usually encountered from the jerks back in my youthful days, Dominique parted my lips to ecstasy as he drove in me. I joined him by lifting my buttocks higher until the grip of my vagina fit smoothly on top of him. More than anything, I had to find a way to relieve the tightness of my sweetness.

Thinking about the conversation we had at dinner, I watched this man in amazement as he gently slid in and out of me. Dominique asked me to tell him what I wanted to happen while we were making love. I told him about some of my deepest and nastiest fantasies of passion and how I liked being held close as he tastefully made love to me. Most men wanted easy access to jump in and out of my body like I was a cup of Jell-O bouncing through the air.

The more Dominique tried to find his comfort spot within me, the more I lifted my buttocks to join him. I lived in a world of fantasy and this night, it seemed my deepest fantasies were about to come true.

Dominique had turned the radio to 102.3 before I arrived. They were playing the hit song from back in the day, "Is It Still Good To You," as I released moan after moan. My passion with older songs drove me completely nuts whenever I made love with any man. Dominique could feel the instant flow of hot juices being released from me.

"D!" I moaned cutting his name down to a single letter. "Make love to me," I said whispering softly in his ears.

"I want you to cum for me baby," Dominique said demanding a response.

Knowing that was where I drew the line when it came to being with a man the first time, I simply replied with, "Take me to ecstasy."

Gripping him ever so tightly, Dominique could hardly stand the heat. My lustrous body and constant licks on his neck sent him into a massive explosion. Trying his best to hold back his release of pressure, he squeezed my legs tightly together, and released some of the most powerful cum ever.

Not wanting the passion to end, Dominique continued to roll until his member had emptied every ounce of the milky substance left inside of him.

"This can't be it, baby! I wanted to see you cum," he said trying to keep his composure. "You got some good shit girl!" He whispered leaning down towards me and giving me a huge kiss.

Whispering softly, "I don't cum for everyone. I hold back because once I release my juices, I fall head over heels in love. Only two men have ever made me cum," I said staring into his large brown eyes. "You are one sexy black man," I said getting myself into a deeper bind. "I can get use to being with a strong man like you."

Granted I was only 5'6", Dominique, well—he looked like a giant lying next to me. Dominique didn't reply after my comment. He just looked into my eyes and smiled.

"Ugh, did I miss your response Dominique? Or, did I scare you off with the sudden come on?" I asked.

"Nah baby! I was just thinking how nice it would be having you somewhere on a beach where it's nice and warm. This place gets kind of cold in the winter. I'm thinking maybe the Caribbean or Cancun."

"When?" I asked excitingly. "I can leave the boys here or they can stay with their father."

"Sometime in February, say—the week of Valentine's Day," Dominique replied.

"That's next month," I said.

"I know baby. Wouldn't it be great?" Dominique said smiling wildly at me. "That's if you can get away."

"Oh, I'll make time for that. I always wanted to go to Cancun. Just didn't have anyone to take me," I replied.

"Cancun it is baby. I'll make the arrangements just as soon as I get myself out of you. I wanna do it again," he said with a desired look of hunger written across his face. "I can lose myself inside you over and over again and then find time to recover."

"You have a lot of bullshit built up inside you, don't you Dominique? I know you like playing with my head, but that's okay. A sista can take it," I said jokingly.

"Bullshit! Is that what you think I'm trying to pull here? Nah, baby. I am going to take you to Cancun. You'll see."

CHAPTER 19

Who Rung the Bell?

Thinking about the chicken I had gotten earlier from Popeye's, Dominique insisted that we go downstairs for a quick bite. He wanted more from me. He wanted to continue his penetrating strides into my heated fortress. As we headed downstairs, I asked if I could borrow one of his robes that hung neatly behind his bedroom door. I wore the white terry cloth and Dominique wore the blue.

"Would you like a glass of wine?" He inquired as he watched me separate the chicken and potatoes.

"Not too much," I said smiling at him. "You know I won't be any good while driving back home."

Dominique headed further downstairs into his basement. He had a great variation of Sherries, but all the wines were gone. I had never tasted Sherry. Dominique reached into his remodeled pantry and retrieved a single wine glass filling it with crushed ice. I told him to pour a drop just in case I didn't like the taste. My first sip sent chills throughout my body.

"I can't drink this," I said crinkling my forehead.

"Ah. I guess you're not a drinker after all," Dominique said with a snicker. Then we dove into our meal. The three pieces of chicken were demolished in minutes. We sat and talked for a while waiting for our food to digest before we would make another venture upstairs. Dominique talked about his recent relationship with a woman he'd been seeing over the past three years. Since they had been together for some time, Dominique hung in there trying not to hurt her in the end. Being able to relate to what he had gone through, I spoke about my many relationships and how each of them led to dead ends.

As we spoke about our relationships, Dominique was telling me how he was with another woman and by chance, his ex-girlfriend knocked on the door.

"Every time I get it in my mind to leave her, bad luck seems to follow me around," he said.

As though she had him in some type of trance, I could see the sadness in his eyes and how he tried his best to be honest with me about his relationship. We both needed comfort at the moment, but all we could do was stare.

Ring. Ring. We looked at each other.

"Was that the doorbell? I asked nervously.

"Yes, baby. That's the doorbell," he said with shock on his face. "Don't move," he said softly.

"Dominique! Dominique." We heard a voice outside calling his name. More rings and more voices. He could see the worried look in my face. After five minutes, the buzzes and voices were gone. He had me come closer to him as I sat quietly in the chair. He motioned for me to get up and then he held me. I was damn near shaking in my pants. I envisioned myself being shot at or it being some type of setup like in the movies.

"Did you call her and have come over without telling me?" I asked.

"Come on baby! Give me more credit than that," he said looking down at my shivering body.

"I'm scared Dominique," I screamed out. "I've never been in a situation like this before."

"I know baby. I'm so sorry for this."

The phone began ringing. He dimmed the lights so that no one could see him if they were standing at the front door.

"She's home now," he said. "She must have gone home."

The phone began ringing again, but he wouldn't pick it up. He ran upstairs telling me to stay put. As he came back down, there was a sigh of relief written across his face.

"That was my sister," he said expressing his concerns. "I hope everything is okay."

Again the phone rang, but this time it was Yolanda, his ex-girlfriend.

"I'm not answering that," he said looking at the number from his caller ID. "She's at home."

Then his cell phone rang. He had left it upstairs.

"You'd better get that before she really gets suspicious Dominique."

"You're right baby," he said rushing back upstairs.

As he answered, I could hear him on the phone. "Whazzup? Whazzup? Whazzup?" He asked quickly and in a very smooth tone. "I'm over my partner's house watching the game. You messin' me up woman," he said jokingly. "I'll call you back later." Then he hung up the phone. "The coast is clear."

"Dominique I thought she was out of your life," I said nervously.

"She is baby. She just won't stop calling me. If she found out that I was dating someone else, she would cause a lot of problems."

"We better end this now Dominique. I don't want her to drive by here and see my car outside. She might mess it up."

"Ah baby! Don't worry about that. But, I think to be on the safe side, we'd better pick this up later," he said. "Damn, I really wanted to get back inside those legs of yours.

"And I wanted you too, Dominique. I'm just glad that God is letting me get out of this one safely."

We got dressed and I went over to this bathroom to wipe myself down. Since Dante was watching Montel, I didn't have to worry about explaining my whereabouts to anyone. I had gotten so use to telling Jamal my every move that having Dante there made things much easier for me.

I couldn't help, but think about the sex Dominique and I engaged in earlier. Then it hit me. How within minutes my life became shambled because of someone coming to the door. Wipe after wipe, I thought about another woman coming over and blowing our cover. I wasn't certain who it was, but I knew that someone wanted to see Dominique desperately. He walked in the bathroom and made more apologies.

"I could see the fear in your face baby. That crazy ass girl just won't leave me alone."

Throwing my head back, I took a deep breath. "Why tonight of all nights?" I inquired. "The very night I decided to come over to your house, this woman terrorizes you."

"I don't know what brought her over here. She hasn't been her in months."

"Do you think one of your neighbors saw me come in and that's how she found out?"

"I don't think any of my neighbors know her. She only came around on the weekends. I had to kick her to the curb. She was too damn possessive. Now a woman like you, I could love forever."

"You're just saying that to make me feel better."

"No kidding baby. You're the best thing that's come my way since.... Well, I don't want to mention that, but you're the best."

"Now you're blowing my mind and making me blush."

"Are you sure you wanna leave right now? I mean, your son is old enough to watch Montel, isn't he?"

I thought long and hard, "I'd better go as tempting as it is to stay. My son will have a fit if I don't come home."

"You don't necessarily have to spend the night, but I would like for you to stay a little while longer and have some wine with me."

"Now you know I can't do that. I told you earlier what would happen if I drove around with alcohol in my system."

"I guess you better go then before I have you do something you might regret."

"Can I take a rain check?" Dominique asked as he walked me to the door. He noticed a familiar car outside and hurried me to my car.

As soon as Chantal was out of sight, his ex-girlfriend walked up to him. "I thought that tramp bitch would never leave," she said pushing him to the side.

"Look here Yolanda, I've moved on with my life and I suggest you do the same."

"Ah come on Dominique! Don't do me this way," she said trying to put her arms around his neck.

"You've been drinking again huh?" He asked pushing her away.

"I just had a little bit. Not even enough to fail a blood test."

"You gotta go Yolanda. I can't be bothered with you again."

"Come on big 'D'. You know you want me. You could never resist me before."

"Oh, but that's where you are wrong. I finally found someone who loves me for who I am and not what I can give them. Besides, she's already rich."

"That lil' scrony wench is rich?"

"Yep, she sure is. She doesn't have to work either."

"Must be nice to drive around in a Benz that's paid for. What her husband died or something?"

"Actually, she won it playing the Maryland lottery some years ago. She is very smart too Yolanda. She invested her money and got a lot more. If she chooses, she never has to work again."

"Some people have all the luck. So I guess I'm not in the running since you found someone with money?"

"It's not even like that. Don't hate her because she has something you'll never have again."

"I'm not hating on her. But she took my property and I want it back."

"First of all, I was never your damn property. Second, you need to be steppin'. I got a lot of things to do in the morning. I don't want Chantal coming back by here tonight and finding you here."

"She's long gone. I doubt if she'll be back."

"I don't want to chance it. Now, just leave."

"Okay, but I will be back for what's mine."

"The nerve of her showing up like she owned the place," Dominique thought to himself. *"Chantal might get the wrong impression if she would have come by here and found Yolanda in my house. Whew,"* he said as he headed upstairs, *"Too much drama around here for me tonight."*

CHAPTER 20

"Cancun by the way of Miami"

By day break, I was up and raring to go. I was already in the kitchen cooking breakfast when Dante walked down stairs.

"Long night Momma?" Dante asked.

"Too long for me," I responded.

"So what's up with you and Mr. Dominique? Are you serious about him?"

I could tell where he was heading with his questioning. He always liked to keep Jamal abreast to any situation happening around my house.

"Not quite. But, who knows. Maybe he will be the one for me."

"I thought you said you were not going to get involved anymore."

"What I said was I wasn't going to get married again. Getting hitched and seeing someone are two different things. Dominique and I have a lot in command."

"That's good Momma. I just hope you're happy this time."

"Oh, we won't be getting hitched for a while. Maybe never. I'm just not ready for any commitments right now."

"Whatever makes you happy Momma makes me happy."

"What's come over you? You didn't use to be like this. Are you feeling okay? Is it Janique?"

"Well—a little bit," he explained. "She wants to move in with me."

"You mean—stay here with us."

"Oh no," he said. "Not like that! She wants us to get a place together. I don't think she's happy at home."

"Dante, you have your whole life ahead of you. Don't do something you will regret later on in the future. I know you love this woman, but think about the situation she would have you in with her family. Arabs are very conscientious people when it comes to their involvement outside their own culture. In other words baby, they normally stick together."

"Not Janique Momma. She loves me unconditionally."

"It will be a disgrace to her family living in sin. Muslim customs are way different from ours. Are you ready to give your life to another god?"

"Momma you're talking as though we were married or something."

"Baby, I'm just getting you ready. If you assume the responsibility of moving in together, then you'd better be ready for a wedding in your near future. They won't allow their daughter to move in with you unless she's married."

"I'm definitely not ready for that. Shoot, I'm only twenty. I have my whole life ahead of me. I mean—I haven't found the job I wanted yet."

"Think about it first okay sweetie. If Janique loves you, she'll wait."

The phone started to ring and Dante raced over towards it. You're expecting a call, Dante?"

"Maybe," he said hoping it would be Janique.

"Hello."

"Good morning Dante. Is your mother in?"

"Sure. One moment, Mr. Dominique."

"Mommmmma—it's Mr. D," he said loudly, screaming as though she was in another room.

"Gimme that phone boy! You knew I was standing right here."

Laughing hysterically, he gave me the phone. "I'm going to my room for a second. If you need me, just call," he said giving me a kiss on my cheek.

"That boy is something else," I said as I answered the phone.

"Having a good morning Chantal?" Dominique asked while listening to me talk to Dante.

"Yeah, he's growing so fast. Before you know it, he'll be out of my hair."

"I know you don't want that day to come anytime soon. I mean, he is a grown man and by now, he should be finding a place of his own."

"What ya'll been talking about this or something?" I asked curiously.

"No, what made you ask that?"

"He was just talking about moving in with his girlfriend. I didn't think it was a good idea. You know how Muslims are with their religion. I don't want Dante worshipping some other god. I brought him up knowing that there is only one God and He is almighty."

"I understand that." Changing the subject, Dominique said, "Look baby, I have something to tell you. Hopefully, you will understand."

I wiped my hands on my shorts and paused. I knew it had something to do with last night and his ex-girlfriend.

"Last night when you left, Yolanda saw you leave. She came over to the house, spotted your car in front of my house, and waited for you to leave. I was a little concerned that she would come after you. I'm glad she didn't mess with your car after all."

"How did she know it was mine?"

"She didn't, but got a little suspicious when I answered the phone and said that I was over someone else's house. She had seen my car out front earlier so she hung around."

"How far does she live from you?"

"About five minutes away. She didn't want to cause any problems though. She just wanted to know why I didn't give her any play anymore. I tried to explain that I have moved on with my life but she wasn't taking no for an answer. I eventually kicked her out of my house. She was getting a little too weird for me."

"It's a good thing I didn't come back. I probably would have put my narrow foot up her scrawny ass."

"Come on now Chantal. You're too sweet to be getting yourself all roused up behind another woman."

"Yeah, but I got a little fight in me you know."

"I don't put that past you. We'll just stay away from Yolanda and everything will be okay. She's just jealous anyway that I have me a woman with money."

"You told her that?" I asked suspiciously. "I don't want everyone knowing my business."

"Didn't have to after she saw your ride. Made her skin crawl with anger knowing that she didn't have a hold on me anymore," he said as he got ready to tell me more.

"I'm just glad I left when I did. If that slut would have touched my car, I would probably be in jail right now."

"Forget about that baby. I got something else I have to tell you."

"Uh Oh—I don't like the sound of this one either."

"It's not as bad as you think. My company needs me to go to Miami for a week. I have a conference to attend. I was wondering if you'd like to go with me."

I sat on the sofa sipping a cup of vanilla tea. "I can't leave the boys here for that long by themselves. They'll kill each other."

"Come on baby. Dante is grown and Montel is getting older now. He'll be outta your hair before you know it. You have to let them grow up."

"I know that I do. But, what's going to happen if something goes wrong while I'm away?"

"We'll cross that line when it happens. Come go with me baby!"

"Let me talk it over with the boys and I'll get back with you."

"Okay. But my flight leaves at 4 p.m."

"This evening! That's not enough time for me to get myself together and plan for the boys."

"The boys will be fine Chantal."

"I'll call you back in thirty minutes okay."

"Okay, but don't wait too long. I already have your ticket."

"Dominique—you weren't going to take no for an answer were you?"

"Nope," he said smiling on the other end of the phone. "I'll still wait for you to call me back though. Talk to you later."

"Okay," I said taking a deep breath before I called Dante and Montel to the room.

I could see the look of concern in their eyes as I started to tell them about the trip. Montel came over and put his arms around me. "It's all right Momma. You need some time alone with Mr. Dominique. You have been so busy over the years that you haven't taken much time for yourself."

"Montel's right Momma. You need a vacation."

"But a whole week? Whose gonna take care of you and cook your meals for you?"

"Ugh—I think both of us are old enough to take care of ourselves and we can cook. Remember, we learned from the best. You go ahead Momma. Montel and I will be just fine."

"Okay. I leave today. I'll be back within a week. It might even be shorter than that. It just depends on how long Dominique's trip will last."

"We'll be fine Momma. You go and have a little fun for a change."

"Okay—okay already. I'm calling Dominique now."

Montel and Dante looked at each. They gave each other some dap and then they went flying off to their rooms.

"Momma's leaving us in charge man. Can you believe that?" Montel said curiously.

"Nah, I can't believe she's doing that. I use to stay over to other people's house, but never alone. I mean—this time, it will be just me and you, but it'll be fun."

"Oh yeah, I can believe that," Montel said. "I know the first thing I'm going to do."

"What's that?" A suspicious Dante asked.

"I'm calling up my homies and tell them to stop by."

"I don't think so. You're not having your friends up in here while Momma's away. It took this long for her to trust me to watch the house. I'm not going to blow it Montel. Besides, you're not old enough for homies. You just turned twelve."

"Man, my friends aren't going to tear the place up. I just wanna have them over to swim that's all."

"Nope, it's out of the question."

"That figures. You're just as strict as Momma."

"You better believe it."

The plane was leaving within hours. I had a lot of things to pack. I called Dominique back and told him the good news. Dominique had two first class tickets on United Airlines. Back in the day, they use to serve single meals to all the customers but something must have happened because all they were serving now were pretzels and soda. It was definitely a step backwards.

Our plane landed at 6:45 p.m. It was a direct flight to Miami International Airport. MIA was crowded with a lot of people traveling from different parts of the world. All stops coming from and going to South America would have to make its way through MIA before continuing to their destination.

"It looks like a war zone," I said as I clenched on to Dominique's arm.

"I know you're not afraid of this place after living in Maryland all those years."

"I'm not afraid of this place. It's just the people. Look at them. You're talking diversity. My God, the women are drop dead gorgeous and the men, I might add, are tight as hell."

"Hey—we didn't come here for you to get your thrills over other men. What about me? My body's tight, isn't it?" He asked expecting a yes.

"Baby, you know you look good. Stop jiving."

"Well then, I say we head over to the luggage area and get to steppin'. This is going to be the best time you've ever had woman."

"I sure hope so," I said remembering my past relationships. "I know you have a lot of meetings to attend, but will you be able to spend some time with me?"

"More than you'll ever know. Actually, I have two meetings on Wednesday and Thursday and the rest of the time belongs to us."

"But, it's Sunday. Why the urgency? We could have waited to leave out Tuesday night."

"I wanted more time with you baby. I'll show you when we get to our hotel."

We checked into the Mercury South Beach Hotel located next to America's number one urban beach. It was considered to be a very upscale resort. Dominique asked for the penthouse house special which included a large king sized oval bed in the master bedroom and a double packed queen bed in the additional room. The bathroom was filled with oils from Bolivia and candles that illuminated once the lights were on. I was deeply impressed by the massive amount of planning and the consideration Dominique had put into our trip. Once we got settled, he asked if I wanted to go to the pool, but I insisted we needed to rest before doing anything extraordinary.

"I'll tell you what," he said pulling me closer to him. "Why don't we take a long bath in the Jacuzzi? I have somewhere special I would like to take you afterwards."

"Ooh, that sounds good. Let's take it a step further. I wanna do something more romantic. How about a little foolin' around while we're in the sauna?" I commented.

"I like that even better." We headed towards the sauna removing all that we were wearing. I got in first. Dominique stood admiring my beautifully smooth caramel body. "Girl, what I wouldn't do to be inside of you right now," he said as he lowered himself into the Jacuzzi.

"Ah, I know you're just talking a lot of mess. Look at my body starting to sag."

"Sweetheart, your body is classic. What I mean by that is, you've been around the world and back a few times and your body still looks like you're fresh out of high school."

"Come on now baby! You know you've gone too far by saying that. My body got marks even a pencil won't erase."

"You're funny Chantal. Come here for a minute," he said as I backed into him. "Let me rub you down for a minute."

"Ooh, that feels so good," I said as he began to rub my shoulders. Gradually making his way down to my back, he leaned forward and kissed me on the back of my neck. "Baby, you're starting to make me heated in here. Don't start anything you can't finish," I said.

"I finish everything I start," he said leaving a huge mark on my shoulders. "If you were cotton candy, I would savor you until you melt in my mouth."

"You're awfully flirtatious Dominique. I can't call you a lollipop because lollipops crack after a minute or so and I don't see you cracking anytime soon."

"Now who's the flirtatious one?" He said reaching around to grab my erect nipples.

I threw my head to the side and started to imagine him all over me. The bubbles in the sauna were moving at a steady pace. The water was filtered to reach a temperature of 102 degrees. It was a bit warm, but was tolerable for the both of us. We soaked for a while longer and I enjoyed every minute of Dominique feeling my body for excitement as his body was starting to take pleasure itself.

"Let's get out of this tub and go where we both can find a lot of comfort," he said lifting my body at heads length.

"I'm right behind you," I said dripping water all over the floor.

"Damn baby, I like it when you're wet.

CHAPTER 21

"Conquered by Passion"

Pushing me gently against the wall, Dominique lifted my legs high and wrapped them around him. Every inch of his 6'5" body was all over me. His pants were half way down his legs making it difficult to thrust. He looked down at me and gently smiled. I wanted this man and I wanted him badly. He was powerful and the thrust of his manhood revived the innermost parts of my body.

With every encounter I had with Dominique, the passion seemed to be quite different. Dominique had a unique way of revealing his lovemaking to me. This time, he stood on his right leg nearly dropping me as he removed his left leg from inside his pants and kissed me. I looked at him and started to smile.

"Dayum!" I said as I looked up at him.

Dominique smiled and put his right leg down repeating the effort with his left leg. I don't know if he was trying to show off or if the man had talent for keeping the passion flowing while undressing. Whatever it was, I was determined to find out the outcome. I was still embraced around his manhood as he walked towards the partially fixed bed. Carefully, he laid me down, lifted my legs, and watched as his manhood glided in and out of me.

"Dominique," I said looking up at him. As I watched the sweat fall from this hunk of a man, I told him that I needed a quick break. My bladder felt as though it was going to burst. "I really have to go…..."

He shssed me before I could complete my sentence. Sometimes I wonder if men are just ignorant when it comes to a woman's body or if they just don't understand when a woman says she has to go, it means she has to go.

"Baby, try and hold it a bit longer. I don't wanna lose this feeling," He said while sweat was pouring from his long dark body.

"But I—

"Shhhhhh! Now, isn't that better baby?" He said requiring a response.

I just couldn't seem to get my rhythm right knowing that at any minute I would piss on myself. "Baby, I can't hold it. You're too much for me!"

"Your bladder is that weak, baby?" He said looking at the fear in my face.

Slowly, Dominique backed away from me giving me the opportunity to make a quick run towards the bathroom.

I sat on the toilet for quite some time. I was holding my stomach as though it was about to fall off. "Ouchhhh!" I said prolonging the word.

"Chantal—baby, are you all right in there?" A desperate Dominique asked trying to open the bathroom door.

I sat on the toilet and stared at the floor. Trying to connect the patterns hidden amongst the tile, I screamed out some more. "Dominique—Help me!"

"Open the door, baby! I can't get in."

"I can't get up," I said in a soft uttered voice.

"Do you need me to call someone?" He asked worriedly.

"Call my doctor! She'll know what to do."

My doctor was on call that night. My previous doctor had gone back to Uganda and now I was stuck with someone who didn't quite know the history of my illness. I was having a relapse of the endometriosis I suffered with some fifteen years ago. True enough I had to pee, but the unbearable pain I use to encounter while making love was back and this time, it wasn't going anywhere anytime soon.

"Take her to the hospital as soon as possible," Dr. Victoria Schuler said.

Prying the door open with a butter knife, Dominique was able to push the latch in and get the door open. I was spaced out sitting on the toilet unable to move. My body was stiff and I had a slight leakage of blood running from my insides.

"Oh my God!" Dominique said trying gently to get me dressed. "Doctor Schuler wants you to go to the hospital immediately."

When we arrived at the hospital, there was a crowd of sick people surrounding the corners and sitting in the waiting area. Dr. Schuler had phone in and had the nurse in the hallway waiting my arrival.

"Take her to Room 1E2 around the corner across from the nurse's station," one of the doctors said. "I'll meet you there."

Almost immediately, an intern took my pulse and retrieved blood. My pressure was extremely low and my pulse slightly high. They took a variety of tests including a pregnancy test. I tried to reassure them that I wasn't pregnant, but they insisted upon taking the test for precaution.

"Is she going to be okay?" Dominique asked.

"I'm sure she will be. But, we need to get the test results from her blood work first," a pretty young nurse by the name of Connie responded.

After a few hours had past, Doctor Schuler walked in, looked at me, and asked if Dominique could leave the room. I wasn't sure how she got there so fast, but was very appreciative. As Dominique walked away, he gave me a kiss on the cheek and told me to be strong.

"Seems like a wonderful man," Dr. Schuler said.

"He's the best," I replied holding my stomach. "Am I going to be okay, Doc?"

"Chantal, I want to do a series of tests including one for a kidney infection. I don't think it's the endometriosis. I believe it's an infection in your bladder."

"How can you tell? You haven't gotten the results back yet," I said reluctantly.

"You're correct. But, I've seen enough of these symptoms to know. It may not be an infection, but I want to take precautions just to be on the safe side."

"That's fine as long as you're straight forward with me. Don't hold nothing back Doc. I need to know if I'm going to be okay."

Intern Connie walked into the room and pulled Dr. Schuler off to the side. Judging by her facial expressions, it didn't look good. Dr. Schuler walked over towards me and told me she needed to do some X-rays. "It's routine," she said.

"Chantal, we need to keep you overnight until all of your tests come back in. I will send for your friend to come in with you."

When Dominique came back to the room, he gave me another kiss.

"Everything alright, baby?" He asked curiously.

Trying not to worry him, I smiled gently and said, "They want to keep me overnight. It's nothing to worry about. They think I might have an infection in my bladder. They want to be certain when the test comes back. It's a routine thing."

"Baby, that sounds serious. I don't think it's too routine. I hope they are upfront with you. I'll be right here with you."

"No Dominique. I think you should go and get some rest."

"And leave my baby here all by herself? Not in this lifetime! I'm staying. No ifs, ands, or buts about it."

"That's what I like about you; your aggressiveness. Thanks for caring, Dominique."

"You know I love you, baby. Don't even sweat it," he said giving me a wink. "Now get some rest and I'll go down the hall and get something to eat and drink. I'm starving."

"After what we've been through tonight, so am I. Sneak me back a candy bar!"

"I don't know about that, baby. It might not be good for you while they're doing tests on you."

"Come on Dominique! If you love me, you would."

"Aw shit! There you go brainwashing a brotha."

I smiled and started to yawn. "I guess it's getting late. Hurry back with my candy bar."

"I won't be long sweetie."

When Dominique returned, the room was empty. Connie had come and taken me to get X-rays. Dominique sat quietly, hoping I would be fine. His luck with women was hitting two for two. He lost his first wife and now I might have a problem. I wasn't getting any younger and the closer I got to fifty, the more my body started to tell on me.

Connie rolled me back into the room and Dominique stood up. "Is she okay?"

"She's gonna be fine. Give her a little R & R, she'll be just fine."

"Whew, that's a relief!" Dominique said rubbing his forehead. "Tomorrow, when they release you, the first thing I'm going to do is make my baby a big bowl of soup."

"I'm not sick Dominique. I mean—I don't have a fever but hey, if you want to make me some soup, more power to you honey."

"That's my girl! Now get some sleep. I'll be right here when you wake up."

The next day, Doctor Schuler came into the room. She motioned Dominique to leave. I was still asleep. I woke briefly as she began checking the readings from my pressure machine. She gave me a nudge on the arm.

"What time is it?" I asked. I was so tired after such a long night. They had been coming in my room all night long and needless to say, I didn't get any rest.

"It's still pretty early. How are you feeling this morning?" Doctor Schuler asked.

"Kinda woozy, but I'll live."

"You sure will. Your test results are fine. However, your X-rays showed a little concern."

I sat up immediately. I was hoping she wasn't going to tell me I had cancer or something bad like that.

"You have a tumor around your bladder. It's not that large, but we will need to operate. The sooner, the better."

"Is it serious?" I asked.

"Serious enough for surgery," Dr. Schuler responded. "I've already spoken with a team and they can perform the procedure tomorrow at 9 o'clock sharp."

"You're not kidding are you?"

"No Ms. Lewis. This is for real. We have to get it right away before it turns cancerous."

"What?" I said as I started to shed a tear. "Please have Dominique come back in here please."

She buzzed the nurses' station and they sent for Dominique. When he came back into the room, I was scared and crying.

"Please call my family back home and get my sons on the phone. They need to be here with me."

"What's wrong baby?" A concerned Dominique asked.

"They want to perform surgery on me tomorrow." I took a deep breath and said, "They said I have a tumor." My mouth started to tremble. "I'm scared Dominique."

Dr. Schuler left the room. Connie came in and showed Dominique where he could find the nearest telephone.

"It's gonna be okay baby. I'll call work and let them know that I won't be in today or tomorrow."

Dominique stepped out of the room and called Dante first. He booked a flight for them to arrive in Miami so they could be with me. They arrived within hours. Afterwards, he got a hold of Denise and Byron. They ordered some flowers and sent their prayers. This was the one time that I missed Mildred the most. Momma always knew what to say to make me feel better.

The next day, they prepped me for surgery and took me away. Dominique, Dante, and Montel stood and watched as they rolled me out of my room.

"That's a good woman right there." Dominique said.

"My mom's the best there is," Montel said.

"She's my life," a worried Dante replied.

"Come on guys. Your momma's gonna be just fine. Chantal's a strong black woman and women like her always pull through," Dominique insisted. But, in the back of his mind, he worried also. If he were to lose me too, I know he would just give up on happiness. No one made him any happier than me. At least, that's what he told me.

Four hours had gone by and they still waited. Connie had left for the day and was replaced by Johns, another intern. He was a short well-rounded twenty-something young man. His demeanor was pleasant yet—on a childish level. He fit right in with Montel. They chatted for a while and then, I was rolled back into my room.

"Momma," a joyful Montel yelled out.

I was still drowsy from the anesthesia. I looked over at Montel and Dante. Then, I looked at a smiling Dominique.

"I knew you'd be okay sweetie," he said blowing a kiss my way.

Dante walked towards me once they got me settled in the room.

"I was worried Momma. I thought you wouldn't make it."

I only murmured. I smiled and went back to sleep.

"She's tired," Dominique said. "Let's let your Momma rest."

"Can we get some grub, Mr. D?" Dante asked. "I'm hungry."

"Sure thing."

They went to Denny's down the street from the hospital. There wasn't much of a crowd, but the few that were there did not make for a good setting with Dominique. Dante was old enough to pay for his own meal, but Dominique wanted to handle the bill. Montel couldn't wait to get a bite into his mouth.

"Man, we need to eat fast and get up outta here. There are too many—how would I put this—low class people in this place for me."

"Mr. D, you shouldn't say that," Montel replied.

"I know I shouldn't, but I've been around the block a few times and these people aren't the kind you wanna be around."

"Why you judging the brothas like that Mr. D? Dante asked.

"Man, it's late and this neighborhood ain't where I wanna be right now."

"Okay, Mr. D. If you say so, I'll just scarf my burger down and we'll be gone," Montel said.

"Your momma's a lucky woman to have two fine boys such as yourself taking care of her. I was hoping one day that would be my responsibility," Dominique said.

"Whatcha tryin' to say Mr. D?" Dante asked.

"Well, I've known your momma a few months now. And" pausing to choose his words carefully, "I was hoping that she might be mine one day."

"You mean marriage, Mr. D?" Montel asked.

"Yep, I wanna make her my wife. Very soon I might add," Dominique responded.

"It won't happen. Momma said she'll never marry again after our father. I guess he just didn't make her happy," Dante said.

"See that's where you are so wrong. Chantal loves me and I know that she'll want to marry me."

"Mr. D, Momma is almost fifty. She's getting older not younger. Don't you think she just needs a little space to be happy instead of jumping into a marriage again?" Dante asked hastingly. "I know you love her, but if my pops couldn't make her happy and that RJ guy couldn't, what makes you think you could?

"Good question young man. But I got what it takes. And, it's called L.O.V.E."

"Anybody can love," Dante said.

"Nah! It takes a special man and a special woman to create love. That's what we have. Tell you what, let's discuss this back at the hospital. I don't want your momma to think we left her all by herself."

"Good idea," Montel said.

They paid for their meal and headed towards the door. Two big husky black men walked towards them. Dominique looked at Dante and told him to be cool. The two guys had no intention of moving. They seem to be looking for trouble. Dominique moved in front of Montel shoving him to the side.

"We don't want any trouble here. We're just headin' back to the hospital," a nervous Dominique said.

"We don't want any trouble either you punk ass nigga," one of the guys replied throwing his hands up in the air. "Can a black man walk in a restaurant without being indignant?"

"Strong choice of words man coming from you," Dominique said.

"Nigga, what's that shit supposed to mean?" The smaller of the two asked.

"I didn't mean it in a dumb way, man. I was just implying that it was a strong word. I probably wouldn't have thought of the word myself."

"Mr. Dominique, I think we should be getting back to Momma," a frightened Montel said.

"Momma—Momma, nigga you walking around here with someone else's kid? Shit, that wouldn't happen in this lifetime. Where the hell is his father?" The bigger guy asked.

"That's none of your damn business. Now, get the hell out of my way so I can get these guys back to their mother."

Dominique was tall, but the bigger of the two guys was at least three hundred and fifty pounds. He probably would have put a good ass whippin' on Dominique, but the manager walked over and broke up the argument before it got uglier.

"Not in my establishment! You guys take that shit somewhere else," he said.

"Aw, come on Pops, we just messin' around. Ain't nothing brawling up here, right Mr. Dominique?" The bigger guy asked looking him in the eyes.

"Nothing at all sir! Didn't mean to disrespect your business," Dominique said.

"You boys run on along. These two men are regulars here. They play a little football for the city. Pretty damn good too, I might say," he said.

"I knew it, Mr. Dominique. That big guy looks like the guy that plays for the Ravens," Montel said.

"Who Lewis?" Dante asked.

"Yeah him," Montel said.

"Nah, he's too ugly for that," Dante said. "I'm not sure who that guy is, but he's not Ray Lewis. Ray Lewis has more class than that. Besides, we're in Miami. Why would Ray Lewis be here?"

"Alright guys, we'd better get back soon. Your momma's probably worried sick about us."

"Okay Mr. Dominique. Let's head back. See you, Mr. Parker," Montel said waving goodbye.

As they headed back towards the car, Dominique's pager went off. He looked over at Dante with a worried look. "It's the hospital," he said. "We better get back."

"I hope momma's okay," a worried Montel replied.

"Oh I'm sure your momma's just fine. Sometimes they call you when she can't reach the phone or they need to tell you something important. I bet she started to worry about us and wanted to make sure we were okay."

"Be real, Mr. Dominique!" Dante said. "If momma wanted to talk to you, she would have called your cell phone. I don't remember you leaving your number with them."

"Ah—you see, that's where you are wrong. I gave them my pager number just in case the batteries died on my cell phone. They probably called the first number that they saw."

"That's possible, but we should get there fast. I bet it's me Momma needs to see," Dante suggested.

"Un-un. She wants to see me first because I'm the baby," Montel replied.

"Baby my foot! You're too big to be anyone's baby."

"All right boys. We're here. Let's just go in and act as though everything is okay. We don't want to scare your Momma with what happened tonight, do we?"

"No sir," both of the boys replied.

As they got off the elevator leading to the third floor, the nurses' station was quiet and no one other than the night janitor was visible. They knocked softly on my door. I was fast asleep when they walked in. His cell phone was in sight so it had to be one of the nurses who beeped Dominique. Dante and Montel stayed in the room while Dominique went looking for a nurse. My eyes opened suddenly as Dante sat at one end of the bed rubbing my feet and Montel sat at the other end rubbing my head.

"Something wrong sweetie?" I asked as I looked over at Dante.

"Hi Momma! No nothing's wrong. We were worried about you," Dante said. "Mr. Dominique's beeper went off. He said it was the hospital."

"Huh, that's funny. I didn't beep him from this room. One of the nurses must have called him."

Dominique had gone around the corner. In one of the rooms where no one was positioned for the night, a nurse—tall with long braided weaves— motioned him to come in. She was beautiful and any man would notice it.

"I told you it's over, Veronica. You need to get that in your head. I've moved on."

There was one skeleton Dominique forgot to mention when they first met. It wasn't that he had fallen in love with someone else, but he had just gotten rid of someone. Veronica didn't care for their relationship to end so abruptly. She wanted the passion Dominique had to offer and the kindness of his heart. She just couldn't keep herself away from the men at the clubs. Dominique walked in on her one night while he was out with some of his home boys. Not expecting Veronica to be wrapped up in another man's arms, his heart was torn. He never told his friends he had been dating her. Now he was too embarrassed to mention it. When Veronica came home later that night unaware that she had been busted by Dominique, he already had her clothes packed.

The argument was bitter and cold. Dominique had just let her into his life after his wife died, but she wasn't there for long. Veronica swore she would win him over someday. When she saw him come into the hospital, she knew she only had one chance to try and win his heart back. She thought by beeping him, he would rush back to the hospital and run into her accidentally. How she ended up in Miami was a mystery.

"The game's over Veronica," he said to her in a cold kind of way.

"But Dominique, could you at least hear me out?"

"One minute. That's all you have," he said closing the door behind him.

At the other end of the hallway, Dante had noticed him going into the room. He wasn't sure if he should follow him or just turn around and pretend that he hadn't seen a thing. *"Nah, that's my momma's heart he is playing with,"* Dante said to himself. "I won't let him break it in pieces."

Dante walked towards the door. He could hear noises as he got closer. He heard Dominique tell her that what happened in the past was staying in the past. "That's why they call it the past," he overheard Dominique say.

"Man, you're a hard one to win over! Stop fighting the passion Dominique. I know you really want me."

"That's where you are wrong Veronica. My life and my heart belong to the woman you see lying in the other room. We're getting married soon. Just leave me alone. You had your chance and you blew it with that guy I saw you with."

"Dominique, please," she said begging for him to listen. "He didn't mean anything to me. I worked at that place. I didn't tell you that because I knew you would be angry."

"Worked—angry? What do you mean by you worked at that place? Are you saying that you waited tables or something," Dominique asked while starting to let his temper rise.

"I was a dancer, Dominique."

"I thought you were a nurse."

"I am a nurse, but at the time, I needed extra income. Dancing was my way of life before I became a nurse. I just did it so I could pay off some bills."

"So you lied to me the whole time we were together."

"I didn't lie to you at all, Dominique. I just didn't tell you the truth."

Dante stood at the door until he couldn't take it anymore. What he thought he would walk in on was a mere encounter from Dominique's past.

He knocked softly and then he walked in. Clearing his throat, he said, "Momma is looking for you. She woke up and saw us, but not you."

"Okay. Tell her I'll be right there. I have some unfinished business with a friend of mine."

"We're not friends, Dominique and you know it. We are lovers."

"Don't start nothing up in here Veronica! Life as you knew it with me was over some years ago. "Hold up a minute Dante," Dominique said as he motioned Dante to stay. "I'm finished here. We'll walk back together. Good-bye Veronica. I hope you find the happiness you were looking for before you saw me tonight."

Veronica threw her head back as she watched him walk out the door and said, "I'll get him back one way or another."

Dominique explained to Dante what he had just witnessed in the room. "That woman was someone I met before your mother. I would have given her the world until I walked in on her with one of my friends."

"The guy was your friend, Mr. Dominique?"

"Yeah, he still doesn't know that I saw him at the club that night with Veronica. It's amazing how you put so much trust in a friend and they turn around and stab you in the back," he said putting his arm over Dante's shoulder.

"Sorry to hear that Mr. D. Momma would never disappoint you like that."

"Oh, I already know that. I knew she was special the very first day I laid eyes on her in the shoe store. You know, that is one of the biggest malls I've ever had to walk my entire life."

"They did build it rather big," Dante said. "But, you know what Mr. Dominique?"

"What's that?"

"My momma's sure lucky to find a man like you."

Dominique grabbed him by the head, put him in a head lock, and said, "Nope, I'm the lucky one." They walked into the room where Montel had laid his head down on my lap. We both had fallen fast asleep waiting for Dominique to come back into the room.

My doctor had returned to Maryland after the surgery. I was getting exhausted being there myself. I asked if I could be transferred back to Maryland and be admitted to Mercy Medical Center. They had no problem with that as long as my doctor would be there to look after me. They kept me in the hospital for another week. I was surprised. I thought everything would be fine after the surgery and I could go home right away.

Montel and Dante were exhausted when I finally came back. They had been in and out of the hospital daily waiting for me to come home. Dominique missed a few days of work, but that didn't seem to matter to him. They knew how much he loved me and wanted to be with me. His company was very cool about letting him take the time off.

My recovery at home went well. Everyone treated me like I was a queen. I thought maybe I should have gotten sick more often. But for now, this would do. I enjoyed the attention I was getting from the boys and Dominique. However, too much attention will spoil the hell out of you.

The Day Our Eyes Met

You didn't notice me sitting there
staring at your inner man.
As you walked gently across the room,
some part of me knew that you wanted me
just as much as I wanted you.
Yet neither of us said a word.
I caught a glimpse of your pearly whites
as you stared deep into my eyes
and that was when I knew
I had gotten your attention.
As I fumbled through my papers
in hopes that you would hang around,
I wanted to hold a conversation with you,
but somehow—you seemed distant.
Pondering the thought of you embarrassing me,
I opened my mouth to speak.
Was I getting ready to make a fool of myself
or was I bold enough to stand my ground?
A part of me boldly said,
"Yes" but the true part of me said, "Continue onward."
As I followed you through the foyer
and into the open air
It was at that moment that I felt a sense of hope.
Sometimes I feel like a child
finding that piece of candy lying on the floor
Yet other times I feel like a woman
chasing a distinctive dream
that often rummage through her mind.
It wasn't until the day I opened my heart
to you that I knew you were still there.
And if our eyes should ever meet again,
at least I know, that following my heart
instead of my mind
was the best thing that I could have ever done.

CHAPTER 22

"A Christmas Sorrow (Shanice)"

It was Christmas Day 2002 and snow had fallen the previous night as I and many desperate shoppers engaged in the rage of finding the last gift. I had worked that night in a nearby mall trying to enlighten many with baskets of delight for men and women. Marcay and I were the only ones to work the cart watching as people scrounged around for their loved ones in hopes of finding the cheapest yet most pleasing gift of all.

Man, our feet begged for mercy as we stood there on the brick surface assisting customer after customer. Young boys stood next to one of the baskets hoping to snatch and run like they had done the previous night. But I was ready for them. I watched him—the smallest of them all—as he stood next to the blue basket with a body wash and lotion. Seeing that they had no chance, the group retired from the area and moved to where the chains were. "Whew," I said to myself. "It's gonna be a wild night."

As the cleanup crew began to shut down the mall, we headed home in the midst of the white crystals falling from Heaven. As I drove down Liberty Road and got closer to Druid Park Drive, my car started to slide and I prayed to God that He would keep me safe until I reached my home. Ahead of me, was an accident consisting of a 4 x 4 and two other cars. I reached for my cell phone and called Frank to see if Frankie was tucked in bed. By the time I reached my house, I could see that the lights were out, but I was in for a nice surprise. Since I didn't have to go to work and Frankie wasn't going to daycare, he was up waiting for me in the closet.

"Surprise," he said as he and his father jumped out of the closet and damn near scared the pants off me.

"I thought he'd be sleep by now."

"Now you know this boy wasn't going to bed without you. He is so anxious about Santa coming tonight that I was starting to believe he exist."

"Well—maybe he'll be more impressed seeing the money I made tonight selling my Christmas baskets." I reached into a gold bag that I had won from my Mary Kay Director a few months prior and poured out several hundred dollars.

"Wow!" Frankie said as he grabbed for the money.

"Put my money down son! Momma stood on her feet all night for this."

"Daddy, look at all that money Momma have," Frankie said snatching a twenty for himself.

In a matter of hours, I surfaced with nearly three hundred dollars made from selling the last of my gift baskets. After Frankie had gone to bed, Frank and I went downstairs and had a cup of tea. We talked for a while until we thought Frankie was fast asleep. After I had assembled the toys I bought for Frankie, I was ready for bed.

"It's after one," I remarked barely able to stand on my feet after a long day at the mall.

"You're calling it a night honey?" Frank replied as he attempted to put the car track together.

"I'm so tired Frank. I'll see you in the morning," I said as I gave him a kiss on the forehead.

I headed upstairs noticing that Frankie was still awake. "I thought I told you to go to bed son," I said seeing that he was struggling with his posture.

"I'm trying very hard Momma, but I can't. See." Closing his door tightly, I snuck out of his room and headed to mine. I gave thanks to God for allowing His only Son to reign from Heaven to save my soul. I thanked Him for many things but mostly, I prayed for my friend, Chantal knowing that this would be her first Christmas without her mother. After I got off my knees, I was knocked out.

When the clock struck 5:48 a.m. on Christmas Day, I got out of bed being careful not to wake Frank. I put on a pair of navy blue sweat pants, my Nike tennis shoes, and a coat and then I headed outside to get Frank's surprise from my car. The snow had turned into ice and the sidewalk was slippery. I knew I had to work fast in order to get Frank's gift from the car. Sleet was falling from the sky and I was getting soaked. The box was heavy, but I had taken a dolly from work the previous day to assist me. As I got the box up the steps, I closed the door slowly trying not to wake my sleeping family.

The plows were outside scraping the roads as the sleet continued to fall. In a moment's time, I was back in bed when a flash of lightning flashed through my room. I immediately sat up and said, "Lord, what in the world?" Thinking that a storm was brewing, I slid under the covers. Suddenly, a small thunderous noise sounded and it was over. The clock showed 6:27 a.m. as a flash of lightning flashed through the room with the metal bunk bed. I sat up unaware of the tragedy that had taken place in an instant. I thought to myself, *"How could there be lightning flashing in December?"* Not even ten minutes later, sirens were behind my house and I looked out the window to see what was going on.

A fire engulfing an apartment had burned a mother and her two year old child to death. I clung to Frank. Jake, arriving home from his midnight shift, stood dumb -founded with two large bags of toys in each hand as he watched the firefighters put out the flames. Falling to his knees, he begged for mercy. "Why Lord? Why?" He cried out as he watched his wife and child being pulled from the fire. They took him over to a bench and asked the names of the victims. "My wife, Alisha and my baby, Brittany," he said crying out louder. "This can't be," he screamed. Jake worked in a factory in the city. They needed him to work Christmas Eve since another worker had called out sick. "It should've been me with them." Jumping to his feet, he said, "I'll be alright." He walked over to his car and there was a loud bang. The door was partially open and Jake fell to the ground. The stress of having to explain what happened to his family overwhelmed him.

Frankie came running to me after he heard the gun shot. "Mommy, mommy. I hear firecrackers," he said wanting to go outside. "No baby. That wasn't firecrackers. See the ambulance and fire trucks outside," I said.

"Yes ma'am."

"Well, something terrible has happened…." Unable to finish my sentence, I burst into tears.

"Mommy, why are you crying?"

"It's Christmas baby," getting away from the subject. "Let's see what Santa bought you this year."

"Santa's been here! Wow! Let's go!" Dashing down the hallway, he searched the tree for his gifts.

From my bedroom window, I could see all the excitement taking place outside. I found it hard to smile knowing that three more lives were gone as my family was blessed to celebrate another Christmas.

CHAPTER 23

"Beauty Times Two"

A week later, I was getting ready for my big promotion with Mary Kay. I had to make sure my makeup was flawless and my suit was together. The big event was about to start and my team had led me to one of the highest achievements in the beauty consultant's world. After only four months of hard work and determination, I was going to debut as an elite Sales Director sporting my brand new candy apple red Grand Am. As a beauty consultant, many prizes are given away and one of the biggest rewards was winning 'the car'.

My excitement echoed throughout the house as I found myself running late as usual. I still had to comb my hair, brush over the chipped polish on my nails, and take the children to a babysitter. Frank had gone away for the weekend and wouldn't be back until the next day. I struggled trying to get them ready. I eventually called Suzette, one of the neighbors down the road and had her come and sit with the children. Suzette was a mischievous teen who always talked on the phone. She paid no attention to the children and having her over was out of desperation. I told her to pay close attention to little Frankie because he liked to bother things that didn't belong to him.

As I ran to my car, I waved at one of my neighbors, stepped in a crack along the sidewalk, and watched as my shoe came off behind me.

"Busy day for you, huh—Shanice?" She said.

"Girl, you just wouldn't believe how late I am for this big event," I replied.

"Another Mary Kay event, huh?"

"Yeah and I'm extremely late. I'll tell you all about it when I return," I said waving good-bye to her.

As usual, I would always say a prayer before I left the house just in case I didn't make it to my destination. I always asked God to keep me safe and if I didn't make it to my destination, to let my soul rest in His presence.

Traffic was heavy on 395. I could see most of it stemmed from the event I was heading to. There were pink Cadillac's and red Grand AM's all around me. I was excited to be sporting my red car as well. As I drove closer to the Convention area, it had already started to get dark. I drove around West Lombard Street and found a parking space nearby. It was rather dark and the parking attendant had left for a break. The ceiling was low and dampness covered the area. In the distance, I saw three men who looked rather suspicious, but since I was already running late, I paid them no attention. It looked as though they were playing craps or some sort of dice game.

I headed down the walkway with my bag clinched tightly at my side. As soon as I got halfway to the convention, I remembered that I hadn't locked my car door. I knew the three men had watched me leave so I took a chance on going back. Something didn't sit well as I moved closer to where I had parked my car. I knew the exact space where my car was parked, but somehow, in a matter of minutes, it was gone. I fell to the ground screaming out loud. I knew it had to be the men who sat off to the side playing games.

As I ran towards the parking attendant's station, noticing that he still wasn't there, someone grabbed out at me and pulled me off to the side.

"Make one sound," he said in a harsh voice, "I'll blow your damn brains out."

My eyes stretched. I kicked and screamed, but the guy didn't let go. Thinking about the training I'd gotten from Frank in abduction protection, I immediately elbowed him in the abdomen. He turned me loose briefly and I started to run. My panty holes were torn and my hair was out of place. I ran and screamed continuously until the parking attendant appeared. He saw the guy run off and that I was hurt.

"Ma'am," he said, "Can I help you get somewhere?"

"You stupid idiot! Can't you see I need help here?"

"That's not a nice thing to say, miss. I'm only trying to help you."

I could see that he was handicapped and made apologies. The guy was about 5'10", slender, and needed a bath like yesterday. I knew I should have parked in a better area. I was reluctant to go to the event. I had prepared so well for my award. I had the parking attendant call the city police, who by the way, took their own sweet time arriving. I explained about the parking and how I was in a hurry. I gave them a description of the three guys and what they were wearing. I also gave them a description of my car. Of course, a candy apple red Grand Am was not hard to miss.

The officer called in the description and the license plate number. Another officer receiving the call spotted the car sitting on the corner of Preston and Calvert. He approached the car slowly and called in for back up. As he got out of the car, he looked around the area for any suspects matching my description. It looked like the men needed a ride and my car was perfect for the taking. The other thing the officer noticed was that the gas needle was on empty. It was possible that the car had run out of gas and it was as far as the car would take them. Then I remembered I needed to stop and get some gas before going to the convention center. Thank God for small miracles.

When the officer and I arrived, I used my keys to open the door. The guys had popped the ignition to get it started. I sat in tears of joy knowing that my car could have been gone forever.

"Officer—" I paused briefly. "Thank you for finding my car," I said giving him a slight smile.

"You know Ms. Lewis it's always best to be aware of your surroundings and lock your doors before you leave. If you had taken the time to do that, it wouldn't have been so tempting for the men to steal your car. I will tell you this much, we will find the guys because this is not the first time a car was stolen from this particular parking lot. We believe that there is a car theft ring operating from that parking garage."

"Do you think the parking attendant had something to do with it?

"We believe he was ma'am."

"But he was handicapped. After I pulled in, he disappeared." Pausing for a second, I said, "Now I get it. He had to leave so that the guys would have enough time to get away with my car. When the other guy grabbed me, it probably was a deterrence as well."

"It's possible that's the way it happened. We'll talk to the attendant and see what we can get out of him. In the meantime, we'll take you to the gas station and get some gas so that you can make it back home."

"I was heading to a special event with my cosmetic business, but with the way I am looking, I'd better head home and change my clothes."

"That's a good idea. I believe you've had enough excitement for one day. Why don't you just go home, get in a hot tub of water, and relax for the remainder of the day? Those events will be there even when you're gone."

"But I promised my team I would be there."

"I'm sure you did. Do what you feel is right. We will contact you if we find out anything."

"Thank you Officer. I will be more careful the next time."

When I arrived home, the house was quiet. I called out to the babysitter who was downstairs in the basement with Frankie. I could hear the stairs shaking as they ran to greet me.

"Mommy Mommy. What happened to your clothes?" Frankie asked.

My makeup was ruined. My mascara was running down my face like someone had taken black chalk and smeared it all over me. The Mary Kay suit with the Purple Sash draped around my neck I was wearing was no longer glamorous. Instead, half the beads were missing and it was ripped. My legs were scratched and my pantyhose had been ruin. I looked like a black Cinderella running away from her ball. "I'm fine baby. I just had a little accident," I said looking over at Delois who sensed something had happened.

Delois knew there was more to the story, but didn't want to question me around Frankie.

"Let's let Mommy go upstairs and change her clothes. It looks like she could use a long relaxing bath.

Frankie was only six, but his concern for me went deeper than I had imagined. "I know something bad happened to you, right Mommy? Did someone hurt you?"

"Baby, Mommy just had a small accident in the parking garage. Yes, some bad man grabbed your mommy," trying to bring humor to the story, "but you should have seen him after I got a hold of him. I roughed him up pretty bad."

"Did the policeman get him?"

"Not yet. But they will and it will all be just one big mistake."

"Frankie," Delois said cheerfully. "Let your Mommy go and change right now. She'll be just fine."

"Okay Ms. Delois. I'll see you when you get out."

Looking over at Delois, I said, "Thank you," in a soft low key voice.

I walked slowly up the stairs. As soon as I looked in the mirror, I shook my head and started to cry. I knew that matters could have been worse, but I thanked God for allowing me to make it back home safely and for letting me know how to handle myself in times of trouble. What I didn't understand was why me? Why something so bad had to happen to me on the day I would finally receive a prestigious award from Mary Kay?

As I began running the water in my jade jacuzzi, I sat off to the side and thought about Frank. Why couldn't he have been there for me? I knew if he was there, nothing would have happened to me. He was cautious when it came to locking doors and setting the alarm on the car.

I could hear my cell phone ringing from afar. I answered the phone and LaVonda Wilson, one of my top Red Jackets was on the other end. "Hello."

"Shanice. Hi. It's LaVonda. Where are you?" She was worried after I didn't walk across the stage with the other new Directors and called to see what had happened.

"I'm at home."

"Why didn't you come tonight?"

God I didn't want to relive the events I've gone through, but thought it warranted an explanation.

"I was mugged in the parking garage near West Lombard Street."

"What? Someone jumped you! Are you okay?"

"I'm better. They stole my car. I forgot to lock the doors and when I realized it, I went back to lock them and the car was gone."

"Oh my God! Did you call the police?"

"Yes, of course I did, but not until after I was jumped. They think the parking attendant had something to do with it."

"What do you think? Do you think that guy would risk his job behind someone's car being stolen?"

"I really don't know what to think. All I know is that I'm tired and I need a relaxing bath."

"Okay. I'll call you later on to check on you. Shanice...I'm glad you're okay."

"Thanks LaVonda. Tell everyone I'm okay."

LaVonda did more than that. She went to the coordinator of the event and they announced what had happened. They were cautioned to be aware of their surroundings and reminded that nothing was more important than their life. The event lasted until 10:00 p.m. and my award was given to LaVonda to bring back to me.

Just as I stepped into the Jacuzzi, my phone rang again.

"What the hell is going on?" I thought to myself. I just let it rang and got in the tub. Delois came to the door and told me that Chantal was on the other end.

"Tell her I'll give her a call when I get out of the tub."

"She said it's important Shanice."

"Damnit," I said out loud. "What could be so important?"

"I'll call her in two minutes."

I got out of the tub in minutes. The long relaxing bath didn't happen the way I planned it. I dried off and put on an exotic robe. I had hoped that Frank would make it back soon to rub me down. I picked up the phone and dialed Chantal's number. The phone rang and rang. "What the..." I thought. "I thought it was an emergency. What could have been so important that she had to leave before I could call her back?"

Since Chantal didn't live far from me, I got in my car and headed over. When I arrived, I saw an ambulance parked outside her house. I threw my car in park and ran to the front door.

"Chantal...Dante, where are you guys?"

Dante wasn't home, but my girl—Chantal was on a stretcher heading to the hospital.

"Girlfriend—what happened to you?"

"My stomach is hurting so bad."

"You're not pregnant again are you?"

Chantal gave me demented look. "Not in this lifetime."

"You and Dominique have been pretty tight these days."

"Girl hush your mouth. Dominique is out of town and ain't no babies happening here. Besides, we're much too old for that."

The ambulance driver motioned for us to leave.

"I'll meet you at the hospital," I told her.

Jamal had stopped by to take Montel and Dante to the Universal Circus. They always seem to have the show at Mondawmon Mall, but this year they decided to have it at Security Square Mall. This year they were featuring the Gabonese Wire Walkers and the Twisted Sistas. Chantal never had a chance to take Dante and now it seemed as though she wouldn't be able to take Montel.

When Jamal and the boys left the house, Chantal mentioned she had told them she wasn't feel well. Apparently, Jamal told her to lie down until they returned. Though Jamal was out of Chantal's life, he still tried to show he cared since she wasn't feeling well.

The ambulance team took Chantal to Mercy Medical Center and a team of emergency crew swoop her off the gurney and led her towards the cubicles. She passed many sick people as they rolled her towards her cubicle. She wasn't sure what her problem was this time, but hoped that it wasn't the endometriosis again. I tried to call Jamal on his cell phone, but there was no answer. His answering machine came on immediately indicating that he had never turned it on. By the time I reached Mercy, Chantal was already stabilized in her room.

Being that Mercy Medical Center was around the corner from the Mary Kay event I was to attend earlier, I was reminded about my incident. I took the route from Pratt Street turning onto Charles Street and followed it to St. Paul's. I was very hesitant to park my car in the closed-in garage, but didn't have a choice. The parking attendants didn't look as careless and harmful as the one close to Lombard Street. I stayed with Chantal until I was finally able to reach Jamal and the boys. It seemed as though she had a bad case of the flu virus. After giving her a prescription for some antibiotics, she was released.

CHAPTER 24

"Moving Away" (Shanice)

With all that was going on in my life, it looked as though my biggest dream was coming true. I was finally going to get out of Maryland and head South where I could feel warmth in the winter and stay cool during the summer months. When I got off work the next day, I thought, "My life's a shamble waiting to happen," I murmured as I grabbed my black Coach purse, a few manila envelopes, and headed straight for the door. "If I have to work here one more day...Ooh, Lord, help me hold my peace. This place—these people, I have to get the hell away from here."

It didn't take much for me to lose my cool. But when I did, everyone or anything in sight needed to get out of my way. Being that it was 5:05 p.m. on a Friday evening, the sky was partly cloudy, and the thought of summer was inevitable, cracked my last nerve. It seemed as though the entire world from the West Coast to the East Coast was feeling the taste of Mother Nature's anger. If there weren't fires burning in Arizona or earthquakes shattering Algeria, then it was floods and thunderstorms ripping through the South and most of the East Coast. People were either burning or drowning all over the world.

I prayed hard that Route 29 would be clear as I drove past the Courtyard Marriott on Route 175. I was listening to Brad Rogers of Heaven 600 as he began preparing himself for the Top Five at Five. "Oh my God," I said looking at the site ahead of me. As usual, the traffic was at a complete standstill. I knew I had to get Frankie from daycare or risk paying an additional five dollars for every fifteen minutes that I was late. I really didn't have time to fool around. My nerves were starting to get the best of me. All I could think about was it being June 20th and leaving the company I had invested so much of my precious time with. I hadn't told anyone at work about my sudden urge to quit the company and move to South Carolina. I smiled as I reached in my purse for my cell phone to call Chantal. I had to see if my girl was okay after her sudden illness the day before.

The phone rang continuously, but Chantal didn't answer. "That's odd," I thought to myself. "My girl always answers the phone. She must be getting her groove on with Dominique or something, cause I know she wouldn't let the phone ring without answering it." I reached back into my purse and put the phone away. The traffic was still at turtle's speed, but I was getting a little closer to my exit heading towards Carroll County. A flash of lightning flashed in front of me scaring the living shit out of me as I passed Route 40 West. "Just a few more exits and I'll be on Route 70," I thought as another flash went across the sky.

"I don't remember the forecast mentioning any thunderstorms for today. This weather pattern is a trip," I thought to myself. The phone rang while I was approaching my exit. I knew it had to be my girl calling me back. I rumbled through my purse almost dropping the entire thing on the floor. A car in front of me slammed on brakes and I dropped everything. "Whew, close call girlfriend," I said out loud. I guess I'd better keep my eyes on the road before I leave this place in a black bag."

The phone rang again. "Damn, it's on the floor and I can't reach it. Better pull off the road before I do something stupid." The number appeared as an anonymous caller and I knew only one person with a number like that.

"What's up girlfriend?" I asked feeling relieved that she had called me back. "Why didn't you answer when I called the first time? I almost got in a wreck trying to get the phone."

"Oh, you tryin' to blame a sista for your lack of driving experience," Chantal said laughing at me. "I was just checking on you. I know you've been going through some things at work. Was today any better?" Chantal asked.

"Girl, those people are picking my last nerves. They knew I had allergies to smoke and they turned around and put me in an office with a smoker. This guy smokes so much that the residue sticks to his clothing. When he walked past me on Monday, I got sick as a dog."

"What?" Chantal said as she cracked a slight giggle. "You're that sensitive to smoke?"

"Damn straight! They knew I was and yet they moved our offices to a new building and gave the Caucasians nice furniture. The black guy and I got sectionals. I went from having two desks in my office to half a desk to do my work on, quarter of a desk for the computer, and a fourth of a desk for the telephone."

"That's some messed up shit, girlfriend."

"I know it is, but I'll fix them though. When I move, they are going to wish they never heard of Shanice Robinson."

"Well, I hope everything works out for you. You don't deserve that mess from them."

"I know I don't. But what I plan on doing is going on vacation with Frank and Frankie and then when I come back, I'm going to slam a letter of resignation on my boss's desk. I can't wait to see his face."

"You sure that's the way you wanna do it? I mean, when I quit my job years ago after winning all that money, I went in and calmly told my boss Mike that I was quitting. I gave him a two weeks notice and I completed all the pending work I had left on my desk."

"That's fine for you. I don't plan to be an ass, but I will do it with a little tact. You know, make it look good anyway so they won't suspect the lawsuit."

"You're planning to sue them?" Chantal asked in a shocked voice.

"Damn straight. They won't even see it coming. Then I'll be rich like my girl."

"Girlfriend, don't leave any burnt bridges while trying to go up the ladder of success. You never know who you might need while coming back down."

"I'll be careful about it. They'll just wish they never met me."

Chantal changed the subject. "So, you're really going to leave the area, huh?"

"Yep...I'm gonna miss you the most—our friendship, laughter, and good times—you know, the things we could and couldn't tell others about us."

"Girlfriend, you better take that to your grave. That was many moons ago," Chantal replied.

"Yeah, but it was fun. Oh and how can I forget the guys we met at the beach that summer while we were getting to know each other better? Whew, if Frank knew about that, I would be dead meat."

"It won't come from me. I can guarantee you that much," Chantal said.

"And I know it won't come from me. My lips are sealed. Look, I better get off this phone before I have an accident reminiscing about the past."

"Okay then, I guess I'll see you over the weekend," Chantal mentioned.

"That sounds good. You wanna go somewhere nice and eat or catch a movie?"

"I'm up for that." Chantal replied.

"I'll call you tomorrow morning and we'll make it a day. I'll tell Frank that he has to babysit."

"Later," Chantal said hanging up the phone. "I'm gonna miss that fool," she said while walking towards the kitchen to prepare dinner.

The next morning when I called, it wasn't because of us meeting up, but to let Chantal know that I had to bring Frankie. Chantal didn't mind Frankie going. She just asked Montel if he wanted to tag along to keep him company while we talked. We decided to catch 'Bringing Down the House' at Arundel Mills. The lines were long and Frankie's patience was wearing thin. Montel grabbed his arm and took him over to the video area until Chantal and I made it through the lines. The attendant directed us toward theatre number six, but we wanted to get some popcorn and sodas first.

The comical part about the whole ordeal was that we were stuck in a theatre with two boys on an afternoon planned for two women. When the movie ended, the boys ran off to the video area again. We gave them a dollar's worth of change and told them that that would be it for the day. Once they were done, we packed them in my car and headed for Chantal's.

Since Frankie loved being at her house so much, and Dante wanted to do something with Montel, we asked him if he wouldn't mind keeping them until we came back from shopping. That was the story we told. We knew we weren't going shopping. Dante didn't mind and told us to take our time. Now you know telling two women on a Saturday afternoon to take their time while shopping might not be so smart. We smiled and told him that the boys had already had lunch and we would be back by dinner. I gave Frankie a kiss and we were off shopping as we called it.

We drove downtown Baltimore to the harbor and took in a little sunshine. It seemed as though everyone had the same idea. We strolled along fancy-free and watched as the eyes of what seemed to be young business men fell upon us. "Look at him staring at us like we're a fresh pack of meat waiting to hit the grill," Chantal murmured.

"Don't hurt to look," I said. "Besides, I wouldn't give him any of this if he begged for it."

Chantal gave me a look that I'd never forget. "Girl, don't you get us in trouble while we're here."

"Whatcha mean by that?" I asked slowing down my pace.

Chantal turned towards me and said, "We're both committed to wonderful men. I don't need any drama coming in my life. Besides, I'll be married in a few months."

"No drama intended," I said. "Sure you wanna go through with it again?"

"More than ever. Dominique is everything I've ever dreamed a man could be."

"Bet he ain't nothin' like Frank," I said smiling at her.

"That's your opinion girlfriend. You once told me that you had a big poppa, well guess what, I do too," Chantal replied as she smiled back at me.

"Don't start talking that freaky shit! We're out here alone with no men at our sides. And you know how I am. I'll jump a man's bones any time."

"You're just nasty Shanice."

"Yeah, but when I freak Frank, he forgets all about the nastiness and takes the prize."

"You still do that at your age?" Chantal asked turning up her nose.

"What the hell do you mean by my age? You're older—much older than me," I replied.

"I only have you by three years. But, you seem to be nastier than ever," Chantal chanted.

"Don't get mad at me if you don't know how to blow any more," I said taking in a deep breath.

"How the hell do you know what I can and can not do with my mouth?" Chantal said getting a little defensive. "Are you ever in the room with me and Dominique?"

"No," I laughed. "Calm down girlfriend. I'm just having a little fun."

"Then shut up and let's go down by the docks," Chantal said putting her hands around my neck.

"Okay," I replied as I placed my head on Chantal's shoulders. "I'll follow you."

We walked along the pier and tossed a few rocks into the bay. From afar, we could see the Science Museum and the Aquarium.

"When's the last time you brought Frankie to the museum, Shanice?"

"You mean, when's the first time?"

"He's never been there before?" Chantal questioned.

"Not with me. I very seldom come this way."

"Don't tell me you're afraid of the city," Chantal said.

"After I got mugged in the parking garage, I vowed never to step foot in this area again."

"You're here now. What's the difference?" Chantal asked.

"You. I wanted to do something special with you. It doesn't seem too bad being down here as long as I am with a friend."

"I made a mistake during my party judging the area myself until I saw a homeless guy return Jamal's wallet. It wasn't as bad as I thought."

"Yeah but, you have to watch yourself with all that money. Somebody could easily knock you across your head if they knew who you were."

"That's true, but I try and stay out of places where I think I would be robbed."

"That's a good thing."

We walked a little more and then decided to finish our conversation on the grass. It was still a little damp from the rain the night before, but Chantal didn't mind it. We had a ball talking about the many men and relationships we've had. We decided to return to my car and head back. It was still a bit early and I started telling Chantal about my future plans. She knew I enjoyed my part-time job with Mary Kay, but she didn't know that I was about to launch one of the biggest deals of my life with a well-known publishing company.

As we drove past the Baltimore Convention Center, I dropped it on her. "When I leave for South Carolina, my book will hit the stands."

Chantal leaned back. "What book?"

"You know—the one that I've been working on since 2000."

"No, I don't know about it," Chantal replied. "Care to clue a sistah in?"

"I know I told you. Anyway, to make a long story short, the title is "The Essence of Innocence…Undeniable Betrayal…Unforgiven Love. It's my first book and I'm so excited."

"When did this come about?"

"I finished it a few months back and turned it in to a publisher. I didn't know that it was one of those publishing companies where your book is printed only when someone ordered it off the internet or walked into a bookstore. Had I known that, I would have tried other companies. Anyway, I was attending an event in Richmond and ran into a publisher. He was thrilled by my enthusiasm to get the book republished. He offered me a deal I couldn't refuse."

"That's great girlfriend. Congratulations!"

"Thanks. I'm working on two more and hopefully, I'll have one of them completed by the fall of 2003."

"You go Shanice. That's what I'm talking about."

"After we get to South Carolina, I don't plan on doing anything but Mary Kay and writing books. When I'm tired of doing Mary Kay, I'll write. When I'm tired of writing, I'll do Mary Kay."

"You seem to have it all planned out," Chantal said looking over at me.

"I sure do. You gotta have a game plan going to a place you've never been."

"Is Frank excited about the move?"

"Gurl, he can not wait to get out of here. Since the job is transferring him down, they'll pick up the cost. The military calls it PCSing."

"Ugh, I think I know a little bit about that since I use to be in the military some moons ago."

"Oh yeah, I forgot about that."

"I didn't," Chantal said looking over at me. "I met Jamal while in the military, divorced Kenyon, and had Dante. I'll never forget my drama days."

"Well, that's in the past now. You have Mr. Wonderful as you would say. I'm sure he'll satisfy all your lusting needs."

"He sure will."

We both laughed as we turned the corner heading towards Chantal's big house. It seemed as though every time I saw her house, it got prettier. I'm not sure if it was from the flowers outside or the spirit she has placed upon it. Either way, it's a beautiful house and no one could take it from her.

Frankie had been bad the entire time I was gone. Dante had had enough of him and made him go to Chantal's spare room upstairs to lie down. When we walked in the house, it was very peaceful. Too quiet for even Montel! Chantal called out and Dante came running.

"You girls had fun?" Dante asked.

"Too much to recount," Chantal replied.

"I see because you didn't bring back any bags. Gotcha." He said smartly.

"Well," I said. "Your mom and I decided to go to the Harbor instead. We'll do the shopping thing another time."

"That's cool. Ms. Shanice I just wanted you to know that Frankie had some problems listening while you were away. He understood me better when I got on him."

"Please tell me he didn't show his little black ass?"

"Yes ma'am, he did. I had to make him go upstairs and lie down. He even got on Montel's nerves."

"I'm sorry about that Dante. Could you get him for me?"

"I guess he didn't want to be here after all Shanice."

"I guess not. I wish Frank didn't have to go out. He could have kept him for me."

"Mommy," Frankie yelled as he ran down the stairs.

"Hi sweetie. I heard you didn't have such a good day."

"No," he said giving her the sad eyes. "Dante was mean to me."

"What?" Dante said lengthening his lips. "I gave you all kinds of stuff and even played around on the floor with you."

"You wouldn't let me play with Montel's game."

"That's only because Montel's game is for older boys. I didn't know if your mom allowed you to play with them."

"I told you it would be okay."

Chantal interrupted. "Dante, you did the right thing. I'm not sure what kind of game it was, but if it's a bloody one or has guns, he knows he is not allowed to play with them."

"Yes ma'am. It was a bloody game."

"Then you most certainly did the right thing." I took my focus off Dante for a moment and turned to Frankie. "Young man, I think you owe someone an apology."

"Maw....Okay, I'm sorry Dante."

"It's okay young brother. I understand how you feel."

"All right Frankie, run off and play for a little bit. I wanna finish talking to your Aunt Chantal."

"Okay Momma." We knew Chantal really wasn't his aunt. But, since he had known her from the day he was born, we had him call her that out of respect. We chatted a little more about my move and then it was off to my crib. Frank finally made it back home and was awaiting our arrival.

"Thought I would have to be home by myself tonight," he said giving me a kiss on the lips and Frankie a pet on the head.

I gave him a kiss back and said, "Whatever gave you that idea?"

"Well, I have been home for a couple hours and was starting to worry. Then I figured you were okay though because you were with Chantal."

"Why didn't you call on my cell phone if you were that concerned?"

"Oh, I knew you were okay. Besides, it gave me some time to finish preparing for our move."

"Like what?" I implied curiously.

"Like looking at new homes in South Carolina and planning a nice surprise for you guys. Couldn't do that while you were here, could I?"

"Maybe. Maybe not. I still wanted to do it with you."

"I know some things you can do with me right now," he said looking down at Frankie. "Hey big guy, how would you like to go down stairs and see what Daddy has in the bag for you?"

"Sure Daddy," he said as he headed downstairs.

"Are you bribing him again?"

"Trying my damnedest if you know what I mean," he said smiling at me. "Why don't you go upstairs and see what's on the bed for you?"

"Ooh, sounds like fun."

"Oh, it will definitely be fun," Frank said patting me on my butt.

Frankie ran back to the second level and gave his father a huge kiss. "Thanks Daddy. Can I play with it now?" He asked holding the latest PS2 game in his hands.

"You sure can big guy. You can play until eight then you must come upstairs for your bath."

It was just past six and Frank had roughly two hours to make his move on me. I proceeded down stairs in the sheer baby blue negligee Frank had lying on the bed. "Is this what you wanted me to find?"

"Ooh baby! It looks just the way I thought it would. Come over here for a second." Sweeping me up off my feet, he hurried me upstairs in his arms and laid me down on the bed. My legs were spread eagled and he still was wearing the pair of jeans he had on earlier. He backed away from me, walked backwards towards the door trying not to miss one moment of my tender thighs, locked the door, and made his was back towards me. I kept my legs just the way he left them as he lowered himself back in place and began kissing me.

I could feel the heat stirring up in his pants as I reached down to unzip them. His moves were smooth and filled with passion. He grabbed both my legs, lifted them high and pulled them closer together so that he could kiss the tenderness of my thighs. I loved this man so much. I loved the way he took his time with me and made me feel like a woman should feel while being loved. Frank lowered my legs and unbuttoned his shirt. I reached up and pulled his arms through. As the moment of passion heightened, a knock came to the door. "Be quiet," he said backing away from me.

"Who is it?" Frank said wanting to scream at Frankie for interrupting his passion.

"It's me Daddy," he said snickering. "You know there is no one else here but me, you, and Mommy."

"What's the problem son?"

"I want something to eat. Can I get a snack?"

"Sure baby. You can have anything you want," I yelled out to him.

"Okay. I'll get a bag of chips and head back downstairs."

"That's sounds good," Frank said as he came back towards me pointing with desire. His flesh thickened as he got closer.

I could feel my insides moisten as Frank walked towards to me. The man had it going on when it came to size, passion, and getting me wet.

"Can we start this again, baby?" He said rubbing his flesh close to mine.

"You can do anything your heart desires. Just kiss me," I said grabbing him down towards my area of passion.

He looked at me knowing that I wanted to be kissed in places other than my mouth. He lifted my legs once again and smiled. I began to moan as Frank continuously kissed my soft spot. My juices flowed as I burned with desire and grabbed for my jugs. The more he kissed, the more I touched my throbbing nipples.

Another knock came to the door. "Damn it," I said burning deep inside. "What do you want now Frankie?"

"I wanna come in. I'm bored."

"I thought you wanted to play with your new game," Frank replied.

"I can't win it. It's too hard."

"Please, can I come in?"

We looked at each other knowing our well-planned time was about to end. "Wait just a minute Frankie. I'm rubbing your mother's back."

"Okay. But just one minute. I'll wait outside the door until you finish."

"Don't say a word honey," he told me as he thought of another plan. "Frankie, will you go and get Momma a glass of water real fast? She's not feeling well."

"Okay Daddy. I'll be right back."

They hurried and put their clothes on and Frank went off to the bathroom to wipe his face. When he came back, I had already put my clothes on and opened the door. "Later," I said giving him a smack on the cheek.

"You betcha baby!"

Frankie came up the stairs holding a green cup of water in his hands. "Are you okay Mommy? He said curiously.

"Sure baby. Why you ask?

"I heard some noises in here before I knocked before. I didn't know if you were sick or not."

Frank and I looked at each other and smiled. "Daddy was giving me a deep massage and he was pressing on some nerves that caused me a little pain. I'm okay."

"Is it eight o'clock yet? I'm getting tired."

I glanced over at Frank and gave him the eye. "Not quite baby. If you want to get in the tub, Daddy will give you a bath and Momma will tuck you in."

"That sounds good," he said yawning a few times.

"Hmmm," Frank said. "Looks like someone had a long tiresome day. I'd better hurry up and run you some nice warm soothing water."

"Yeah, I think that's an excellent idea honey," I said winking twice at him. "We'll take good care of you sweetie. Just you wait and see."

We knew we had the rest of the night for love-making once Frankie got tired. "No more interruptions," I said to myself. My area was still fired up from all the attention Frank was giving me. As Frank marched him off to the bathtub, I thought about the move again. I looked around the room and said to myself, "I'll miss this room the most." I knew it was where Frank and I spent most of our time before Frankie came in the picture.

Frank came back into the room after about ten minutes with a tired six year old and put him in our bed. I pulled out the oil and rubbed his back until he fell asleep. "Looks like it's just you and me baby," I said handing him over to Frank.

"Looks that way," he said picking Frankie up and taking him across the hallway to his room. Frank turned on his nightlight and came back to where I was lying. I was waiting for him once again with nothing on.

"That was fast," he said pulling his clothes off as well.

"Knowing that you are near makes the freak come out suddenly," I said giving him a smile of intent.

"I like the sound of that," Frank said luring his body towards me.

"Do you think we'll make it this time?" I asked smiling at him.

"Oh, nothing's going to stop us this time," he said unplugging the phone. "Come here girl!" He turned on the radio to 95.9 FM and held me close. They were playing "Betcha By Golly Wow," by the Stylistics. It was as though the curtains had risen and they were performing live in the mist of us. The mood came back suddenly and the heat was back in place. Frank lifted me back into a world of pleasure I hadn't felt in a while.

He lit a couple of candles and undid the laces on my negligee. I could feel the passion that was about to overcome both of us. Gently, he lifted my legs and massaged my inner thighs. The look on his face made my soul soar. I was comforted in knowing that my husband was about to drive me to another level of ecstasy. He leaned in towards my heated vagina and began licking the juices inside. My body was wet and I had no control of the liquid seeping out. "Ummm…" my lips parted as he kissed them gently. I motioned for him to come towards me, but Frank was hungry for my love. He knew the right spot to touch and he wanted the explosion to last a lifetime. After I came, he was up for a quick breather and moved slowly towards me. I could taste my insides all over his lips. He smiled at me as I flipped him over. My eyes must have had the fire of a tiger the way I looked at him. He was long and hard and the moisture in my mouth was for the calling. He tried his best to hold back on the leakage, but the gentleness of my tongue drifting up and down on him begged for more. I wanted as much of him as I could possibly take without gagging. He lowered my head trying to get me further down the pathway of his veins. I could feel tears in my eyes as I gagged slightly telling him that I couldn't take any more. I mean…he had way too much for me to deep throat all of his love. But, I did my best to make the most of it. Before long, Frank let out a loud, "suck it baby" and his cum was all in my mouth. I was like a pro swallowing every bit without a single drop. I drained him so badly he couldn't move another inch.

"Let me catch my breath for a moment," he said. "Then I will be ready to make love to you all night. You took my breath away baby."

The way I looked at him gave him the impression I was ready for more. I said, "You take all the time you need baby. My legs are right for the picking."

By the end of the night, we were exhausted from being over sexed and the constant kissing and caressing of each others body. I lay there rubbing my erect nipples and massaging Frank's drained head.

The next morning, I knew I had to go back to the one place I had no desire to be. The closer I drove towards that company, the more I wanted to turn around and say 'the hell with it.' Three cars were in the parking lot at the time and my newfound roommate had not arrived yet. I separated my workload and headed towards the kitchen to get a cup of tea. Mitch, an older gentleman, accompanied me while I ran hot water over the Lipton tea bag daggling inside my cup.

"You're in mighty early," he said as he poured himself a cup of coffee.

"Got a lot of things to take care of today. I don't wanna waste time dragging along before everyone shows up."

"That's good work ethics. They must really appreciate the work you're doing around here," he said smiling heavily at me.

"Don't I only wish that was true! They don't know how to appreciate us around here. Only certain people move up in this place and it ain't me or my kind."

"I won't comment on that," he said looking at me strangely. "So Shanice, how do you feel about the move? I know Winston wasn't pleased about it."

"I feel the same way he does. I mean, I've been at this company the longest and I got screwed royally up the ass."

"That's putting it kind of harsh, don't you think?"

"No, I think I hit the donkey on the nuts."

"You're funny," he said as he headed in the direction of his office. "I'll be over to see you guys later. Tell Winston I'll check him later."

"I sure will," I said as I walked past the office of the girl who placed me with Winston. Patricia sat cozy looking in her office filled with plants and other pictures she had ordered with company funds. Her only job was to take care of the office management and she had a hard time doing that. All day long, Patricia and Kandy would stand around the front desk gossiping about other people including one of the girls who was supposedly her best friend. Hell, if that was a black person doing some mess like that, we would definitely get walking papers. Instead, Patricia would be rewarded with monetary gifts while the people who worked the hardest got nothing.

Eventually, I got tired of the same day in and day out shit from certain people claiming to befriend me. When you weren't watching, they'd stab you so hard in your back you could feel the blood rushing through your veins. At the end of the day, I always looked forward to going back home to be with my family and getting with my girl Chantal. That's when I felt my comfort zone kick in. The sad part about it was in a few weeks, I would be leaving Chantal behind and moving on. I knew we would see each every now and then. But I would want to see her everyday. It's a good thing that she finally met someone that she could share her life with and be happy for a change. It's a shame it took her damn near a lifetime to find him.

True Friends

True friends will be with you no matter what
They are there for you when you fall flat on your butt
They give you advice when you're doing wrong
They let you know where you belong
They will be with you until the end
They are there because they're your friend
They won't put unnecessary pressure on you
They won't tell you what to do
They make you feel that you are needed
They are there for you when you're mistreated
A true friend will love you for no special reason
She's there for you through all seasons
When you're feeling down and don't know what to do
Call on your friend she'll be right there for you
A true friend won't invade your private space
And they won't try to take your spouse's place
Being a true friend comes in many forms, shapes, and sizes
They won't come with any surprises
Now that you know how to be a friend
I hope you will be mine until the very end

Copyright ©2003 Donna Marie Brown

CHAPTER 25

"Chantal's Breakdown"

As soon as Shanice got home from work, she gave me a call. She was in such a strange mood. I don't know what came over her, but she was starting to worry me. I tried giving her advice, but she wouldn't listen. She was adamant about leaving her job. I suggested that she confront her boss and tell him her intentions. She wouldn't have it. We got off the phone and I started feeling a weird sensation in my hands. *"Here we go again,"* I thought.

At first, I thought I was having a stroke, but later realized I was trying to carry too much burden on my chest. Dante came in the house and I was shaking. He kept asking me what was wrong, but my lips seemed to be locked. He called for Dominique to come and they took me to the hospital. I was having a breakdown.

It hadn't been long since we came back from our vacation in Miami. I started having weird headaches. The only thing I could think of was the migraines I occasionally suffered when I ate pizza, bananas, or drank sodas. But this was different. I started to feel really strange like people were talking to me inside my head. Come to think of it, I really never came to terms with my mother's death.

One of the doctors, Kilborne—referred Dominique to a hospital in Chattahoochee. I knew I wasn't crazy just stressed. We headed down 95 and my headaches got worse. I must have passed out because I woke up in one of the hospitals outside of Tampa.

We arrived about 7:30 p.m. that night and were greeted by a host of nurses and interns studying behavioral medicine for the summer. Dominique flew the boys up to be with him while I was resting. We entered my room which was filled with pastels and woven blankets. Kinda odd to have blankets during the summer, but I didn't pay it any mind. There were pictures hanging on the walls with people walking through a passageway and dogs barking at children while they walked to school. The one that caught my attention the most was the one of a body of water covering a land filled with people and animals. I wasn't sure what it meant, but it damn sure caught my eye. God said He would never again destroy the world with water, but the picture seemed as though the ending was near.

I went over to the bed and placed my baggage down. The view from my window wasn't so great. All I could see were damaged trees and a trail that led to a wooded area. It was as though a dream some time ago was visible through the scene.

Dominique thought I should lie down and take a breather after such a long trip. I was told that this was the best place to be for mind relaxation. I was not sure how true that was, but I was comfortable.

Dominique took the boys to Bennigan's for a bite to eat. As I rested for a few minutes, I could hear the birds chirping outside on the window sill. I could hear various noises in the hallway and then one of the nurses came in and gave me some Paxel to calm my nerves. I felt dizzy immediately and fell asleep.

After seeing that picture hanging on the wall, I fell into a deep dream. I was on a boat along with my mother and sister, Denise. Water was covering the surface and starting to come into the boat. We went under the deck until it settled down. We drifted into another land and sea gulls were flying about. When we came from underneath, mounds of white dunes covered with green grass appeared before us.

Momma suggested that we get off the boat and take a look around. I was hesitant at first because sea gulls and storks were everywhere. Mind you—my mother had already passed and I was a little weary of a dead person trying to guide me into a strange land. As we walked on the shore, the surroundings were familiar to me. After seeing the white dunes and big waves, I knew somehow I was on Pensacola Beach on the Gulf Shores. There was a puddle filled with flies swarming around a dead fish. I was starting to get scared as we walked towards a wooden screened-in house further on the shore. Momma invited us to come in and Denise glanced at me. She was just as terrified as I was.

The house was pitch black and had a musty smell. The further we walked in, the more nervous I got. Before I could finish the dream, I jumped up and stared at the picture on the wall. I must have screamed along the way because one of the nurses came in to check on me. She saw that I was sweating and grabbed a towel.

"The medicine," she said, "sometimes tend to make you have nightmares."

I stared at her and said, "But this was not a nightmare. It was too real. I saw my sister and my mother."

"That happens ma'am especially when other people are on your mind before you go to sleep. Just lie down and try and relax." I tried taking her advice and drifted back into dreamland. Momma and Denise weren't present—just the big boat and a body of water.

Dominique and the boys came back after a great meal a Bennigan's. They snuck me a piece of double chocolate cake and some hot wings. Now you know they smelled those wings lingering through the halls. Although I was still drowsy from the medication, we decided to walk around the complex so I could eat my wings in peace. We walked for roughly twenty minutes and I told them I was going to pass out.

I didn't want to be in that place, but I needed to rest. There were so many sicko's running around screaming shit like, "Damned the Torpedoes! Full speed ahead!" Another one yelled, "You see Jesus on the wall? He's there you know." I felt sorry for this lady. She was a little short stocky black woman wearing a flannel dress and a pair of open toe slides. She scared the pants off me.

Then I said, "Jesus is all around us. Trust Him and He'll set you free."

That woman turned her pudgy nose up at me and said, "He doesn't exist. I say that all the time. He's the devil in disguise."

Now I knew this woman was half out of her mind. I asked her, "Ma'am, do you know Christ? Has anyone ever taken you to church?"

She looked at me with her big brown eyes and said, "I reckon when I was a little girl my Momma took me. Then she spat some tobacco from her mouth and I almost puked. "She died in an airplane crash in 1988 and my father died in his sleep from an overdose of alcohol and cocaine in 1992. God doesn't exist in my eyes."

My heart went out to her, but she was wrong about Christ. I felt compelled to speak to her about Him. "My momma passed recently, but her health was really bad. I don't blame God for taking her away no matter how much I miss her. We all have to go some day."

She looked at me and asked, "You the devil?" All of a sudden, this woman started to scare me. Her eyes turned a violent red as though the devil himself had swept through her soul. "God does not exist and I can prove it."

At that point, I didn't care to talk to her anymore. She had to be possessed with demons or something. I bid her farewell and told her that Christ really did love her despite her feelings for Him.

Dominique came back to the room and had a bouquet of flowers with him. I was never so happy to see him in my life. "Where are the boys?" I asked.

"They are outside roaming the grounds."

"Please get me out of here," I begged him. There are some really sick people here. The boys shouldn't be wandering around the premises on their own."

"They'll be fine. Don't worry about them," Dominique said.

"You're such a wonderful man "D". How did I get so lucky?"

"You think it was luck sweetheart. God brought us together in that mall and I'm forever grateful."

Then I told him, "I think I just ran into the devil." I grabbed his body tightly and started to cry. I begged him to get me away from those Looney people.

"Baby," he said lifting my head back slightly. "What's wrong sweetheart?"

I couldn't hold back any longer. My mind wasn't getting the rest I had expected to get. "There are some strange things going on here. This lady just told me that God was actually the devil."

"Slow down sweetheart. The medicine is making you talk out of your mind."

"It's true Dominique," I tried explaining. "I'm really afraid to be here."

"Relax honey. I'll get a nurse."

When Dominique came back, I was fast asleep. The boys were with him. They left me a note saying they were heading to the hotel room and would return in the morning.

I was awakened by this strange figure lingering over my body. All I could see was a blur of what seemed to be a teenage boy bound with chains. "Help me," he murmured.

I immediately sat up and asked, "Why are you bound like that?"

He looked at me and smiled. Most of his teeth were brownish green and missing. "They say I'm trouble."

"Get out," I screamed. This guy was a total nut. He wouldn't leave so I jumped out of my bed and ran into the courtyard. I could feel the skin crawl on the back of my neck as I tried to make my getaway.

"Stop her!" One of the interns yelled.

I ran further into the courtyard and hid behind a tree. There was no way in hell I was going to stay one more night in that place. Some of the residents stayed to themselves, but then there was Pricillia—who watched as her mother went on a killing spree when she was eight. She hadn't said a word since that very day. She stood there clapping her hands and stomping her feet furiously as I struggled to stay hidden.

"She went into the courtyard," another intern yelled.

I was hiding behind this huge oak tree and felt something on my head. As I reached my hands upward to investigate, a big ass cockroach was on my hands. I was terrified of those things and tried my best not to scream. Sam—a big time schizophrenic spotted me. "I see you hiding behind the tree," he said leading the interns my way.

"Scat—Go you dumb asshole. You're gonna get me caught."

He was jumping up and down laughing with a stupid grin upon his face. "They're gonna get you…lalalalalalala. She's over here," he said laughing wholeheartedly.

When they reached around the tree to get me, I was no longer there. Sam stood there and said, "She's gone and I'm not tellin'. Then he started fussin' with himself. "Hehehe—she ain't comin' back."

I managed to find a safe place where a phone was visible. I called Dominique's cell phone and pleaded with him to come and get me. The staff searched the hospital, but to no avail. I ducked into a room where several patients were either tied up or sedated. As I walked over to one of the patients, I could hear voices in the hallway.

"Check the psycho ward Brandon!" One of them yelled.

I panicked and hid under one of the beds.

"Come out…Come out wherever you are!" Brandon sang.

I was breathing hard. My skin was pouring in sweat as I hoped I wouldn't be discovered by Brandon. I rolled under several beds until I reached the end. Standing at the end of the bed was a tall well built man with a long white robe draping in his hands. He grabbed me by my hair and stood me in front of him. I was scared to death as I was dragged from the psycho ward through an open tunnel. My screams for help went unnoticed. Then suddenly, if by fate, an older administrator knocked the perpetrator unconscious.

"Come with me," he said as I was lead towards the front lounge where Dominique and a shit load of cops from the Chattahoochee police department were standing. Dante and Montel ran my way.

"We were so worried about you Momma," Montel cried.

I looked at Dominique and asked, "Can I please go home now and get some rest?"

He smiled joyfully knowing that I was safe and said, "Yes dear. Seems like we didn't make the best choice for you after all!"

"Go figure," I replied slapping him playfully across the head. Don't ever do this kind of shit to me again without asking me first."

CHAPTER 26

"Mother's Day Delight (Shanice)"

After Chantal got back from the hospital, she gave me a call. It was around 11:00 p.m. on a Friday night. I could tell she was embarrassed by the whole ordeal and told her if she needed me to call. We hung up the phone and I fell asleep. I was awakened by the cool feeling of slush as I watched Frankie jump from his sleep as though he had gone through the worst nightmare. He sat there in a daze as the last of the yellowish liquid flowed from his midsection. I jumped in complete surprise as I looked at the small black clock sitting on the pedestal next to my brown cabinet as it read 2:37 a.m. Frankie had wet his pants and the right side of my polka-dotted night shorts were drenched. The long pillow on his side of the bed was completely soaked.

I had gone in his room that night to tuck him in, but instead fell asleep at his side. Of all the nights I climbed into his double bunk bed, it had to be the one where he peed his pants. I immediately rushed him off to the bathroom, nearly falling on my face from being tired. I had been on my feet all day selling MK baskets at Mondawmin Mall in Liberty Heights. On my way there, the rain was coming down quite hard and I was trying my best to drive carefully. Two minutes away was all I could think when the traffic light at Wabash Avenue turned yellow and suddenly red. Trying to brake slowly, I slid into the traffic and saw a horrific light flash before me. All I could think was, *"Damnit, I slid right through the light and it caught me!"* I knew I would have to pay a fine of seventy-five dollars. The city of Baltimore had found a new way of ripping off people and I was their next victim. People started to get angry saying that the state had sat a trap and was banking their hard earned money. I knew I had a chance to fight it, but if I lost, I would lose a days work and would probably have to pay an extra fine for court fees. As I arrived at the mall, the parking lot was nearly full. People started to gather for the big rush and last minute shopping for Mother's Day.

That morning when I left the house at nine, I didn't realize that my blessings were about to flow so heavily. I was the first to arrive and began setting up the carts so that when the first customer came to purchase a gift all the baskets would be neatly arranged. An older gentleman with grayish hair and a long beard came over to my cart and complimented me. His clothes were torn and he desperately needed a bath. I smiled at him as he told me that I must have just stepped out of a salon because my hair was so neatly combed. To me, it was nothing fancy outside of grabbing a big wand hair curler and bumping it out a little.

"You're such a classy woman," he said as he tilted his hat to me and looked down at the big rock I was sporting on my finger. "Your husband doesn't know how lucky a man he is."

I was stunned by his remark knowing that I was just an average woman trying to work as hard as I could to bring money into my house.

"Thanks for the compliment sir. I believe in my heart that he knows. If the truth be known, I'm the lucky one…not my husband," I said as I continued to move the baskets to my liking.

"You look mighty busy ma'am. I'll leave you to your work. You have a blessed Mother's Day."

I thanked him as he drifted into the crowd of people who were heading in the other direction. "Some people are so kind and yet, have so little," I thought as I continued on. All the lights on the other carts started to illuminate as the big clock struck ten. Many of the carts were highly decorated with balloons and flowers while others had jewelry and other fragrances. My cart was filled with many international perfumes, body lotions, and facial creams that would beautify even the simplest woman. All day long, another woman and I worked until we sold many of the decorative baskets. She told me to brace myself for the crowd of people that would come after the rain stopped falling. It poured for nearly four hours, but it didn't stop the show that took place behind us.

One of the local radio stations, 95.9 had shown up for the annual mother/daughter look-a-like contest. The people gathered watching as the last contestants got on the floor. One of the young teens told the crowd that she never imagined herself without her mother and that her life just wouldn't be complete without her. "Never take your mother for granted," she said. "You never know when you might have to live without her." She then turned to her mother and gave her a huge kiss on the cheeks. A tear fell from my eyes as I heard the young girl speak so well of her mother. I knew once I got back home, I had to call my mother.

Frank arrived at my cart close to four thirty. Frankie ran towards me and leapt into my arms.

"Mommy," he said giving me a huge hug and kiss. "I really missed you today. Daddy took me over to the circus and I saw three big elephants. It was really loud in the tent Mommy."

I smiled and told him, "Soon, Mommy will be home and we will have our special time together. Mommy's very busy right now, but since I have been here for a while, I guess I can take a little break. I saw a neat place around the corner I know you would like."

"You did Mommy? Will you take me there?"

"Sure baby. Just let me tell the other women and I'll be right back." I glanced over at Frank, gave him a wink, and off we went. As soon as Frankie saw the motorized rides, he ran towards them.

"Mommy...Mommy, can I ride the jeep?"

"Sure baby. Let me find a couple quarters and you'll be set." I realized that I had left my purse back at the cart and asked Frank if he could help. All he had were dollar bills. He walked over to the change machine and came back with four quarters. Frankie's eyes lit up as I helped him get into the jeep.

"This is a long ride," he said with a smile on his face. "You're great Mommy!"

I smiled and told him, "It's because you make me that way."

Frank put his arms around me and we walked towards the end of the mall. It wasn't a big mall, but it had more shoe stores than some of the bigger malls. He knew that Frankie needed bigger shoes. As soon as we made it back towards the Mary Kay cart, Frankie spotted a cart carrying snowballs. He wanted the lime, Frank ordered a combination of cherry and blueberry, and I ordered some hot tea. From the looks of things below, the Mary Kay cart was really picking up with customers. I told Frank I needed to get back to work. They left and headed towards the Payless Shoe Store. He chose a nice pair of loafers and went home.

By the end of the night, I had cleared over eight hundred dollars selling Mary Kay baskets. I was amazed as I counted my money realizing that I could do this daily and not have to work hard. My feet were sore as hell when I took off my shoes. Frank told me to stretch out on the sofa. He took them one by one and massaged them until I started to fall asleep. He knew I was tired and had had a long day.

"Honey," he said. "Why don't you go soak for a while and I'll rub you some more when you get out of the tub?"

My eyes lifted as I thought about the possibilities of Frank rubbing me in places other than my feet. "You promise," I said smiling at him with my eyes thickened.

"Just leave it to me baby! I'll take care of you."

Unfortunately, Frankie was sleepy and wanted me to put him to sleep as well. He was sitting on my bed when I got out of the tub. Frank looked at me standing there wearing my Victoria Secret's burgundy two piece sleep wear. The top had buttons down the middle and Frank knew he had easy access to my breast. "I'll be waiting for you when you come out of the room baby," he told me as I closed the door to Frankie's room. He commenced to heading down and got on his computer. Completely forgetting about Frankie and me, he watched playoffs of the NBA teams competing for the National Championship. It wasn't until Frankie wet the bed that I realized I had falling asleep without Frank in my arms. I jumped up and raced him off to the bathroom. He still had a little urine left inside of him. I talked to him about wetting the bed and then I took two thick towels from the pantry and placed them on top of the wet spot until the next morning.

At six-thirty, I heard an alarm go off but turned back over and went to sleep. Frank had gotten up early and went down stairs. Unaware of his plans, he went to Frankie's room and had him wake me up. "Happy Mother's Day," he said standing there with a plate filled with bacon, eggs, and toast. He had already set up a TV tray and placed a cup of hot tea with Equal in it. "Rise and shine Mommy. It's your special day," he said giving me three cards. One of the cards he had made while in school. He wrote me a special poem and told me how much I meant to him. The other two cards were store bought. The one from Frank had a bunch of twenties.

My eyes were filled with tears as I told him he didn't have to do that. I would have been satisfied with a card.

The breakfast was demolished quickly and then I went downstairs to join Frank and Frankie as they ate their breakfast. "This is the best Mother's Day I've had so far," I said with tears in my eyes. "You two are the greatest." They smiled at me and continued eating.

CHAPTER 27

"Saying Goodbye" (Shanice)

Three weeks later, my worst nightmare came true. I had to say goodbye to the best friend a girl could ever hope for. It was the hardest thing I ever had to do. We stood outside her house and talked for a long while. Mosquitoes were bad that night and we both kept popping our legs trying not to let the bugs have their way with us. Chantal was my very best friend and she would do anything for me if I asked. It didn't matter how far away I was or how late at night, she was always there when I needed her.

As the night drew longer and the bugs bit more, she pointed out the different houses in the neighborhood that had been having some problems. I guess even in the uppity neighborhoods there were drug dealers and some ruthless people. I laughed at her and told her that she would be missed dearly. Sometimes I felt as though if I had never met Chantal, my life wouldn't be so meaningful. She taught me a lot of things, but mostly, she taught me how to love and respect other people. That was a hard thing to learn after living in Maryland amongst the most diverse people I had ever encountered. I'm just so glad Chantal and I found each other and I could rely on her for friendship. We said our goodbyes for the night and then she told me that she would be over to pick me up the next morning to take me to the airport.

When we arrived at the airport, Chantal couldn't resist stopping to have her usual at Starbuck's coffee shop. It was crowded when we arrived, but I got through the line in no time flat.

I caught a glance of this distinguished looking man as I sat with Chantal who had an unbelievable craving for some mocha blend coffee. Mocha wasn't my passion, but Chantal always liked to relax while driving through the city.

Somehow, she'd find the nearest Starbucks and have her usual Mocha on a daily basis.

She had placed her order before me and the sound of mocha sent vibes through my soul. I was hooked on the first sip. She smiled at me and told me that it was always a pleasure being with me. That was the day I realized how much she meant to me. She had so many problems while growing up and if I could have been there for her during the hard times, I would have.

I often think about the day Chantal and I got so drunk that we almost did something we'd both regret. Since she had so many problems, I really didn't want to push the issue with her. I mean—I like her and everything— but my forte' was men. They didn't have to have a lot of money or even look good for that matter. As long as they knew how to take care of me, I was truly satisfied.

As we sat there at the Starbuck's in the BWI airport, I could hear them calling for my flight. Chantal reminded me how much she would miss me and not to forget to write. Frank had already taken the kids to South Carolina to find a place, but I wanted to stay behind for a few days to gather the rest of my belongings and to be with Chantal.

"Last call for Charleston," I heard the announcer say as I told Chantal goodbye and ran as fast as I could to my flight. They were already boarding and it looked as if I was the last to get on the flight. I'll never forget the sight I saw next when I arrived at my seat.

"Wow, a window seat!" I said as I gazed into the eyes of the man who had passed by me while I sat with Chantal earlier.

"I take it you like sitting by the window," he said as into my eyes.

"Yes," I said staring back at him. "I tend to think better while looking out into the clouds."

"Oh, well—I'd better leave you to your thinking then," he said as he turned away from me.

"No—please, don't do that!" I said. Our conversations were beautiful and filled with so much laughter. He was much older than me, but to look at him, he looked every one would think he was in his forties. The more he spoke to me, I realized how wise of an individual he was. His build was approximately 5'9" and I at 5'6" was the perfect match for him. His skin was ebony bronze and his eyes were soft like the morning dew. The one thing I noticed the most was his chest. This man's chest was unbelievably solid. Most thirty and forty year old men could only dream of having one like his.

We talked the entire flight. Ironic as it may seem, this guy and I were born and raised in the same area. We started talking about people we knew and the places we've been. The funny part about the whole conversation was when we started talking about syrup sandwiches, sugar water, and day old Krispy Kreme Donuts. We laughed our ass off about that and then he looked into my eyes and said, "I can't believe you did that too!" That's when I realized I wasn't talking to a stranger, but a friend from the past.

"Glamorous," he said as he continued to stare at me. "If only I could have the pleasure…" Then he paused. "My name is Ron."

He was married and so was I. At the time, I wasn't looking for a companion, but a friend with a friendly ear. To feel myself being snatched away by this wonderful man, in a way, frightened me. It seemed as though he was trying to steal my heart away from Frank and he didn't even know it. Mind you—the offers he made were enticing, but the thought of losing Frank bothered me.

As the flight came to an end in Charleston, he checked his schedule to see when his next flight would be. He had another two and a half hours before he got on his next flight and I only had to get my luggage and meet up with Frank and the kids. It was a difficult choice, but I chose to be with Ron.

He offered me a T-Bone steak dinner smothered with onions and mushrooms. I was in awe. Then he smiled, looked down at the pretzels and soft drink given to us by the flight attendant and said. "Here you are my dear. The best steak dinner I could find." We both laughed about his joke and then he looked into my eyes once more and said, "May I have the pleasure of buying you some coffee, tea, or some lunch?" I covered my face in flattery.

"Certainly," I said trying not to show the embarrassment lingering in front of me. "Just let me make one call and everything will work out fine. By the way, I'm Shanice." In just a brief hour, I was mesmerized by the gentleness of someone old enough to be my father. We went over to the Miami Grill inside the airport and placed our order. We decided on the Classic Philly Cheese Steak sandwich with the exception of onions and green peppers. To watch this man eat was like watching a child with a sucker. It was though he had never eaten a cheese steak sandwich a day in his life. For a moment, he looked at me while I tried to eat my steak in front of him and made fun of the way I was chewing. I had to cautiously explain my reasoning for chewing so slowly. After telling him about the many luncheons I've attended and the men sitting in heat waiting to bust a nut, he said to me, "I can see how this might affect your mind." Then he took another bite of his sandwich. "I personally would have never given it a thought."

I smiled at him as he told me in his next words how beautiful I was and how if neither of us were married, he'd pamper me with gifts, love, and a shrimp scampi delight. I was on cloud nine as I listened to this man tell me how the younger men like wild sex but he, if ever given the chance, would make slow passionate love to me starting with my head and ending at my toe. Now I don't know if all of that came from me telling him about the hot dog scenario or if he was just a man filled with love. He embraced my heart with words, "If only I knew you a couple days ago, we could have sat on the beach watching the tides roll in and the sun set in the west." He pulled out a postcard showing condos located in Baltimore and pointed to the one he owned. He kept blowing my mind over and over again with words that totally captivated my heart. But, all I could think about was Frank and my kids.

Sometimes God will place a person in your life for a reason to make you appreciate what it is that you already have. There isn't a day that goes by that I don't think about Frank, but Ron somehow will always be a vague memory to hold on to. I could have easily given myself to Ron that day. Not because I'm a whorish person or anything, but because in an instant, he swept me off my feet through passionate conversations. I mean—you don't just meet someone by chance and you pour your heart out to them without a mere thought. You embrace every moment and capture the feel of what he is saying inside of you.

The more I listened and the closer it got for us to say goodbye, a part of me felt as if I was losing my best friend. You know—how can you sit and talk about syrup sandwiches and sugar water with someone you never met and laugh about it? In my opinion, that could only mean one or two things: Either you grew up poor as hell or you were from the south. Don't think just because you are high and mighty now it couldn't happen again. I thank God daily for all the blessings He bestowed upon me. I count it a blessing every day knowing that God blessed me to succumb the system while I was younger and move to higher grounds with Frank. If there is one thing I know for sure, it's the mere fact of putting God first and the rest of the world second. I would love to give myself credit for making it this far, but all the glory goes to God.

Ron and I spoke of Christ and how He affected our lives. I couldn't believe through all that we said, our religious beliefs remain the same. Sometimes, you just have to take your spiritual blessings and hold on for dear life. Before we stood up to say goodbye, Ron said, "I don't know what you look like from the chest down, but if it's anything like the beauty I see in your face, I'd like to hold a vivid thought of it in my mind for the next three to six hours." He then reached over, looked into my eyes and said, "I can't stand up and give you a hug or kiss like I want to, but when we depart I will realize that out of all the women I've met in my lifetime, you are the most beautiful, kind-hearted person I've ever encountered.

Then by chance, we stood up and I thanked him for the honor of his presence. He smiled and said, "Oh—what the heck?" He asked for a hug, gave me a small kiss on the cheek, and started to walk away. I couldn't help myself when I saw him standing there waving goodbye. There was no way this could be the last time that I saw him. Somehow, we'd have to see each other for more than just a steak sandwich. He motioned for me to come over and then he gave me his business card. When I looked at his complete name and realized I had seen him before on TV, I almost fainted. He wrote his cell phone number down and asked me to call him. At that moment Frank was distant in my mind and Ron—my new found friend had entered.

As I walked away, I tried not to look back. But when I did, he was just a memory that kept me company for a while. He meant well and wanted a lot in return that I couldn't give him. I couldn't promise him the world, but I knew if we had the chance, I'd give that middle-aged man a run for his money.

CHAPTER 28

"Ron"

After I arrived home that night, I greeted my family with hugs and kisses and told Frank I needed to call Chantal to let her know I made it home safely. To my surprise, she had already called and when Frank told her I would be arriving later, she was appalled. According to Frank, she didn't question my tardiness, but was anxious to talk to me. "I'll give her a call after I freshen up a little," I said as I gave Frank a hug and a simple kiss.

"What's that smell honey?" He asked me curiously.

"Excuse me," I replied knowing it had to be the expensive cologne Ron was wearing.

"The smell on your clothes Shanice, what fragrance is it?" He asked again releasing me from his arms.

"Oh that!" I said with a worried look on my face. "I'm not sure honey. It must have been from the older gentleman that was sitting next to me on the plane. His cologne was very loud," I said coming back with a strong lie.

"Oh. For a minute, you had me worried about another man." He said trying to pretend it didn't matter.

"Baby, you never have to worry about anything like that," I said lying my ass off.

"When you finish talking to Chantal, I have something I want to show you," he said heading towards the stairs.

"I won't be long. Just have to let my girl know I made it home okay."

I couldn't wait for him to clear the room. I had so much I wanted to tell Chantal about Ron. When I dialed her number, it rang twice.

"Speak to me," she said knowing that it was me on the other end.

"Whassup girlfriend? Miss me yet?" I said waiting to tell her my good news.

"I sure do. I know it's only been a few hours, but knowing you won't be close is killing me."

"Me too. Guess what?" I said.

"What?" Chantal replied waiting suspiciously.

She knew right then and there I had done something wrong. "Remember the guy I had been watching from the coffee shop?"

"Yeah," Chantal replied waiting patiently.

"I met him."

"What? How? When?" Chantal asked excitedly.

"On the plane, heading back from BWI."

"He was on your plane?" Chantal asked in amazement.

"Yep. He is absolutely wonderful," I said jumping on my couch and kicking my legs back.

Frank had come to the top of the stairs. To my surprise, he just sat there listening to my conversation. He had never done anything like that before, but he was curious as to why I was wearing another man's cologne on my clothing. I was completely unaware of him being there.

"How's that?" Chantal asked.

"Well, as we sat on the plane, we talked about a lot of things. Some things we actually had in common. He offered to buy me lunch after we got off the plane and I took him up on his offer. We talked about a lot of things including Frank and his former wife. After we finished talking, he gave me his business card and asked if I would give him a call sometime."

"You're not thinking about calling him, are you Shanice?"

"I'm not sure yet. He was just so gentle with his words and he had the most beautiful smile I've ever seen on a man."

"You are so happily married to Frank. I'm sure you wouldn't blow your marriage over someone you met in an airport."

"Oh hell no. But if I was to ever run into him again, I would be willing to have a nice dinner with him or even..." I was cut off abruptly by Chantal.

"Listen to yourself Shanice! I know you better than this. You wouldn't do anything so foolish to hurt Frank. You just couldn't."

"Calm down Chantal. I'm just making conversation. I don't think I'll ever hear from this guy again. Besides, it's not like he has a way of contacting me," I said brutally.

"Tell me something! I thought you were about to do something you'll regret," Chantal said.

"Girl no! Ron is just someone I met by chance. In fact, I threw his business card in the trash can as I was heading back towards the baggage claim area," I knew that was a big lie also, but if Chantal had one less thing to worry about then I would say anything to settle her mind. I knew she was getting married soon and I didn't need her worrying about me. "Listen," I said to her. "Frank wanted to show me something upstairs so I'll call you tomorrow.

"Okay. I'll be waiting," Chantal hung up the phone and shook her head.

As I put the phone away and headed towards the stairs, Frank stood up. He had a messed up look on his face and wasn't too pleased with me at the time. "An old gentleman sitting next to you," he said. "Why lie Shanice?"

"There was an old gentleman sitting next to me. After we had lunch, he gave me a quick hug. I wasn't lying about him. I just didn't tell it the way it really happened because I knew you wouldn't understand."

"How can I understand when you lied to me? I thought we could talk about anything Shanice."

"We can," I said trying to get myself out of harms way. Frank wasn't a violent man, but sometimes when he got angry, he'd lose his temper. I wasn't trying to be the one he lost his temper on.

"Then tell me baby, did you really throw the business card away?"

"Yeah, I actually ripped it into pieces so that no one could find it and give this man any prank calls. He was just a passer by. I swear to you." I knew it was a lie, but I had to tell him something. This man was angry as hell. I had plans to call Ron back as soon as I got a chance. I wanted to see if his number actually worked. I wasn't trying to score with him.

"Come here," he said. "I do trust you Shanice. If you said that was all that happened, I believe you. But, if for some reason you are trying to deceive me, I'll never forgive you."

I was sweating on the inside. "You can trust me Frank. I'll never deceive you." I said trying my best to squeeze in between his arms.

"Follow me. I have something for you."

For a minute, I was relieved knowing that I had told Frank the biggest lie ever and he believed me. I guess it's the way I told it that made him believe me. I hated lying to my husband, but this guy Ron—had stolen my heart so quickly. I had to see what he was all about.

I followed Frank up to our bedroom. He had it fully lit with scented candles and had run me some nice warm bath water. I guess he wanted me to get rid of the smell on my body before he touched me. "You went out of your way for me huh?" I said feeling guilty as crap.

"Anything for my baby. I have something special planned for you." He smiled at me and I knew the incident was forgotten.

I couldn't think of anything else, but Ron. I was looking at Frank, but was hoping that it was Ron I was getting ready to make love to. He had a vase filled with pink and yellow roses sitting at the bedside. It was the first time for me being in our new home, but I was loving it already. We had four bedrooms with an extra room in case I needed to do my Mary Kay or he wanted to work on some of his projects. I was amazed at how big this house was. The stairs wrapped around spirally and were trimmed nicely in redwood.

Frank bent down to pick me up and took me over to the bed. "Stay put. I'll be right back."

I was excited knowing that he had something else up his sleeves.

"Well now," he said pulling a bottle of wine from behind his back. "Let's have some fun."

The kids were downstairs in the basement so I knew we wouldn't be interrupted. He came towards me and for a minute, I was hesitant to be with him. "What's wrong baby?"

"Nothing," I said. "I just had a long tiresome day. I'm still up for what you have planned. I really need to eat something though. I haven't eaten since lunch earlier and I'm starved."

Frank smiled and said, "I'll be right back. Don't go anywhere!"

I didn't move, but when he came back, he had a rib-eye steak in his hands and a fresh salad. Now I know I'm not crazy, but Ron had offered me a steak dinner on the plane. This was too much of a coincidence. I didn't care. I was hungry as hell and that steak dinner looked great. "Thank you honey," I said gulping down the entire dinner within ten minutes.

"Damn baby, you were hungry! Care to rendezvous for a bit?"

"Don't mind one bit! That dinner was fantastic baby. Thanks for thinking of me."

"No problem whatsoever."

He took away the tray with the plate with nothing, but a piece of fat from the steak. I would have eaten it too, but I didn't want to show my greediness. He returned and lay beside me. I knew Frank was about to make some strong love to me after sensing another man could have moved in on his territory. He gently kissed me on my neck and started to pull my shirt over my head. My body was ready after the conversation I had with Ron. "You look so good baby," he said placing his hands between my thighs. I could feel the heat and knew I was getting ready to get it good. My breasts were very tender and my nipples stood at attention. He removed my bra and held them firmly in his hands. He kissed my lips and then bent down to kiss my breast. All I could do was close my eyes and moan. Frank was always so gentle with me. He knew how to rock my world and leave me wanting more.

I scooted back further onto our bed and he spread my legs so that he could fit inside them. I was still wearing a pair of Capri jeans from earlier.

"I have to remove them," he said as he unbuttoned my pants. Gently sliding them off, he placed himself in between my legs once again and brushed up against me. I could feel him protruding as he held on to me. "I want you so bad Shanice."

"I want you too," I said finally telling the truth for a change.

He stood up and motioned for me to unzip him. I didn't mind pulling his pants down since he was standing there pointing directly at me. "Someone wants it bad," I said giving him a smile.

"You just don't know how much I want you right now."

"Oh, I know baby," I said as I kissed the arrow pointing right in my face.

Frank loved it when I kissed him there. I figured if I could make him feel better about what happened earlier with Ron, I'd do just about anything to please him.

It didn't take long before he was fully aroused. I removed my mouth and slid backward. Frank came at me with hunger in his eyes. He wasn't wanting food either. I had on a 'G' string so he pushed it to the side and placed himself inside of me. Man was he hot and hard as a rock! I liked that in him. It didn't take long before we both reached our boiling point. We laughed about that. Normally, we'd be making love for a long while, but this time was quite different. Within minutes, we were through.

For a brief moment, I thought about Ron. I wondered about him being just as good as Frank or if he was better. Then I said to myself, "There's no way in the world he can top my baby." We lay there caressing each others body and soon fell asleep. I'm not sure what happened while we were sleeping because when I woke up about three to go to the bathroom, Frank had already gotten dressed and was on the other side of the bed. I was still naked as a newborn baby. Our love had dried up on my inner thighs and I washed until it was clear. "What a night," I said as I emptied my bladder and got back in bed.

I immediately went into a deep sleep and the next thing I knew, Ron had entered my mind. I still remembered his gentle smile and the way he held me when he said goodbye. Just that fast, he had come into my dream and was about to take me away. We were at a resort somewhere in the Pacific and Ron had arranged the whole thing. I told Frank that I had a Mary Kay trip I needed to take. It sort of took the suspicion away. Ron said that he wasn't interested in making love to me right away, but wanted to capture the beauty of my smile. I was flattered, but would much rather feel him inside of me. He wined and dined me just like he said he would.

As the evening got shorter, we went back to our room and talked about our relationships. Ron asked me if I would mind if he gave me a soft kiss.

I didn't think anything of it so I allowed him. His kisses were soft and passionate as hell. I wanted to be with him badly. "I'll go further if you want," he said. "I don't want you to feel uncomfortable with me," he was smooth as hell.

"I want you," I said pulling him closer to me. I wanted him to feel my breasts and to taste my thighs the way he had described at the airport.

After we undressed each other, I was amazed how thick this man's middle leg was. He was fine as hell. I thought Frank had it going on, but Ron was much bigger for an older man. I would have thought that men his age would need Viagra to stay up, but Ron had it going on with his piece. Ron turned me onto a whole new level of foreplay. It was the first time I had actually played with myself in front of a man. I was so deep into my dream that I had starting sweating while lying next to Frank.

As the dream continued, Ron removed my hands from my inner legs and parted my legs so that he could get inside of them. I guess my movements were swift because they woke Frank. He watched as I was touching my breasts and moaning. I was completely unaware that he had awakened. Ron moved slowly allowing me to feel all of him. I screamed loudly as I reached my climax and called out Ron's name. I was holding my breasts and climbing in the bed.

Frank jumped up and walked away. I could see the anger in the eyes and tried to explain that I was dreaming. It didn't matter to him. In his mind, I was thinking about another man in our bed. For the rest of the night, Frank slept in the guest room. He barely said two words to me the next day. I can't believe I screwed up so bad. I went to the kitchen and started breakfast. I put on the kettle to make some tea and picked up the phone to call Chantal. At that point, I really could use a friend. Chantal didn't answer the phone right away, but when she did, she didn't seem thrilled. I guess I messed up her beauty sleep. She'd warned me of the dangers I would encounter messing with another man. The funny thing about it was I hadn't seen Ron. It was just a dream. Somehow Chantal didn't see it that way. She said she would call me back later because Dominique was over and she didn't want to disturb him.

It was only two months away before their big day and my marriage was already falling apart. I had to find a way to calm Frank down and explain my dream to him. I started with an apology. Then I looked him in the eyes and said, "Have you ever thought about someone…say a movie star for so long that you've made love to them in your dreams?"

Frank was shocked by my words. "No, I can't say I've done that Shanice. You really disappointed me. I felt secure knowing that I had an honest woman. I don't know what I have now. Leave me to myself for a while until I can think of what to do next," he said walking away from me.

"Aren't you going to eat breakfast with me and the kids?"

"No, I'll just get a cup of coffee if you don't mind."

"But I do mind Frank. It was just a dream."

Frankie walked into the kitchen. "Good morning Mommy and Daddy," he said yawning a little bit.

"Good morning sweetheart," I said.

Frank smiled at him and gave him a hug. "Good morning buddy. How's my big guy doing this morning?"

"I'm fine daddy. Wanna go outside and play with me later?"

"Let me think about it for a minute. Okay, I guess I can."

"Great! Hurry up and fix my plate Mommy. I'm starving"

I stared at him for a minute and said to myself, "My little boy is growing up. But I know he didn't just place an order for his meal. He is demanding already. He must have gotten it from his father because I never taught him to be disrespectful like that."

"Ugh, I think you can come a little better than that Frankie," I said to him.

"Yes Mom. Could you please fix me something to eat because I want to go outside and play with Daddy?"

"That's better. Sit at the table and I'll have it ready shortly."

"Thanks Mom," he said as he looked at Frank. Frank gave him a wink letting him know that it was okay. Somehow, he didn't look at me for the rest of the morning. Our conversations were very short. Frank wanted to let me know that he didn't appreciate me calling out another man's name while we were sleep. In his mind, if I dreamt about him, I must have been thinking about him before I went to bed. I explained to him that this guy was as old as my father and I would never allow myself to be with him. Frank still didn't buy it. He knew I loved men and I was a big flirt. Can't help myself there! My mom was a big flirt and now that she's in her sixties, she continues to be one. I guess I got it from her.

That afternoon, I got a phone call from Chantal. She and Dominique had been making love when I called her first thing that morning so she really couldn't talk. I know how she felt because I sure hated when she'd call and interrupt me and Frank. Our love making wasn't the kind that could be put on hold for a minute or two. When we got together, we went full force. I guess that's why it's so hard to imagine myself with Ron. I've never made love to him except in my mind and in my dreams. One day I will get up the nerve to call him, but until then I'll keep things just the way they are.

Secret Lies

Lies are told when we are fast asleep
Lies told here were much too deep
Sneaking around during day and night
Replenishing our bodies with sexual delight
Getting caught up in the heat of the night
Giving them pleasure with all our might
Was it worth the pain, the shame and embarrassment?
Brought to you in the form of virtual harassment,
The secrets you kept to keep your body warm
Knowing if they found out it would bring you physical harm
There's a secret in lying and every lie has a secret.
But if you choose your words carefully
You might find ways to defeat it.

CHAPTER 29

"Fate"

Several weeks later, I found the nerve to call Ron. He was quite surprised to hear from me. I told him that I had been trying to email him, but somehow his email address always came back in the form of an error.

He laughed and said, "I've been thinking about you for a while now. Since you didn't give me your number, I had no way of contacting you."

I gasped and said, "You touched me that day our eyes first met. There was something about your smile that drew me nearer to you."

"Is that a fact?" He said smirking as he gathered his next words. "I feel a connection between us. I know we've only seen each other once, but you called me and that just let me know that I was on your mind."

How was I to respond to this man? I mean—I've only seen him briefly, but yet there was something about his words that capture my sense of nature. I responded with, "I really don't know what I feel, but I do know you seem to be a sweet man and a part of me would like to get to know you better. Oh shit," I thought to myself, "why did I say that so soon?"

He paused and said, "Shanice, only good things could come from our relationship. I'm a very romantic man with a passionate heart. I can make love to a woman over and over again giving her every desire she had in her heart."

I was in a rut. Now how was I going to respond to that? Why did I make this call in the first place? My number showed up on his caller ID and knew he would write it down. "Well," I said taking a deep slow breath. It was almost like I was about to exhale. He was talking about romance already and we've only been on the phone five minutes. "Other than my husband," emphasizing the word husband, "I haven't been with anyone else. I really wasn't looking for romance. I get plenty of that at home. I was only looking for a friend."

"I'm not asking for your hand in marriage," he said appallingly, "I only want a chance to see you one more time over a cup of tea or a bottle of wine."

I paused this time because I know I just couldn't be with another man and have a glass of wine. My body would start raging and then I'd do something stupid like sleep with the guy. Maybe that wouldn't be such a bad thing. I caught myself and then said, "That would be nice. I would like that." I thought, *"Damnit, I cannot believe I gave in so fast."* I placed my hand over my face sliding my fingers down gently. He couldn't see what I was doing so he didn't know that I had a slip of the tongue.

"Okay," he said. "We'd have to set this up very carefully and make sure no one knows about this but us."

I didn't have any problems with that because if Frank found out about some mess like this, it would crush him and he would leave me like a hot potato. I still had to think about my kids. Although Miranda and Justin, my kids from a previous marriage, were older, Frankie was still a bit too young to understand if I messed up. *"Oh God,"* I thought—*why do I always get myself into trouble like this?* Then I responded to him after hearing, "Shanice, are you still there?"

"Yes," I said. "I was just thinking about what you said and how it would affect my life."

"We don't have to do anything you are uncomfortable with. I don't want to pressure you. We can always sit and talk."

"Oh, I'm not pressured," I said as I sat on the floor on top of a blanket. I didn't feel right talking to another man on my bed. My legs started to shake as we spoke more about the subject. "I really would like to be with you. It doesn't have to be a sexual thing. We both are adults Ron. We can handle ourselves," I said knowing damn well I didn't mean what I was saying.

"Can I call you sweetheart?" He asked in a soft voice.

I was overwhelmed by his sudden request to call me sweetheart. "You can call me whatever you like. And," I asked returning the favor, "what would you like for me to call you?" I asked with a snicker.

"I don't see anything humorous," he said. Then he laughed. "Just kidding sweetheart. You can call me whatever you like, but I would prefer 'honey or baby.' But if you wanna call me Ron, I'll be okay with that too."

I was good about calling people sweetie so that's what I decided I would call him. I told him that I had to get off the phone because my husband would return at any time. He asked if he could call me at the number that appeared on his cell phone. Since I was using my cell phone and no one ever answers it without my permission, I didn't see anything wrong with it. We just had to be discreet about it though. I didn't need any slip ups and Frank being all over my case.

All night, I thought about this Ron person. He had sucked me into his realm and I didn't know what hit me. Maybe it was his voice or maybe it was just the way he came across to me. Whatever it was, I was hooked.

I fell asleep thinking about him again, but this time I wanted to make damn sure that I didn't call out Ron's name. Frank excused me the first time, but I'm not sure he would do that again.

I did dream about Ron though. We were on a cruise to Jamaica and Ron had paid the way. Of course, in my dreams, men would always pay. Ron had taken me to the starboard side of the ship and we were looking into the deep sea. Ron said to me, "I'm so glad you were able to find time to be with me. I was thinking I'd never see you again."

My response was, "being with you was the only thing I could think about." I know that blew his mind. He smiled and stood behind me. He was slightly taller than me so he was able to pull my hair to the side and kiss me on the neck. His kisses were soft and meaningful. Every man can't just kiss your neck and you feel something behind it. My body felt the warmth of his touch and I could feel him rise up against me. I turned around leaning against the metal frame of the rail and looked into his eyes. "You're not getting excited already are you?" I asked and then smiled at him.

"Oh, you can say that. You make me this way." He held on to me squeezing my body so tight that my breasts were pressing firmly against his chest.

I didn't want to hurt his feelings so I said this in the sexiest voice I could, "Ron, I can't breathe."

Letting go of me slightly, he said, "I didn't mean to wipe all the air from your body! You just felt so good in my arms."

He sure had a way with words. I said, "Oh, I didn't mean it sarcastically baby. I just needed to breathe a little that's all." I gave him a sexy smile and kissed his lips.

"Care to join me in our cabin for a glass of wine?"

"That sounds nice," I said knowing once again we've laid eyes on each other without any clothes on.

We walked back to our cabin hand in hand. I started to feel dirty just knowing that I was letting another man touch me. Ron ordered a bottle of Chardonnay. It was the only kind that I preferred. I knew there were better wines out there, but I just loved the way Chardonnay made my inside tingle. He poured me a glass and we sat on the bed and toasted each other. I took a gulp and a little drip ran down my lips. Ron leaned over and removed the excess wine starting to drip from my chin. "Excuse me," I said. "Guess I was a bit clumsy with the wine.

"Not a problem sweetheart. I enjoyed kissing it from your chin," he smiled at me and told me, "You look so lovely Shanice. I only wish we both had the opportunity to live freely and explore the world together."

I was flabbergasted. "Sometimes in life we just have to live for the day," I responded. "It might be the only moment we have together or it may turn into a lifetime of love."

I knew my words were right on the money. He took the glass of wine from my hands and placed it on the table. "May I have the pleasure of dancing with you?"

I looked at him as he took me in his arms and said, "I don't hear any music but..." He cut me off suddenly, "We can make our own music."

My eyebrows stretched forming a crease in my forehead. "Indeed we can," I said to this man of many words. We started to dance and he began humming a soft tune in my ear with sweet words following thereafter. I didn't have a clue what he was humming, but the melody was beautiful. I was mesmerized by his mellifluous voice. "You make me wanna leave everything behind and be with you forever."

Ron stopped singing and said, "That's the way you are supposed to feel sweetheart." And then, he continued to sing. When he had finished, he lifted my chin and his eyes fell towards my nose. We kissed for a while and he asked if it was alright to unbutton my shirt. "I don't want to move too fast," he said.

I gave him a sign that it was okay and started to unbutton his shirt as well. We continued locking our lips together until he pulled my shirt back. He reached around my back and unsnapped my bra. I had been waiting for this for quite some time and now the day had finally come.

"You have beautiful breasts," he whispers holding them firmly in his hands. As he lowered his head down to kiss them, my alarm clock went off.

"What the?" I jumped turning it off quickly.

Frank had already gone to work and I had to get Frankie ready for school. I tried my best to get back into that dream, but it was all gone. "Damnit! So much for the romance part," I said rolling myself out of bed. I got up and walked over to my bathroom. Frank had left the light on again letting me know he had already been in the bathroom and out the door. I did my business noticing a wet spot in my silk panties and shook my head. "Girlfriend, you gotta get a grip!" I said out loud. I knew what I had to do and what decisions needed to be made.

As soon as I got Frankie out the door, I gave Ron a call. He had just made it in to his nine to five. He was sipping a cup of black coffee and reading his morning mail. "Good morning Ron," I said in the most intriguing voice I could find.

"Shanice," he inquired. "Is that you sweetheart?"

I knew right then I was getting ready to get myself into some deep trouble. "Yes," I said to him while lying flat on my stomach kicking my legs back.

"To what do I owe this pleasure?"

Thinking about the dream I had about him, I commented with, "I woke up with you on my mind. I was wondering if our conversation yesterday had any affect on you."

"Baby," he said, "you are all I've been thinking about."

Then I sat up on the bed, pulled my feet to the carpeted floor, and walked over by the mirror. I was staring at myself as though I was God's gift to every man on the planet. "I have some free time coming up soon and I was hoping that we could spend a little of it together."

Ron, stunned by my last reply, said, "Are you sure you wanna move this fast? I mean—I wanna be with you intimately, but I want to make sure you are very comfortable with it."

I didn't need to think any further. Besides, this man was a good catch in my dreams and I sure wanted to make my dreams a reality with him. So I said, "All I can think about is us being together intimately. I can't seem to get you off my mind Ron. Please don't get me wrong. I love my husband and we're very happy together, but I have no problem being with you."

Ron took a sip of his coffee and I could hear him turn a page. "Am I boring you my dear or holding you up?" I asked. I said a lot to this man and he didn't seem to be the least bit interested in me.

"Sweetheart, I heard every word you said. I have a report I have to get out for a morning meeting. But, baby," he said. "I want nothing more than to be with you. I want to hold your breasts in my strong black hands and wrap my hands around your luscious ass. However, I need to get this report out and I'll call you later."

Immediately, I felt like a fool wanting to be with someone that didn't seem to have any interest in me or my body. Yeah, he said that he wanted to hold me, but my words to him were sincere. I was willing to sacrifice my family to be with him for a day or so. "Okay," I said. "I'll be waiting for your call."

I hung up the phone and immediately it rung back. "Hello," I said.

The voice on the other end tripped me out. "Now sweetheart," he said, "there is one thing you will soon realize about me and that is, never end a phone call without saying, I love you."

I smiled and it hit me that Ron did care about me. "Okay," I said to him. "I thought you didn't care."

"I'm not finished talking to you. When I say my last I love you, then you will know that I have ended the call. Until then, don't ever hang up the phone."

Again, I was taken by this man, his sensual way of handling his words. "I just wanted to hear your voice and invite you out to lunch with me. I didn't mean to stir you up or get you excited while preparing for your meeting."

"Sweetheart, you can call me anytime. I'm never too busy to hear your voice."

I felt a little better about those words. "If you're not too busy, I'm free next weekend. Frank is taking the kids to see his family and I decided not to go with him."

"Well—let's see—you live in South Carolina and I live in Baltimore. There is a lot of distance to cover. I will have to set something up with my wife to where I am going on a business trip and won't be back until Monday or so. Can you make it work for you as well?"

I thought about it for a minute and then I said, "Yeah, I think I can come up with something. Maybe I'll say that I will be visiting some relatives that live about an hour away. I really want to see you. I had a dream about us last night and if real life is anything like this dream, we need to be together to see what the outcome will be."

"I take it you didn't get to finish the dream."

"How did you know that?"

"Well," Ron said, "you wanted to know the outcome, which in my book means a conclusion wasn't met."

The man was right on the money. He knew me well and I'd only met him once. "You're right about that," I said.

"I'll find a spot and let you know where to meet me. I'll pay for your flight and the hotel accommodations."

"Oh no," I replied. You don't have to put yourself out like that. I'm very capable of taking care of myself."

"I'm sure you are, but I insist," Ron said.

I wasn't about to argue with him. If the man wanted to pay to be with me, then by all means, I was going to let him. "Okay. I give in," I said. "Can I call you later when you're not too busy?"

"Like I said sweetheart, you can call me anytime. My heart, my mind, and my phone will always be opened to you."

Ron was so zealous. No wonder I was falling for him. "It's settled," I said.

As we got ready to end the call, Ron said, "I love you," in the softest voice I've ever heard.

I replied with, "I love you too." I must have been out of my mind telling another man that I loved him. Something wasn't running right in my head, especially if I was getting ready to mess around on the one man who meant the world to me.

We ended the conversation and I put the phone back on the charger. I watched myself in the mirror circling my entire body making sure I looked good enough to be with another man. I could see flab around my waist area, but what woman with kids didn't have a little flab or jelly rolling in her front. My stomach didn't shake like jelly, but it was a little pudgy even for me.

I went into the kitchen and made a fresh cup of tea. Then, I called Chantal. When she answered the phone, she said she had just gotten out of the shower. Her day was getting closer and she was getting a little anxious to get it over with. I reminded her that Dominique was probably the best man she'd ever encounter. She told me she had some running around to do and wondered if I could call her back. Man, this calling back thing was wearing a hole in my ear. It was the same song I'd just heard a few minutes ago from Ron. "Sure," I said and then I got into the shower myself and did a little breast exam. Women should always check their breasts at least once a month for any lumps. Once again, everything seemed to be fine with them. I got out of the shower, got dressed and headed out the door. I wasn't sure where I was going, but I had to get out of the house. Thinking about Ron all the time could hurt my image.

South Carolina was so different from Maryland. Rush hour was a moving thing for the people in Charleston. There were no such thing as stop and go traffic. All the traffic ran smoothly and the people were courteous when changing lanes. Shoot, in Maryland, you try changing lanes and you might get run off the road by someone thinking they owned the damn road.

I saw a sign saying the mall was one mile away. I had about two hours before I picked Frankie up from school so I decided to go shopping and buy something for myself for a change. I went inside Lerner's and spotted a pair of hip huggers that I was dying to try on. Unfortunately, my belly hung just a tad bit over my stomach and the jeans were screaming, "Don't even think about putting one foot inside me!" I smiled to myself and wished for a moment I was the size of a teenage. Being that I was almost forty, maybe a couple years over, but who's counting, I didn't need those jeans anyway. I'll just leave them to Miranda and the girls her age to wear. I hardly ever saw her since she turned sixteen. If she's not with her friends, then she is hanging with some boy wanting desperately to get inside her pants. Although she is my daughter, the girl got it going on when it comes to style. Me, I'm still a little too plain for that.

I left Lerner's and headed towards the food court. It wasn't much of an eatery area, but the pizza was good. I sat in the center of the food court and watched the people as they were passing by. I know people were saying, "Now she know she's wrong by sitting there stuffing her face. She needs to be at work supporting her family."

I didn't mind a little work, but I had been working for the past twenty three and a half years and frankly, I was on my break to reality. I was wearing a pair of jean shorts and a Jesus shirt that I had gotten from a carnival event at the First United Church of Christ in Baltimore. I checked the time on my watch noticing that I had to get Frankie by 3:00 P.M. I had about thirty minutes so I hurried to my car so I wouldn't be late picking Frankie up.

On the way back from Frankie's school, I decided to treat him to McDonald's. If I'd known the boy was going to pull a Dr. Jekyll and Mr. Hyde on me, I would have kept going home. Frankie picked the seat next to the front entrance of McDonald's and we sat down to eat. I was all into my Quarter Pounder with cheese and he was eating his cheeseburger happy meal. The boy jumped up and started shouting something about, "Here we go," stretching the word 'go'. Then he started jumping up and down like he was possessed or something was in his pants. At that point I realized he was trapped inside his Mario Super Smash Bros. game. An older white gentleman turned around and started to stare. "Kids," I said. "You never know what they will do next."

I encouraged him to eat as fast as he could so he could go outside and play on the jungle gym. He kept saying, "Here we go," and moved his arms and legs like he was trapped inside the game. The older gentleman kept looking our way and I knew it was time to go. I packed what was left of his happy meal and headed out the door. I put him on the jungle gym and then I sat at the stone table adjacent the activity center. Frankie kept running back and forth across this man's foot which was wrapped in an ace band midway up his calf. I told Frankie he had to say excuse me whenever he crossed him.

The man looked at him and said, "would you like to see my leg?"

Frankie replied with, "Why would I want to see that bumped leg?" I chuckled from the embarrassment and said, "Be careful sweetie. You don't want to bump his leg."

The man wearing the Tennessee Titans ball cap said that he had had an accident while cutting some wood. He accidentally cut his leg on the drill saw and had to get twelve stitches. Being the joker that I was, I said, "Why would you want to do something so foolish?" Then I smiled noticing that, he nor his wife thought what I said was funny. *"Some people wouldn't know sense of humor if it was to stare them in the face,"* I thought. I guess they didn't like my type of humor because when I bent down to tie Frankie shoes, they were gone. I told Frankie he had five minutes then we would have to leave also.

My phone rang and I answered with, "Whassup girlfriend?" I knew it was Chantal. She finally had time to talk to a sista. She was checking to see if I was still going to be her Matron of Honor. I told her, "Try and stop me!" Then she wanted to know if I had heard from Ron and if so, I had to give her the spill. I said I would keep it to myself, but I needed to let someone know where I would be in case I turned up missing. I didn't think Ron was like that but I had to be sure. Her wedding was set for Valentine's Day 2003 and she was getting anxious about her gown. Since she had been married twice before, I didn't think she should be wearing a gown this time, but a T-length dress instead.

"Ugh, just because a sista's been around the block a time or two doesn't mean she can't look good going down the isle," Chantal said.

"I didn't mean any harm by my words. You'll look good in anything that you wear girlfriend, but I was just concerned about the whiteness of your dress." I said trying to reverse my original tone.

"My dress is cream with diamonds down the middle. There is no whiteness to my dress. It has a train, but not a long one. You'll see."

"Alrighty then girlfriend! I can't wait to see you in it. Now, about Ron?" I knew this was the main reason Chantal called in the first place. "Girl, I keep having all these weird dreams about him and I making love. We stay in touch with each other all the time, but I'm just afraid of what might happen if things should go badly for us."

"What do you mean by that?" Chantal asked out of curiosity.

"I really don't know this man and I'm just afraid that after being with him, we might fall into something we can't get out of so easily."

"Maybe you should tell him that you think things are moving too fast for you. It won't hurt to be honest with him."

"I know Chantal. But he sounds like such a romantic man. I just wanna see how he feels or if he is hung like Frank."

"See, that's what got you in trouble the first time. You are always looking for a man with size instead of him being capable of love. You better watch yourself Shanice. One of these days, you are going to get yourself into some serious trouble messing with a man's mind."

"I'm not worried about that," I said. "As long as I know Frank is at home waiting for me, I could care less about these men passing through the night."

"Okay. I warned you. I'll call you back later. Got some things to take care of," Chantal said as she started to hang up the phone.

CHAPTER 30

"Stranger Calling"

I was awakened not by the sound of an alarm clock or footsteps in the hallway, but by the loud ringing sound of the telephone. I dashed down the hallway realizing once again I had fallen asleep in Frankie's room. Almost slipping on the carpet nearly breaking my neck, I answered the phone with, "Hello. This had better be good," I said hoping that it wasn't bad news about the death of a loved one.

"Did someone just dial this number?" The other voice at the end of the phone asked.

"It's 1:34 a.m. in the morning and I can assure you that everyone including myself was asleep."

"I'm so sorry to have awakened you ma'am," an apologetic male's voice said softly. I hung up the phone, peeped in on Miranda, Justin, and Frankie and got in my bed. Frank was lying there sound asleep. He didn't even hear the phone ringing next to him. After I crawled back into bed, I noticed a slight pain around my right ankle. I asked, *"Why me Lord?"* Whatever happened to people respecting your sleep time or you for that matter?" I thought while lying next to Frank. Man, I was pissed.

It took me a few minutes before I could fall back to sleep only to have the alarm clock go off at 6:30. "Damnit!" I said. "It's just not enough hours in the night to get my beauty rest." Then, I smiled, said a little prayer and thanked God for giving me life once again. I got the kids out the door and was home all by myself trying to relax when the phone rang again. Since it was after eight, I knew it could only be one person. "Whassup?" I said thinking it had to be Chantal.

"I saw you this morning heading off in your big fine car," a heavy breathing voice acknowledged.

"Who is this?" I asked out of concern.

"You were wearing those sexy pair of black Capri's and a red tank top weren't you?"

"I'm going to hang up this phone if you don't tell me who you are," I said starting to get worried.

"You're so beautiful," the voice on the other end of the phone said.

I was terrified and began checking my doors and looking out the windows. I didn't see any parked cars outside my house or any strange guys lurking in the streets. "Please!" I pleaded. "What do you want?"

He laughed out loud in the strangest voice. "Is Frankie okay? When is the last time you checked on him?"

I knew he had to be some wacko because I'd just dropped Frankie off at school. "I'm hanging up now," I said and then slammed down the phone. It occurred to me that the nut on the other end of the phone could've had my son. Frantically, I called Frankie's school and I was reassured that he was in his class. I told the counselor not to release him to anyone, but me. The thought of someone getting a hold of my baby sent chills up my spine.

I hung the phone up and double-checked the doors and windows. I could see Mr. Johnson outside raking his grass. He was a much older gentleman and had lost his wife to cancer several years ago. I peeped out the door and got his attention. "Fine morning for raking the grass," I said nervously.

"Yes—Yes—Yes," he said gumming on a chicken bone.

"You haven't seen anyone hanging around here in the last thirty minutes or so, have you Mr. Johnson?"

"Can't say I have Shanice! Expecting a guest?" He asked curiously.

"No sir. Just had a strange call earlier and got a little worried! That's all."

"Well now," he said. "Don't go worrying your pretty little face! I'll keep an eye out for you. If I see anything suspicious, I'll give you a call."

I started thinking to myself as to how this man was going to call me if he didn't have my number. It's not like it was listed in the phone book because I haven't been too long in Charleston. Then I said, "Oh, I think I'll be okay Mr. Johnson. Some prank caller probably."

"You let me know if I can help out Shanice. I'm right next door."

I walked back into my cozy mid-size brick house looking around just in case the caller had come inside while I was talking to Mr. Johnson. I'm not sure if it was someone playing a sick joke on me or someone was actually watching my every move. I picked up the phone to call Frank, then suddenly realized how stupid I might sound telling him about the call. Frank might think I'm just exaggerating or feeling scared because we just moved to a new house. Then, I thought about Ron, his sensitivity to my needs and the way he always seemed to have the right words to say. I picked up the phone and gave him a call. The phone rang once and he answered with a smooth hello.

"I was waiting on your call sweetheart," he said with a slight chuckle.

"How did you know I would call you?" I asked out of curiosity.

"I know my baby. She always calls me when she needs to hear my sexy voice."

At first I thought, "What a conceited prick!" Then, I realized that he was being his same old loving joking self. "I thought you wanted to hear from me about our plans to meet."

"Oh baby, you're right about that!" He said eager to listen to what I had to say.

"I was thinking that we could meet up this Saturday around 10:00 a.m. I could meet you half way between South Carolina and Maryland."

"I have one better for you," Ron said. "What if I come to South Carolina on a business trip?"

I got a little scared knowing that this was my territory. "I really don't know my way around here that well. But, I think I can find somewhere secluded enough for us to hang out."

"If it's gonna cause any problems, we could find a half way point. I just want my baby to be comfortable wherever we are."

Then I felt a little selfish. I knew I wouldn't have to spend any extra money if he came here so I agreed to meet him about forty five minutes away from my house. "It won't cause any problems at all sweetheart. Let me clear things here first with my family and then we can get together later."

"I can't wait to see you Shanice. Seems like a lifetime ago."

"I'm sure it does, but we both know it wasn't. I'll call you when things are clear on my end."

I hung up the phone and tried to come up with as many excuses as possible to tell Frank why I would be away for the weekend. After calling Ron's name out a couple times in my dream, I knew Frank would be skeptical about me going out of town on a business trip.

Frank came home about six, tired and drenched from work. I met him at the door and gave him a big kiss. "Long day baby?" I asked.

"You wouldn't believe how those idiots are at work. Man sometimes I wish they would just think before doing things."

I gulped for a moment and asked, "What happened?"

"One of the guys was working on a software program for the site and erased the entire file. Now we have to work this weekend to fix the problem."

I took another gulp. "This weekend huh." I had to come up with something quick. "I was planning to meet with Chantal this weekend. She wanted me to come and get measured for the wedding."

"I don't know baby. I guess Justin and Miranda would have to watch Frankie until I get back home. It might be kind of late though. You sure it have to be this weekend?"

"Chantal called earlier and wanted all of the wedding party to meet with her. I can call and see if we can meet another time."

"No, don't do that. She's waited long enough for her happiness. I won't take this from her. You go. I'll take care of things here."

Frank tried not to show his concern about me being away after I called another man's name in my sleep.

"Thank you honey. I'm sure Chantal will be happy about this when I call her back."

I gave Chantal a call and informed her of what was happening. Chantal wasn't pleased that I would sneak out on Frank the way I was. "Against my better judgment Shanice, I'll go along with this, but you better be real careful about sneaking around. It can come back and bite you where it hurts."

"Don't worry Chantal. I'll be careful. I just want to see if this man is all he says he is."

"You barely know him Shanice. I hope you use protection."

"Look, it's not like I haven't screwed around before. I know what I'm doing. I just wanted to let you know where I will be just in case something goes wrong and Frank calls checking on me. Can I count on you?"

"You know you can. But listen girlfriend, a word of advice. When I was married to Kenyon and Jamal, I snuck around and had men coming out the ying yang. I was happy for a moment, but I woke up one day and thought about all the wrong I had done. It's not a pretty scene Shanice. Once you start having affairs, it's hard to stop."

"Yeah, I know that. But, I'm good at what I do. I haven't got caught yet. When I was with Rick, Frank wasn't the only man I messed around with. Shit, I can count on both hands the amount of men I've been with."

"You see, that's what I'm talking about. You have to give that shit up or it will bite your ass so hard you won't know what hit you."

"You mean…like Rick getting HIV from screwing around so much."

"Exactly. HIV and Aids are some serious diseases once you have them."

"I will be careful Chantal. I don't plan on contracting any diseases anytime soon."

"Okay. Can't say I didn't warn your greedy ass. I ain't never seen a woman that was so desperate to be fucked that she had to go two states over to get it. You have a wonderful man at home just waiting to give you everything your heart desires."

"Maybe that's the problem. Maybe I don't want everything from one man. Maybe, I want it every time I run into a sexy man."

"You see, that's non-sense. You're too old and smart for that kind of shit. You need to make up your mind before you end up on a situation like me. What if this man is some kind of rapist or murderer? You don't know. He might kill your stupid ass soon as he walks in the door."

"See Chantal. You're scaring me now. I'm just going away for a day. That's why I told you all the information just in case I turn up missing."

"You should be afraid Shanice. It's a dangerous world out there and I want my friend to be with me forever. But, if it will make you happy, I'll keep my mouth shut. Just be careful okay."

"I will. I'll call you when I get back."

CHAPTER 31

"Seeing Ron"

Two days later, I was packing my clothes getting ready for my rendezvous with Ron. I was nervous as hell. I didn't know what to expect or if he would show up. I knew what I was doing was dangerous, but I was so curious about Ron. He talked a lot of mess on the phone and I wanted him to put his money where his mouth was.

I left the house around five and drove to the Westin Hotel and Resorts in Charlotte. It was one of the most beautiful hotels I've ever seen. After I checked in, I took my bags to the room and just fell back on the king-sized bed. I stared around the room for a few minutes, got up, and freshened up for Ron.

Ron arrived around seven. His plane had gotten in a little late, but he called me to let me know that he still was coming. The closer he got to the Westin, the more nervous I got. When he called to say that he was in the parking lot, my body froze solid. I ran to the sink, wiped myself with a wet rag, and pulled my skirt back down.

Ron knocked on the door and I tried not to show that I had been standing there waiting for him. When I opened the door and saw him standing there, my insides started melting right away. *"Damn,"* I thought to myself. He was finer than I remembered.

He came in and greeted me with a soft kiss on the lips. I had worn my hair up in a ball, but when I saw him, I immediately let it down. I figured sooner or later, it was going to get messed up.

I lit a candle, turned on the CD player slipping in *We Both Deserve Each Other's Love* by Jeffrey Osbourne, and slowly walked towards Ron. I was wrong as hell being with this man, but at the time, I didn't care. I gave him a quick kiss on his lips and smiled heavily.

"Umm," he said asking me if I was certain this should be happening.

I smiled and told him it was my first time having an affair on Frank since we've been married and I was starting to enjoy myself already. "My body deserves the touch of another man," I said sliding one of my legs in between his.

"Listen," he said as he held me closely. "The magical touch Jeffrey Osbourne has with his words always seems to relax my body and make me wanna love a woman with all that I have. As much as I would like to have you right now, I think we should get to know a little bit about each other over dinner. We have plenty of time for romance.

He was so right. Here it was five minutes since the man had walked in the door and I was all over him. I sho' nuff was showing my horniness. "Okay," I replied with a sigh of relief. We went out and ate at Lone Star and returned. At that point, Ron was ready for me. He unbuttoned my shirt and slipped it over my head. He stared down at my chest and kissed me.

"I love your chest," he said as he continued to undress me.

"You do?" I responded wanting him to kiss me in other places.

Ron was great. The way he'd positioned my legs and gently slid himself inside of me showed the experience this man had in making passionate love. All men can't make love. Most of them just want to jump in and out as fast as they could to bust a nut and to hell with making a woman feeling good. Not Ron though. Ron did everything right from kissing my inner thighs to caressing my butt. From start to finish, Ron made love to me over and over again. I didn't think he would ever go down. He didn't take me by surprise though. He warned me ahead of time about being a real man and knowing how to make love to a woman all night. I didn't believe a man could keep a hard on for so long. Shit, Ron proved me wrong. He wasn't going down anytime soon until he was ready to stop making love to me.

"Damn," I said. "What a man!"

He smiled and said, "You didn't believe me did you sweetheart? I told you I could make love to you all night."

I was totally mesmerized by him. After a night of nothing but romance, we ended it the next morning by him waking me up with a complete hard on. By then, my legs were sore as hell. I didn't let on though. I wanted Ron to screw my brains out and he did.

We laid and talked for a while before we both had to head our separate ways. "I must go and shower now," he said smiling at me.

"One more time," I said. I could not let this man get away without giving it to me from behind. He turned me around and with every ounce of strength he had left, he tore my ass up. "Now we can get in the shower," I said staring into his sexy eyes.

"Okay, I like the water kinda cool," Ron replied.

"That's fine with me."

He stood under the running water until he got it at the right temperature. We only brought one washcloth into the shower with us so I took it from him and asked if I could bathe him. He was shocked by my question and said, "Sure baby. I'll just give you some room." He didn't know I was about to wash his feet and everything else in between. "I would have been finished with my shower by now," he said getting a little annoyed.

"I just wanna give my baby a good washing off from head to toe," I said going down on my knees. With soap covering his entire body and me on my knees, I reached up, grabbed a hold of him, and gently gave him a quick kiss where it counted most.

"Ooh," he said. "I wasn't expecting that."

"I know you weren't baby. It's just my special gift for you to take back home with you."

"I will treasure it," Ron said smiling at me.

Then Ron got out of the shower and left me high and dry. I thought he would return the favor and wash my body down as well. I guess he wasn't use to taking a shower with another woman. Maybe he was starting to feel a little guilty about the whole matter.

"I'll be out shortly," I said washing myself thoroughly. If ever there was a time that my dreams and fantasies came true, it sure was with Ron. I always wanted someone to love me the whole night through and wake up in the morning with extra dessert. I got exactly what I had dreamed of my entire life.

We got dressed and headed out for some breakfast. Ron brought me back to my car, fought off a bee that was hovering around us, gave me a kiss, told me that he loved me, and walked away.

The entire drive back, I tried to think of what I would tell Frank if he asked about my trip to Chantal's. I had lied to him and told him that I was going to Chantal's to get fitted for her wedding. I made sure that it would be late when I got back so he wouldn't get suspicious. I hated lying to my husband. I don't think I could ever do that again. I even had the nerve to pack my bags as though I was really going to meet with Chantal. The guilt seemed to be overpowering me. What a liar I turned out to be!

It had been a week since Ron and I had made love. To me, it was almost like Betty Wright's old hit song, *Tonight is the Night*. Ron was a very passionate man and had a lot of love to give.

I was in the kitchen preparing dinner and all I could think about was him. After I fixed dinner for Frankie, Justin, and Miranda, I went into my room to freshen up for a bit. I was tired as hell. That's when it hit me. I looked at the clock and realized that at that very moment a week ago, Ron and I was deep in each others arms. I still remember him walking into the hotel room wearing a pair of cream color khaki's, a dark polo style shirt, and a beautiful smile.

No sooner than I started to remember all of this, my mind snapped back into reality when my cell phone rang. I looked at the number seeing that it was Ron and headed straight for my secret closet just in case someone walked in on me. "Hello," I said waiting to hear his sexy voice.

"Hi sweetheart, I just wanted to give my baby a call and let her know that I was thinking about her."

Man, if this wasn't déjà vu', I don't know what was. "How did you know I was thinking about you at this very moment?" I asked out of curiosity.

"Well," he said. "I was doing so many things today and then I said to myself, *I haven't talked to my baby today.* So, I decided to give you a call."

"It's funny how that happened. I was just looking at the clock and said to myself, *this time last weekend my baby and I were wrapped in each others arms.*"

Ron chuckled for a bit. "You're right about that sweetheart. It was such a marvelous time we had together. Ummm," he commented. "We had a wonderful time especially when you asked me if you could kiss my lollipop."

"Yeah, it was so tasty," I said as I walked from the closet to my king size bed. I sure was hoping Frank or one of the kids didn't follow me to my bedroom.

"You do that so well," Ron said. "I think you're very tasty also."

I tried to change the subject since he had just called and I didn't want to start our conversation off sexually. "So, other than me on your mind, how was your day?"

"It was busy as hell baby. I had to do some things around the house since Isabel tore up our neighborhood. We didn't get it as bad as the people in Virginia from what I was told, but we did get it pretty damn bad."

I paused for a moment. "Sure wish I was there to help you out baby! We didn't get an ounce of rain or the winds in South Carolina."

"Then count yourself lucky sweetheart. Listen, I just wanted to give you a call and see how you were doing. I will call you back later on tonight and chat a little more."

"Okay baby. I will be looking forward to your call. I love you," I said.

"I love you too."

We hung up the phone and I headed back into the kitchen as though nothing had happened. Frank was heading my way and asked who was on the phone. I came up with a quick lie and said it was Chantal. I didn't like telling him lies like that. Frank is such a good man and I don't want his trust in me to fade.

I stood at the kitchen sink and filled it with water. I continued thinking about that night I spent with Ron and what happened after we came back from Lone Star.

As I continued to stand there washing dishes, Frank put his arms around me and whispered in my ear, "I wanna make love to you tonight."

What the hell was I supposed to do? All night long I was sitting here fantasizing about a man I was with the previous week and then my husband comes into the kitchen wanting to slip inside of me. I've never been one to turn Frank down.

"Sure honey," I said instantly. "Let me just finish with these dishes and I'll be right up. Where are the kids?" I asked suspiciously.

"They're in their beds and we are all alone."

"Then, I will definitely hurry up with these dishes," I said.

"The dishes can wait baby. I want you now." Frank said, being adamant about making love to me.

"They sure can. I didn't want to wash these dishes anyway," I replied with a quick lie.

We headed upstairs and all of my memories of Ron from the previous week vanished as Frank took control of my mind and body. I know it's something thinking about another man and then making love to your husband. But, the most important thing was I was in the arms of my husband and not giving my love to some stranger.

CHAPTER 32

"Southern Living"

A couple weeks had gone by since I last saw Ron. He had been on my mind constantly and I was about to go completely insane thinking about him. Everything was so peaceful around our two story brick home and I was lovin' the slow pace of southern living. Justin and Miranda came into the living room while I was sitting back lounging on my black leather chaise watching a rerun of The Cosby Show and sipping a tall glass of lemonade.

It was at that moment I realized how much they had grown up. They seldom spoke their father's name since he had hung himself in jail. I didn't do anything to try and entice their thoughts or try and bring back the memories of him. I'm sure I could have done better, but I figured since Frank was in their life, he'd pick up the pieces of fatherhood.

Justin had a football game that night and Miranda was cheerleading. It's a damn shame I'd never attended any of his games or watched Miranda cheer. I guess I wasn't the good momma I was supposed to be. My focus seemed to always be around Frankie and satisfying my own self. Besides, I couldn't see myself going to something so meaningless and boring as a football game without having someone by my side. Well—that was until I met Ron. Frank had to work extra hours to try and make up some time he'd taken off previously that week. So, I was left all by myself with Frankie at my side watching this football game that I had no interest in.

When we first arrived, the crowd was going wild over an announcement of some ex-pro football icon from many blue moons ago attending the game. It didn't make my body quiver at all until they flashed a picture of him across the screen and I almost wet my pants. It was Ron. I couldn't believe my eyes. The same man I had shared my insides with a couple weeks prior was in South Carolina attending the same game. I didn't make my presence known immediately because of the kids being there. I wanted so badly to run to him and be held. Was I that foolish to take such a risk? I gave Frankie a twenty and sent him over to the concession stand to get some drinks and a couple hot dogs. I told him that I saw an old friend and was going over to speak. I knew right away what my intentions were, but Frankie didn't know. He was growing up just like Justin and Miranda and in a few years, they would all be out of my house. At least, I hope it would be that way. I'm not trying to get rid of my kids early or anything, but it's time for me to start enjoying the rest of my life with Frank.

When Ron saw me, the seriousness in his face, turned to delight. "Well, hello sweetheart," he said smiling as he walked towards me.

"I didn't know that you would be here," I was shocked by him being there.

"My nephew is playing in the championship game tonight and he asked if I would come to his game. I never imagined you would be here."

"Did you bring any company with you?" I said hoping it was an absolute 'No.'

"Well," he replied, "if you're asking if I brought the wife, the answer is no."

"Yes," I said with a huge grin on my face. "I mean…not that she shouldn't be here, but I was hoping to have a little time with you." I muttered. "How long will you be in town?"

"I have a flight back to Baltimore tomorrow night, but I could delay it if you make it worth my time."

"Ooh," I said expressing the excitement in my face. "I think I can get away for a few hours or so."

"I'm staying at the Renaissance two miles down the road," Ron said.

"I'll call you when I get settled in," I said. "Justin is coming this way so I'd better make myself scarce. Love you baby!"

"I love you too," Ron said and walked away.

That night, I gave Ron a call from my room. I hid deep in my closet so that no one could hear my conversation. He informed me where to meet him and to be as discreet as I possibly could. I decided to wear something appealing, but not too revealing in case the kids got suspicious. Since Frank was away, I figured I could slip out and be back before he arrived home.

This time was no different with Ron. The man had it going on and he knew it. As usual, he wanted to be a gentleman and feed a sistah before he laid the hard loving on me. I didn't mind. Something told me not to eat anyway. When we came back, Ron said that he didn't have much time because he had to make an early flight. It seemed to work out fine for both of us because I knew there was no way in hell I could spend the entire night with him and Frank not get suspicious.

It was something about Ron's eyes that drove me totally out of my mind. The way he stared at me made me want to do nothing, but love him. It was as though he had me completely wrapped around his finger. He came over to me and gave me a long soft kiss and started to unbutton my shirt. At first, I felt a little uneasy knowing that Frank was in the same town and could have easily had me followed. But when Ron took my shirt off and looked into my eyes, I wanted him just as much as I wanted him the first time.

There didn't seem to be much of a conversation between us, just sex after sex. I lay flat on my back as he climbed on top of me. He eased himself inside of me smiling the whole while. My legs trembled at the thought of this man getting ready to love my thighs again. I really didn't think I could take anymore. I mean…this was round five and I was nearly out for the count. I looked at him thinking to myself, "Damn, where did he get so much energy from?" He was hard as a rock and was about to crack at any given moment.

"You're not tired, are you sweetheart?" He said grinning from ear to ear.

I gazed into his sweet brown eyes knowing that my thighs were sore as hell and was starting to bruise. "No," I replied lying through my teeth. "Bring it on!" My lips were saying one thing, but my mind was saying, please go down soon mister! It didn't though. All I could think was I only had a chance to see him every so often and I could endure the pain a little while longer.

I knew there would be repercussions after this because of this daring attempt to be with Ron. But come on now, a man like Ron come along every once in a lifetime and if I could get it from him and still have Frank, I'd try it again and again. We ended the night with a long wet kiss and said our goodbyes. In a way, I sort of wanted this to be the last time. I felt so guilty cheating on Frank like that.

Frank was already home when I arrived. He and the kids must have been downstairs at least I thought. I headed to the kitchen and picked up something to eat. I retired to the living room and was sitting on the lounge chair when Frank entered the room. His mind seemed to be far off in a distant land. I was completely relaxed at that point sipping on a tall glass of ice water, eating a bowl of dry Frosted Flakes, and watching Law and Order SVU. "Damn," I thought to myself. Frank's in another one of those I wanna talk to you moods.

The look in his eyes told me I'd better chew those Frosted Flakes and chew them fast. I started to get discouraged by his silence.

"Everything okay sweetheart?" I asked trying to break the ice.

He looked down upon me as to say, we only been married a few years and you… "Something's not right with your trip you took a few weeks ago, Shanice."

"Oh shit," I thought to, "he's gonna whip my black ass. "What do you mean honey?" Trying really hard to be as innocent looking as a baby making his final push of poop out of his system.

"Did you have a good time sweetheart?" He asked still keeping me in suspense.

"I sure did. A lot of people got recognized that night including me."

"You don't say Shanice!" Frank confirmed by a slip of paper in his hands. This came in the mail today and I usually don't open your mail. But the outside said Mr. and Mrs. Williams. Since I'm Mr. Williams I thought by right I could open it. To my surprise, it was receipt from the Holiday Inn in another state. I thought you said you went to a seminar here in town for a couple days.

Damn, I was completely busted. I had to find a quick lie and fast. "I know it looks bad Frank, but I don't know why that came here for me. I was at that meeting. I swear to you."

The look Frank gave me told me to duck fast. "Don't lie to me Shanice. Did you meet someone at a hotel or not? It's a simple answer, yes or no."

Was I going to be honest with my husband and let the cat out of the bag or was I going to keep my lie straight? "Frank if you don't believe me, you can call one of the girls that attended with me. They will vouch for me."

"Enough Shanice. You can't even look me in the eye without telling a lie. All this time, I thought I had found the woman of my dreams and you turned out just like Monique, a lying whore. Look where it got Monique! Six feet under!

"I am taking a trip to South America on Saturday. Have your things out of my house by the time I return," Frank said angrily.

I stood there with my eyes stretched to the extreme. "Frank, you can't mean that!" I whimpered hoping he'd tell me that he was just kidding or pulling my leg. I'd never seen Frank so distraught or saddened until this day. I really broke this man's heart this time.

"I mean it Shanice. I want you completely packed and out of my house.

"Frank, I won't do it. This is my house too," I pleaded. "I didn't mean to hurt you baby. I didn't lie to you about the meeting. I just chose not to go."

"Who is this man that you would risk your entire family for?" Frank asked demanding an explanation.

I could sense him softening a bit so I begged him to sit down and allow me to explain. He was hesitant at first and I don't blame him. Fortunately, he chose to hear me out. "His name is Ron Long. I met him on a flight on my way to Charleston while we were moving. He was really nice and ..."

Frank cut me short of saying all but he was great in bed. "How dare you Shanice?" He jumped from his seat angry as hell. "How dare you insult me like this in front of my kids?"

I tried to go after him to calm him down a bit, but he pushed me clear across the room. I tripped on the throw rug and stumbled to the floor. Frankie was standing at the top of the stairs.

"Mommy," he screamed out. Although it wasn't as drastic as I made it to be, I pretended to be hurt so that Frank would come to me. He watched my reaction for a minute or two then walked over towards me and Frankie. Frankie had already beat him there and was sympathizing with me.

"Are you okay Momma?" I could see the fear in his eyes as he looked over at Frank and rolled his eyes. "Why'd you do it Daddy? Why'd you hurt Momma like that?"

"I got angry for a second. I didn't mean to hurt her. I guess I'd better learn to calm down a little before I strike."

"I'm okay sweetie. Your father and I had a misunderstanding." I explained.

"Do we have to move Mommy?" He asked sadly.

Frank butted in. "I have to take a trip and I don't want you guys here alone. Your Momma has agreed to go and stay with your Auntie Chantal until I return."

I stared at Frank for a moment confused as ever. "We'll discuss this at a more appropriate time," Frank said as he left the room heading out the door. I knew I had ripped this man's heart into several pieces. And, unlike a jigsaw puzzle, the pieces weren't coming back together so easily.

We visited with Chantal for a couple days and then returned back to South Carolina. Although I had to decide to make every effort to make my marriage work with Frank, I couldn't get Ron out of my mind. It was as though I was addicted to this man.

"I have to do something with my time," I thought. I had entirely too much time on my hands to get sneaking around with Ron.

After seeing Ron one more time, we decided to call it quits. It broke my heart knowing I couldn't be with him again, but Frank and the kids were very important to me. Fortunately for me, Frank never found out about the other visit and I just kept pretending that I was so in love with him. Funny how you can work the mind when you're guilty as hell!

CHAPTER 33

"Hell's Pervert"

A few weeks after settling down in South Carolina, I decided to take a job at a local call center. I must have been a desperate individual because working in a call center was against my morals. This place was filled with freaks, gays, and lustful people. Chantal laughed at me when I told her where I was working. But unlike Chantal, I had to work to make a living. They made me attend three weeks of training and man I never knew how it felt to be in customer service until I became a Customer Service Representative myself. Our trainer was a very attractive Caucasian male. However, I believed in our African American culture and would never trade it for the likes of a white man.

The class seemed as though it would never end. But, when it did, all the chaos began to happen. I'll never forget the one time when I was working and the phone calls wouldn't let up. All I could think about was going home to be with my family. Day in and day out for about a week, the calls wouldn't stop.

My first paycheck was a shocker. I didn't know moving down south would be so depressing. I wanted to see if my paychecks would improve so I continued working for the call center. The shocker of my life came when I answered a call from a pervert. We had been taught how to handle such calls while in training, but nothing could ever prepare me for this one.

I picked up the phone with my usual greeting, "Thank you for calling the National Marketing Center. This is Shanice, how may I assist you today?" The voice on the other line was soft and very seductive. "Shanice," he said and then started to laugh. "Would you like to have a little phone sex with me?" I about lost my damn mind. I know my face turned pure red after that question.

I composed myself and with a straight face, I replied, "No, but I do thank you for calling the National Marketing Center. Have a great day!" As I was about to hang up, he said, "Then, would you like to suck my cock?" By that time, I was furious. The nerve of this asshole calling me to ask if I would suck his cock. It probably was all small and shit anyway. I figured a person like that either, didn't have a girlfriend in his life because he was too small and floated inside of her or he just had too much time on his hand and was jobless. After I picked myself back off the floor and came back to reality because of that senseless question, I said, "Well…you know…maybe a little phone sex with a pervert like yourself wouldn't be so bad after all." Knowing all along that I was getting ready to mess with his head.

"You would," he said not knowing what was getting ready to hit him.

"Sure," I said raring him up for a knockdown.

Judging by the sound of his voice, I could tell he was hispanic. "Can you open up your legs and describe what the inside of your vagina looks like?"

Oh he was fishing now! But again, I didn't allow him to get to me. "Well," I said, "It looks just like yours."

He was shocked to hear that I wasn't playing his little game anymore. "Listen, you slut! I know where to find you and I'll blow your ass away if you keeping fuckin' around with me."

I was a little frightened, but I chuckled and said, "And, then you'll miss all the fun of me blowing on your small limped penis."

"You messed up this time lady. I know your name and I'll find you."

I wasn't afraid anymore. "When you find me, I'll make sure to have my binoculars with me so I can see just how small you are."

"You slut," he said and then hung up the phone. Not sooner than I hung up with him, the lady sitting next to me received the same call. She was so frustrated that she ran to one of the managers and had them come and talk with him. The manager insisted that she didn't have to put up with the call. The next time he called, we were ready for him. They immediately put the phone on emergency and were able to record his call. The call came from a little place in South Carolina called Aiken. His voice was strong and powerful. He wanted desperately to talk to me, but Shakyra, one of the girls that had received the call, told him that there wasn't any Shanice working at the place. That only intimidated his integrity. "I know where you work," he insisted. "I will blow you and all those hoes in there away if you don't let me talk to her. Shakyra waved for Charena, one of the team managers seated nearby to come over. Shakyra was shaking like hell after talkin' to him.

"No need to worry about him," Charena said. "He calls all the time and make the same threats," she said with her lips curved slightly.

"But you didn't hear him this time, Charena." Shakyra said. "He was mad as hell. Shanice really pissed him off."

Charena told me to put my phone on meeting and come over to her cubicle. After I told her what the guy had said, she took me to an office where they made recordings of all the calls. She played the call back and my eyes stretched knowing that I was actually carrying on a conversation with him.

"You know the rules Shanice! This man made threats to kill you and now he is planning to come here and blow up the place."

"You don't believe him, do you Charena?" I asked.

"I don't know what to believe Shanice. Shakyra is scared as hell to leave this place. We have to make this right and fast."

Charena called an all hands meeting with her group and informed all the team managers to do likewise. I was starting to get scared myself. I mean, this man couldn't be serious about killing me. I called Frank on my cell phone and told him about the situation. He was still a little teed with me but told me to be careful. He just reassured me that his love for me was true.

The phone rang again. A girl by the name of Wendy Hart answered. "It's for Shanice." Charena looked at me and told me to go and get it. It was him again, but this time he was persistent.

"I'll give you another chance Shanice," he said bold but firmly.

"How may I assist you sir?" I asked trying to be calm. By now, the call was being recorded by our security people and the police had been informed.

"I want my phone sex Shanice," he demanded.

"No," I replied. "I won't let you coerce me into doing something against the rules.

"Well, I think you should suck my big fat cock then."

I was pissed. The nerve of him telling me what he thought I should do. "You must not have one since you have to call a place like this asking women to suck on you."

"I wanna nibble on your stuff," he replied.

Before I knew it, I slammed down the phone. It wasn't enough time to get a trace on him. His location had changed and he was heading our way. They just couldn't figure out how far away he was. I glanced over at Charena and said, "I think he's on his way. What do we do now?"

"Clear the place now!" Charena demanded.

I ran through the building yelling for everyone to leave there post and place there phones in meeting. The administrator came through and insisted that there was no threat. Charena didn't want to take any chances. By the time he arrived, the place had cleared half way. Most of the employees had gotten in their cars and trucks and got out of dodge. They made me hang around just in case this fool was pulling everyone's legs.

I heard some loud noises outside the lounge area and peeped around the corner. Man was I wrong about this guy! He was fine as hell. He was a tall Puerto Rican with a long braid in the back of his head. The guards were trying to calm him down, but he wanted to see me. They told him that no such person worked at the place. We couldn't understand how he knew where to find us.

Charena came out and called out his name. "Shaheed Rodiguez," she said.

He looked at her and said, "Yeah, I remember you. You that ho that fired me three months ago! Yeah," he said again shaking his head. "You thought I was an airhead and couldn't do my job. Guess what ho, I'm in control now."

He opened up his coat and was strapped with TNT. "Oh my God," one of the guards yelled out. "This man is nuts." He told him to stay calm and no one would get hurt. We knew no good would come from this and tried to sneak around the kitchen area. Unfortunately, there was only one way out. The back gate was locked and the security guard had the key.

"I want that ho that talked all that shit to me earlier." He was persistent and threatened to blow up the place if they didn't turn me over. I was scared as hell but they wouldn't give me up. You just don't know how relieved and thankful to God I was having them working on my side and not his. "You got three seconds and I'm going to blow this place to smithereens," he said.

"She's not here," Charena insisted.

"Then I guess I just have to prove my point." He pressed a button and everything went up into flames before we knew what hit us. There I lay covered in blood over a misconception that a pervert caller endured. So many people lay beside me and scattered throughout the hallway. In the open lounge which no longer existed, this caller that had harassed so many women was found shattered into severed pieces still holding a fried stem from the TNT in his hands.

Fire trucks, police cars, and ambulances arrived within minutes. By the time the news had spread, three different news helicopters were flashing images of the bodies and the site across the nation. People were starting to fear that it would be worse than 9-11 or the D.C. sniper case.

Moments later, Frank and kids had arrived. For him to relive the tragedy of Monique all over again in me took a toll on his faith. Every ounce of faith he had in God was starting to dissolve.

Frankie was torn when he saw me lying there in all that blood. I was unconscious and they didn't know if I was amongst the dead or not. Fortunately for me, I still had a little life in my soul. They took me to Roper Hospital North in Charleston. Most of the others were either there with me or carried to the U.S. Naval Hospital. In all, fifty five of us were injured, twenty eight were killed, and five others received minor wounds.

Charena and Shakyra were amongst the dead. I was still listed in critical condition. Frank and the kids stood by my side the entire time. They took me to surgery because I had a huge gash in my forehead. Somehow through all of this mess, Ron saw what happened while in Baltimore and kept calling my cell phone. When he was unable to reach me, he headed to Charleston. He knew where I worked and wanted to be with me.

He arrived at the hospital and told Frank he was an uncle on my father's side of the family. Frank hadn't met all my relatives yet so he believed him. He wanted to sit with them until I came out of recovery. When I saw his face, he gave me a look as to say, "Keep your mouth shut, everything was going to be okay."

I couldn't believe he had come so far to see me. "I was telling your husband that you should start introducing your relatives to him." Then he smiled at me and said, "I'm going to get some coffee." He asked if Frank wanted some, but his reply was "no."

It was a clever thing for him to say that he was my uncle because truly he was old enough to be my father. But looking at him, you couldn't tell. I was glad that Ron had showed up. It only let me know that he still loved me after we had broken things off. Frank and the kids decided to leave and go get something to eat. Ron hung around a bit longer. He came closer to my bed and said, "I thought I had lost my love. I had to come and see you."

I was flattered. "I'm not going anywhere anytime soon." Then I started to yawn. "I still love you Shanice," Ron blurted. "I would love to be with you again."

I didn't know what to think. I was so drugged from the medications that I told him to meet me around the corner in two minutes.

Ron smiled and said, "I think I'd better let you get some sleep. You're talking off the wall."

"I know what I'm saying. I was just seeing if you were paying attention." Then I was starting to fade again. "Please don't leave before getting with me again."

Ron smiled and said, "I will get some accommodations for the night. You sleep tight sweetheart." He loved calling me that. Said it was my pet peed for being beautiful.

When he came back the next day, Frank and the kids were in the room with me. I had just had my lunch—hospital food as usual. Frankie brought me a bag of chips and a cold strawberry soda. Ron was holding a large bouquet of flowers and said, "Good evening. Just wanted to stop by to see how my favorite niece was doing."

Frank looked over at me and said, "When did Shanice become your favorite niece?" I cut him off quickly.

"Uncle Phil, so glad you could come back to see me again."

"Actually," Ron said. "Shanice has been my favorite niece for as long as I could remember. We lost touch for a while. Guess I wasn't being a good uncle at the time. But, I'm here now."

Frank looked at me suspiciously, but didn't say a word. I'm sure he wondered how come I never mentioned him. I did a lot of wrong in my lifetime, but it wasn't on purpose. I guess I just loved men too much. It's one of the things I made clear to Frank when we first got together.

Ron told us he had to get back to Virginia and take care of business, but he would stay in touch with us for now on.

I was released from the hospital two days later and made contact with Ron. "Why?" I thought to myself. "Why can't I just be faithful to Frank and leave Ron alone?" If Frank ever had any doubts about me and Ron, this should have been the time. I wasn't sure if he knew that Ron was from Virginia, but it was a dead giveaway when I mentioned it.

*Special note about this particular chapter. Although this chapter is fictional, in real life, I had received an actual call from a pervert while working at a call center. Parts of the call were true until Shanice started playing with the callers head and he made an attempt to come and blow the place up. The call center where I used to work had received several bomb threats after I had spoken with this guy twice and it's one of the reasons I am know longer there. When the fear of this caller coming after me started to set in, I gave my two weeks resignation and began working for the government.

If you receive such a call, under no circumstances should you react the way I did. You never know what kind of person you are dealing with.

CHAPTER 34

"Flames"

It's been a month to the date since we've heard from Ron or Uncle Phil as he would call himself. Frank hadn't mentioned him and I didn't bring him up again. Just when I thought everything between Ron and I was clear, he called my cell phone and asked if I could meet him at a nearby hotel. I was hesitant, but wanted to be with him. "How can I come up with another lie?" I asked him.

"Have you ever heard the term cat and mouse?" He said. "We've been through a lot and when I want something badly, I continue to pursue it."

"Ron, we have to stop this. I love my husband and I love my family. I can't keep lying to them."

"Shanice, I don't want you to do anything that you don't want to do, but I promise you, I will make it the last time if you wish."

"Shit, shit, shit," I repeatedly said. "Can you give me some time to think this one over?"

"All the time you need, but I will only be here for briefly."

"What's briefly?" I asked.

"I'm leaving two days from now. If you don't show up, then I'll know that you couldn't make it or you decided that it would be the best thing for your situation."

"Ron, does your wife ever get suspicious about you leaving so much?" I asked.

"I'm sure she does, but I don't worry about that Shanice. My wife is ill and she doesn't want to have sex anymore. I don't blame her, but I can't put my life on hold. I love sex and with you, well—let's just say, you keep me youthful."

"I'm flattered Ron, but I still need an excuse to be with you again."

"Let me see," Ron said. "How often do you go shopping?"

"Not that often, but you have given me a great idea. I probably won't be able to stay any longer than three hours. Is that okay with you?"

"That's perfect. Call my cell phone. I'll be at the Clairton Suites."

"I'll call you soon."

I met up with Ron around eight. I was hoping this would be the last time being with him, but every time I see him or be around him, I change my mind. I wasn't sure what kind of hold Ron had on me, but I was hooked.

We were only in the room five minutes before Ron started to undress me. It seemed he was more anxious this time to be with me than ever. I was still in a lot of pain from the blast, but I decided I would get over it. After Ron got me completely undressed, I did likewise to him.

The inside of my legs trembled as Ron allowed himself to glide in and out of me. I thought to myself, "What passion could overtake the love this man holds within himself?" He continued his soft gentle thrusts as my legs tingled more. I knew I was about to reach my climax but wanted to hold back for him. I couldn't hold it much longer. The juices inside me burned like the fiery flames of a volcano about to erupt. "Come with me," I whispered gently in his ears. He looked down at me as the leopard filled comforter surrounded our bodies.

"In and out," he smiled and said, "Together it shall be!" Our passion flared hot as the mere eruption of our souls left our bodies.

That was the point when I distinguished real love making and the act of foolishness I tried to release when I was with Frank. I love making love with Frank. Yet, at times, it got a bit redundant. But Ron, on the other hand, was always gentle as a bird. I guess that's the difference between wisdom and just wanting to get a hold of some sweet stuff.

Ron wouldn't release my body just yet. He wanted more and so did I. It was almost like it was going to be our last chance for pleasure and Ron wanted to make sure that my body was well pleased before he let go.

I could feel the growth of him as he continued to lie on my overheated body. "Round two?" I asked feeling myself thickening from the explosion that had just taken place. One thing for sure, my body wasn't meant to have a man stuck inside for a long period of time. I was starting to rub raw in just that little time. Mind you—had I not came so quickly—I could have lasted all day. Soft strokes from Ron and my body filled with hot liquids as it had intended to be. He leaned down and kissed my pulsating breast as he stroked gently against my inner legs.

"Pop pop," he said and my body lit up like candles. I didn't know what the hell hit me.

"Have mercy!" I said and smiled at him.

"What's that sweetheart?" He asked looking at me as though he could my inner thoughts.

"Just thinking out loud baby!" I said not wanting him to ever quit. I wanted to feel like this with Frank, but somehow he never brought me to this level. I guess the true distinction between them both was obvious. If a man is used to getting it all the time, he'll just do what he needs to do to get his. But a man hungry for love and devotion will drive you to another level and each time would be better than the time before.

Ron stood up and opened his arms. As soon as I saw him standing there, I rushed into his arms for comfort. His eyes had a luring effect that I couldn't shake. I wanted him badly. I asked him to sit in the opened arm chair so that I could climb on top of him. He was hard as a rock and I planted myself neatly on top of it. My movements were slow at first, but the stiffness in his groin made me want more of him.

"Slow down," he whispered. But I couldn't. He drove me to full climax within minutes and I fell to his chest. Ron smiled knowing once again he had pleased his baby. "Play for me," he said. At first, it shocked the shit out of me to hear Ron say that.

"Okay," I whispered softly in his ears. I had a seductive look on my face. My lips were wet and so was my vagina. I lifted myself off him and got back onto the bed. I turned face down as though he was going to doggie style my ass from behind. Instead, he stood there and watched me as I put my index finger on top of my clitoris.

I started slow at first because my vagina was already sore from the intense love- making we had endured earlier. The heat immediately built and Ron was chanting, "Fuck yourself baby," over and over again. I tried to block out what he was saying and entice my mind with words of my own.

I knew he was enjoying himself as I lifted my ass high into the heated air. If only he would have joined in, it would have made it better. I was turning into a mother fuckin' freak around Ron. Who would have thought this middle aged sex machine would stimulate me so?

As though déjà vu' had struck suddenly, Ron bent down, spread my butt cheeks, and started eating away at my ass. I screamed loud when he bit the bottom of my vagina. "Oh my God!" I screamed again.

"Everything okay sweetheart?" He asked.

I came up with a quick lie and said, "Yes darling, it feels so damn good," I didn't want to let this wonderful man down.

He came up for a quick breather. He had this look on his face, then slid himself inside of me. My vagina was raw as hell. I just bit my tongue and continued to please him.

We must have made love all night long. Ron was by far the best man I've ever slept with. We ended the night at Outback Steakhouse. Then Ron took me back to the hotel. I made a promise not to have sex with Ron any more after this time. I had deceived Frank so much that it was pathetic.

When I arrived home, Frank was waiting at the door. He asked, "How was your trip to Chantal's house?" and I burst into tears. I had to come clean. I couldn't deceive him any longer. He seemed distraught about the situation. I told him I needed help and would check myself into counseling or a clinic if it would help save our marriage.

Frank must have felt sorry for me and finally came clean himself. When he told me that he had been seeing someone else and that she might be pregnant, I was livid. "All this time Frank," I screamed. "Damn you Frank! Damn you!" My heart dropped.

"Calm down Shanice! It's not like you didn't see it coming. I mean— the nights away, even the recent trips. Did you actually believe I was going on all those trips? I'm sure you had some kind of suspicions, right?"

"A dog will be a dog Frank," I continued to scream. Seems like I wasn't the only one getting' my groove on. My man was having just as much fun as I was. That goes beyond two can play the same game.

"You don't need to leave Shanice. I'm moving out. You can have the house and well—since Frankie likes to hang with you so much, you can have him too!"

Man, I was stunned! What the hell just happened? "You can't be serious Frank?"

"I am baby girl. It's just not going to happen with us."

Oh shit, I thought. Ron wasn't planning on leaving his wife. I wouldn't ask him to do such a thing anyways. "Can't we work this out Frank?"

He glanced at me and rubbed my forehead. His lips made a—so sad too bad type motion—then he said, "It's the best thing to do Shanice. Now you can have your cake and eat it too!"

"But Frank, that's not what I want. I want our family to stick together."

"Should've thought about that when you were out having fun. You had everything right in front of you. All you needed to do was take it. Don't chase something that don't want to be caught. Cut your losses and move on Shanice!"

I know he didn't just say, in so many words—fuck off. "Are you trying to tell me to go to hell in a gentle way Frank?"

"No baby, don't look so deep into my words. I'm leaving and that's all to it."

Then just like that, Frank walked out the door and out of my life. I just knew he would be right back.

Days went by and no word from him. I sat at the bottom of the stairs. Miranda came and sat with me. I hadn't told the kids yet in hopes Frank would return. Miranda asked me why I was crying. I didn't have the guts to tell my daughter that I screwed up and Frank wasn't coming back. Instead, I told her that I was still grieving over Rick's niece. I couldn't understand why someone with such a great future ahead of her would be snatched away like a thief in the night.

Miranda put her arms around me and shockingly said, "Momma, it's gonna be alright. I know Frank left you for another woman. He told me and Justin before you came home. You pushed him out there Momma. He told us about your rendezvous with another man."

"It wasn't like that Miranda," I tried denying the fact that it was true. "Ron happened upon me on day and I couldn't shake him loose."

"I guess grownups have love problems just like us teenagers."

I looked at my daughter curiously. I didn't need her telling me that she was involved with someone just as she was about to finish high school. "What does that mean Miranda?" I knew where she was heading but curious to see if she had been having sex.

"No Momma," she said. "I haven't had sexual relationships yet. But, I am very closely involved with someone."

I explained the mishaps and consequences that could follow if she wasn't careful. Miranda was no dummy though. She knew how to keep those sex craving piss tail boys out of her pants. On the other hand, I was a sex freak.

Miranda and I walked towards the kitchen and I noticed a picture of Frank and me hanging on the mantle. I shook my head and said, "I screwed up royally. Frank is such a good man."

We made it to the kitchen and fixed a couple of peanut butter and jelly sandwiches. For a brief moment, I felt like a kid again. Then we heard the door to the living room open and shut. I put Miranda behind me and walked slowly towards the living room. Frank was standing there half beaten and drunk as hell. He was barely gone a couple hours. I've never known Frank to get drunk and knew something had to happen.

"He tried to kill me," Frank said frantically. Miranda and I rushed to him. He was badly hurt.

"Who tried to kill you Frank?" Thinking to myself, "Let me get my hands on that son of bitch."

"Her husband," he replied. "I didn't even know she was married."

"Amazing how something seems too good to be true turns out to be not good for you after all," I remarked strongly looking at his wounded face. "Come sit in the living room and I'll clean you up."

"I don't deserve you Shanice. I'm so sorry baby," he replied.

For the first time, I felt remorseful. Miranda went upstairs to get a wash cloth and I grabbed some gauze pads from the linen closet to patch Frank up a bit.

"Look at us Frank!" I said hastily. Can we find love again?"

He gazed keenly into my eyes with a tear running down his cheek. Somebody kicked his ass pretty damn good. "I want that Shanice," he responded kneeling on one knee. "Let's start this love over and put our sins behind us. From now on, no more lies, sneaking around or skeletons in the closet."

Easy for him to say now that he didn't have anyone else in his life. As for me, I agreed to his terms knowing damn well Ron was no closer out of my life than the bruise over his left eye. "I'd like that Frank." Then I shook my head, smiled at him and walked him towards the stairwell.

CHAPTER 35

"Conspiracy"

Two hours later while Frank and I were lying in the bed, my phone rang. The caller ID let me know it was Ron calling. I paused and answered, "Hello Chantal," knowing it was no closer to being Chantal than me becoming a multi-millionnaire writing books.

"I need you baby," a very quiet spoken man appealed.

I sat up in the bed and said, "What's wrong?"

"My wife is very ill. She…." Then he burst into tears.

I told Frank this was a serious call and I needed to take it elsewhere. "It's Chantal and something seems wrong with her."

"Go ahead sweetheart. I'll be waiting for you."

"Thanks for understanding Frank. I'll be right back." As I walked away, I kept saying, un huh over and over again until I was no longer in sight.

"What happened to her baby? Is she going to make it?" I asked curiously. I always tried to show concern when it came to her because I knew it wasn't right sleeping with her husband. But I couldn't help myself when it came to Ron.

"I don't know," he replied. "She was fine. We were eating dinner and she said she couldn't breathe. I called 911 right away. I am following behind them in my car."

"Why didn't you ride with her?" I asked. "I mean—she might need to see your face to keep her alive."

"I panicked and jumped into my car. I knew I couldn't call you from the ambulance."

Frank yelled out, "Is everything okay Shanice?"

"Not really Frank," hoping he wouldn't come near the bathroom down the hallway. "Just a few more minutes."

"We're almost at the hospital. They're taking her to Sinai. Can you come and be with me? I'll pay for it."

Shit—how could I explain this one to Frank? I keep going back and forth to Baltimore. He's sure to get curious over this one. "I'll see what I can do. Keep me informed of her condition okay."

"I will sweetheart. I love you Shanice. Please try and come. I don't want to be alone."

I hung up the phone and told Frank that my girlfriend from my Mary Kay unit in Maryland was losing her father and wanted me to come there and be with her.

"I need you here. We need our time Shanice."

"I know we do but…"

He cut me short of saying that I wasn't going regardless. "Not this time Shanice. Our relationship needs to heal."

"But Frank—," he cut me off again.

"It's final Shanice."

Now this man had given up on us and walked out of my life. Then all of a sudden, he comes back telling me what I can and can not do. I gathered a blanket and went into the spare room.

"Shanice," he called out. "Shanice."

I closed the door and said, "Good night Frank." Then I heard a bang at the door. He must have kicked the door and walked away. I *69'd the phone and called Ron back. His phone kept ringing. I figured he must have made it to the hospital and turned the cell phone off. Minutes later, my phone rang again.

I sat up because the news was worse. "She's had a massive stroke and…" (he paused) "They don't think she's going to make it. Can you come baby?"

I wanted to tell him what he needed to hear, but all that came from my mouth was, "It's not appropriate baby. How can I explain it to Frank…my children?"

Ron took a deep breath. "I understand if you cannot get away. I wanted some company. Don't worry about it sweetheart! No harm intended. I should say goodnight then."

"Shit. Why did he put me in such an awkward situation?" I knew he would be hurt if I didn't come to him. I gathered my thoughts, but the complexity of my mind took me in another direction. "No wait baby!" I demanded. "You've been so kind and tender-hearted towards me. The least I could do is be with you in your time of need."

Ron relieved by my sudden change of mind said, "I'll send for you."

Now wait a minute! This man not only wanted me to be with him, but was paying for it as well. "You don't have…"

He cut me off suddenly with his keen authoritative voice. "You're sacrificing a lot to help me. The least I can do is pay for your trip."

Ron always told me that he was working in corporate America making six figures, but dayum did he always have to be so modest? "As you wish sweetheart," I said. I gathered some things and said, "I'll be there tomorrow morning."

Frank walked in the room as I was packing. I could tell he wasn't pleased about me taking another trip. He just threw his hands in the air and said, "I really don't like this Shanice. It better not be another one of your lies. I promise you, I'll leave if I find out it was something other than your friend needing you."

"I'm not lying this time Frank. It's the honest to God's truth." *God please forgive me for telling another lie,"* I thought to myself as I gave Frank a hug. "I really do appreciate you Frank. I'll never deceive you again."

"I just don't know Shanice," he said as he was leaving the room. "I'm sleeping in the spare room tonight."

"Damn, I just keep fucking up," I said out loud.

I got up the next morning and headed to the airport. When I arrived at BWI, Ron greeted me with a sweet smile and gave me a loving kiss. That was pretty damn bold if I had to say so myself. We had a late breakfast and Ron drove up to a house that made even Chantal's look like a homeless shelter. My mouth dropped as I looked at the mansion we were driving up to. *"This fuckers' filthy rich,"* I thought to myself.

"You like it sweetheart," he asked smiling back at me.

"Like," I replied. "Baby your house is beyond being da bomb!"

Ron squint his eyes. "da bomb?" He asked curiously.

"You know…got it goin' on… off the chain."

"You're too funny Shanice," he said as we walked into his big luxurious house. Ron had to literally close the bottom of my lips. There were statues, plaques, a room filled with oriental designs, and my favorite, the living room. His living room set had swayed back neck rest so your head didn't fall off the back of the couch while you rested. "I know it's nice baby. I worked long and hard for it to look like this."

Ron had two sets of stairs in his home. One led to the side of the house where overnight guests slept and then there was the one that led to his room. Ron had one side of a house to himself. There was a huge workout center adjacent to his bedroom door.

"Ron your house is fantastic. I would have never imagined it looked like this."

"I didn't want to tell you everything about me. Your interest in me might only be for my money." Then he chuckled and said, "I'm just kidding baby. Sit back, relax, and enjoy my house."

I had to think long and hard about this one. The last time I was with another man while his wife was in the hospital, she died. I couldn't bare that guilt anymore. "So when is your wife going to get out of the hospital?" I asked.

"We don't know. Her heart is not stable yet."

All I could think was—not again Lord. Please don't let that woman die. I felt like I was some type of bad luck queen or something. He took my bags to the guest room only because his son Deshon was staying there until his mother got well.

As we started up the stairwell, I said to him, "You really have a lovely house Ron." I found myself repeating my words over and over again.

He glanced at me and said, "You haven't seen the half of it sweetheart."

Things were definitely going well at this point until he took me upstairs to the side of the house where the guest room was located. The room he led me to was the most intriguing room I've seen in my entire life. The bed was canopied with burgundy drapes and armed soldiers stood in the corner of each wall. The room had a view that overlooked a rose petal garden leading to a small pond. My first instinct was to pack my damn bags and move in with Ron, but I knew he was married and so was I. I told him that I wanted to freshen up a bit and he went back across to the other side of his mansion. My mistake was forgetting his son was staying at his house at the same time and on the same side as me.

I thought we were alone in the house so I made myself comfortable by taking a shower and deciding to walk outside the room with just a night gown and a green sequin G-sting strapped between my legs. When I stepped outside the door, Deshon was going inside his room. I tried desperately to dash back into my quarters, but he followed me. He didn't know I was having an affair with his father and wanted to test the waters. I tried to explain that I was married with three kids, but that didn't seem to phase him one bit.

The thing about it was Ron wasn't going to let me be free in his mansion without getting a taste of me. I bargained with Deshon to leave me alone until later. Just as he was walking out Ron was stepping in.

"What the...?" Ron gasped." Deshon, what the hell are you doing in here son? You're a married man."

I still had on my see through nightie waiting for Ron to show up.

"I saw her in the hallway and wanted to chat a bit."

"I see," Ron said. "Couldn't you have waited until she put on something decent?" Ron gave me a disappointed look. He seemed a bit agitated with the way I was dressed around his son. I meant no harm by it. I was actually on my way to find him when Deshon caught me. "Tell her goodbye son. We don't want our guest to feel uncomfortable, do we son?"

Deshon waved at me and said, "I'll see you around. I didn't catch your name."

"Shanice," I said and focused my attention on Ron. "I do apologize for my appearance.

"My son's a nice person Shanice. I'm sorry he startled you."

"He seems like a very nice person Ron. You should be proud."

The next words that came from Ron's mouth kinda pissed me off. "Would you have given him some if I hadn't showed up?"

I was offended by such a question. "No sweetheart," I responded. "My heart belongs to you." Knowing that he thought because Deshon was much younger than I, he would have jumped at the opportunity to be with him. My days with momma boys were history.

"Can't say I believe that Shanice!" Ron said. "My son graduated with honors from Harvard you know. He's a big shot lawyer in Rhode Island." Then it dawned on me that we were actually having our first fight in over six months.

"What's not to believe Ron? I love you." Then I captured Ron's hand and said, "Just because you graduate from an Ivy League College doesn't make every woman trip over herself for you. My heart belongs to you Ron."

Ron changed the subject. "Gimme some sweet stuff baby!"

I didn't know what to think. A part of me wanted to, but the other part was still crushed. I lifted my nightie and showed off my G-string.

"Yeah," Ron yelled out. "That's what I'm talking about." Ron got over my appearance around Deshon fast. He didn't seem to care about Deshon seeing me in my nightie. We made passionate sensual love all night. When we had finished, Ron lay on top of me until he fell asleep. Thank God he wasn't a heavy man.

The next morning Ron's housekeeper had breakfast lined across the counter. I stuffed my belly with grits, eggs, bacon, and a slice of bagel. Ron didn't each much. He said he had to run an errand and would return. I wanted to go too, but he insisted I stay and keep the bed warm.

Deshon came from his room wearing a pair of long pajama pants and a blue muscle shirt. Damn he was fine! I usually don't dig momma's boys, but Deshon was an easy catch. I mentioned that I would be up in the guest room if he needed me. I walked the spiral stairs and noticed I was being followed. Hurrying to the room, Deshon caught up with me short of me closing the door.

"Ms. Shanice, can I have a moment of your time?"

He was laying out his strategy and dividing the cost all at once. "Just one moment," I said. "I don't want your father thinking I'm some kind of whore or something like that."

"I'll be brief. You know you're a sexy woman to be only thirty five."

He was fishin' now. I caught a hold of his game earlier, but fell right into his trap. "Closer to forty five," I replied.

"You look tensed. I know you can use one of my special award winning back rubs."

Good thing I had changed my clothes. "It shouldn't hurt anything," I responded.

"Great! Can you lie downLye on your stomach for me."

I did like an idiot. "No freaky business Deshon."

"Scouts honor," he replied smiling down at me.

He sat at the bottom of my butt, grabbed some oil from the nightstand drawer as though he had done this before, and pressed firmly on my back. I could feel him as he leaned forward. He was starting to get an erection as he rubbed my back.

"Shit shit shit," I said trying to turn over. Deshon was placing me in a very indignant situation. My reaction was compulsive and I just wanted him to stop. I wasn't comfortable at all.

"Relax, I don't plan to hurt you."

"I think you should end this now." I replied. "Your father will be home shortly."

I heard the doorknob turn and Ron was standing in the doorway.

"Told you she'd let me get next to her daddy."

That bastard set me up big time. "What? You followed me up to this room. You were not invited in here."

Ron was highly disappointed in me. I let him down. It was innocent though. I didn't know his son would come on to me. Ron turned and walked out the door. I saw him dialing on his Motorola T720 cell phone and I didn't think anything of it.

"Yeah, my name is Ron. I need to see you immediately." I wasn't sure who he had called and didn't ask questions.

He came back to the room and said to me, "You have to leave now. I'll make sure you are well compensated for your troubles."

"There's no trouble Ron. Nothing happened. Your son brought this on."

"Enough Shanice. I asked you to come and help me in my time of trouble. My son knew you were coming. It was only a test and you failed horribly sweetheart. Please gather your things and I'll take you to the airport."

Deshon breezed by me. "Pops don't blame her. She's cool. She wouldn't let me touch her anywhere, but her back."

"You said she let you get it."

"No, I didn't say it like that. I was just jivin' you dad. She straight. She's a true friend of yours."

"I just don't want her ruining your marriage to Janeesha."

"You don't have to worry about that Ron. My girlfriend lives about twenty minutes from here. Please take me to her."

"No sweetheart, you can stay here."

"I wanna go Ron. I thought you knew me better than that."

Deshon left the room. He turned around and said, "You have to trust someone sometime daddy."

CHAPTER 36

"Chantal, Shanice, and Dominique?"

The phone rang as we were talking. Ron answered and then said, "Oh my God no!" I could tell by the conversation it wasn't good. Ron said, "Thank you, I'll be right over." Then he started to yell to Deshon to come back into the room.

"Sit down son," he said sadly.

"What is it dad?" Deshon thought it had something to do with Shanice and the misunderstanding they'd had before.

He looked at Deshon and then burst into tears. "Your mother is gone son."

Deshon paused and jumped up. "We should have been there daddy."

"I know and I feel really bad that we weren't. She would have wanted it this way."

I went over to Ron and asked, "Is there anything I can do for you and your son Deshon?"

He looked at me and smiled. Then he said, "No sweetheart. I've already imposed upon you too much."

"I would like to go with you Ron if it's okay," I responded.

"It's better if you didn't, but I appreciate your offer." Then he took me over to Chantal's and said he would be back to get me.

When I arrived at Chantal's, I was extremely happy and torn at the same time. We embraced and she invited me in. Girlfriend was getting ready

211

for her big day with Dominique. No one was home except her. We went through the foyer and straight to the kitchen.

"What's wrong Shanice?" She asked.

I didn't want her to know that I had seen Ron again after I made her a promise. It was obvious that something was bugging me though. We sat down and I began to spill the beans. As we sat in her huge living room sipping on our favorite drinks—French Mocha cappuccinos, I asked her not to judge me. I had on a pair of blue sweats and a long pull over jersey and Chantal was wearing a pair of black leggings and a long green sweater. We sat directly across from each other giggling about the old times and talking about how men took advantage of our kindness.

The more we talked, the more I knew I had missed my best friend. When Chantal asked about Ron, my heart fluttered thinking about the many times we had gotten together and I was finally going to leave this man alone. I tried to be discreet, but she could tell that I was hiding something. Most of all, I didn't want her to think badly of me because Frank was such a nice person.

"Gurl, I still think about the very first time we met on that plane and how we sat and talked about sugar sandwiches and Krispy Kreme Donuts."

"Have you at least left the man alone yet?" Chantal asked.

I didn't know whether to tell her the truth or to tell my best friend the biggest lie ever. "Frankly," I thought hard before answering her directly. "Ron thought we should cool it for a while."

"What? You're finally coming to realization that this man is married and you can not have him." Chantal said.

"It wasn't like that," I said dropping my head in shame. "Ron asked me to come to his house this past weekend. His wife had gotten ill and he didn't want to be in the house alone."

"Tell me you didn't go over to another woman's house and stay there Shanice. Please tell me you didn't do something so stupid."

"Yes Chantal. Ron's son was there also which made matters worse."

"You went there knowing that his son would be there?" Chantal asked furiously.

"Come on now! Give me more credit than that. When I got there, Ron introduced me as one of his wife's friends from her sorority group in Atlanta. He offered me a place to stay for the night and I took the bait."

"Bait, what bait Shanice?"

"They set me up. Ron had planned to come to the room where I was staying for that night. But, when I got ready to go to his room for a quick sneak, his son Deshon was walking in from the club. He saw me in one of my teddies. I didn't even know the man was there. I was embarrassed as hell standing there like that in his mother's house."

Ron walked up about that time and said, "Mrs. Williams, I see you have met my son."

I was stunned. His son was fine as hell. "This is your son." I replied.

"Yep. My one and only."

I felt invaded having the father and son watching over me like I was a piece of chicken waiting to be devoured. But then again, I wasn't wearing a bra and my chest was hanging slightly out."

"I can not believe you were walking in that woman's house like that. I thought you were better than that Shanice."

"I am. I had gotten myself together since I've been with Frank. But, Ron just brought out a new kind of freak in me."

"What about Frank? Does he know about Ron?"

"Yeah, he found out when I was supposed to go to that Mary Kay conference in Charlotte, but I went in another direction. Somehow, the stupid hotel sent me a confirmation from our stay in a hotel."

"You slipped up bad that time girlfriend," Chantal said.

"Damn sure did! Now, Frank doesn't trust one word I say. And to top it off, Ron walked in on his son giving me a back rub. Blew my cover big time!"

"How in the world did that happen, Shanice?"

"Ron said he was going back to his room so I thought our little meeting for the night wasn't going to take place. As soon as Ron was out of sight, I heard a knock at my door. Thinking it was Ron, I ran to the door only to find Deshon. He invited himself in and asked if he could rub my back."

"You didn't fall for that one did you?"

"Sure did."

"Girl, I thought you knew better."

"So did I. As soon as Deshon sat on the bottom of my back to rub me down, Ron walked in the room. Deshon immediately said, "Told you you couldn't trust her dad." He still was unaware that Ron and I had a thing going on. He thought I was going to try something on Ron or take advantage of his kindness.

"Oh Shanice! I know you were hurt girlfriend."

"That's not the half of it. Ron made Deshon get out of the room and told me to get my things and he would take me back to the airport. I begged and pleaded with him, but he was too upset to listen. I asked him to bring me over here instead."

I fixed my face into a semi smirk and Chantal walked over to me. She lifted my head and told me that I had nothing to be ashamed of. I knew that

I did because I not only let myself down, but Frank as well. I mean—how was I to explain this one to Frank?"

"Are you going to tell him?" Chantal inquired.

"I don't know," I responded.

Then Chantal gave me a long hug as tears developed in my eyes. She pulled back from me slightly and wiped away my tears. "Are you okay girlfriend?"

"Not quite." Then I burst into a sudden cry.

Chantal kept saying, "Please don't cry Shanice. It's going to be okay. I promise."

"I've ruined everything Chantal. I have such a loving husband and caring kids. How did this happen?"

"I don't know girlfriend. But, you'll make it through."

What happened next through me for a moment! Chantal lifted my head again and kissed me. I was shocked. She would never let herself that close to me before, but this was personal. I broke from her and said, "Chantal?"

Then, as if by a stroke of courage passing through her heart, Chantal kissed me again. She could feel my pain and wanted me to know that she cared about me. *"Oh my God,"* I thought. Chantal didn't just kiss me again. It wasn't a smack on the cheek or the lips, but a strong kiss with her tongue. I always wanted to know how it felt to be with my friend and now it seemed I was going to get my opportunity.

(Chantal)

When Shanice came in my house and I saw how torn, distraught, and upset she was, my first instinct was that someone had fucked her over. She was fucked over alright by that damn Ron person. All I could do was console her, but a part of me wanted her, not for any particular reason at all, I just wanted my best friend to know that I loved her and I would always be there for her. It had been ages since I had sexual encounters with a woman. There I was, reverting back to my first time with Michelle and Keisha. We were girls then, but now that I was a woman; curiosity was getting the best of me. It's my belief that when something traumatic happen to you as a kid, you either "A" take it to another level and become gay, lesbian or bisexual or "B" try your best to cover it up and let it get the best of you. Seeing my best friend torn the way she was only meant that she allowed people like Ron to fuck her over and I wasn't having it.

I decided to go against the odds knowing we were alone in my house. I always wanted to see how it felt to be with Shanice. I mean—the woman was drop dead gorgeous two times over. When I held her in my arms, feeling her breast pressed all up against mine and shit, my panties got soaked. It was at that point I finally accepted that I was a bisexual. I didn't need a damn therapist looking into my past like most people trying to find some traumatic shit that happened umpteen years ago. I already knew. Hell, I knew that shit when I was in High School, but wouldn't accept it. If those girls knew every time they took their clothes off I was catching a glimpse, they would have opened up a can of whip ass on me. Of course, I never acted on it until I met Terrice. We really didn't go all the way, but got close several times. I guess her looking like a man and shit threw me way in left field. But Shanice, shit—she had it going on with those big firm ass tits and luscious ass. I don't even know why I felt such an attraction since I was getting married to Dominique soon. Guess I was just reverting back to the little girl that had her virginity ripped away at ten. It's sad to say that sometimes being in love is not all what it's cut out to be. You can love someone with all your heart, but still have the desire to be with someone else.

As I held Shanice closer, I could tell she felt something too. Maybe we both needed a little piece of mind, but we really didn't know how to break the ice. I took charge though. If I was going to be with a woman, it would be on my terms.

(Shanice)

Chantal lifted my jersey and pulled my bra upward. "I always wanted to see your chest," I remember hearing her say.

"You did," I replied.

She seemed fascinated by my nipples and the thickness of my breast. I closed my eyes and went along with her. Somehow, I knew it was right and the right moment for us. Fate must have brought us back together this last time. Since she was a bit taller and older than me, I let her take charge. We were both in pretty good shape and for her to be close to fifty, she wasn't such a bad catch.

Man, Chantal had me steaming. Then she asked, "Do you want to go further?"

I didn't know how to answer that one so I said, "I'll follow your lead." We looked at each other and burst into laughter.

"You didn't think I was serious did you Shanice?"

Then my heart softened and I said, "Nah, just wanted to see how far you would go before you called it off."

"You're too good of a friend for us to do something as ridiculous as that Shanice."

"You are too. But aren't you at least curious about it Chantal."

Now another cans of worms were about to stir up. "I've thought about you a thousand times and wondered about how we would be together" and then I told myself, "Shanice would never fall for something so foolish."

"You don't know that. I've been around the block once or twice with women before," I said expressing myself in a liberal manner.

"What about our men Shanice? Dominique and Frank would be devastated if they knew we did something crazy like that."

"Frank would be thrilled to death. He expressed himself about you not allowing me to get with you some years ago."

"Girlfriend, that was some years ago. You're my best friend Shanice. I don't want to ruin our friendship behind a one night stand."

"I pondered the thought of knowing that I could have had you and let you go again."

"You're serious aren't you Shanice?"

Then I lifted Chantal's sweater and unfastened her bra. Chantal dropped her eyes and thought about Keisha when she first saw her breast and how disgusted she was. But this was different because she was a grown woman now and could make her own decisions without someone pressuring her.

"Let's try it and see if we like it before you knock it okay," I replied a little bushy eyed.

"With you, I think I'll give it a whirl." Then Chantal smiled and we kissed each other on the lips. It was quite different kissing a woman after all this time, but Chantal just closed her eyes and went with the flow. We both simultaneously started to fall back on the bed and rolled over.

We grabbed at the comforter and pulled the sheets back. I was appalled that we were actually getting ready to bump each others Kitty Kats. We were both wet and well experienced in the field of love making. However, I believe I had more talent than Chantal. She might be older, but I believe I have been around the block more than she'd ever imagine.

I held her for a while and a knock came to the door. We looked at each other and then the doorknob turned. *"Oh shit,"* I thought. If Montel was at the door, we were going to look like fools lying in the bed together.

It was Dominique. He walked in and seeing us together, he dropped his mouth so hard that we had to scrap it off the floor. "What the hell?" He said and then came towards the bed. Ironic as it may have been, Dominique asked, "Can I join in on the fun?"

We looked at each other and burst into laughter. "I don't share Dominique. You know me better than that." Chantal grimaced.

"Nah, no threesomes for me either. Chantal and I was just lying her reminiscing about the past."

"And I bet it was a damn good one too," Dominique said smiling at me. "You ladies sure you don't wanna see how it would be?"

"I'm positive," Chantal replied. "Why would you want to be with me and Shanice anyway?"

"I know you women have a past and this would be your final opportunity to live it out before we got hooked. Once we are hooked, Chantal's all mine."

I looked at Chantal for a moment, made somewhat of a smirk, and said, "Don't hurt to try! I won't tell if you don't."

"Yeah, but can we trust Dominique not to spill the beans?" Chantal replied.

"Now you know me better than that baby! Tell you what, I'll watch you and Shanice go at it and then if you like, I'll join in."

Chantal looked at me and then I said, "Just this one time. But, you can't sleep with my girl."

"That's fine by me," I replied.

(Chantal)

We all got butt naked and I watched Dominique at first to see how he would react seeing Shanice without any clothes on. His reaction never changed and that let me know that he still thought the world of me. I commenced to touching Shanice's breast knowing how it felt years ago touching Michelle and Keisha. It was quite different this time because I was with my girl and I was a grown woman.

I leaned down and put Shanice's right breast in my mouth and then Dominique came over to me from behind. I guess he couldn't stand watching his woman kissing another woman that way. He squatted down and started to kiss my butt cheeks. I was hot and wasn't trying to cool down anytime soon. Shanice opened her legs and I inserted two of my fingers inside. Dominique stood back up and inserted himself inside of me. I started to moan and we had a wild orgy going on in Chantal's house.

I could feel the moisture of Shanice's vagina all over my fingers and then I removed them. I looked her in the eyes, she smiled, and then I started to kiss her lips. I had never enjoyed myself so much until this day. We were damn near fifty and having the time of our lives. The mood was steaming and then the freaking doorbell rang. We stopped right in our tracks and put our clothes on fast.

(Shanice)

Ron was standing at the door. He came back sooner than I expected him. I had to introduce him to my girl and Dominique. I felt guiltier than ever at this point. Our faces were flushed. Ron looked at me and then he said, "You're not cheatin' on me are you Shanice?"

Oh shit! He busted us big time. "No Ron," I lied quickly. "This is my girl Chantal and her soon to be fiancée Dominique. We were wrestling around on the carpet. It's been a while since I've seen them."

He asked if he could speak to me for a moment and we went outside to talk. "I know what sex smell like Shanice and I interrupted something major just then."

"You're saying that I'm lying Ron?" I responded.

"No, I'm just saying that you're not telling me the truth. Remember, I've been around for a while. I know certain smells when I smell them."

"Too bad you can never trust me Ron. I think you should take me to the airport after I clean myself up."

Ron thought for a moment. Then, he said, "Sweetheart, my wife just died. I'm not thinking clearly. Forgive me please."

What was I to do? I came here to console this man and now I've cheated and lied to him. "I'm sorry baby. I know you're under a lot of stress right now. Is there anything I could do to help out?"

"Come back to my place with me," he sighed.

"Your son is there Ron. Is that wise?"

"He went back to his house to be with his family. I'm all alone. No one will bother us. I'll park the car in the garage so no one will know that I'm home. I can't be alone Shanice."

I didn't know what to tell him. I still had another day or so before I was expected back in South Carolina. Frank was getting a little agitated with me being gone. Although Frankie, Miranda and Justin were old enough to take care of themselves, I felt bad leaving Frank there thinking I was at one of my girlfriend's house. I decided to go with him and explained the situation to Chantal and Dominique. Chantal whispered in my ear, "It was fun wasn't it girlfriend."

I smiled back and said, "Damn sure was." Then I gave Dominique a hug and told them that I would see them in a couple weeks for the wedding. Although Dominique interrupted what was supposed to be a woman thing, a part of me was grateful that the ordeal didn't go down as plan. Chantal's my girl and all, but for two grown ass women (one married, cheating, and hurt) and the other about to get married and bisexual, bumping coochies was out of the question. It was much nicer the way it all played out with Dominique intervening when he did.

Ron wanted to get some dinner so we stopped by Ryan's steak house and had some grub. I didn't want to fill up because I knew Ron would probably want a little bit. I was exactly right. As soon as we got back, Ron picked me up and took me upstairs. After we reached the room I had been staying in, Ron turned out all the lights except the one from the bathroom so that we could see.

"I don't want anyone to see us up here," he said.

When Ron took my underwear off, they were soiled from Chantal's fingers being in my cat. "You're awfully wet sweetheart," he said looking at me curiously.

"Must have come from all that wrestling me, Chantal and Dominique was doing."

"Oh," he replied and continued to undress me. Ron was no dummy. He knew something was up, but he still wanted to be with me.

We made mad passionate love over and over again until Ron fell asleep. He had a slight snore and then a sudden cry. I could tell he was still asleep and I didn't want to awake him. *"Poor man,"* I thought. *"Now that he's lost his wife, what will he do?"*

It was hard for me to fall asleep right away. I kept thinking about me, Chantal and Dominique. That was freaky as hell, but I enjoyed it tremendously. If only we could have continued.

Morning came and I got up and fixed Ron a big breakfast. He wasn't that hungry. He ate as much as he could and said, "I have to get a lot of things straight today. Can you hang around and greet the guest for me?"

Now that was odd. I didn't know these people, but when they came in, I introduced myself as Ron's cousin. He was fine with that except for when Deshon came over and saw that I was still in his mother's house. It didn't take long for him to put two and two together.

He pulled me off into the kitchen and asked me point blank if I was sleeping with his father.

I looked at him and said, "Your father is old enough to be my father. I don't think so. We are just really good friends."

I don't think he bought it, but went along with it. I couldn't wait for Ron to get back so that I could clue him in on what Deshon was suspecting.

I gave him a call on his cell phone and told him about it. He said, "Wait until I come home and I'll explain everything to you."

Apparently, it wasn't Ron that had all the money. His job tied him over pretty well, but his wife was an heiress and he stood to inherit a few million dollars and some property. I understood at that point. Deshon was getting his also, but he wanted to make sure that his daddy didn't do his mother in for the inheritance.

Ron came back and explained that his wife had married a high priest over in Africa a year or so before they got married. Soon after they were married, he was court- martial and never seen again. Word got out that he was beheaded for perjury. She had to wait several months before she inherited her fortunes. His royalties were tied up before she could get a hold of them.

She and Ron met a couple years later while Ron was on his way to work. He saw her at a traffic light and asked her to pull over. When she stepped out of her car, she was hit by another car and Ron ran to her rescue. It was a slight fracture in her ribs, but she made it. They were married after a year and had been married for the past twenty five plus years.

Then it all made sense. I told Ron I had to make a call and would return shortly. I called and spoke with Frank and the kids and told them I would be home soon. I returned back to Ron and his guest. So many people filled that room. I offered to make desserts and get drinks. Ron was delighted and said "yes".

CHAPTER 37

"Your Wife is Cheating on Us"

When I got home, I saw a strange car parked in my driveway. My first instinct was some woman had moved in on my territory while I was whorin' around with Ron. I rushed through my pathway rowed with two rose bushes and a flock of mulberry bushes on the left side of me. I stuck the key in the keyhole and to my surprise Ron was standing in my living room holding a conversation with Frank. *Oh shit!* I thought not knowing what Ron could have told him. "Good evening honey. Who's your friend?" I asked trying desperately to pretend I didn't know him.

"Baby we need to talk," Frank replied with somebody-spit-in-my-face kinda look.

"I just got home sweetheart. It's been a very trying day," I replied trying to ease the pressure that was built up in the room.

Ron was standing in the mist with a disappointed look upon his face. "Hello again sweetheart."

I played him off and asked, "Do you know me?" Shit I'd try anything to keep Frank from wanting to kick me out flat on my ass.

"All too well," he replied. "Don't you remember last night and the night before? Even I couldn't forget them."

"Ugh...Ugh..." I couldn't do nothing, but stutter. I gave him a startled— you son of a bitch back stabbing bastard look. "Vaguely," I finally replied.

"I guess I have to since you brought it to my attention." Then I came up with something fast. "Didn't I see you in Maryland at my friend's house?"

Frank glanced at me with tears in his eyes and said, "Why are you cheatin' on me again Shanice?"

I didn't know how to answer that question so I turned to Ron and said, "What made you tell him that?"

Then Ron dropped a few tears and replied, "You baby. I need you in my life. I know you did something wrong with your friends, but I'm willing to let that go if you give me another chance."

Frank, stunned by Ron's inappropriate behavior of begging his wife in his own house said, "Wait one damn minute! I don't give a damn how old you are. Nigga, I will kill. You know that? Coming up in my damn house talkin' bout' you need my wife. I've put up with enough of this shit already."

I turned to Ron again and screamed, "I can't believe you told Frank on me. You're a stupid asshole."

"You cheated on me Shanice. You hurt me and embarrassed me in front of my son. You don't do that to people you say you love."

Frank looked at me as though he was going to rip my head off.

"You lied to me again Shanice. You were with another man?"

"Don't blame her," Ron said. "I lost my wife about a week ago and Shanice came to help me out. She ended up half naked in front of my son and doing something with her girlfriend and her fiancé."

I stood hopeless with my bags still dangling from my armpits and my mouth wide enough to catch a fly. "I'm so sorry Frank. He really needed me."

"Go to hell Shanice. Take this tramp off my hands before I kill the both of you. I can't believe you chose this old ass man over me."

"Frank please!" I begged. "Give me a chance to explain."

Ron shook his head and said, "Don't you think you've done enough sweetheart?"

"I don't want to be with you Ron. I want my family back."

Frank turned to me, arched his shoulders back, and said, "You made your bed. Now sleep in it. You and this old timer need to get the hell out of my house before I get my gun."

"Let's go Shanice. I have a big mansion waiting on you. My mission here is accomplished."

"Accomplished?" I grabbed Ron's face and spat on him. "Damn you Ron! You ruined my life. My life was fine until you came along. Why did you have to tell Frank on me?"

Ron's next words were tough to swallow. "Why did you have to cheat on us?"

"I didn't cheat on you. Chantal, Dominique, and I were wrestling on the carpet when you showed up."

"Funny how you see things that way when I saw them clearly from the window. I guess my son was a convenience to toy around with also?"

Man, I was crying like hell. Frank and Ron were crying louder than me. I ran upstairs with my bags in hand. I could hear Frank and Ron going at it. I barricaded myself in my room, but soon heard footsteps coming towards the door. "Mommy," I heard a soft weary, little voice say.

"Miranda sweetheart," I said trying to wipe my eyes dry.

"Yes Mommy. Please open the door."

I rose from the bed and stumbled across the floor. Frank had left a shoe in the middle of the floor and I stubbed my toe. "Damnit," I screamed.

"Everything okay Momma?" Miranda asked as I opened the door.

"Everything is fine baby. No need to get upset."

"Who's that man downstairs arguing with Daddy Frank?"

I had to think about my answer carefully. "He's a good friend of mine."

"Daddy said you had an affair with him."

"He told you that?" I responded hastily.

"No ma'am. I overheard them yelling and the man told Daddy that his wife was cheatin' on them."

I about flipped my lid when she told me that. "It's not like that at all sweetie. He is someone I worked with in Maryland. I had to go there because one of my friends mother got really sick. I ran into him at Auntie Chantal's house. He got angry because I wouldn't go home with him."

"Momma, I appreciate you trying to protect me, but I'm not a little girl anymore. I can take it."

I grabbed her by her head and started playing with her hair. "You sure are a big girl Miranda. But some things are better left unsaid." I knew she would figure it out, but one thing for sure, my baby loved me.

After Miranda left out of my room, I was compelled to write Frank a letter requesting his forgiveness. I knew he couldn't quite forgive me of all my wrongdoings, but if anything was obvious, it was the mere fact that I loved my husband and would do anything to win his love back. I started my letter off the usual way, softening him up a bit.

Dear Frank,

Honey, I know things have been bad between us lately, but I need you to know that I never intended to hurt you or *our* family. I don't know how it happened or where it first began. All I know is that I was wrong trying to love two men at once. What satisfaction did I receive? A lifetime of hurt and confusion for our family. I guess it all started with Rick and Monique. They say what goes around comes around—once a cheat, always a cheat. It was down right preposterous for me to think that I could get away with having someone on the side. But, it wasn't all my doing Frank. You did your dirt, but I was made the villain. You see Frank. I accepted that you had another family in another country because I knew they couldn't harm us. But you took it to the limit with me and Ron. Yes, I rubbed him in your face, but it wasn't on purpose. All I ever wanted was for you to love me and you did a damn good job at that. But part of me wanted more. I wanted to feel like I was invincible and had complete control of my thoughts and feelings. Unfortunately Frank, I was just a time bomb waiting to explode.

I hope you can find it in your heart to forgive me. Frank you are my life—I mean—no man has ever appreciated me the way that you have. I know you've done wrong and have some skeletons in your closet. But for me to continue to hurt you the way that I have is disgraceful. You know maybe if Rick and Monique didn't cheat on us, we probably wouldn't be in the predicament we're in now. I can't help but feel I was a part of Rick's infidelity. I thought I was giving him all the love he needed, but apparently, Monique gave him more. I'm not trying to blame others for my wrongdoings, but I just want you to know that I get it now. Ron was a thing of the past that happened for a moment, but you're my future Frank. Please understand that as long as I am alive, I will never do anything to hurt you like this again.

You're my light when dark clouds seem to circle my path. When I fall asleep at night, I don't want another man in my dreams, I want you Frank, lying next to me holding me like there is no tomorrow. When I awake, I want to see your smile brightly shining in my face saying 'you want to make sweet passionate love to me.' Let's get past this Frank. I placed a damper in your heart and it might take a lifetime to close it, but I'm willing to wait just as long as you would have me, just to be in your life. I've said a lot Frank and I hope you know by now that I love you more than words can express. Please don't walk out on our love Frank. Give me another chance!

Your loving wife,
Shanice

I never heard from Ron again and Frank—well, once again because of the kids, he found it in his heart to forgive me. We had gone through a lot, but in order for us to move forward, we had a lot of work to do.

Chantal's wedding was coming up soon and we prepared ourselves to make one last trip to Maryland. I knew Ron would be there, but I didn't let him know I was coming.

CHAPTER 38

"Reliving the Hell"

After all that had happened, I insisted upon going back to work. The first day I walked back in, if looks could kill, they would have. Everyone in the room paused with silence. No one said a word to their customers. They just stared at me. Shit, who did they think they were to stare at me like that? I didn't do anything to any of those assholes. I could hear voices from a distance saying what kind of nerve does this woman have coming back here after causing so much chaos?

I just kept my head high as I strutted across the multi-colored carpet. Someone balled up a piece of paper and threw it at me. "Damn it!" I screamed out. I heard someone yell, "Go home ho! We don't need any trouble here."

I guess they had some nerve. They had remodeled the place after the blasting and I was scorned by my peers. To feel like no one ever wants to see you again is a hurting thing. "It's not good to judge someone before you know the facts damnit." I continued to walk towards a seat in the far corner of the room. It was a small cubicle facing a cream-colored wall. Toujuana, a good friend of mine, walked towards me. She always sat in that corner and greeted me with a smile.

"Hey girlfriend," she said. "I heard you were damn near blown to pieces by that jerk."

"You could definitely say that!" I responded with a slight ache in my face. "This fool had my face messed up. I had to get quite a few stitches across my jaw."

"Girl, you should have stayed home. What possessed you to come back here of all places to work?" Toujuana asked.

I looked at her and said, "You and Taquana. Every time I think about having fun and keeping myself young, ya'll come to mind."

"Thanks for the compliment. But, you shouldn't be here. The people are very upset about what happened."

I glanced at Toujuana and told her, "They will have to escort me out of this joint—cause a sistah ain't leavin' anytime soon." I sat my black ass down and gathered my composure. I knew they were hatin' on a sistah but hell—I needed to make a living just like them. I didn't know that jackass was going to come to South Carolina and blow up the NMC.

The phone clicked over and I began my greeting, "Thank you for calling the National Marketing Center. How may I be of assistance to you today?" I asked.

The voice was strong yet comical on the other end. "Hello ma'am. I have a quick question for you," he said.

"Uh oh," I thought. Get ready for the next pervert. "Sure," I replied. "What would you like to know?" Setting myself up for a real blow.

"First of all, my name is Yuseff and I was wondering if there is a limit on the amount of times you can use a credit card on your account?"

Whew, that's an easy enough question to answer. "Yuseff before I go any further, could I get you to verify some information on your account?"

"Sure," he said confidently. "Whatcha wanna know?" All slang and shit.

"I need your full name, address, and telephone number."

"My pleasure," he said with smooth laughter.

I knew this was going to be a pleasant call and would carry me through the end of my shift. The call started at 7:20 p.m. and I got off at 7:30 p.m. There's nothing better than ending your day with a call like this one.

After he verified all of his information, I asked him if he wanted to use one of his credit cards on his account.

"Gladly," he said laughing again.

"Great!" I responded. "What's your credit card number?"

When he gave me the number, it came up as 'insufficient funds.' I started laughing my ass off and he asked what was so funny. My response to him was, "How can you call here asking such a serious question about credit cards and your shit popped up with 'insufficient funds?"

He burst into laughter. "I like you," he said. "You're funny. Nah though, for real, how much can I put on there?"

Again, I laughed. "I told you it came up as though you were a broke nigga. Why's that?"

"I'm not sure why that card did that, but can you help a brotha out?" He asked laughing his head off.

He knew damn well before he called here he didn't have it like that, but wanted a freebee. "Sorry my brotha. But I can't just put money on your account. They'll throw me under the jail for a mere $5.00 transaction.

He laughed again. "How will they know?"

"Man don't you know they record everything around here and I can see it now, Shanice went to jail over $5.00. NO THANK YOU!"

"Can you at least look into my account and see how good it is? That should at least count for something."

I looked into his account noticing that in a month's time, he had used his credit card more than twelve times.

"It's no wonder your credit card comes up as 'insufficient funds.' You've gone way over you card limit."

"Oh," he said. "That explains everything."

I was compelled to help him at that point, but his account had a zero balance and you can't add credit to a zero balance. He understood at that point and decided to ask me out. "Come on now!" I said. "You won't have any money to take me out."

"Oh see—you trying to be sarcastic."

"Nah," I said. "Just having a laugh or two with you."

"Okay, I see. Well, maybe next time I'll have some money to take you to Burger King or something like that."

Man, my Burger King days were over. He had to be young talking about taking me to B.K. Anyway, I told him I had to go because I had several calls waiting and I had been on the phone too long. Actually, my time was up and I didn't have time to be talking to some broke ass nigga who wanted to take me to Burger King.

Finally, my break came. Two days off and no more headsets attached to my ears. The bad part about it though, I had to get the Christmas shopping done fast. It was only a couple days left before Christmas and I only had gifts for Frankie. Miranda and Justin would kill me if they knew I hadn't gotten them a gift yet. They were much older and didn't need much, but Frankie was about to turn six soon. I had to get my son something even if it was just clothes. I hurried off to Sears and Wal-mart trying to find some good deals. Justin ended up with two pair of blue jeans, three shirts, and *Enter the Matrix* game for his Game Cube I had bought him for his birthday. Miranda got a fifty dollar bill, a couple pair of outfits, and prepaid cell phone with Sprint.

Then there was Frank. I thought about the usual PJ's, shirt, pants, and a nice card. But this time, I was really going out. He saw me through all the shit I had gone through. I decided that I would buy him a nice DVD system for his car.

So much money spent and bills to pay. My day was shot. I still had dinner to fix and a huge ass house to clean. Not that I kept a dirty house, but the breakfast dishes were still in the sink and the beds were unmade. Taking a deep breath, I made myself scarce and left that shit just like that. I wasn't about to clean up behind teenagers. I made a few calls—one being to Ron and the other was to Chantal. I had my laughs for a while then decided that I was going to cook some shrimp scampi with rice and a lemon meringue pie for dessert.

The next day, I went shopping again. Figured I'd better buy myself a little Christmas gift as well. I ended up purchasing a nice pair of black jeans, something I've never owned, a hunter green pullover sweater, and a pair of black ankle boots. Then it was back to the home front to do some wrapping. Everyone was curious as to what I had gotten them especially Frank. He could tell it was the usual clothing, but he didn't know what else I had in store for him.

CHAPTER 39

"Rejections"

Rejections...Rejections...Rejections.   I tried so many publishing companies and had the door slammed literally in my face again. I knew my books were good. I mean—I'm not Maya Angelo or Zane, but come on—there should be enough room at the top for everyone. I called Chantal trying to find a logical explanation for this madness.

The phone rang twice and Chantal said, "Whassup my friend?"

It cheered me for a minute hearing her voice. "Nada dayum thing!" I replied fearing I would burst into tears at any given moment. The thing about Chantal was that she had gone through so much and I didn't want to put my burdens on her.

"Ooh, someone's in a bad mood today!" Chantal commented.

"Yeah. I'm just trying to figure something out." I responded.

Chantal broke the ice and said, "What gives girlfriend? Spill the juice already, won't cha."

I cried louder, "I don't get it Chantal. I just don't fuckin' get it."

"Hey...hey...hey, girlfriend," Chantal yelled. "Please don't cry. I was just kidding."

"You don't understand Chantal. I work in this place where I'm constantly being cursed out and perverted men calling to ask if I would suck on their nasty ass penis."

"You shittin' me, right?" Chantal replied.

"No," I cried more. "You just don't know how many times I wanted to walk away from the NMC and say the hell with them. But, I kinda like it

230

there. I've sold so many books at that place. The people are loving me and my books. I didn't feel that kind of love in Baltimore."

"Is that the real reason why you left?" Chantal asked.

"Oh no. I just had to get to a warmer climate and friendlier people."

"What about the friends you left behind here in Baltimore? Don't we matter?" Chantal whimpered.

"Of course you do. I'm just going through some issues with publishing companies right now. One minute they want me and the next minute, I'm being rejected again."

Chantal started coughing, said excuse me, then asked, "What about the big book deal you were about to cut?"

Ashamed to tell the truth, I said, "It fell through."

"I'm so sorry sweetie. They don't know what an influence your book would be to so many women who have been molested, raped and abused by men." Then she paused and said, "Tell you what, let's go somewhere nice. Just me and you."

My spirits lifted a little. We decided to go away to Chicago. Chantal told me that she happened to run across two tickets to the Oprah show. Ecstatic as I might have been, I still had Frankie and my family to worry about. I know Frank didn't trust me after the Ron ordeal, but I tried to ease his mind so that he'd be able to trust me again.

Chantal was such a great friend. She always seemed to know what I needed. I continued telling her about the jackass who called me asking if he could cum in my mouth. The nerve of him. Chantal burst into laughter and said, "Sounds like a really wild place to work?"

I chuckled finally and said, "I mean—it was quite hilarious having someone other than Frank or Ron wanting to cum in my mouth."

"Yeah, the place is wild alright. You have women dressing like hoochie mommas and men queer as hell."

"I need to get you as far away from that place as possible."

I agreed wholeheartedly. We hung up the phone and I went upstairs to my bedroom. It was raining something awful outside and I could hear the neighbor's dog Zena barking. *"Poor thing,"* I thought to myself. *"How could someone leave their dog outside in the pouring rain like that?"* The rain continued harder and the lightning flashed. I heard a loud clatter outside my window and was scared to look, fearing that Zena was struck by lightning.

Something was dangling from my window sill and I peeped through a small crack in the curtains and noticed that one of my shingles had fallen. "Dammit," I declared. "This cannot be happening on such a perfect day."

Frank and the kids were away. It was my day off and you know a sistah was tryin' to rest. But how the hell could I get any rest with the noise Mother

Nature was performing outside. The clatter continued and Zena yelped. I wanted desperately to bring her in my house, but I didn't care for dogs. I mean—she was all wet up and shit and I know Shavonne would have thanked me dearly. But, let's face it, I wasn't tryin' to go outside in the rain, get my 'do messed up for some stinking ass dog. Zena would have to soak.

Another clash of thunder and I heard a loud yelp. The curiosity was killing me. *Dammit*, was Zena struck or not? I thought feeling like shit knowing I could have saved her.

Outside in the tall grass lay the 80lb pit bull. Skin crispy as toast! "Damnit," Why couldn't I just bring the stupid dog in?" I picked up my Nokia 5185 and called Shavonnne. She rushed home at the sound of the news. I didn't let on that I heard Zena's cry for help. Shavonne was devastated. She blamed herself after hearing the forecast and ignored the warning.

She called the vet and they came over to pick Zena up. Unfortunately for her, she was arrested, charged for animal neglect, and fined $2500.00. Shavonne had to spend five days in jail. Such a harsh sentence for a damn dog. When she came home, girlfriend didn't have two words to say to me. Somehow she felt I could have done something to prevent Zena from being struck.

The next day, I went back to work. I was thinking, *t*his will probably be my last week after working here for four months. It was noisy as usual and I was greeted the same fucked up way. *They all can kiss my black ass.* I thought as I walked to my cubicle. I completed my logins and waited for the calls to roll in. One by one they rolled in nonstop. Not a relief in sight. We had 114 calls in the queue.

My next caller rung in and made me change my life. Although we weren't 911, I took the caller seriously. After going through the riffraff of questions, she screamed, "He's going to kill me!"

I was terrified and didn't know what to think. "Calm down ma'am!" I said. "Who's trying to kill you?" I asked out of fear for her life.

"My son," she said screaming louder.

My first instinct was that she was playing a senseless prank on me. Then composing myself, I asked, "Are you sure he wasn't pulling your leg?"

She started to whisper, "He's in the other room. Got himself drunk and wanted me to give him my purse. I worked hard for my paycheck and I'm not giving it to him."

"But ma'am," I cut her off. "He's your son. Should I call 911 for you?"

She gasped and said, "He's threatened me several times before, but this is different."

I heard a loud noise then the phone dropped. She started to scream and the phone died. *"Oh my God,"* I thought thinking the worse. I put my phone in system problems and headed towards one of the supervisor's desk. My supervisor ran to my workstation and called the number back. The phone rang once and then there was dead air. She called 911 and we were kept on the phone until they reached the resident. The site inside wasn't a pretty one. The son had made good on his promise. They found the lady, her son, and a two year old still gasping for life inside. The child was rushed to the hospital and remained in critical condition.

At that point, I decided my job was overwhelming and I couldn't take the pressure any longer. My supervisor and I were commended for a job well done and given a promotion. I decided to stay on a little while longer and tried to block out what had happened. I knew somewhere out there someone needed me and I wanted to be there for them.

CHAPTER 40

"Beat to Shame"

A week later, I walked into the open space and her face looked as though someone used it as a punching bag. I went over to her and asked what had happened. She had tears in her eyes and said, "He got so angry. I couldn't keep my mouth shut."

My heart softened for her. Knowing how vicious men could be and seeing what had happened to Chantal, I sympathized with her. "Girlfriend, God didn't put us here to be anyone's punching bag."

She looked at me and said, "It was my fault. I wouldn't keep my mouth shut."

"Oh hell no," I replied. Why do women think they are the cause of men kicking their ass all the time?" I have to be thankful though. I've never had that happen to me before.

I walked her over to the service desk and told her how the next time she might not be so lucky. Just seeing the bruises on her face and the front row of her teeth mounted back in place reminded me of how so many women are trapped into relationships being abused and are afraid to leave. Some are told that it'll never happen again while others have their children to protect. I went home that night and cried for her. I couldn't seem to shake the feeling especially since Frank had pushed me to the floor. My excuse was, he wouldn't have done it if I hadn't lied to him.

My phone rang as I lay flat on my flabby stomach. Chantal was on the other line. The news wasn't good at all. Rick's niece was found dead after a brutal struggle with her ex-boyfriend. They had gone out to Applebee's on Route 40 in Catonsville and he told her that he wanted to work things out.

When Kahneshia refused to be with him, an argument ensued and one thing led to another. He beat her so bad that when they found her she was laying in a puddle of blood. A couple hours later, Michael turned himself in, but was let go a few days later because they couldn't find any evidence of him being at the crime scene. The only thing he suffered was a blow to the head and some minor scratches on his face and arms. None of Kahneshia's DNA was found on him so they let him go.

I wept hard for her. I remember taking her to the park and the mall when she was little. I hadn't seen her since Rick went to jail and prior to his funeral. I couldn't believe this shit was happening to me. Chantal tried to calm me down, but I was furious as hell. The nerve of that fucker beating her down like that! I told Chantal that I would be back in Baltimore, but would see if it was okay with Frank to go. We hung up the phone and I wept some more. This asshole had the audacity to beat my niece like that. I mean—technically speaking, she was no longer my niece because Rick and I were no longer married, but I still saw her as my niece. I fell asleep with tears in my eyes and bags under both. My eyes had swollen just that fast from crying over Kahneshia.

The next morning, I was eager to talk with the girl that had been beaten by her boyfriend. After looking at her face and seeing the scars left behind, I gave her a hug and told her about my niece.

"He left me for dead," she yelled.

Some of the people turned around and looked at her. "Why do you put up with that shit?" I asked.

"I don't know why. He said he loves me," Benita insisted.

"Girlfriend, don't believe that shit! Anytime a man beats a woman to damn near death especially the way yo ass was beat, that ain't nothin' but hatred," I replied.

"You don't understand. I was mouthin' off."

I cut her off real fast. "Don't you dare blame yourself for this! Your boyfriend is an asshole and he should fry for messin' up your face like this."

"He didn't mean to…"

I cut her short again. "Girl you must be out of your mind. Your face looks like you just stepped out of the ring with Roy Jones Jr."

She smiled and said, "Who is Roy Jones Jr.?"

Now I thought everybody knew about the pound for pound boxer from Pensacola, Florida. "Girl, this guy boxes with fierce fiery flames coming from his gloves. I truly would hate to be on the other side of his gloves when he is throwing the punches."

"You seem to know a lot about him," Benita said.

"Not really," I said. "I just tend to follow his boxing events since my girl Chantal is from his hometown Pensacola."

"I don't know Shanice. This man sounds more brutal than Selmo."

"Selmo?" I laughed my ass off. Benita didn't think it was too funny. In fact, she called me a skank bitch and walked away. Shit it didn't hurt my feelings. At least, my face was still in one piece.

After all this mess, I really was starting to lose interest in the NMC. The people didn't amount much to anything. There were people walking around with rings in their noses, eyelids, multi-color hair, queers, and lesbians all over the place. I knew my book deal was going to come through real soon and I was going to be on top of the world. I had my kids and my two men. What else could I want? My world couldn't get any better than this.

I went home that evening, walked into my room looking around at some of the finer things I had accrued in life and walked over to my mahogany dresser and pulled out my purple Victoria Secrets lounger. Sometimes I just like to kick back and relax after a long day at work.

Frank came in and saw the tears where I had started back crying again for Kahneshia. "What's wrong honey?" He asked trying to be sympathetic.

"My niece was killed last night," I replied getting ready to hit him with the obvious question.

Frank held me for a while and I cried harder. "That bastard didn't have to kill her. She was only twenty-one."

For the first time, I could feel Frank hurting for me since the incident with Ron. He asked if I wanted to go back to Maryland to be with Rick's family. Playing it off, I said, "You think I should Frank?"

He said, "Sweetheart I know you are hurting and if it makes you feel better, I think you should go."

Frank was such a kind-hearted loving man. How could I continue messin' him around the way I was? "I would like to go and pay my respects."

"That would be great honey. Maybe you should take Miranda and Justin so that they can be with their cousins."

I was not trying to hear that. I suddenly replied with, "They'll have to miss out on their classes and we know how they feel about that." Great cover up at the last moment.

He smiled and said, "The kids will be fine. It shouldn't bother them one bit."

In a way, it probably was best for the kids to go with me. That way, it wouldn't be so tempting for me to end up in Ron's arms. I mean—it's hard to think about Ron and not get totally excited…his warm sexy eyes that seem to mesmerize me every time I look into them. Sometimes I feel as though I'm in a trance and no detected vibe could snap me back to reality. There's not a day that goes by I don't think about the man. You know, love is a funny thing and you boast about not getting enough. A stumbling block will fall into your path every time and you are left picking up the pieces.

When Frank asked me to take Justin and Miranda to Maryland with me, all I could think about was finding Ron despite the fact that this man tried to ruin my marriage. I couldn't help myself knowing that I would be in the same area as he. So my cover up was, "If you think it is okay then I'll check with the kids and see what they think about the situation. What about you Frank? Do you plan on attending your friend's funeral?"

Frank wasn't expecting that question and his reply was, "I'm not sure if I could take the time off from work."

He covered himself well and I didn't pressure him any further. I just told him that I was going to take a long hot shower and would be out shortly. I would have invited him in, but I had Ron on my mind and I didn't want my last thoughts of him ruined by Frank.

When I got out of the shower, I wrapped myself in my navy blue towel, my body dripping with excess water. My mind immediately drifted back to Ron and I smiled. If only Ron was near me to caress my slippery brown body, I know we would be rolling all over the sink and possibly the floor. But for now, I had to get myself prepared to go back to Maryland, face Rick's family, and be ready to attend Chantal's big wedding in a couple of days. My girl had it good. Through it all, she's endured a lot of pain, but in the end, she found the man of her dreams. If only I could remain as faithful to Frank as she has to Dominique.

CHAPTER 41

"Chantal's Wedding Day"

In my previous life, I had misery, heartache, and pain. My day of reckoning soon came to past when my long lost love from Pensacola showed up. It was a beautiful day outside. The church was filled with people from my family and Dominique's. We chose to be married at the Hyatt located in the heart of Baltimore, MD. Most of the people knew me as a sweet victim of molestation, rape, and abuse. But, they didn't know that I too had a hidden secret that would one come day out of the closet and bite me on the ass.

We had the ushers seat our family members according to our wishes. My family members wore hunters green with a touch of gray and his mother wore a baby blue gown sequenced in beige lace. The spot where Mildred would have been sitting was occupied by my Aunt Clara. Since my sister Denise was in the wedding and Byron was to give me away, the rest of our family sat on the second row awaiting the ceremony. Each chair was uniquely decorated by a local florist with big white bows accented in baby's breath.

The ceremony was to start at 6 p.m. that Saturday because I wanted a candlelight ceremony. The sun was still beaming heavily outside as more and more guests arrived complaining about the heat. You could see the make-up running down some of the women's faces. After the final guest arrived, the doors were closed and the music started. By the time I walked down the aisle and was handed over to Dominique, the preacher asked if we both would kneel down for a little prayer.

In my excitement, a lot ran through my mind. I thought about how proud my mother would be to finally see me acquire the happiness I desired. Dante looked over at me and smiled generously. He knew I had finally found that special someone who would take me to a whole new dimension in life. I wouldn't have to worry about having my needs fulfilled—that's for sure. Dominique was more man than I could handle at times. He was so good about being there for me when I needed comfort or just needed that special someone to talk to. This was it—my final opportunity to be happy.

A sudden burst of fresh air came through the door and there stood a tall dark, middle-age hunk from my past. I couldn't believe my eyes. After twenty-seven years of longing for this man, he finally appeared on the day when my future would be decided. He stepped in, sat off to the side, and waited for the appropriate time to announce his desire to have me—his long lost love. When I first left my native Pensacola to join the Navy, I left Al behind in hopes of finding him again one day. Our day never came and I tried to move on with my life.

Standing in his white tuxedo, Dominique glanced over at me. He could tell that I was weary, but excited to see this man. He probably wondered what impact this man had on my life and why he suddenly appeared on our wedding day. Al stood up and made his announcement in front of our guests. They sat in awe as he started to talk.

"I have come for my true love and I won't leave until I have her."

"Who, may I ask are you looking for?" A tall clean cut Dominique responded.

"He wants me Dominique," I said wanting desperately to run down the aisle towards Al.

Dominique pulled me off to the side. His voice was harsh and I was embarrassed by the way the guests looked at me. "Please explain this man to me," he said. "Who is he and why does he want to take you away? Have you been cheating on me?" A hurtful Dominique asked.

"Oh no sweetheart. Al is from my past. Some twenty-seven years ago, we had a love so strong that only fate could tear it apart."

"But why now Chantal?" He asked me. "Why after all these years he wants to profess his love for you?"

"I couldn't find her. I've searched high and low. I didn't know her married name. Chantal, please come to me."

With my mouth open, I could only stand and stare at him. It seemed that Al hadn't changed a bit. It must have been the martial arts that kept him fit.

"I can't walk away from Dominique. He's my pride and joy, Al. How dare you come here and interrupt something so right, so sacred!"

Al's destiny was torn. He was determined more than ever to have me. "I found out about your wedding just days prior. There was an announcement back in Pensacola about a native woman who won such a large amount from the lottery that was getting married. After I retired from the Navy, I headed back your way trying to find you. I served my country for over twenty-five years. I need you in my life, Chantal."

"It's too late for us Al. Dominique's everything I ever want and need in a man. It's just too late. Please, leave before you make it too hard to say 'no.'"

"I was hoping it didn't come to this." He pulled a huge ring out of his pocket and kneeled down on one knee. *"I'll give you the stars, the sun, the rain, the moon, and the mountains, I'll give you the world and all that you reach for and even more..."* Singing a few lines from After Seven's—'Ready or Not.'

"Get up Al! Please, don't make a mockery of yourself," I yelled out.

He continued. "Girl, I love you more than words can show and that's for sure. I'll cross the highest hills, swim the widest sea, nothing could discourage me and I'll pray that you will be always there for me forever more. Ready or Not, I'll give you everything and more."

I interrupted him. "Al, please, don't do this," I begged.

Again, the door swung open and there appeared, RJ. His smile was even wider than when Al walked through the door.

"What's going on around here?" Dominique shouted.

"I come to reclaim my love," he said demanding me to speak.

"I don't understand. Why is this happening to me?" I questioned.

RJ following the lead of Al, kneeled down, and pulled out a 24 karat diamond ring with my initials engraved. "I did this just for you. Forget the others and be mine, Chantal!"

"No, No, No—this is not happening to me." I held my hands to my face.

RJ started, "If you won't be mine, then listen to what I have to say before you shut me out."

"What is it RJ?"

He started—*Just to be close to you, girl.* Just for a moment—well—just for an hour." He was singing one of The Commodores oldest melodies.

I shook my head from left to right. "This is impossible. There is no way this can be happening to me. This just isn't possible."

"You better believe it!" Another voice sitting inside the church yelled out. He stood up and I was devastated. I ended up passing out. Kenyon had a harsh look upon his face. He pulled out—not a ring—like the others, but a long leather belt and began snapping it. "Thought you got rid of me forever, didn't you bitch? Well guess what? *I Can't Get Over You...*I tried and I tried, but I can't get you off my mind.'

I couldn't believe it. He was singing too. He actually sounded good. Then like an old woman at a funeral, I passed out again. I'm not sure for how long because the next thing I knew, I was pouring in sweat. I jumped realizing it was just another frightening dream haunting me on my wedding day. Dominique rolled over and asked me what was going on. I was too afraid to tell him about the horrible nightmare I had just had.

"It's okay, honey. I was just having a weird dream about our wedding day. I think everything will be just fine," I said smiling at him.

"You're not getting butterflies on your wedding day, are you baby?"

"Nope—just bad dreams! I know this is going to be the wedding of a lifetime. I truly love you Dominique."

"And, I love you too, Ms. Chantal Lewis-Jenkins. I hope to change that name really soon."

Dedication and Praises

I give my total praise to God Almighty for giving me the desire to become a writer and for blessing me with so many people who continually pushed me to become an inspiring author. I would like to thank the following people for their encouragement and support during my past few years of writing.

First and foremost, to my mother, Annie Wright, who is now deceased, I want to thank you for all the love and discipline you embedded within me as a child. They say, "Train a child when he is young and when he is older, he will not depart from it." I truly believe in that. My mother was my best friend and my comforter for thirty five wonderful years. Although she is no longer here, I can feel her presence around me daily pushing me to move forth with my writing. Thank you mother for your struggle to keep a roof over our heads and for the undying love you gave to each of us. We'll never forget you. I love you with all of my heart.

To my father, James Wright Sr., I want to thank you for being there for me when I got off the school bus and you always had a crisp ten dollar or twenty dollar bill waiting in your hands. Thanks for the love you gave me over the years.

To my husband and children, Stephen, Darius and Stephen Anthony: I want to thank you for all the wonderful years of support and love you've given me as my journey towards a more inspiring life opened. You guys are truly the backbone to the foundation that I am working on to build a better life for my family. I love you so much.

To my sisters and brothers, James, Sharon, Frank, and Lorie: Thank you for your support and the sibling rivalry we encountered as children. It really helped me to grow up.

To my Uncle Raymond Jones and Aunt Mable, a special thank you for letting me know that when one door closes, you'll always have one open for me. I'm sure you know what that means.

To my Aunt Claudell McGee, I've always admired you for the wonderful mother and aunt you are. Thank you for putting up with my stubbornness and ungrateful attitude while I was a child. Your teachings made me the woman I am today.

To my Uncle John (Peter) Jones and Aunt Erma, thank you for all the support you've given over the years and for inspiring me with my writing. Thank you Uncle Peter for that Thursday night before Momma passed and how you were there to comfort me when everyone else had left me alone. I'll never forget that night.

To my uncles Eugene and David Wright, thank you for sticking by me when I came over and the door was shut in my face. I want to thank both of you for the support you've given upon finding out that I had become a writer. The phone calls are unreal.

To my special friends in Maryland, first, Larry McDowell—had it not been for you, I wouldn't be where I'm at today with my writing. You started this with, "Donna please send me some encouraging emails or some good writings that I can read because I'm bored." Had it not been for the push in Powerpoint slides, I would still be sitting at ACS wondering where my next step in life was heading. Thank you Larry for being there for me.

My best girlfriend, Shelia Burley: It's hard to find words for you because no matter what was going on in my life, you were there to encourage, advise, and lend a helping hand. The day I left Maryland was by far, the hardest day of my life. I love you girlfriend.

To my other best girlfriend, Joyce Harley, when I needed a friend with a listening ear to be objective, to encourage or just needed to laugh, I would choose you over and over again. I thank you for being a great friend and motivator. I miss you more than you'll ever know.

To my good friend Rodney Wellington, if ever there was a person to say, "You can do it Donna." It was you. I value you as a friend and I miss hearing those words face to face. Thank you Rodney for supporting my writings.

To my good friend, RM, your ambition to support me while writing is overwhelming. I have met many people in my life that encouraged, supported, and pushed me while writing, but your prayers and confidence in my writing ability is what drives me to accomplish my goals the most. Thank you for being a great friend and advisor.

Last but not least, to my good friend, GLA, thank you for the memories from yester year. You started all of this and I am truly grateful for you wherever you might me.

Although there are many people who have supported me, please don't feel as though I didn't acknowledge you in a special way. I want to thank all of you and especially my fans. It's because of you I had the perseverance to finish up my second book. Although I knew I would finish one day, my friends at Sitel Corporation in Augusta, GA and my friends and family back home in Pensacola, FL, I thank you also.

About the Author

Portuguese was born and raised as Donna Brown in Pensacola, FL. She graduated from Escambia High School. She is married with two children and currently resides in Georgia. She is currently pursuing studies in Business Management.

Her book Secret Lies was written as a sequel to her first novel released in 2003, *The Essence of Innocence...Undeniable Betrayal...Unforgiven Love.* Donna's passion is writing romance novels that inspire, stimulate, and captivates the hearts of both men and women. She is currently working on two other romance novels and a screen play. She has completed two children's books *Crippled Like Me* and *The Perfect Father* which she hopes to have released in the nearest future.

Printed in the United States
38654LVS00003B/67-84